To Believe in Peter Pan

Book One

Monica Shantel

TO BELIEVE IN *Peter Pan*

TO BELIEVE BOOK ONE

MONICA SHANTEL

This is a work of fiction. Names, characters, and incidents either are the product of the author's imagination or are used fictitiously. Any resemblance to actual persons, living or dead, or events is entirely coincidental.

To Believe in Peter Pan

Book Cover by Monica Shantel

Illustrations by Monica Shantel

ISBN 978-1-960696-96-0 (Paperback) ISBN 978-1-960696-06-9 (Hardcover)

Second Edition

For those who were told they couldn't.

Fee
Zeeslang
Waters
Cannib

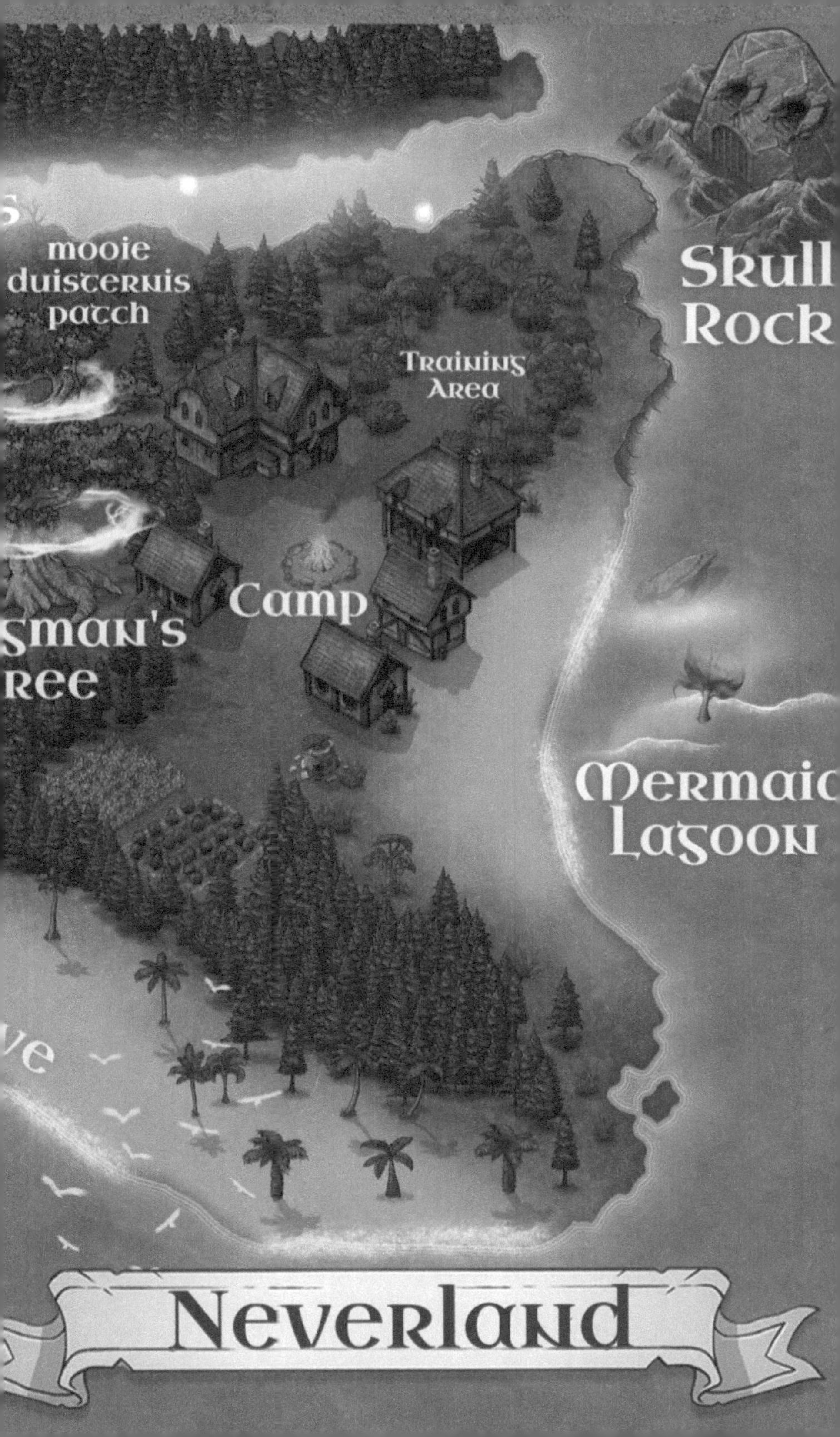

mooie duisternis patch

Skull Rock

Training Area

Camp

Mermaid Lagoon

Neverland

Liliana
Stone

5/11/22

5/14/22

Peter Pan

MONICA SHANTEL

NEVERLAND NEEDS
A SAVIOR.

00: Monster

THE STREET BEYOND ME was as silent as the ghosts that haunted this town, as silent as the parents who'd turn the other cheek when a child was thrown onto the streets and begging for some kindness.

Buildings, lights, and the clouded sky reflected off the freshly wet pavement. The air smelt of rain and the salt that carried from the ocean just a mile from the town.

My stomach grumbled. I took my cue and approached a skip. A quick glance told me no restaurants had thrown any recent food out.

A raindrop pelted against my skin. I hurried down the street and to the underground where the tracks were. No metros were running at this hour, but it provided me with some shelter and quiet.

Screaming pierced the air, traveling down the railway. It was difficult to pinpoint the direction it came from, but I knew right away someone needed my help. Unfortunately for them, I was not in any shape to help at all. A boy once stepped in to defend my lack of honour against his father, but I couldn't return the favour. Not with stabbing pains erupting inside my abdomen.

The screams grew louder—closer.

A young girl came shooting from the left side, headed face first into the tracks. I'd say mother taught me better than to allow a girl to fight her own battles but I had no such thing as a mother. She'd abandoned me the day I came into this world.

Something unusual croaked. Something inhuman. I didn't believe in such fairy tales, ghosts or otherwise. But this wasn't a fairy tale, was it?

I nearly jumped out of my skin when the girl's head popped up as she climbed up onto the floor. A shrilling yell echoed through the tunnel.

"What the bloody hell is happening in there?" I stood on my feet as the girl ran towards me. I didn't need her to shout it. We both bolted from the underground and up into the pouring rain.

When we rounded the corner between a few buildings, I leaned my back against the wall, waiting for an answer.

She lifted her eyes to meet mine. "That thing in there was not human. Believe me if you will, but I was certain I'd lose my heart."

"Did you see its face?"

As she caught her breath, she nodded slightly. "I saw it all right. It had to be at least three-hundred centimetres tall. Long chin and all black. Gaping mouth. Glowing eyes."

"Like a shadow," I whispered.

She nodded again. "Almost like a shadow."

Whatever had taken residence down in that railway was not human by any length, and I was certain it was not here to make friends. It wanted something or *someone,* and however it was going to get that would put London in danger.

01: Deal

Voices echoed from every direction. I questioned if they were coming from my own head and I'd been hit one too many times this year. However, they were all male voices—and last I recalled, I still had a mother *and* a sister.

"...where'd she come from..."

"...why's she here..."

"...who is she..."

"...what'll Pan do with her..."

The whispers continued quieter as echoed from a distance. I couldn't grasp where, or who, they came from, but I knew a small crowd when I heard one. Few voices were begging to be discovered.

Darkness engulfed my vision. Trying to open my eyes was a struggle, but being in the presence of unknown males was one hell of a motivation.

While prying my eyes, the voices got louder, and words came out faster. For a moment, I wondered if I had been in an accident and nearby citizens were sticking their noses where they didn't belong.

However, they weren't citizens. They were *just* boys.

Trees surrounded us. Tall, and luscious green. From behind me, waves rolled against the shore while crows cawed up above—circling. I'd never been to the ocean, nor did I live near one, but weren't seagulls the bird of the ocean? Maybe a dream, but no. It wasn't. I knew what a dream felt like and this was far from it.

Just last night I had begged to be taken to Neverland and escape my home life. But I hadn't expected it to come true. I guessed Pan's shadow decided I was worthy, and I couldn't lie and say I wasn't excited about it.

Studying these boys, the caked-on dirt and unkempt hair stood out. They all displayed very confused, shocked, and even some irritated facial expressions. Towards me? A little rude, no?

"Step aside, lads," someone said from the back. His English accent dripped thickly. As they scrambled out of his way, he stopped a foot before me. "Who do you think you are coming to my island?"

Taller. Somewhere between lean and muscular. His ghostly complexion had been slightly tanned, and hair almost as dark as the crows. This boy was certainly older than the others. The looks he shot back were laced with intimidation. He'd been crowned king.

I sat up as the boys stepped back again, their leader not moving an inch. Eyeing him, I said, "I'm pretty sure that's not how you're supposed to treat your guests. You know, since I passed your shadow's test? What about my qualifications has you treating me like I'm an intruder?"

His back straightened, eyes narrowing on me. "I'm Peter Pan," he paused, "and this, Love, is Neverland. I *created* it."

My suspicions had been correct. I had ended up in Neverland and Peter Pan himself stood before me. I had been given *freedom* from my family. "Thank you." I shot him a small smile before jumping to my feet and dusting off my backside.

I took in the new faces, my suspicions confirmed. Not a single girl resided here, and there were at least ten boys already. They wore more raggedy clothing, but Peter Pan had slightly more modern clothes. A brown belt with black leggings, a *dagger* hanging on the right side.

He deflected any looks I gave as he crossed his arms. He was barely older than I was, and with a smooth chin, he couldn't have been any older than eighteen. Did he shave? What a thought—Peter Pan using a razor.

"So, what makes me special? I happen to be the only girl around." I wanted to say more but first impressions were everything, weren't they?

He appeared bothered by my observation. A tad offended. Annoyed, even, like he had somewhere else to be and I was just a bump in the road. "You're really not that special. You're here because you asked to be."

That didn't answer my question, but I couldn't ask for direct answers from the guy who said he created Neverland—a place full of magic and mystery. "All right, I'm the only girl who asks to come here."

He lifted his eyebrows in amusement. "There's another girl here. Allow me to warn you, though, most girls who end up here don't last a day. I don't expect you to be here by tomorrow." He waved the back of his hand, dismissing my strengths.

You don't mean anything to anyone, remember?

Shutting the voice up, a small smirk formed. "Is that a challenge? I do love a challenge." Nature calmed me in ways Peter thought wouldn't be possible. I was a woman—yes—but the outdoors was home to me more than a house with four walls could ever be.

Surprise encased his eyes. "If you'd like it to be." His demeanor relaxed. "But let's make this a little more interesting, shall we? What will I get if you don't last?" He let out a chuckle. "I'm not exactly too fond of you, but I don't ignore the fact that I do appreciate your presence for one reason."

Judgment swirled around in my eyes. "Don't even tell me; I already know. If I don't last, you want me to sleep with you?"

"What's that mean?" a boy asked.

Peter's laugh drifted into the air like smoke from a flame. "Really? That's what you think of me? I love your presence because you're fun to hunt. You could call it bloodlust."

I rolled my eyes.

This Peter didn't appear so welcoming, and he was about to learn I was far too used to the feeling. "Oh, fantastic. My only options are to win or be killed." I took a step closer. "Since this is a deal, what do I get when I win?" I didn't let his height scare me.

"To stay here, of course." He gestured to the island.

"No, a *real* prize. What do *I* get if I win?" I repeated the question again, slower, more pronounced.

He glanced at his lost boys. Curiosity killed the cat. He faced me with a promising end. "I'll give you the third biggest cabin."

"The third?" I asked to annoy the hell out of him. Two could play this game of his.

His eyes narrowed just a bit. "The biggest cabin is mine and I'd be a fool to let you have it. The second belongs to my second-in-command, and he won't be losing his bed just because you may or may *not* win a game."

I nodded a bit. "Sounds like a good deal to me." I carefully eyed the boys, questioning who his second-in-command was. My best guess was on the other big guy who sent the nastiest looks. Peter 2.0.

Peter's eyes moved up and down my body. "I'll be testing you on every skill you'll need to survive. I will very much enjoy hearing you scream. Don't hesitate to beg for mercy, because oh how I'll relish every last attempt." He didn't give a wicked smile, but his eyes darkened. I'd sworn I saw a cloud of black smoke spilling into his irises.

"Why, you believe I'll win? I've already got the sun beat. I can't burn." I'd survive. I'd prove myself. "So, what's going to be the official sign for when I give up? Do I say I surrender? Do I cry?" Neither of which I did often.

Not counting last night.

He came closer, his icy breath fanning my face as he stood merely inches away. He was *far* too close for my liking. "You simply beg me to take your life. Neverland is nothing like your world."

"No, it's not. My world is worse."

I'd show him I was worthy to live here, whether I had boobs or not. At least here, I had a chance to earn respect. Back home, I never would have gotten as far as a basic hello. Just accusations and threats.

He turned away to face his boys. "A game begins." He twisted his head back towards me. "Let's not keep the new girl waiting."

I didn't know what he had in store for me, but I'd take it. Introductions and tours wouldn't be part of my first day. Fitting, if anyone asked me.

The lost boys yelled while Peter circled me. "The first rule is do not disobey. There will be *deadly* consequences."

To his insane satisfaction, that was a literal threat.

"Second, call me Pan. Peter is a name I no longer go by." I wanted to ask him why he didn't like Peter, but I could only guess that Peter Pan himself, *too*, had a past he did not want to associate with anymore.

"Third, you always respect me. Are we clear?"

I had to respect him because he was the leader? Respect was earned, not something you could force. I'd respect him if he was a good leader, and not the one standing before me now. He gloated over his power far too much.

"I said, are we clear?" he repeated louder.

I sucked up my pride because I wanted to be here as much as I didn't want to admit it to him. "Crystal."

He halted, his crows falling eerily silent. "You will get only one meal to eat for the next twenty-four hours. I also don't want to hear a single word about how my lost boys treat you. They are free to do *whatever* they want." He waved his lost boys over. "We'll begin with training."

He turned and walked off. The boys started to follow, and I studied each of them as they passed by. They either glared or laughed, but one of them licked his lips while his eyes lingered below my neck. All that washed over me was nausea.

I followed them to the training center, eyes glued to the one I was sure to steer clear of.

Being around a bunch of boys was nothing new. I had two brothers, one more than I had sisters. I'd lived with them before, so this would really be a walk in the park.

They might have hated me now, but I could work with that.

We arrived at a clearing with targets, bows and arrows, swords, and plenty of bushes and trees that circled us.

Peter, or Pan, stood between us and the targets. "Everyone starts off with what they left off with yesterday. Have fun!" The boys scattered within seconds, finding their stations. Pan approached me. "As for you, new girl—"

"Lili," I corrected him.

"*If* you win this challenge, I just might call you by your name." He nodded his head towards my left. "I want you to start off over there."

The bows and arrows.

I made my way over, tilting my head as I faced a target. The boys stopped to watch my every move.

Grabbing a bow and arrow, I pulled the nock against the string where it fit perfectly. My elbow bent, my feet planted a few inches apart, and ninety degrees from the target. Position ready, I drew back the arow.

They all made the mistake of assuming I didn't have even a little knowledge.

I aimed just above my mark.

And I let it fly.

It landed near the bullseye but not quite in it.

Where I came from, my older brother happened to be into archery. I would use his weapons to practice just in case things went too far with our father.

Boys whispered to each other and Pan let a cunning little smile dance on his lips. "Impressive, Love. Let's see how you run." I put my bow down as he called another boy over. "Levi, you're going to race her."

Levi was a tall kid, but probably younger than me. Maybe fifteen at most. When he got into position, he said, "Don't let the thorns bite on your way out."

Removing the black frames on my face, I hooked them onto the neckline of my tank top. "I'll do my best. My short legs only go so far..." I leaned forward, bracing my feet.

When Peter said go, we ran.

Short legs were not a hinderance. Not when I used every ounce of speed to carry me to the end. I focused on that finish line that waved a comfy bed in the air. I *needed* to belong.

I barely passed it a second before Levi.

Maybe next time. If his masculinity wasn't already crushed.

The boys watched with wide eyes while Levi narrowed his. "I thought you said you weren't a great runner."

With a small smile, I shrugged. "Oops, I guess I lied."

It had been too easy to fool them. Being a fast runner was not that hard and I didn't need the practice to do it. Now being able to run for long periods of time was not a strength I had, but that thankfully hadn't been the battle here.

Pan watched me with curiosity. "Let's see how well you do when you're fighting one of us."

We moved to the center of the clearing. He'd pick either the smallest or the largest boy. "Jacob."

Jacob stepped forward. This couldn't be *too* hard. He was the same boy who'd been eyeing me from the start. If I didn't warn him now, he'd think I was free game. I could send him just the warning he needed.

I put my glasses over to the side where nobody could accidentally break them. Wouldn't that just be my luck, huh?

Whatever knowledge I had would need to be enough to leave without a broken rib.

He took the first swing, catching my side. I grunted while twisting from his view.

I blocked my face to dodge the next blow. Success.

He sent a hit to my stomach before I could predict the move, and I doubled over long enough for him to smack my boob. As I yelled out in pain, he wrapped his arm around my neck and tightened.

I struggled for a few seconds but managed to elbow his ribs. He stumbled back. I took a strike to his knee and when he collapsed onto both, I sent *my* knee to his face—and down he went, like a broken man.

Heavy breaths passed through my lungs as the boys stood in shock. Pan seemed to be the only one not amused by my victory.

"Where did you learn that? A girl can't fight like that!" a younger boy shouted.

"I just did." I wiped my hands on my shorts and found my glasses, watching the world come into perfect focus as I placed them on my nose.

When your father despised your existence, you learned to defend yourself in desperate times. Knowing most people had knees that were fragile was just common knowledge.

As I locked eyes with Pan, my pride swelled. "What's next?"

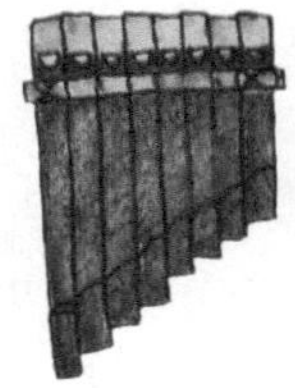

02: The Cage

No matter what they did, I'd never leave. "We have twenty-four hours to make our new girl regret coming." Pan stalked, shoulders reeled and chest pushed out just a bit.

As I crossed my arms and rolled my eyes, I said, "I can hear you."

"I know." He came to a stop and faced me. "You don't belong here, and I'll ensure you don't survive. Happy ending for everyone."

"No." I snickered. "I'll end up dead. How would they be 'happy for everyone'?" I quoted with my fingers. Then, as a thought hit me, I tapped my chin. "I thought Pan knew everything?"

I lifted my eyes to meet his when he approached.

Forefinger and thumb, he grabbed my chin, applying a little pressure. "You'll shut your damn mouth if you know it's good for you."

Laughing off his threats, I swatted his hand. "Or you'll kill me?" A threat was just a threat. "Does it really matter? No matter what I do, you're set on making my life here difficult for your amusement. There's be no use in forfeiting my personality if my outcome is the same." I gave him a shrug.

He stepped back, peering over at his boys. "Take her to the cage."

Pan was all bark and no bite. When I talked back, he'd order to lock me up like the coward he was, and he'd have the boys do the dirty work *for* him.

Two of the older boys gripped me by the arms, and I did yank as hard as I could but my strength was hardly comparable to double theirs. "Get your hands off me!"

They laughed. "We take orders from Pan."

My dad was back home—far away from me. He instilled more fear than the two bozos to the sides of me. I had finally gotten away from him just like I'd asked for. At least Pan's *shadow* understood my cry for help.

They dragged me over to a cage that had been handmade by the king himself. The entire structure was made of bamboo and vines. Once they shoved me inside and locked me in using those vines, I sat against the back wall. The cage hadn't been any bigger than a metal dog kennel made for an extra-large breed. I concluded from all this that the construction itself couldn't hold up.

Testing my theory, I started kicking at the door, using the heel of my foot to force the blows. I gave up after a few minutes when I hadn't even made a dent in the bamboo.

An accent traveled through the bars, "Love, this cage isn't as weak as you'd think. You're not getting out of here. I have to show my lost boys that I don't let someone go unpunished for the way they speak to me." *Pan.*

So much ego. Such a reputation to want to uphold. "Who is this other girl?" I asked.

"There's no need for you to worry much about that. You won't see her around. She cooks our food and does our chores. She's very useful for that type of stuff."

The cage dug into my spine as I leaned against it. "You must be really old if a woman's place is housewife."

His eyes pried, never faltering. "She's no wife. here, I am immortal. I control everything, including the residents. Don't expect me to go easy on those who disobey. The other girl obeys, and so she stays." A smile danced on his lips, but not genuinely. It reeked of bitterness.

"But does she get any respect?" I crossed my arms, eyes darting down his body before returning to his face. "Without women, you wouldn't be here. Unless you poofed into existence, it's safe to say a woman carried and birthed your ungrateful ass, and a woman did the same for your lost boys. You're welcome, on behalf of the population who can have kids." I mirrored his smile.

"I understand how we are made. It also takes a man to help that woman get pregnant." He cocked an eyebrow.

"No shit, but we're not talking about sexism against men. I don't judge any of you. I could get along with you easily, if you weren't treating me like the worthless human being you think I am. However, you hate me because of my DNA—because I have parts different from yours." I released a sigh and a head shake. "Can I ask something?"

"No—" he started, but I interrupted him anyway.

"You're obviously old enough to have gone through puberty and hormones but you hate women." I shifted my body. "You're a sexual sadist, correct?"

He kept his gaze glued on me, but he didn't seem moved by my words. "You keep saying I hate women, but that is far from the truth."

Ignoring his lie, I waved my hand around. "Sexual sadists are people who get off on hurting others. Our pain is your gain."

He chuckled a little. "What are my other options?"

Glaring daggers at him was an understatement. He was testing my buttons, and I was going to return the favor.

He walked off.

I didn't know how long I'd be in here, but I was not about to give up for him of all people. I would prove my worth. Girls could handle just as much as boys, and more. No lost girls seemed like such a ludicrous standard to live by.

Night fell over the island. In the center of the camp, I heard cheering—a celebration. Why were they celebrating if my arrival was such a bad thing?

A sharp pain shot through my stomach. The early signs of starvation.

The cage opened, but I hadn't expected Pan. "Your time has come to an end." Wait, did he mean death? "We're moving onto the next part of the test soon." He waved me out and I complied.

I admired the bonfire to my left. "What is this?"

"A celebration."

"For what?" I watched the boys dance around the fire. It appeared to intrigue them, to excite them. Bonfires could be fun, if they didn't include your power-hungry Peter Pan of course.

"Why do we need a reason to celebrate? There are no rules." He walked back to the fire, but he didn't join in on the dancing. It looked ritualistic if you asked me.

Pan took out a wooden flute, and as he began to play, something changed my perspective of him. How could he play stunning music?

I stared, completely lost to the tune. As soon as he caught me, he pulled the flute away from his lips. I didn't understand why. I wasn't anything *special* according to him.

When I turned to the right, I noticed a new guy—one who I hadn't seen before—his face hidden in the shadows under his hood. Then I counted the bodies of all the boys, stumped. There'd been ten before, and now eleven stood. Who was this guy? Why wasn't he there when I arrived? Maybe I'd been locked up so long that a new lost boy arrived after me and that was why they danced around a bonfire.

Once I won this challenge, I'd explore all I could. I wanted to know where these boys came from and their biggest dreams. Most importantly, I wanted to know more about Pan.

Someone tapped my shoulder and I turned around, utterly confused when nobody was there. At least until I lowered my eyes to see a younger boy in front of me. He'd been very short to somehow go unnoticed that easily. "How did a girl get on this island?" he asked, a puzzle written on his face.

I didn't know how to answer his question other than shrug. "The shadow brought me here like he brought the rest of you." Scanning the boys again, I pointed to the cloaked figure whose face was still impossible to place. "Hey, can I ask you who that is over there?"

He sat on the log to my left. "That's Kace. He's Pan's second-in-command. They've been here the longest. He's super friendly once you get to know him." *Ha*, friendly? Anyone who served Pan—and especially as his right-hand man—was not friendly by any means.

I nodded a bit, eyes still stuck on the guy. That was his second-in-command. That still begged the question of why he wasn't there when I had arrived.

"All right. What's your name?" I gave the kid my full attention.

He lowered his head, a small smile creeping up. "Hunter."

I smiled in return. "Hello, Hunter, I'm Lili. Don't worry, I don't bite. I ended up here the same reason the rest of you did." I gestured to the rest of the island.

He looked at my arm. "I once had a sister, but she was mean to me."

"You boys have judged me since my arrival. I didn't do anything wrong, did I?" He didn't know what to say to that, so I patted his shoulder. "I know what it feels like to be the victim. Although Pan deserves to know the same sentiment. He doesn't deserve my blinded respect."

"What?" More puzzled looks.

I shook my head, shooing away the idea. "Nevermind."

I wasn't too worried about losing. I used to go to school while sick, seeing as my parents never gave me any other choice. I'd had a period for at least six years of my life. This was nothing compared to that.

A shiver ran up my spine even though I stood near the fire. Apart from the daring flames, some thoughts from the eyes piercing my soul sent chills down my back.

I pushed some of my hair behind my ear just as soon as the boy grabbed my frames. “You wear glasses?”

I looked at him, blinking away the blurry vision as if it would make a difference. “I do. I was given the gene of poor eyesight and now everything is way out of focus without glasses or contacts. It’s a curse.” I gently took them back, the hint of a headache slipping away as the world became crystal again. “Without them, I get headaches. I think the last thing I need on this island is another reason for a headache.” I nodded a bit.

Mom had horrible eyesight. She’d been wearing glasses since she was a teenager and now, she was legally blind in her right eye. It was her bad gene I attained.

Glancing at Pan, he watched us with cunning intentions. He was planning to torture me but I wasn't going to back down. He didn’t play so nicely, and neither did I. I’d been raised to believe nice was something one had to fight for.

“Hey, why don't you go dance with the others,” I told Hunter.

“Okay!” He jumped up before joining the circle of wild animals.

I didn't want Pan to think I was bonding well with the boys, in turn bringing them punishment. I couldn't live with myself if he hurt a kid just for enjoying my company. Maybe once I showed him that I was just like them, he'd accept me. That was at least twelve more hours to go before that could become reality.

He wouldn't be letting me sleep somewhere decent just yet. I wouldn't even be surprised if I was made to sleep in a pit of snakes. Could he read my mind? In case he could, I needed to be careful about what I said. I wouldn't give him any ideas.

I kept my knees together to ensure what little body heat I still had left would stay with me.

My stomach began singing the songs of hunger in an attempt to appease the gods.

Don't bother, stomach. We won’t get fed until we win this challenge.

I would make sure Pan lost if it was the last thing I did, even if he killed me in the end.

Once the event died down, the boys retreated to their own cabins. I refused to budge. The clearing was empty—cold—dead silent. Not even a cricket could be heard.

I was going to crack Neverland open like tectonic plates shifting. On a mission. Underground. Spreading like tree roots. Bringing Pan to his knees. I aimed to be an *earthquake*.

"Let's go." I twisted to see Pan wearing a face of his oh-so-lovely irritation.

My brows knitted together. "Where are we going?"

"Back to the cage. Your bed awaits you, princess." He didn't bother to hide the satisfaction in his eyes. He took great pride in *what* he was. A monster.

03: Mooie Duisternis

I tapped my foot to a random beat, swaying my head a little and humming an upbeat tune. This cage wasn't getting any more exciting, so, to pass the time faster, I had been playing nonstop songs in my head. It was moreso a challenge to myself to see how many I could recall all on my own.

I sang quietly, the trees my only audience. Music had been one thing aside from nature that helped keep me sane. Unfortunately when my family would scream at each other, even my music couldn't block that out.

"What are you doing?" The only voice I didn't want to hear. Just my luck.

I let out a snicker. "Oh you poor, poor boy. It's called singing. You should try it. It makes people happy."

He opened the cage to reveal his icy, river-green eyes. I'd be lying if I said his eyes didn't sparkle when the sun hit them just right. "Singing? It sounds musical," he joked.

Regardless of what he wanted, I didn't move, my arms resting on my knees, hands dangling. "That's because it is. It's music with a voice, with words. Words can add a hell of a lot more meaning to a song." My lips curved up on one side. Pan could be a jokester, and so could I.

He grabbed my wrist and pulled me from the cage. "Tonight, you can be our newest member—if you can last that long." He shooed me forward. "Go on."

"Where am I going now?" I turned my head back to give him a disgusted look.

"We're eating breakfast and you get the honors of begging for it." A little smirk formed as he led us over to the firepit. The lost boys were all ready to eat their hearts away.

"Oh, joy." I rolled my eyes as they started to scarf down their food.

I turned my head to search for any signs of the other girl. Yet, there was no trace of her, almost as if she didn't exist. Did Pan make her up? Who was she?

Pan forced me forward by my chin, his nails digging just a little too deep. "I said you're watching us eat." When he let go, he used his hands for his salad. Well, without dressing I suppose one had no real reason for utensils. Why waste the resources?

Of course, my stupid stomach grumbled.

This damn thing needs to keep quiet.

I forced the humor I could into my laugh. "I can watch people eat and be fine. Where I come from, we have the TV. It's a thing that shows moving pictures and I watched a lot of people eat while dinner was still cooking." Courtesy of my sister or my older brother—rarely. "This isn't new to me." I gestured to all the boys who's just about finished.

He shrugged. "If it doesn't bother you, you wouldn't have needed to explain that it doesn't."

I couldn't quite confirm that Pan was born sometime before the invention of the TV. Weren't they invented in the fifties? Maybe I was off, but I'd always been terrible at history. Pan, however, could be nearly a century old.

When he finished up, he headed over to the fire and doused it in water.

"When your bowls have been put where they go, go train. I won't be far behind. I need to deal with our newcomer." He turned to me during that last sentence.

The boys ventured towards the training area for the day and I faced Pan. "What are you going to do now?"

Arms crossed, his eyes gleamed. "I'll let it stay a surprise until it comes."

Pan must have understood horrible parents to some extent. Why else would Neverland exist? Why would adults be banned? Assuming they were anyway. The only answer was Pan's secret and I couldn't complain much about it—whatever *it* was.

I followed him through the trees, crows perched high up above, and we came upon a patch of dead bushes. Rose bushes without the roses.

A mist of sea salt drifted in the air. I could taste and smell it, strong like a freshly brewed pot of coffee. Unlike coffee, the sea was pleasant.

The humidity didn't help the plants thrive. Everything in this path had been nearly rotted and dried out. Right before winter and after the leaves had shriveled up. Before the snowfall.

A sound couldn't be heard for miles. If he killed me, my scream would never reach another living soul.

"What is this? I have to crawl through a bush of thorns?"

"Oh no. No, no. You wouldn't survive. This is mooie duisternis." Whatever he'd just said, I certainly couldn't pronounce. "It's the deadliest plant to exist, only native to Neverland. One cut and you'll die an agonizing death, and there is *no* cure."

I swallowed. "Oh. What are we here for then?"

"One last test. If you can pass this, I'll call you the winner. If you don't, you die."

I gave him a single nod. "What do I have to do?" I only needed to make it through this, and I'd get exactly what I wanted. I would finally get to *belong*.

He put his hand out, a rope appearing from thin air. A little surprising, given magic was still new to me.

He tied my wrists in front of me, then brought me over to a tree that stood tall in the center of this plant, just as barren. "And you may not need these," he said, pulling my glasses and pocketing them. He made another rope appear, throwing it around the branch directly over the bush. "You might want to sit or lie down," he said.

Every bone in my body was desperate to teach him a lesson. Defy him.

Pan shrugged and tied the rope around my ankles. "I did warn you." He pulled the other end down, yanking me up as if I weighed nothing. With magic's help, I probably *did* weigh nothing.

Hanging upside down over the venomous thorns, terror filled me.

He tied the empty side around the trunk of the tree. "Make it to camp alive and unscathed." He left, my pounding heart the only sound heard for miles.

I looked up at the rope around my feet. First, I had to get the rope off my wrists.

When I began using my body weight to swing, I noticed the bush climbed up the tree—and I was dangerously close to hitting it. I covered my face the best I could, and the bush missed me. Now at a stop, I eyed the rope I hung from. With no other options, I'd have to climb up it.

After some failed attempts, I caught it and grunted. "Come on, you can do it." I huffed and pulled myself up ever so slowly. It took a lot of arm strength, and it hurt my abdomen.

I slipped and fell back where I started, groaning in frustration.

Looking up with wide eyes, a small strand of rope snapped. "No!" I had little time. My death was inevitable if I wasn't fast enough.

I swung my body back up and grabbed onto the rope, fingers tightening. I swallowed my fear as the rope weakened. I needed to prove that women weren't weak. I'd change their minds about *me*.

I pulled myself up, and slowly. Mostly because the restraints hindered me. Yet I still had to think fast and steadily.

I gripped the branch as soon as the rope snapped. My legs dropped, weighing me down. I forced all of my strength into my biceps and forearms to pull myself up. To the lost boys and Pan, this was impossible for a girl. As a girl, I knew better than that and I'd love to see their faces as soon as I made it back.

Using that knowledge to motivate me, I hoisted myself up. If I fell now, I wouldn't catch the branch this time.so I made sure to keep a firm hold on the tree.

Trying to find something sharp enough to cut this rope was a tough challenge when the only sharp thing around were thorns that could kill. I had to cut it before I got back to camp if I'd shock them all.

I looked up to see a small, but thick, broken branch above my head. I slid my arms over it, between my forearms right below the rope. I started to move back and forth to saw the rope.

Ten minutes must have passed before it finally came off. Taking a deep breath, I scanned my surroundings. I would have to swing and jump seeing as this tree was being ravaged by the deadly bush.

I stood—carefully—and hugged the tree, looking around to the other side. A thick branch became my new plan. Moving my left foot over onto it, I made sure the branch was stable before scooting my right. I let go of the trunk and kneeled onto the branch, crawling over as much as possible before the branch was too thin to carry me further.

I held on with both hands and slipped down until I was hanging, but I wouldn't cry out for help just yet. I started to swing my legs until my whole body was in motion. Letting go, I landed on the ground where I had always been meant to be, not on my feet, but Pan would never know.

Getting to my feet, a little smirk appeared while I glanced at the venomous thorns. *I was so close to victory.*

Pan wouldn't be too ecstatic, but a deal was a deal.

Everything here went in every direction as I strode between trees. I had to find my way back to camp, but that was easier said than done. If Lia were here, she would've been able to help. Direction was her strong suit.

Despite walking through trees in a straight line, I swore I was going in circles. I was officially a *lost* girl.

The sun had started to set by now and going back in the dark wasn't an obstacle I could face right now. I had already been useless without my glasses. "Damnit!" I yelled to the forest, and seemingly its crows that I had noticed watched from a distance.

I sped up, but a twig snapped from behind. I spun around in a defensive stance, fists ready. "Who's there?" I looked around, prepared for whatever was about to come my way.

Sure, if you call basic combat skills preparation.

A hooded figure exited the woods. "Nobody who's going to hurt you." His confidence radiated. We both knew I couldn't actually fight him and win.

I was slow to retreat, crossing my arms to keep my guard up. "All right then, who are you, and why are you here?"

He pointed in a direction diagonally to my right. "Camp is that way—southeast. Don't mention it." He started to walk into the trees but paused and at a slight turn, met my eyes. "I'm Kace, by the way." He disappeared into the woods.

I stayed put, dumbfounded. Kace? As in, Pan's second-in-command? Why would he help me? Pan wouldn't allow it, and surely his second wouldn't defy his rules.

I didn't waste any more time thinking about it, at least for now. I headed in the direction towards camp, and sure enough, it wasn't a lie. It took me right back, where the boys ate around the fire and Pan stood over like a protective older brother.

Clearing my throat to get their attention, their eyes grew wide. "I passed your test."

Pan's eyes narrowed as he walked over. "No cuts? Show me." He nodded his head towards my body.

Assuming he meant to undress, I complied, spinning for a three-sixty view. “See? No cuts. That means I get the third biggest cabin.” I pulled my shorts back up. “Looks like I will be staying. And for the record, I'm hungry.” I pulled my tank top back over my head. “I’ll take my glasses back, too. Suppose I will need them after all.” I walked over to the campfire.

I grabbed a bowl of food and started to eat, savoring every bite of soup. I peeked over at Kace who sat by the fire on the other side. I’d thank him later for his help.

Giving Pan a once over, I said, “Don't look so heartbroken. You'll learn to stand my presence.” A smirk crawled onto my face as I watched his transform into a scowl.

Fun was an understatement. Messing with Pan would be the *highlight* of my new home.

04: Fairytale

I neared the center of camp, a bit surprised by the empty nest. Pan must have had them training.

Taking a seat in front of the fire, the flame danced for me, and I picked out a song to sing to it in return.

I started off easing my way in and pouring my heart into it every note. It referenced the characters of Neverland, about being a lost boy. When I attempted to sing higher on that note I had trouble reaching, I squeaked.

I finished, letting Neverland hear about what a free lost boy I was now.

Crickets croaked in every direction. The stars twinkled while the fire illuminated the logs around me. Being out here where I would be camping every day of my life wasn't as scary as some people made it out to be. Relaxation was all my muscles now knew. City life became too chaotic. Stressful. Overstimulating. Everyone had gone about their lives in a panicked and rushed manner.

Here, nobody panicked aside from Pan. But that had been his own fault, really. Nobody but him told him I didn't belong.

That must have been why Pan chose a whole island for Neverland. The ocean and the wilderness surrounded us all, but nobody showed fear. What was there to be afraid of? We all felt at home here and that was something that city life could never have given me. Something my family could never offer was peace of mind.

A boot scuffed along the dirt as someone stepped out from the trees. Pan didn't say a word for a minute or two, but when he did say something, it stung a little. "You don't have a very pleasing voice."

I pressed my lips together, tempted to say something witty but nothing came to mind. "I've been told." Nobody liked to listen to my singing which is why I usually sang in private.

Shock took over my body as Pan approached me. "That song—did you write it?" he asked. He was very interested in my music and the words associated with it.

With a shake of my head, I said, "Another girl did. In my world, your life here is a fairytale," I paused while he sat down on a log, "a fairytale with a happy ending. There are two versions of Peter Pan. There's the happy one, where he finds Wendy and takes her here. They enjoy the magic where they fight Captain Hook. Then he has to take her back home, and she grows old."

The strangest look crossed his face. It was a mixture of admiration, confusion, and *heartbreak*.

I lowered my head. "In the original version, Pan kidnaps the lost boys and treats them like shit. It's sometimes believed he kills them to get rid of them because they're said to be gone by the end of the story." I looked up to catch his reaction. The fire highlighted his cheeks and darkened the shadows in his eyes. "That's how we know about you." I swallowed and waited for another question.

"And you still begged me to take you here." His stare sent chills down my spine.

"I didn't think it would be real."

He released a deep chuckle. "You must believe to make it to the island.

You knew it was real."

I dropped my gaze. "Well, I suppose a small part of me did believe and hope this provided me an escape. I was already in a horrifying home situation. This would *never* be a downgrade from that, whether you turned out to be a murderer or not. Which I suppose you are, just not in the way most might think. Maybe it wasn't the lost boys but I'd bet it was Hook or Wendy."

"You know about people I haven't even told you about yet," Pan said.

I wanted to ask him about these people and what they were like in *his* story, but I knew he'd never answer.

Something was on his mind and if I could just lift his scalp and peek inside, we'd get to the root of the problem a lot sooner.

But that wasn't how men worked, nor magic. I couldn't just use it to look inside someone's head. I'd have to crack the wall he built for himself, and he couldn't keep me locked out forever.

Pan nodded, lifting his finger at a cabin on the other side of the fire. "That's yours."

Compared to the other cabins, this cabin was nicer. Mostly. I had to admit it took balls for Pan to come through for me. There was a sliver of a chance to train him. He had to be teachable, or else I had no reason to live here.

Once Pan left, I took a brisk walk to the garden. It was close to the well where we got our water from, and one day I'd check that out, too.

A small boy kneeled in the dirt. So innocent and pure, depending on how much Pan stole from him already.

As I approached, I sat beside him. "What's your name?"

He straightened up and whispered, "Eric."

I nodded. "Eric. I'll remember that. What do you do out here in the garden?"

Eric pulled out a head of cabbage. "I farm." A little laugh escaped me. With a smile, he handed me the cabbage. "Don't tell Pan I gave you this.

He'll get mad."

I zipped my lips. "Understood. It'll be our little secret."

Eric turned his body away and as soon as I wanted to ask why, someone walked by. I turned my head to see the lost boys arriving. Standing, I headed to my cabin to drop off my cabbage before anyone else saw.

I smiled to myself at the memory of Eric giving me something to eat. It was a sweet gesture, and hopeful that I could make friends despite Pan's hostile environment.

Jacob and Levi shot me glares as I passed them. Boo-hoo. Boys didn't take too well to women emasculating them.

I turned my head as Kace walked over. He waved me to follow, and so I did.

"So you helped me. Why?" I asked.

He didn't look at me as he said, "I have my reasons."

"And I suppose you're not going to tell me those reasons." I faced my cabin.

We stopped at the door. Certainly not as big as Pan's, but not as small as the other boys'. "This is yours now. You earned it."

"Thank you for helping me. I know it was a risky choice. I didn't think someone would find me worthy of defying Pan." I glance up at him.

Dark curls sprung from under his hood, but he'd been just a tad tanner than Pan.

When he did finally give me his attention, his brown eyes held some animosity. Towards me? "I didn't have to help you, and I would not call it defying Pan. Don't take my one kind act for rebellion. That's not what this is." He swept his arm towards the room. "Get a night of good sleep. Goodnight, Lili." He twisted his heel and disappeared into the cabin one over.

He knew my name. Kace knew *my* name. Someone had to have told him, which meant someone else remembered it. Was it Pan? Would Pan even remember, or tell Kace? Either way, Kace had known. Contrary to everyone else, he wasn't as bad as Pan. Hunter had told me, and I hadn't listened. Kace had some humanity in him. A sign of good health. Pan couldn't get to him, at least not completely.

I stepped inside my new room. It was decent, and I had no complaints there. In it stood a dresser and a bed, and an extra door which I assumed was a bathroom. Having my own bathroom was a green flag, considering I'd been used to sharing with my sister and two brothers.

Wood covered every inch—to be expected. A few candles and matches laid on the top of the dresser in case I'd need them. Someday, perhaps, but I'd spend most of my nights out and about.

He had come through with his promises and that was something I couldn't fault Pan for. He wasn't so bad and yet he chose to play the villain of his own story.

According to the fairytales, I now had forever to find out why.

My father had intentionally done the same. Become the villain in my life.

As a child, I made my first art project and I brought it home to my dad. I hadn't realized what a big mistake that was. He ripped it up in front of me and tore my heart. To this day, it still needed stitches, and that was the first memory I had of him.

Fortunately, Pan didn't rip up my heart—at least not yet.

The dresser whispered my name, so I went to dig through it. The clothes would work just fine.

There were shorts, mainly in brown and black. There also happened to be two pairs of leggings, also in black and brown. No sense of style from Pan.

In the middle drawer were shirts in a teensy wider variety of colors than the bottoms. By wider, I meant white. A white and black tank top, then two more shirts in the same shades.

Next to the dresser sat a pair of black leather combat boots. Practical. Stylish. "You gave a girl something to work with," I said as a crow landed on my windowsill. "It'll do."

In the top drawer were things I weren't expecting. Underwear and bras. Pan had given me underwear and bras. A gesture he didn't need to show, but I appreciated it nonetheless.

But after checking the tags on the garments, I released a sigh. "These aren't the right size."

The crow cocked its head.

"Oh, don't give me that look. This underwear is too small, and so are the bras. The thought was nice while it lasted."

The crow cawed to announce his departure. A little rude.

I removed my glasses and put them on my dresser. Everything around me blurred, but I could still make out its shapes. A useful skill for surviving in the wild.

I lay down in bed, studying the ceiling's every crack, wondering when I would get a tour. I didn't even care if I got one, but I'd love to know where to swim if not the beach right behind my Pan's cabin.

What made Pan who he was? Nobody could keep a secret forever.

When my eyes began to droop, I closed them and turned on my side, pulling the blanket over me. I was going to sleep tonight, and I'd sleep well. I had my own bed, and it wasn't in a cage anymore. It was the result of being a thorn in Pan's side—the kind that came out victorious when he was the only one left scathed. It was the privilege of being a *lost girl*.

05: Mountains

Settling in, my eyes fixated on the fire—flames licking the wood that crackled, embers drifting into the night sky. "The story begins...with a mechanic. They repair cars for people." I snickered. "Imperfect humans, I tell you."

The boys all leaned in to listen.

The clouds floated by and the sun burned everything in its path—human skin and asphalt alike. At a local mechanic shop, things seemed to be going as stress-free as one would like until a woman returned to get her car.

As she entered, she told them her name and which car she came to pick up. The mechanic got everything in order, but not before long, the price added up. "We noticed some extra things..." The words she always dreaded to hear. Going to the mechanic was more stressful than a family gathering for the holidays.

After everything was said and done, she asked for the total price. She almost had a heart attack, knowing she wouldn't be able to fix it. Who had that much money on hand? So she paid for the current repairs and turned to leave.

"Ma'am?" the man asked.

When she looked back at him, her breathing shortened. She feared what he would say next. Would he tell her that her car was done for?

"You lost your earring." He held out a small stud.

She grabbed it from him. She asked herself if it was even possible to go without a car. No more car expenses again, right? If only it were that easy.

When she went out with friends, she was always the one driving everyone around because of how much she put into her repairs. She had the working windows and AC. That was enough to remind herself she was lucky to be able to afford a car and repair it at all.

While leaving, she muttered, "Thanks for nothing."

As she walked out the door, the mechanic wondered if he would ever see her again. If he could give her discounts and keep his job, he would.

She continued to visit when her car needed repairs, and every time, she dreaded the news. The mechanic learned so much about her through fixing her car. What had him intrigued about her the most was how she treated the mechanics with respect, despite how angry she would get at the mention of problems.

This woman always did her best to work with what life handed her.

He was finally going to work up the nerve to ask her out. Maybe he could relieve some stress and fix her car outside of work. He wanted to see her smile for once.

She walked out the door for one last time. Neither of them knew it, but after that day, the shop never saw her again. The mechanic hated himself from that day on for never asking her on a date. What he never learned from her car was how sick she'd been and now she was finally somewhere better where bills didn't exist, and stress could not enter. She was now where people flew, and time never moved. She was free.

The boys smiled in awe. "She went to Neverland!"

I laughed a little. "Yes, indeed."

Pan rolled his eyes and scoffed, leaning against the cabin. "Don't be silly. Adults don't come to Neverland. They die here."

Everyone went quiet.

Pan exited the camp not long after. Even after he left, his presence lingered, and nobody wanted to say a word. Damn him and his power. I'd eventually do something about it. *Eventually*.

I retreated to my cabin.

My mind wandered back home. I tried to suppress the memory, to avoid letting myself down but I couldn't erase *her*. Nana was the one friend I had who wanted to help me out. She wanted to get custody of me—and she almost had it. Mom and Dad were just too smart to let me go. Nana truly loved me and that was what I missed the most. I missed her beautiful storytelling and funny jokes.

Five minutes later a knock echoed from the other side of my door. When I opened it, surprise painted my expression when I found Kace waiting.

As he lifted his hood from his head, I first noticed the dark hair that wanted to spiral out of control—literally in spirals. His eyes were just as unruly and yet they never screamed *run* the way Pan's did.

"You look like you need someone to talk to," he said after minutes of silence.

I laughed a little and gave him a shrug. "Should I remind you that you're Pan's friend, and not mine?"

Kace stepped back. "Do you want to go on an adventure or not?"

My grin widened. "I do."

We ventured off into the forest. We had walked straight behind the camp and beyond, passing some areas that caught my attention right away.

The largest tree I'd ever seen passed by, as well as a little waterfall that looked ever so inviting.

Kace kept moving so I never had time to stop and smell the roses. We stopped at some lush mountains, as far as he'd go. "Pan doesn't trust you yet. But keep showing him that you're not who he thinks you are. Eventually, he'll warm up to you."

"Why are we here?" I glanced up at the overwhelming mountain before me.

He nodded his head towards them. "There are some things to teach you that Pan praises. Climbing the mountains is great exercise and he doesn't have to know I told you. Now, it's totally up to you whether you do climb but if you want to show Pan that you belong here, the exercise would be good for you."

I gasped, looking down at my body. Was I that out of shape? Of course not, seeing as I'd beaten Jacob *and* Levi in tests.

With a twist of his head, his eyes were back on me. "I know what you're thinking, and yes you do need exercise. Everyone needs to keep up if they wish to be part of the army that fights pirates and the hunters who gather food."

Which did I want to be? Regardless, he had a point. I didn't want to be the lost girl who refused to exercise along with the lost boys. I *chose* to be here, and it was my decision to make sure I'd fit in.

Kace shrugged. "Or you can be the kind of person who wants to be credited for the hard work they don't do. It's your choice, Lili."

Before I could catch it, the question slipped from my tongue, "How do you know my name?" Hearing it out loud made the question sound disappointingly stupid.

A laugh erupted while he rolled his eyes in a more playful manner. "Word gets around. Believe it or not, most people here remember your name. Pan may act like the bad guy, but he isn't all wicked. You earned your spot as a lost girl, didn't you? You passed the tests, and when you surprise people, they never forget your name."

I tilted my head.

I'd become memorable. Even without Pan's trust, I'd already begun to win the respect I'd always craved.

"Climb some mountains and we'll see if you really do want to be one of us." He left, and as he did, a little smile formed. As if he knew I was *home*.

Placing my first foot against the base where the mountain met the ground, I heard, "Trying to fit in?"

I stepped back and turned to look at the guy. Jacob, of course. Still feeling cheated since I beat him at his own game. Maybe not my proudest moment, but it had certainly been high up there.

"It's more than just fitting in. I need to exercise if I want to survive here in Neverland. We're in the wild, Jacob. So do you mind?" I gestured to the mountain.

He stepped forward and lifted his chin as if he had another idea in mind. "I do."

Snickering, I said, "You want to fight me again? What is that going to prove after I won Pan's challenge? Get over it."

He closed the distance between us, backing me up until my feet caught where the mountain met the ground, sending me against it. Jacob grabbed my wrist and pushed it into the rock covered in a thin sheet of greenery. "Pan only let you be one of us because he wants to fuck you."

I struggled against his grip, but his fingers only tightened. Pan despised me, and he made that much fairly clear. There was no way he'd ever want to sleep with me. Kill me, I could believe. Like a cat waiting for the right moment to take out the mouse.

"Just a girl on an island of boys with raging hormones." Using his other hand, he started to lift my shirt. Every muscle in my body withdrew from his touch, my own breakfast about to head back up for seconds.

Slipping one hand free, I shoved against him.. "Get your hands off of me, you disgusting prick." I spat on his cheek.

He slammed my other wrist against the mountainside—the shattering of bones the only sound ringing in my ears. I yelled out, my knees buckled beneath me.

Jacob pressed his hips against mine. "You keep holding back like you don't want this." He dragged his filthy mouth down my neck, earning a gag from me. I'd need to burn that area.

I needed to burn my entire body to erase his touch.

He gritted his teeth, grabbing my shirt and ripping it from the back. "Admit it." He forcefully held my chin and lifted my jaw while burying my head into the side of the mountain. "Admit you want me."

I used my good hand to get his pants undone. "I want you," I started, "to rot in a fucking hole." I reached in and gripped his balls, twisting and yanking.

He screamed from the pain and backed away until I let go of him. He grabbed hold of his crotch with a satisfying fall to his knees. "You stupid bitch."

I lifted my foot and slammed the bottom of my boot against his face. "That makes two of us." A pleasant sound. His cries. His insults. Had he not remembered that I knew moves better than he?

I took off running back towards the camp before he could regain his stability.

When I returned, some of the boys gave me looks but I made it to my cabin before the questions started. Sliding down the inside of my door, I inspected my hand. Humiliation was an understatement. I'd allowed the ass to get his hands on me and now my hand paid dearly.

I ripped the rest of my tank top up and wrapped strips around my palm and wrist, tucking it.

"Our little secret, Jacob. Lucky you," I said with a scowl.

A crow cawed as black feathers flashed by my window.

After I changed my shirt, I left the cabin to get myself some lunch. Food was all I wanted to focus on right now. If I could force it down, that was.

Once I had my bowl in hand, Jacob entered and shot me a dirty look. Although, he had it coming for trying to force himself on me. It was *my* body after all. Did he really not expect a girl to fight back? Foolish of him. I'd go down kicking and screaming if I had to go down at all.

Pan stepped out of his cabin and looked at the black cloth around my hand. "What happened?"

Before Jacob could throw me under the bus, I replied, "I was trying to climb a mountain and I fell. I need a better grip."

It wasn't entirely a lie, but it would suffice. Pan was the last person I wanted to cry wolf to. His lost boy was a rapist, but I wasn't about to let him know it.

I didn't fear that Pan would turn out to be a predator, too. He didn't strike me as that guy. What I was afraid of was being a victim on an island full of boys. Like Jacob said, I'd been the only girl where boys with raging hormones resided. The less who knew I was a target, the better. It wasn't their business that after becoming the first lost girl, I'd already been targeted by one of their own.

A babysitter's daughter used to do the same. She would get me into trouble because her mom would believe her over me, and I'd never done anything wrong to her. I still never figured out why she hated me so much. I'd just been a child and she a teenager. However, from that experience, I knew never to cry wolf to a parent about their own. They'd always defend their family first.

I wasn't quite family.

When Pan glanced at Jacob's broken nose, he wanted to ask him about it, but he kept his mouth shut. Maybe he did know what Jacob did, but he never said a word about it.

This was my battle and I'd fight it alone. It was safer. Less mentally and emotionally exhausting than telling a man his friend was a woman's worst nightmare. Too many women knew what it meant when a man defended the abhorrent things his friends did. I was not about to become another.

06: Menstruation

It hit like a boulder. Once the boulder stopped, it hatched into a dinosaur with tiny claws, stabbing endlessly. My insides screamed for it to stop, blood gushing. Everything contorted in a way that became normal, yet not any less painful. The kind of pain could never be forgotten. It happened too many times, month after month. Always unannounced. I would never be any more prepared than I was.

I rolled over onto my side, curling up and squeezing my eyes shut.

I needed something—anything at all, really.

Dragging myself out of bed, I left my cabin. Slow steps, but not steady by any means. I held my lower abdomen, stumbling over small things that were never there to begin with.

The boys piled out from their cabins, chatting amongst themselves. They kept in line much like an army, until one little boy stopped in front of me. "Are you okay?"

His question gathered the attention of another boy. "She's bleeding! Oh my gosh, she's going to die!" All the boys started to panic. Their ruckus led to Pan coming out to see what all the fuss was about.

"What are all of you crying about?" his voice shouted over everyone.

The collective chaos halted.

"Pan, she's dying," a boy said, pointing in my direction. Hunter, I presumed.

He lifted his eyebrows when he faced me, but his eyes didn't show any signs of confusion. "Go train. I'll be there soon."

As soon as they cleared out, he closed the large gap left between us.

This pain, the one thing that made me weak. It was all I had to come apart at the seams. "I'm going to need somewhere to bathe. And if you have anything at all to..." I didn't know how I would explain to Peter Pan what a period was. It was barely explained to me with any sensible reasoning, and even then, I needed to experience it myself to understand it in its entirety.

"You need something to stop bleeding all over the bloody place." He turned to walk to his cabin, so I decided to follow him. As soon as we got to the door, he turned to me. "You stay out here." He disappeared inside.

How did he know what it was? As soon as the question came, it hit me. Of course. How could I forget? There was another girl here and she had a period, too, if I had mine. That was the only explanation.

When he stepped out, he tossed me a box of tampons. "Here. Just one more girl I'm required to take care of."

Required? He provided me a place to sleep. Clothes. Food. Now, tampons. I supposed he did take care of me, but that was putting it lightly. I fought for my rights to be here. And given his tone, he didn't particularly enjoy having to go on tampon runs. So why was I here at all, then? How did I slip through when millions of other girls called upon Pan himself?

I scanned the area. Where did she sleep? And did Pan really keep tampons in his room?

"I still need a place to bathe." My cheeks reddened. "I should also mention I, uh, don't actually know how to put a tampon in." I'd always worn pads instead of tampons. Mom and Lia never taught me, and Nana would never have known how to.

He groaned, rubbing a hand down his face. "You've got to be pulling my leg." He grabbed my wrist and pulled me along. "So needy, aren't you?"

"I resent that."

"It's mutual."

We passed the same large tree and stopped at the waterfall I'd been wondering about when Kace took me. "You can bathe here, and I'll send someone to help you with your...*problem*." He shooed me off before he vanished into the trees.

The crows surely gave me no privacy as they circled the area.

I stripped down to my undergarments, wading through the cool waters, washing the blood.

Crystal clear had been one way to describe it. Chill, but not chilly. Mesmerizing. Hydrating. Serene.

If only I could have enjoyed it to the fullest extent, and not the reason I was here for.

Being clean during my period was a feeling I could never replicate, but the cramps made everything worse. Maybe I could talk Pan into a jacuzzi for the winter.

Twigs cracked behind me. I whipped around and came face to face with a girl.

She smiled, and I swear I heard the birds sing. "Pan told me you needed my help." I got closer as the blue-eyed, blonde beauty put her hand out to shake mine. "I'm so pleased another girl lives on the island." She was everything men wanted. The lady mothers would raise their daughters to be when impressions were life or death for a family's future. How could any woman be this perfect? "I'm Wendy—Wendy Darling."

My ears twitched. She was *the* Wendy. Wendy Darling was the *other* girl. I should've seen it coming. It made perfect sense and yet I never even considered the possibility. Were they dating, or was that just wishful thinking from the humans who stumbled upon fairytales?

"Can I know your name?" She had the attractive accent that Pan did, and no doubt she executed it perfectly. Thick, and poised.

"Lili." I cleared my throat and shook her hand.

"Is it short for anything?" Her voice was as soft as a feather and as smooth as silk. Pan hadn't broken her quite yet. I admired her for the strength it must have taken to keep up that reputation on an island of boys. Who knew how long she'd been residing here.

Shaking away the questions, I said, "Liliana." I grabbed my dry clothes off the rock to my right and stepped out of the water. "Pan sent you because I don't know how to use a tampon."

She grabbed the box and pulled one out. "Don't be embarrassed." She held it up and showed me how it worked as I put my tank top on.

"Thank you. Now I'm going to put one in, before I start bleeding again." Wendy spun the other way. I put one in, adjusting my legs.

Strange feeling—what an understatement.

I finished getting dressed before she turned back around. "Where does Pan get them from anyway?"

She shrugged a little. "He has magic, so my best guess is as good as yours." My best guess what that the guy visited the mainland. How frequently, I couldn't tell.

"Where do you sleep?" I asked.

She walked with me while I carried my box of tampons. "In the cage."

Mouth agape, I looked at her. "Are you serious? You always sleep in the cage? That's cruel. Where do you sleep when someone else is locked in the cage?"

She lowered her eyes. "I sleep in his cabin. I heard you got your own. No lost girl existed before you, and now you've managed to snag a cozy cabin of your own."

"Maybe I can convince Pan to let you stay with me. I have room," I offered.

We couldn't share clothes, seeing as what she wore was a white dress with dirt stains. Frilly. Ruffled. Proper for a woman of her time if it had been washed.

"Oh, no, that's not needed. I don't want your cabin privileges taken away." She nodded rapidly but smiled only a tad. Much like someone refusing a drink but hoping they'd ask one more time so they could revoke the refusal.

I shook my head anyway. "No, I'll ask. I'll keep an eye on you if that's what he's worried about."

We stopped at the firepit, and she turned to say her goodbyes. "Nice meeting you, Lili." She disappeared near Pan's cabin, feet away from Mermaid's Lagoon.

Tempted to follow and see where she was going, I bent over in pain and brown leather boots appeared in my line of sight. "What do you need now, *Little Flower*?" Where in the hell did this nickname stem from?

I lifted my head up to meet Pan's eyes, sighing with added flair. "I just need warmth and a place to curl up in pain. Painkillers would be amazing, but you have no idea what those are."

His face hardened from the insult. Was it any less true? "I'm giving you two hours."

I choked. "Two hours? Do you not realize that this type of pain lasts two days for me?"

"Wendy has pain for merely a few hours." He shrugged, fingers wrapped around his biceps with his arms folded.

Another sigh, this one much more exhausting. "No, Pan. Believe it or not, but every woman's period is different. Some last longer, some shorter. Some women don't get cramps, some have cramps that last days. They all vary. It can make a woman capable of *murder*."

He threw a look back at his cabin with a sneer. "Lovely. Now you're rendered useless for days on end. Why did my shadow even bring you here? You don't belong."

"My family didn't love me a single ounce." I shot him a glare. "And for the record, you think you're hurting because I'm dealing with my period?

Try being the one who's bleeding from your damn genitals."

He came closer and leaned down near my ear until I could feel his breath fan across my cheek. "The next time you give me attitude, I won't hesitate to starve you and work you until you pass out. I will make you wish you were hunted and killed for sport instead."

I closed the gap, showing him he had no effect on me. "Try me, Pan. I'd love to see you damn well *try*."

Asking him about Wendy sleeping in my cabin wouldn't happen tonight.

He clenched his jaw but didn't budge. "Go. I don't want to hear from you. You're wasting my time."

With a smirk on my lips, I spun on my heel and walked back to my cabin. When the door was closed, I sat down on the bed, warm tears rolling down my rosy cheeks.

Lack of emotional control was only a symptom, I told myself.

Pan hated me so much, and for no reason. How was it possible that a man could hold so much hatred, and how could he project it so well?

He took us from our homes where we felt neglected, unloved, and unwanted.

How horrible were his parents? What had they put him through that taught him it was okay to treat others with such little disregard?

He was a man who had no heart—a man unloved and unremembered. He was a man who held so much power over those who pleaded for his security. Everyone here looked up to him—thought he was what they strived to become. He set a terrible example for the young boys.

Curling up in the bed, I tried putting pressure on my cramps to help alleviate some pain, but it didn't last long. My cramps found a way to make me suffer, just like Pan always did. Relentless. Unapologetic.

I rolled onto my back, staring at the ceiling. "Make it stop. Please, make it stop."

Whether I was asking for the cramps or Pan's ruthlessness to end, I wasn't entirely sure.

I begged for it to end, but it wouldn't help, and it never kept me from trying.

I was weak underneath the armor. It'd all been just a front to never let anyone see me beg. Even at home with my father. Everywhere I'd ever went, I put on a mask to hide whatever I felt deep down. Emotions made one vulnerable. Emotions could lead to destruction, and I refused to be the debris left in Pan's path. As long as nobody ever saw, I'd always be seen as a warrior.

During the hours of pain, I would contemplate all that time I spent without it, and how much I took it for granted. I never realized it when I was free of the chains.

That explained exactly how I was living on this island. While I was here, my only goal was to make the pain disappear.

I wanted Pan to be a better version of himself.

I believed in redemption. It had been something I always wished for my father, but it never came true. As for whether or not they deserved forgiveness was a whole other ballgame. People didn't have to associate themselves with someone who'd hurt them, even if they did change. However, I still believed that Pan changing for the better would benefit the boys, Neverland, and most importantly, Pan himself.

As much as I despised him, I also knew if I was going to live here, he needed to be a better king. Getting him to admit that would be the hardest part of all—but it was also the only way any of us would survive. We all deserved the happy endings fairytales promised us.

07: Beware

Two days of suffering had finally passed me by. I had three weeks to myself before I would become immobile once again, and I'd spend them *well.* In the meaningful sunlight, basking in the glory that would become Pan's loss. Save him, sure. Provide hope to the lost boys. Restore Neverland. But I'd take great pleasure in my victories.

Long gone were the days when Nana would aid me through the misery. I'd gotten my first period when I was at her house and she'd been so kind to explain what I needed to do. She kept painkillers, a fresh pitcher of tea, and a rice bag at my disposal.

I misunderstood how they worked in sixth grade during that class where we learned about our changing bodies. I thought periods lasted forever, and I hadn't realized there were three weeks between each one. Oh how Nana laughed so hard when I told her I'd need lots of pads that first time.

Everyone sat around in a circle around the fire while we ate our breakfast—berries and salad.

I loved both, and the fruit salads were a genius combination. Whoever made them here, I needed to thank them personally. I'd thank Wendy.

Eric looked at Pan. “Peter, is she going to live? She was bleeding a lot...”

After minutes, Hunter spoke up, too. With a sorrow-filled expression, he said, “Please tell me Lili's going to be okay.”

Pan gritted his teeth out of irritation. “She's going to be fine. Now shut up, will you?”

“Why was she bleeding?” Hunter asked.

He stood up in one motion. “Ask her yourself!” He left the circle. His fuse box tended to short out often. It wasn't a surprise of any sort. Boys couldn't handle their emotions the way girls could, and that was probably because we were more in touch with ours, and they were taught *not* to be.

Hunter walked towards me and stopped. “Please, tell me, are you going to die?”

I shook my head. “No, no. This is normal for me. I know you guys don't know a lot about girls, but we are different. We're built to bleed. I promise you don't need to worry about me dying.”

He grinned. “Good! Don't tell Pan, but I think you're cool,” he whispered close to my arm.

I chuckled, patting his shoulder. “Your secret is safe with me. I think I'm cool, too.”

Hunter got up and joined another boy in conversation.

I'd spent my past two days in bed, and now I was feeling energetic. I wanted to get up and do something productive. The question was, what?

A shadow fell over me and I turned my head up to Kace. He stood still, eyes focused on something behind me. “Come on. Pan told me to give you a tour and a rundown of how things work around here in Neverland.”

“I already know how things work around here in Neverland.” I furrowed my eyebrows.

“No, you don't.” He started venturing off behind our cabins.

I hesitated, just for a moment, before jumping onto my feet and running to catch up with him. I followed closely behind, avoiding the plants on either side of us as much as I could. In case those too were poisonous. “All right, then. How do things work around here? Time stands still, correct?"

"It doesn't exist. Time standing still is a totally different subject. This island runs on Pan, and vice versa. The two are forever connected. If he dies, the island goes with him. If Neverland dies, he returns to the bones from which he came." He glanced back. "There are certain places that we should avoid altogether." He pushed branches out of his way.

"If time doesn't exist, how do I get periods?" A branch filled with countless leaves smacked me in the face.

Kace laughed at me. The bastard. "Periods are not a result of time existing. Yes, indeed, your eggs shed because your clock is ticking but in Neverland, you aren't aging. You're just going through the normal motions and your body doesn't lose memory. Neverland isn't that powerful, not against mother nature at least."

I pressed my lips together.

"Pan is connected to the island. They thrive off each other. He has all the power, Lili. Do you hear me? You always obey him, or he punishes you. He doesn't go back on his word, and he won't allow anyone to make him look bad in front of the lost boys. He has no remorse when he kills. You're walking on a thin wire right now." He halted.

I stopped and cleared my throat. "So, why exactly does he hate women? Mother issues, or is he just prejudice?"

Not a hint of muscle dared to move on his face. "That's a story I'll let him tell. It's his—not mine."

"He's never going to tell me. He never tells me anything." I crossed my arms in protest.

A small smile formed. "I'm just letting you know you should really try to stay on his good side." He started walking again.

"That's his good side?" I scoffed.

"For you, yes." He stopped at the edge of a cliff. I screeched to a stop before I walked off the edge.

The creepiest rock stood in the distance on the ocean. Two eyes. A mouth. "What is that?"

"Skull Rock. That's off-limits. If you ever attempt to go there, I won't be able to save you." He peered at me.

I swallowed and nodded my head towards the rock. "What's over there?" Waves crashed against the rocks in a fit of a storm, but no storm had been present. Maybe it had just been the pure sin that reeked from that cave.

"Only Pan'll tell you under his terms, and it should stay that way." He turned around, starting off in another direction. I trailed behind him, back down the path. "This next place is another area you should avoid. You'll be tempted to come, seeing as it's directly behind Pan's cabin, but I warn you not to." We came upon the beach east of camp, and I gazed out on the waters. Soft. Pleasant to the ears. Sparkling under the sun.

"Is this Cannibal Cove?" I asked.

"Mermaid Lagoon, actually. They don't like newcomers *or* Pan. That's why he placed his cabin here, to keep watch. I wouldn't risk it. They won't hesitate to kill you." He looked me over. "And Pan doesn't like it when one of his campers is threatened by the mermaids. He hates having to save anyone."

"Right, because he's a killer. I get it. Steer clear of everyone because everyone on this island wants to kill me." I let out a little laugh.

I understood that it was serious, and my life really was in danger no matter who I met or pissed off. I wasn't about to go test the waters and piss people off just because, but I wouldn't let the fear control me, either.

Kace didn't smile, not even a little. Did this guy have any humor? "Let's go." He walked off to the next area.

We approached another beach after a few hours of silence. Much needed on his part; a little lonely on mine.

I pointed to the waves rolling against the shore. "Cannibal Cove. I know this one. This is where Captain Hook lives, right? And Captain Hook is a cannibal? That's where the name comes from."

"Yes, this is Cannibal Cove. I'm warning you to also avoid Hook." He clasped his hands together in front of him in a calm manner. None of this bothered him. He was used to danger, and possibly reveled in it the way Pan did. Hm. Maybe there was something about the two of them I was sensing...

I nodded a bit. "I get it. Everyone is dangerous. Avoid these places. Pan rules everything. You could've just said that."

"I could have, but I'm showing you which directions not to take so you don't get lost and stumble upon these areas. We've lost many by telling them rather than showing them where not to wander off to." He turned his head to his left. "I have a few more places to warn you about."

There were more? Of course there were. Neverland was dangerous on its own, nevermind every single spot filled with murderous creatures.

As Kace strode while I struggled up the cliffside west of Cannibal Cove, I noticed something moving in the waters beside us. Something large, with gray-blue scales.

"You forget that I'm a woman. I don't think like boys. If you tell me something important, I listen. I don't just let it go in one ear and out the other." I gave him a little smirk.

He returned with a sly smile, retorting, "You demonstrate the opposite when you speak to Pan."

"That's different. Pan makes it hard to want to listen to him. He is all threats and no kill. He wouldn't hold such words of importance if they fell out of his mouth without his permission. You, however, have proven to me that I can trust you. You haven't given me a reason to not want to take advice from you. I understand you work for Pan, but you're still different people based on your actions." A rock tumbled down into the ocean below.

Kace gestured to the water. "This is Zeeslang Waters. You should avoid it if you don't want to be eaten."

"Eaten?" I asked.

He sent a grin my way as he gripped my arm and pulled me back before I fell in. "Yes, eaten by the sea serpent. Let's head back before you get yourself killed." He led me the other way.

I glanced at the water one last time, but nothing showed its face. A bit disappointing to say the least. I'd hoped for a tale to tell the others.

We made our way back to the camp where Pan was waiting. "Good, Kace warned you about which places will get you killed. It'll be best if you take his words as commands and *not* suggestions."

Kace went to do his own thing for the rest of the day.

Looking at Pan, I said, "Upon my observation, Kace is different from you. He's trustworthy. However, he still defends you. Why is that?" I paused to give Pan a chance to answer but he didn't budge. "I wouldn't be surprised if you two were lovers. It'd make sense as to why you two are so different, yet he still has your back every chance he gets." I kept my eyes locked on him to capture his true reaction.

Nothing. Not even a blink.

He reached out to fix my hair, pulling it over my shoulders. He let it go, down my chest in its unkempt state. "My relationship with my second-in-command is none of your business. Even if it were, you shouldn't just go assuming things about people because sometimes you could be far off. Is it so hard to believe that I have a loyal man at my side? We've been friends forever and our bond is really that strong, Little Flower."

"It is, yes, because of how different you two act around me. Maybe you're right, maybe your sexuality is none of my business. But what about your hatred towards me? It still makes no sense. I'm trying to understand you, Pan." I began to circle him.

He grabbed my arm, planting me where I was. "Don't. Don't understand me. Kace and I share a pain that nobody else here understands and *that* is all you should know. My secrets aren't yours to go digging around in. I'm warning you to not get yourself into this mess." He loosened his grip and for the first time, his face softened. "And I don't hate you."

I let out a sigh and dropped my gaze, then glanced back up at him. "If you're my leader and you hate me for no real reason, I think it's my place to know why." I stepped back. "You're a terrible leader." My eyes never faltered from his, because if they did, he'd take every bit of confidence I had left in me.

A crestfallen smile appeared. Who had hurt him this much? Could someone really be this way on their own?

I allowed him time to process his thoughts and form them into sentences. I could *obey*, too.

The melancholy left him as soon as he said, "Love, I am not romantically involved with my best friend. I just don't trust the sex I'm attracted to. Do you need proof?"

I choked. "Do I need proof? I don't think I need to see you struggling to get it up for me. Sorry, Pan, but that's just sad. I'll spare you the humiliation." I snickered. "I wish you'd just tell me why you hate me so much." I turned away as the man formed from thin air right in front of me.

He leaned closer, whispering against my upper cheek, "I'm not a genie so be careful with what you wish for."

The corners of my lips twitched, but I kept myself as still as possible. He hated me, so how could he turn that into something that resembled attraction? But Pan could do anything he wanted, and *I* was on the wrong end of this game.

08: Waves

I finished getting dressed before setting out to go talk to Pan about Wendy staying with me. I promised her I would get her a better living situation than a cage.

On my way to his cabin, someone tugged on my shirt. I stopped and turned to see Eric. I smiled, bending down to his level. "Hello there."

He pushed the toe of his shoe into the dirt. "Pan says you're dangerous."

"I'm only dangerous to him because I don't obey him like he wants me to. Is it so dangerous to have free thought?" He had to be the youngest boy here, given his baby face and short legs. No older than seven or eight.

He finally returned the smile. "I want to be your friend."

I'd cry if I'd still been on my period. "That's so sweet. You for sure can be my friend. You'll make a great friend." I straightened and grabbed his hand. "All right, what do you want to do?"

He scanned the trees around us before his eyes finally rested on me. "We can go explore the island! But only the good parts."

"I'm ready for that adventure." My smile grew. An adventure was much needed for a girl like me right now.

"That won't be necessary," Pan said from behind.

I spun around to face Pan. I scowled, cursing him for ruining my first real *adventure* with a lost boy. He was such an asshat.

A small smirk danced on his lips. "What's wrong, Love? I get to choose what you do and who you do it with. I think Eric should go off and do something else."

I frowned as I looked down at Eric. "Maybe next time. I'm sorry."

He nodded quickly. "It's okay." He ran off towards the others.

Facing Pan, I folded my arms across my chest. "We both know we don't particularly like one another. What's this about?"

He stepped closer, leaning towards me. "Did you forget about *my* next adventure? You." He walked off with a smile plastered on his face. I hadn't seen Pan smile like that before. It was playful with no ill intentions lurking behind it. Impossible. Some kind of *trick*.

I followed, keeping my distance. "You're forgetting one thing. I already know about your little bet. It doesn't exactly make a woman want you when she knows you're only being nice to win your own game."

He shrugged me off just like that. "I don't expect it to be permanent." He changed the subject to spare me the humiliation. Was I embarrassed? Hardly. "I dislike you, but I was attracted to a woman once. I don't dislike *all* women—just certain ones."

I couldn't picture Pan with a woman. Absurd. Him? A woman on his arm? Even as attractive as he was, he wasn't all that alluring to be around, from a woman's side of things. If she was interested in men, that was. I couldn't even picture a woman choosing to be with Pan at all. That was laughable at best.

"Certain women, as in...me?" I gestured to myself, referring to the color of my skin.

His eyes lingered on my complexion, but I didn't witness any prejudice in there. "Your race has nothing to do with it. It's about intentions, and not every woman has good intentions." He turned on his heel and fixed his posture. Feet planted, hands clasped behind his back. “I certainly didn’t hate my last partner.”

Partner? As in, friend? Or did he mean a girlfriend? Had Pan dated before?

Rolling my eyes, I said, “Okay, Pan, you hate me—for whatever reason you won't say—how do you expect to put that aside for a game? If you hate me so much, you can't just hide that, and you can’t make me believe you can either. I've known from the start that you feel nothing but hatred towards me. Isn't your deal supposed to be showing me you're attracted to women?” I gestured to myself.

He twisted his head my way, tilted back a bit, an eyebrow cocked. “You think because I don’t trust you that I can't be attracted to you. Tell me, do women not love bad boys in your world? You can dislike someone but still want them.”

I pressed my lips into a thin line, stumped. I despised knowing he was right. How did he know women loved bad boys in my world? Had other girls come through here? Did they throw themselves at him? “But if you still feel attracted to us, then why don't you ever want more?” I gestured to my body. “You mean to tell me you have self-control when men older than you lack all of it?”

“My bloodlust is stronger than my lust. Serial killers are the same way. They can be married, but they are more inclined to kill than have sex with their wife.”

I huffed. Right, yet again. How did he know so much about my world?

Something in my brain clicked and I felt uncomfortable knowing Pan could actually be attracted to me. I had to remind myself that he wanted to kill me more than he wanted to kiss me. *Why* did that make me feel better? If anything, it should've been worse. It was a game of marry, smash, or kill. He chose to kill and somehow, I preferred that option.

He started walking away from me. “Let's go explore now, shall we? The good parts,” he added on with a hint of laughter. He barely looked back, a playful smile moving across his lips.

I proceeded with caution. "Who does he think he is? Oh right, a king," I mumbled to myself.

He chuckled. "I am."

I sighed, exasperated. I was not one to enjoy being wrong. I especially didn't want to be wrong compared to Peter Pan, the Demon King of Neverland.

"Do you sunburn? Genuine question." I glanced at the sun. Seeing how pale he was, he had to burn.

Pan sent a look my way but never gave me his full attention. "I don't burn. Do you?"

"Nope," I said with confidence. "That's why I fit in so well. I don't turn into a sundried tomato. I flourish like a tree." I twirled my index finger towards the sky to mimic a tree growing.

He snickered but never said another word on the topic.

We ventured through the trees in silence the rest of the way, until they cleared out to the ocean.

"Is this Cannibal Cove? You're going to threaten my life to win?" A roll of my eyes. "Typical."

His eyes swept the shallow waters along the shore. "Neither. It's just a beach. There are other access points to the beach that are not full of monstrous creatures."

"Oh, great. Pan is trying to be romantic. This is rich." My laugh echoed in sync with the waves.

He didn't even chuckle.

I cleared my throat. "You're going to fail. I won't fall for Peter Pan."

"Who said anything about falling for me? Are you afraid I'll be that charming?" He bent down and unlaced his boots. "You might want to take your shoes off for this." He removed his boots, then socks. He undid the tool belt around his waist and placed it in the sand next to his shoes.

I complied but not without a groan. I removed my boots and socks. "All right, Pan—" Pan grabbed my wrist and pulled me down to the water faster than I'd seen anyone move before. My feet splashed through the coolness, the salty ocean soothing them over. It was refreshing in this heat.

He let go, studying my relaxed expression. "Have you ever been to a beach?"

I shook my head. "Never. Where I lived, there wasn't a beach nearby. Driving to one wasn't an option either. With shitty parents, you don't take family vacations."

He backed into the water some more. "What was your family like? My shadow may come when summoned, but we don't see your memories. We know nothing about you when you come here except that you had a horrible life, enough to call for my shadow."

I lowered my eyes to the water, admiring the way the sun reflected off the surface. "It's strange to think you and your shadow aren't attached. My shadow is controlled by me. It's not a person."

Sliding into the water, my body soaked in the depths of the ocean. All its cries. It's fears. Every person who's ever fallen in love and every heart that ever broke.

A wave crashed against me before I had a chance to run. It took my glasses right off my face and I reached into the water to grab them, but they weren't around me.

He shrugged and waded through the seafoam. "You avoided my question."

"Pan, my glasses are gone! I can't see without my glasses!" I couldn't go blind for eternity. What would I do? I moved my hands around in the water to see if I could touch them, but nothing came up.

He reached down and grabbed something from the water, handing me a pair of black frames. "These?"

I put them back on and swallowed. "Thanks..." I wasn't happy about thanking him. "I won't tell you about my personal life. You don't get the privilege." I looked up at him.

His jaw tensed. The anger I incited was relieving. I could still do that. All because I wouldn't obey him. What a lovely thought to live by. And yes, it did help me sleep at night.

There was a grumble in my stomach. "I guess I'm hungry."

Pan narrowed his eyes. "How can you be hungry? We already ate breakfast." A man in charge of "growing" boys was asking me that question? Did I hear that correctly?

Standing up, I cupped my hands together while I scooped up water, throwing it at him. "My stomach is bigger than my eyes."

"I'd hope your stomach was bigger, or we'd have a real problem on our hands." When I scooped more water at him, he scowled. "What the bloody hell was that?"

"It's called splashing, Pan. You should learn to be less serious sometimes." I did it again, and again, until he copied me, splashing me in return. More laughter filled the sky. "That's the spirit!"

We both got into a splashing war which eventually led to Pan trying to throw as much as he could. His body came with him, and down into the waves we went. His dark hair dripped into my face as he grabbed my glasses before they could drift off to another island. Despite ice-cold water encasing us, his breath warmed my face. Up close, he didn't look so bad. Underneath the hard exterior, he could almost pass as a misunderstood man—the one Kace had been so loyal to.

Bright green eyes. A blush to his cheek. Lips that needed something to warm them up.

But everything got shoved away as Pan jumped to his feet. Eventually I hurried to my feet so he couldn't see whatever-the-hell-just-happened written all over my face.

I'd accomplished today's task if I could teach Pan to have fun again. That was what I'd focus on, and not his blemish-free skin. Or his pleading smile.

We exited the water, beginning to dry off. "See, wasn't that fun? I hope you enjoyed being young again. Since there are no adults here, I think it's fair that you boys have a little fun." I laced my boots while he buckled his belt.

He walked over as I wrung out my shirt.. "I've never *been* young, Love."

I didn't question what that meant for too long. "Can I ask why it's so important you prove to me you're into women?"

He gave me a look as if I asked the stupidest question ever. "Because I don't need you to tell my boys that I have a romantic relationship with Kace. I'm their leader. I don't play the game of love, and I don't need you to ruin my reputation."

"So, you would rather them think you like me instead?"

He grabbed my chin, locking my gaze. "What happens between us will never get back to camp. This is our secret. A challenge to prove you wrong. It doesn't involve them, and it never will." He let go, his touch still tingling my skin long after.

I put some space between us before he could do it again. Why was he insisting that we didn't tell anyone? Was he embarrassed to be soft?

I was beginning to figure out why Pan was so cruel towards me. He assumed if he wasn't, he'd be seen as some emotional man and not a real one. Maybe he wasn't hateful, and maybe all along he was just scared to show his true feelings. After all, men had been taught what a man should be, and lacking emotions was one of them.

I wanted him to admit I was right, for once. "Is there a rhyme to why you are like this? When you created this island, did you have to be the bad guy to survive, or are you vicious on your own accord? Do you hate women because that's what they taught you, or do you hate women because men were taught it wasn't okay to let your guard down?"

He lifted both brows. "Do you always ask many questions?" He mocked my words, "you don't get the privilege."

I hated when he did that. He was *always* right, too. "You won't win this. I'll make sure of that." I balled my left hand into a fist and put it up in front of my left cheek, pretending to cry. "Boo-hoo."

He dropped one eyebrow. "What are you doing?"

Rolling my eyes, I answered, "Of course you don't understand. You're a grandpa."

"Last I checked, I didn't have any kids." He cupped his elbows, arms splayed across his torso.

I studied his reaction—pure. He wasn't amused. "It's an expression, but I'm sure you don't understand that either. You pride yourself on being so powerful and great, but you don't even understand that I called you grandpa based on your age." I gestured to him.

His eyes drifted off to the trees. "Physically speaking, I'm eighteen. Your expressions don't apply." He turned on his way, disappearing into the forest back to camp.

He thought he would win this bet, but if he couldn't even follow the number one rule of winning a woman over, he was a lost cause at this point. *Apologize* and tell her she was right.

09: Concussion

Walking over to the well, I peered into it as footsteps approached me from behind. I stood and faced the only logical culprit. "Pan."

"What are you doing?" The expression on his face was genuine curiosity blended with some disappointment.

If I told him the truth, his disappointment would grow. Nobody truly wanted that, not even from Pan himself. "Just checking the well. What else does a lost girl do around here?"

His lips curved up in the corner. "You don't want me to answer that." How considerate of him.

I faced the well and attempted to see the bottom. It was useless. There was only one way to see for myself if the well was the portal between Neverland and my world.

Before I could get a leg over the wall, I heard, "Don't fall in the well." Was he going to stand and watch?

Mentally scoffing, I shook my head. He could do what he wanted but my mind was settled. I threw both legs over and jumped down before he could say another word.

Everything went silent as water engulfed me. I broke the surface and gasped for air. My theory failed as Pan's head appeared in the small circular opening. What a lovely wish one could make. Certainly wasn't going to be me. The skies unfortunately looked the same from both worlds. I was not going home, which meant I could *never* visit Nana.

"I believe that was the very thing I told you not to do," his words vibrated against the walls around me.

I grabbed for a stone and searched for a route to get out of here. "Did you really think I'd listen?" Pan knew better by now. I defied every rule he set in place.

He disappeared. What the hell?

"Hey! Aren't you going to get me out of this?" I yelled up.

Climb mountains.

Of course.

Just as I started to climb, a rope came down. I twisted my head back and lost my grip, falling back down into the well. My head hit the concrete. I barely made it to the surface before the rope was pushed against my face. "Grab onto it," Pan said with frustration lacing his voice.

I grabbed the rope as he pulled me up out of the well. I landed on the dirt and closed my eyes, rubbing my head. There had to be blood, and if Pan saw the blood, he'd want to kill me right here and now.

Kace approached us and bent to my level. "What the hell were you thinking?"

Groaning, I said, "I was thinking I could get out of Neverland if I ever needed to."

Pan rolled his eyes. "She hit her bloody head. She needs medical attention, and I'm not using my magic on her."

Kace helped me off the ground. "I'll get to it, then." He took me to his cabin and placed me on his bed.

His cabin didn't look much different from mine aside from the size of it. It lacked just as much personality.

"Eyes open," he said.

I opened my eyes and frowned. "Kace, I'm tired. It would be wrong not to let me sleep."

He dropped his hand against his leg, a sigh passing his lips. "You hit your head, so I can't let you fall asleep for a few hours."

Once I followed his rule, he looked at my head and cleaned up the blood. The pain would surge through my head every time he touched the site.

"How do you know about concussions?" I asked.

He lifted an eyebrow in question. "How old do you think I am?"

A lopsided smile found its way onto my lips. "The real question is how old do I think *Pan* is?"

He shook his head before allowing himself to laugh a little at that. So the man *did* have a sense of humor. How wonderful. "I want to know."

He wanted to know? I think this could be the start of a real friendship. He was allowing me to make fun of Pan and boy, did I take joy in that. I'd abuse the hell out of that.

"I think he was born sometime in the early 1800s. Right around the Victorian era. Oh boy, imagine Pan being born in the Victorian era!" I laughed, but it faded quickly. I didn't think Kace knew what that era was. "Sorry."

He handed me a brush for my hair. "For what?"

I grabbed it from him, eyeing it. If I used this kind of brush, it'd work in Pan's favor. His crows, too. My hair was a literal bird's nest. "You don't know what the Victorian era is."

As if it were his turn, he laughed on cue. "Yes, I do. Do you think I didn't take history lessons in school? And I wanted to point out that you're just a hundred years off from Pan's era."

Pan's era. Oof, that did not sound good at all.

"A hundred years? Oh my gosh, he was born before America was even discovered!" I widened my eyes and choked. "He's so old. He has no idea what America is. How did you guys explain to him why some have different accents? How did you explain what Independence Day is?" I leaned closer. Assuming Kace knew what both were. He must have if he knew what the Victorian era was.

Kace was no American and that was true. Where he came from was a mystery to me, but he had a hint of an accent that came from a place of Hispanic roots.

Kace shook his head. "Who the hell taught you history? America was not discovered in the 1700s. It was discovered in 1492."

My cheeks heated up as I lowered my eyes. Was it really? Then what the hell was 1776 for?

He continued, "And no, I did not mean go back one hundred years. I meant to go forward. Pan was born in 1905. He would have seen the Great Depression had he not ended up here. He's not that old and I am much younger."

"Much? How much?" I tilted my head, wincing.

He shot me a look. "That's my business."

If it was his business, why did he mention it? Now I was curious to know.

"Why did you jump down a well?" he asked as he scooted his chair back.

I furrowed my brows and tapped my chin. How did I explain to Pan's best friend why I wanted to escape Pan if it ever came to it? Now he was the stupid one, and I'd hold that over his head for a while.

"Well, it turns out that I don't belong here, and I want to go home." Ah, yes, *that* was the truth...

A laugh bubbled from his throat. "You don't belong here? You've stopped at nothing to prove your worth, so I don't believe that for a second. Pan is not that bad."

Honestly, Pan wasn't even the reason. Nana was. I just wanted to see her and tell her about my best adventures for once. I wanted to see her eyes light up as the smile reached them—proud of her granddaughter for being a strong woman. "Yes, it is all his fault." As well as Jacob's, who was going to stop at nothing to destroy me.

Just last night, he'd come into the room and tried to rip my clothes off. He hadn't taken the hint the first time that I wasn't interested in having sex and so I sent another message—a thumb to the eye.

I couldn't tell Pan that his lost boy was trying to assault me. I couldn't even tell Kace despite us being friends in some way. That was the thing about being a woman. I couldn't tell anyone here when I was being targeted because I would be blamed for it all—but Nana would never make me feel like a criminal. She always believed me. She never made it out to be my fault.

Kace sat forward and rubbed the refusal from his eyes. "I know he's something different to deal with, but he'll get there. He can become your friend. If you just let him."

I leaned back against the wall. "That's because you're a male. Pan likes you. He trusts you because you both have penis'. I don't. He doesn't trust me, and he is very intent on making sure I know this."

He wasn't sure how he could respond to that because I was right. He couldn't continue to tell me that Pan would warm up to me because the truth was, I was a woman and that wouldn't change.

This was why I couldn't tell him about Jacob, either. He'd find a way to make it sound like I could fight him off, as if I was in the wrong. He'd tell me to just cover up more or avoid Jacob, instead of telling Jacob to back off. It was always about teaching the girls how to not be a victim, and nothing about teaching the boys to not do unspeakable things.

Jacob was in good with the group, and I the new girl. It was not so simple to tell them that he was trying to steal something from me. Not as easy as expecting them to take my side over his. Much like where I came from, rarely did men ever take a woman's side on a matter like assault.

"I'm sorry," I said. I wasn't sure as to why I was apologizing. It wasn't my fault. Maybe I was just afraid of ruining the one good friendship I had here.

Kace leaned forward and removed his hood. "You don't get to choose what parts you're born with. Trust me when I say I know how that feels.

Sometimes people refuse to accept you as you are because they're too close-minded to see what is right in front of them."

I stood and grabbed my head to ensure I didn't lose it. "You're a guy. You don't have to deal with being judged for your sex."

Kace shrugged. "You don't know what I've dealt with. I experienced it. You can't tell me what I experienced wasn't real."

I stepped forward until I had his attention. "Then stop telling me that being the only lost girl on Neverland is so easy. Neverland's king hates me. He judges me. If you know how it feels, then do something about the culprit, and stop telling the minority that they can just get over it as if it doesn't hurt deep down." Being the only girl wasn't all that bad if men didn't royally screw it all up.

Kace got to his feet, swallowing. I assumed he was about to tell me off. He was Pan's best friend after all. "You're right."

I choked. Did he say I was right? Even Pan refused to ever admit that.

"I don't know how you feel because I'm not you. I don't have to worry about being accepted because I'm not the only girl on an island of boys. I'm sorry for making you feel like your feelings don't matter," he said.

I was speechless. How could I say something after that? He'd apologized. He admitted he was wrong and that was more than Pan could say.

He lifted his head some more to show that he wasn't going back on his word. Why would he?

"Thank you," I whispered. I was thankful that he could admit his fault and if I told him that, he would learn that it was truly a fault and not something to be okay with.

Kace smiled a little. "Are we still friends?"

I laughed, nodding. "Yes, we're still friends."

A huge weight had been lifted when he saw the error of his ways. It was always a constant build-up of frustration and stress when everyone else made me feel like I was the one in the wrong. Hearing one person admit that I wasn't just on my period, having mood swings, was a breath of fresh air.

If Pan ever used that against me, I'd kill him. As if I didn't already want to.

"I guess now I'm a walking accident." I lifted my wrapped hand to show him my broken bones. A broken hand and a busted head? I could survive it all.

"What did you do?" he asked.

Shrugging, I said, "Tried to climb the mountain and fell." Same lie I told Pan. If my lies were consistent, they'd appear more believable. Cover all my bases.

Kace checked outside the cabin. "Do you want dinner before you leave Neverland?" he joked.

I shrugged and walked out of the cabin. "I guess I could eat. Although I do want to go hunting one of these days."

He glanced at me. "Hunting? Why hunting?"

Was it that I found joy in killing animals? No. But my other option was to join an army of those boys who killed people and I'd rather kill animals for food than kill people for fun. "Because hunting isn't just a man's job. Women have to eat, too."

He chuckled. "You got me there. I'll let Pan know that you want to train for hunting. I'm sure he won't mind."

If he did mind, we'd have yet another problem. I was here to be a lost girl and if hunting was an option for anyone who lived in the camp, that included me. I could also handle the sight of blood far more than any boy on this island.

Pan caught sight of Kace and I walking beside each other. Was he jealous? He could deny it, but I saw the truth. The harder he tried to prove me wrong, the easier I saw through his façade. Why else would he be so adamant to have an island full of men? Why push away women? Maybe because if the boys saw how Pan chose Kace over a lost girl, they might question it—might judge him. He could choose Kace over me any day and

I wouldn't bat an eye. What sent my blood boiling was the way he treated me as if I were his *ex*.

10: Hangman's Tree

I made my way back to camp alone. Pan had gotten a head start by leaving me at the beach so soon. We'd went for *another* swim and I couldn't deny that I enjoyed it. As soon as I arrived, the first thing I noticed was that everyone was eating food.

I quickened my pace and made it over to the fire. "Lunchtime already? Great, I'm starving." I plopped myself down on a log.

Pan came out of nowhere and gave me a nasty look. "You're late. You won't be getting lunch today."

"That's not fair! You left me behind!" I jabbed my finger in his direction.

"Maybe next time you'll remember that we have lunch at a certain time around here. We wait for no one." He disappeared back into his cabin. What did Pan have in his cabin that entertained him for so many hours in a day?

I turned back towards the fire when a presence appeared next to me. A smile appeared when I recognized Eric. He handed me his bowl of soup. "Here. You can have mine."

"Oh no. That's okay. It's yours." With a gentle push, I moved the bowl back his way.

He smiled and set it in my lap, nestled in the space where my thighs met. "I don't need it. Please, take it."

"How about we share?" I suggested. I couldn't eat his soup without guilt. He needed it as much as I did.

With a nod, he said, "That works." He grabbed another spoon from his pocket and scooped up some of the vegetables.

I took a bite. After swallowing, I said, "You're going to go far with compassion like that."

He giggled. He was such a sweet boy, and I felt sorry for him because Pan was his leader.

"What all can Pan do? What are his abilities?" I asked.

"I know he can transport himself! He's also strong. Undefeatable. The boys hate fighting him. He can get anything he wants and make it appear out of thin air. There's nothing he can't do." He nodded his head a lot as he seemed fascinated by Pan's powers.

I tapped my chin, deep in thought. "Interesting. So, the guy is completely undefeatable. Great," I said, my voice dripping with sarcasm. It was useless trying to make him admit he was the problem.

Eric gave me a look of sympathy. I didn't enjoy being here as much when their own king hated me. Even at home, they despised me just as much, and I wanted someone to simply love me for me. Even after proving I was strong enough and worthy to live here, Pan wasn't giving it up for me. I had to survive here or not live at all. There was no option of going back home.

It wasn't so much that I wanted to go back to just see Nana. I was going to be eighteen soon and that meant I'd have a chance to move out, and that was what I missed. I missed freedom. I didn't want Pan to control me for the rest of my days here. I craved *independence*.

We finished our bowl of soup. He took it back before Pan figured out he shared. At least all his lost boys hadn't had their minds corrupted by his piss-poor leadership skills.

Eric's presence returned. I said, "I'm glad you're back. I was thinking maybe we could finally go on some adventures like we had planned to do the other day before Pan interrupted." I looked to my right, but it wasn't Eric this time. Instead, Kace sat beside me.

Confusion displayed on his face but he shook his head. "I came to tell you Pan wants to see you. He wants me to take you to him." He got up from the log. "And he doesn't wait."

"Why can't he come to get me himself?" I was tired of Pan. He always pushed my buttons. He always made me want to scream to the heavens.

"He's planning something. It's easier to deliver you to him." He scanned the boys.

"Deliver? Excuse me, I'm not a package," I snapped. Maybe I'd been harsh, but I *wasn't* a package to be delivered.

He looked at me. "Do you not consider yourself a package deal?"

I made a face of defeat. "Oh, how sick." Sick indeed. To prove me wrong. Why did everyone do that?

He added on, "When you're born, you are explained as having been delivered."

Huffing, I said, "Okay, I get your point. Let's just go, shall we?"

He began walking back behind the cabins. After a moment of letting Pan's crows grow anxious in the trees, I ran after Kace.

"You told me you haven't been here as long as Pan. Do you miss your family?" I asked. I glanced up at the sun for a moment and reminded myself we were headed west. I needed to learn to read the sun like a clock in case I got lost. Again.

He kept his eyes on the trail ahead of us, but his words were as clear as day. "What family? The family that didn't love me?"

I didn't know what to say to that. "Well, I..."

He stopped, and I didn't notice until I ran into his back. He turned around and awkwardness ensued from being so close. It wasn't awkward because we were a boy and a girl, but because the anger radiating from him was impossible to miss.

"My family did not accept me for who I am. They wanted a girl. They didn't want a son. They tried to diminish my masculinity. They tried to hinder my ruggedness. Here, I can be the man I was born to be, and I am accepted for it." His stare cut deep into my soul.

It wasn't until now that I realized how scary he could be. I now understood why he respected Pan. He was capable of anything. Pushing the wrong buttons could turn him into Pan himself.

Swallowing, I focused my eyes elsewhere.

He continued, "I know that you want to pretend that you're moral and perfect, but you have to come to terms with this at some point. You must accept why you came here. You came here of your *own* accord. Nobody forced you. You came here to get away from the family that hated you. We all came here for the same reason. This is what connects us. Stop treating us like the enemy simply because we, too, asked Pan to take us away, and we choose to *obey* our savior. We are just like you, only less resilient." He turned on his heel and vanished into the brush.

I hurried to find him. I couldn't handle another half-of-a-meal tonight.

Somewhere inside, I wondered if Pan had parents like us. He created this island, and he was filled with magic nobody else here possessed, but someone had to have given birth to him. He must have started to collect lost boys from abusive homes to give children a place where they could be themselves. He must have taken them in because he wanted his own family. I wanted to see humanity in Pan somehow. I *needed* to see it if I was going to stop myself before painting Kace as the villain, too.

We stopped at a giant tree. This had been the largest tree on the island I'd wondered about. It was stunning compared to most regular trees. We were on an island full of them, but this tree stood out.

Tall. Large trunk. Roots that twisted like forming a crown. Leaves that shined bright for eternity. You'd never find them succumbing to the harsh winters or delicacy of autumn.

"What is this place?" I asked, turning to Kace.

"This is called Hangman's Tree," someone said. Kace hadn't opened his mouth to say anything. The voice that answered me had a thick accent attached. One with a bit of gravel to it. My eyes fell upon the source of the voice where Pan stood, leaning against the trunk of this magnificent tree.

Kace nodded out of respect and left us.

Pan pushed himself off the trunk and approached me. "Hello, Love."

"Why did you call me here? Also, what the hell is Hangman's Tree?" I gestured to the huge tree behind him. Of course I'd heard of it. But I wanted to know what it had been in *his* world.

"This tree provides me a quiet place to think to myself." He admired the beauty, eyes glimmering.

Confused, I said, "I thought that's what Skull Rock was for."

"No. That serves me a different purpose." He faced me again and walked around the tree with his hands clasped behind his back. "I hear women like nature. The pretty kind."

I choked on a laugh. What was this moron smoking? "Who told you that?" I crossed my arms, not at all moved by his words.

"That isn't important." He stalked over to me, much slower this time. I did not like the look of this one bit. Then again, did I ever enjoy being alone with Pan? Better yet, did I enjoy being around him at all? No. The answer was always *no*.

He grabbed my hair, fixing it. This time, it wasn't just being fidgety on his part. There was a deeper motive to it.

Clearing my throat, I said, "Pan, if you plan on assaulting me, it won't end well."

Both eyebrows shot up in surprise. "I'm offended that you'd assume something so horrid of me. I'm many things, Little Flower, but I'm not a rapist." He shook his head and began circling me. What was the point of walking in literal circles?

Him and his stupid reputation.

"Then what the hell do you plan on doing? Trying to woo me is laughable at best. You're not a romantic kind of guy. You're a sadistic man and you said so yourself. Just admit it, Pan. You hate me."

He halted in front of me. "It truly intrigues me as to how well you think you know me." He stepped closer, *way* too close for my liking.

"I have to guess because you won't tell me anything else." I backed up to put space between us.

A stupid little smirk formed. "I am not obligated to answer your questions or tell you anything about myself. Assuming things about me doesn't make me look any worse than it does making you look better."

Change the subject, now.

Stepping around him, I walked up to the trunk. I knocked on the wood, amazed by something of Pan's creation. "This is just a tree, correct?" I looked back at him.

He tilted his head.

"Nevermind." I shooed the question away and blew out a deep breath. "How do you plan to show me you don't hate me if you refuse to trust me? Most people learn right away. Are you going to kiss me, Pan?" I snorted.

He closed the gap between us, getting my full attention. "I plan to torture you."

I didn't even have a clue what he meant. He was trying to prove he wasn't sexist by torturing me?

"I can tell by the look of confusion on your face that you need a demonstration. Just remember, I feel nothing for you. This is purely a game for me. Don't act surprised when you get hurt."

I blinked and then squinted through my glasses. I still didn't understand what he was talking about.

He came closer and I stepped back to get away from him. This continued until he had me trapped against the tree. He could murder me right now and I'd be powerless in this position. He could almost taste my blood, and I could most certainly taste his satisfaction.

My eyes almost fell out of my head when something soft brushed against my arm. I peered down at a red rose that stood between his fingers. "Roses are romantic, are they not?" he asked, tipping it forward.

What the hell was he doing? It was *just* a game to him. What did I get myself into? I put myself in the position of being romanced by Pan. This was truly a punishment. This was what I deserved for having to butt into his business.

A shiver ran up my spine when he put the rose between our lips, the only thing that really separated us from a closer connection. A kiss.

I did not enjoy this, and I think he noticed. He took great pleasure in my lack of enjoyment—or to be more precise, my frustration towards myself for falling for it.

He held my chin between his fingers with the same delicacy he held the rose, his fingers sending sparks. "I hate to break it to you, but I'm the Demon King and demons *always* win on Neverland."

"No. You won't win." I pushed his hand away from my chin.

The rose disappeared from his fingers and he placed his hands on either side of my head, palms flat. "You have no say in this. You made it clear that you think I'm in a relationship with my best friend, then keep insisting I hate women—and I'm anything but sexist. I'm a lot of things. A villain. A demon. A king. But I'm *not* sexist. I will make you feel things that even you cannot control until you'll have no choice but to believe me and to believe *in* me. Because I am Peter Pan, Love. I've never been anybody else."

Nothing would please me more than getting my personal bubble back to myself. Kace brought me here for this? Did *he* hate me? And here I thought we'd become friends.

He chuckled at the sight of my fear. "You're afraid to lose. I take great amusement instilling fear into my opponents. You are merely a pawn in my game. Do not forget that."

With a clear voice, I said, "Likewise."

I wished he would back the hell up already. I wanted nothing more than to get his stench away from me. I had never been more scared in my life of what Pan thought would count as romance.

"Give it up, Pan. We can end this bet, go our separate ways, or you can continue this bet and accept losing. It's your call. I can spare the humiliation, but this offer is only on the table for a short time," I said.

He chuckled as he leaned close, whispering in my ear, "You make the offer, hoping I'll take it, and all because you're scared of losing yourself. I don't take bets I can't win, Little Flower."

I released a sigh, attempting to ignore the warmth of his breath and the tickles from his lips brushing the top of my lobe. "And yet, you took this one. Shame."

His words came out in one breath, "I *never* fail."

11: Shame

I couldn't even look at Pan without feeling uncomfortable. It was worse now. Before, I loathed him, but now I just questioned *everything*.

Maybe if I faked believing him, he would give up this little game. Being Pan's challenge was not a fairytale. It was a nightmare waiting to devour me until I couldn't take another breath of my own. Like possession after sleep paralysis. I was probably overreacting but there was something awkward about the villain trying to win my affection.

As Pan turned and walked out of the training area, I followed on a very confident whim. "I think we need to talk."

He looked back at me and lifted an eyebrow. "About what?"

"About your sexuality."

"And what about it?"

"I'm sorry for assuming things about you. Sometimes I just do that because I try to understand those around me, and I thought maybe you were gay and that explained why Kace was close with you. I thought if I could figure you out, you could tell the truth to the lost boys and be more of yourself. You could show them who you really are." A branch smacked me in the face. What the hell? Did all the branches around here hate me? And why were the crows laughing?

"There's a difference between telling them the truth, and exposing your secrets when it isn't their business," he said.

I wanted to ask him what he meant. Was this his confession? Was he trying to tell me that he and Kace were together?

Pan stopped and grabbed my arm to keep me from leaving him behind. "Why is it so hard to believe a man on an island of boys doesn't hate women?"

I shrugged.

"I don't hate women. I just don't trust you because of how manipulative you can be. Women tend to only want me for the power I hold."

A laugh escaped me without permission. "Tell me you're not serious. Pan, you are exactly what you claim to hate! You do this so damn well. You are evil; you are manipulative. When have I proved to be those things? I'm talking about me as a person, not me as a woman. You are more of those things than I am." It was astounding how blind he could be towards his own projections.

He lowered his eyes and scanned the area. "Let's talk about this somewhere else." He must have been afraid of his lost boys hearing. Was I getting through to Pan? Could he possibly be about to do something kind?

We found ourselves more privacy in front of that thinking tree of his.

He took a few seconds to make sure the area was clear, then faced me. "You're right."

I choked on my own saliva. "Did Pan just say I'm right?" Being told I was right in a short, few days—I was truly living a dream.

"Yes. Don't make a big deal about it." His eyes almost rolled out of his head.

"But it is a big deal! I'm getting through to you." I let a big smile form.

He narrowed his eyes. "No, it's not. You'll shut up if you don't want to sleep in the cage," he threatened.

I sighed. "Well, it's a baby step. Will you at least tell me why you believe women are so evil? Did a woman use you for power?"

Silence.

"Peter."

He shot me a glare, eyes flashing gold. "Do not call me that."

I put my hands up in defense. "Okay, I'm sorry."

Both of his eyebrows had been lifted high on his forehead. "Did you just apologize to me?"

Ignoring his question, I said, "If we're going to work to be better, it needs to be a two-way street. How about we make a truce?"

He shook his head. "What is a truce?" he asked.

Ah, yes, a truce wasn't a thing in the 1900s. Or, at least not for Peter Pan himself. "A truce is a neutral compromise. I was proposing that maybe we could make a compromise. I'll follow you if you agree to work with me."

"How does this benefit me? I don't want to work with you," he paused. "Why don't we just forget this?" He gestured between us.

My hopes raised themselves far too high. "Yeah, I can. Does this mean the challenge is off?"

He chuckled as if I'd said the funniest thing. "Oh no. No, I will not forfeit this. I told you I never fail. This challenge is on until I win."

"Why must you feel this need to prove to me that you think I'm pretty?" If I could use words in a way to irritate him, I'd take the jab. Anytime, anywhere.

He coughed, almost choking on his wishful thinking. "I don't think you're pretty. I just think you're attractive."

"You think I'm attractive? That's exactly the same thing, Pan. You just called me pretty using another word." The corner of my lips curved up.

He sent a similar smirk my way as he grabbed my hand and pulled me closer. He held my left hand in his and put his left hand on my waist. He began to move his feet in a pattern.

"Pan, what are you doing?" I tried to pull away.

He turned me around. "Don't women like this?"

"Yes, when it's romantic. This isn't romantic. This is just the game of a wicked man trying to dance with a woman who hates him." I escaped his grasp. "I said I was sorry, and I shouldn't assume things. Please, stop this."

He laughed and I thought maybe I was hallucinating. It was a genuine laugh. "You can't escape the consequences that easily." He pulled me against his chest. "You'll be entertained, but not the victor."

I was just trying to end this. I realized my mistake and wanted to reverse it. I couldn't let him play me.

I couldn't be *his* pawn.

He hummed, and hearing Pan make any pleasant sound wasn't rooted in a fairytale. Not even reality. I was somewhere else, wherever unicorns galloped. Unbelievable. "I must find your romantic weak spot. Every woman has one. There has to be one thing that you can't resist."

I kept my mouth shut. I wouldn't cave. Of course I knew what my weak spot was. Would he? No. He still couldn't read minds.

He disappeared in the blink of an eye, appearing once again in a tux. It amazed me that Pan could dress in such an outfit considering his morals. Then again, the bad guys pulled them off the best.

I put space between us, despite the fact there was already plenty. "I don't have one," I lied.

He saw right through it. I forgot I was a bad liar.

He vanished, returning with a rose this time, still suited up. "What about now?"

A big sigh. "Nope."

He leaned very close to my ear and whispered into it. "I will come out victorious, Little Flower."

It gave me chills, but I refused to let him know what made me melt. A weak spot was more than some goosebumps. He needed me to cave, which I'd never do in his line of sight.

He pulled back. "I must be getting close."

Pan brought one of those little devices from my world, an MP3 player. A song echoed into the sky and bounced between trees to reverberate the perfect sound. Was that also magic, or just physics? I failed physics.

I left his bubble and invaded the tree's instead. "Let's just call it off. I won't tell the boys about it. I won't tell a soul that you failed. I won't even mention it ever again." I could keep to that promise.

He approached me. "The fact that you're begging only makes it much more tempting to win." He pushed my hair back. His finger barely brushed my cheek, and it made my heart speed up, nearing the speed of a puma.

His eyes lit up as if he could hear my heart pounding. "Oh, did I find it? Is this all finally wooing you?"

"No," I said firmly. It took strength to say that without stuttering, because deep down I was cursing myself for falling victim to his ways.

He brought his hands to my waist and pulled me closer to him, leaving little space between us. He danced to the music, leading the way, and I was amazed that Pan could move like this. I didn't stand a chance against his persistence.

I didn't dare say anything though. I'd never intentionally boost his ego. My words would completely fail me, so it wasn't worth opening my mouth.

He lifted my chin with the tip of his index finger. "I think it's fair to say I'm winning. Don't you agree? No woman attracted to men can resist what I have to offer. Just the right mood can change the way you see me. It can change how you react." He moved us both to the rhythm, his fingers pressing into my waist. I swallowed as he relished my undoing of his making. "Admit that you're enjoying this."

Keep my mouth shut, and I might've actually survived this humiliation.

It was tempting to lay my head against his shoulder, but why the hell would I give him more leverage?

He let go of my waist. "You insist that I'm with Kace, but you can't fathom that just maybe two men could be close *without* being gay. This challenge started because of that simple accusation and then, you realized you'd lose. I came to prove to you something you refuse to believe. I'm real, so is it hard to believe my best friend is, too?"

I'd begun to realize my mistake. If I was close with a girl, how would I feel if people just told us we were dating? I was the very person who assumed two close males had to be gay and I knew how wrong I was now.

I took a deep breath and lowered my head to the dirt. Was this finally over?

"Shall we further this challenge? I say if I can get you to admit I'm romantic, I win. It proves Kace and I are close and nothing more." The heat radiated off his body, seeping underneath my skin.

My blood boiled, skin flushed. After I thought it was all over, he proved me wrong. He just couldn't get enough.

He smirked upon seeing the pink tint on my skin. "I take that as a yes. I do love a good challenge." He leaned in closer until his lips were near my own. He wanted this win because I'd shown him up when I became a lost girl. Now he'd stop at nothing to take back his crown of twigs.

Pan wrapped his arms around my waist once more, moving our bodies to the beat of the music. I'd forever hate and despise this moment on this timeless land—and I wasn't just trying to convince myself of that.

"Oh, admit you enjoy this, Love. I very much love the reddening of your cheeks. Knowing how you feel about me. You're attracted to me in every way possible."

"Yeah, because it's working in your favor. I'm not attracted to you."

"No?" he teased.

"No," I spat. But those green eyes were far too mesmerizing up this close.

He was just goading me, and I was falling for it. Hook, line, and sinker.

His dark waves fell across his forehead as he pressed his body against mine. His lively eyes buried themselves in the depths of my lifeless ones, causing the red to deepen. Something was wrong with me. Being messed up in the head was the only explanation for how this made me feel.

He whispered, "I'm getting there." He continued to turn, spinning me.

I almost gasped. I didn't want him to be the victor. This entire *date* was abnormal. Pan was dancing with me and succeeding at his own game. I screamed for help in the abyss of my mind. "I know you can do it."

I didn't want to say it. I couldn't look more foolish than I already did. If I failed, he'd tell everyone, and I'd be the joke of the camp. I wouldn't be respected as a lost girl—assuming I was respected at all.

"I don't wanna do this with you."

"Do what?" his words came out in a low vibration.

"This! Dance!" I shifted my eyes to other areas around us, not daring to look him in the eyes again. He let go of my waist and grabbed my hand, putting us at two arms' length. I feared what came next. He spun me around and pulled me back, pressing his chest against my backside. "Am I romantic?"

"No."

He twirled me again, held me, then dipped me. His hair dangled from his head, his lips dangerously close to mine. And those *eyes*. Only a god could sculpt such perfection. He chuckled as he watched my entire demeanor melt away at this moment. "Admit it. I'm romantic."

The words rolled off my tongue before I could catch them, "You are." I lost the game.

He pulled me back up and let go of me.

I collapsed, holding my head.

He squatted and gestured to himself. "I told you, didn't I? Now, why would you think a woman who hates me would enjoy that so much? Aside from being attractive, there's something more to this going on inside your head. Deep down, I think you enjoy my wickedness no matter my intentions. *You* have a dark side, and that dark side will come out sooner or later. I don't fail, and I *won't* fail for anyone. I'm best at bringing out everyone's demons." He stood on his feet, snapping into his regular attire. "Oh such great fun that was! We should do this again some time, Little Flower," he said with a cunning smile and mischievous look in his eye, before disappearing into the trees.

Hating him was easy, but admitting he was onto something was the difficult part. Sometimes, I wanted to murder him. I didn't want to help him, or to believe he was redeemable. I wanted to rip his heart out—and that was the thought that scared me.

But I would never let my darkness win. Everyone had a little dwelling inside them like a cloud of black smoke. Mine just happened to be thicker than most, all thanks to the man who'd contributed to helping it fester and infect my mind just a little more each day.

However, some of us just knew how to control ourselves. I didn't like my wicked side, and I wouldn't let it take hold.

Picking myself up off the ground, I went back to the camp.

I wouldn't let this loss of mine tarnish my reputation. I was going to prove myself. If anything, this only strengthened my desire to piss Pan off and break his rules. He may have won the battle, but he would not win the *war*. Pan was going to get what was coming to him.

I vowed to make him suffer to no end—no mercy. Pan was going to wish he'd never met me.

12: Lia

As I walked into the training area, the boys were separating into small groups. Pan was nowhere to be found and I was thankful for that. If I saw the demon, I wouldn't hesitate to kill him.

I joined a group of boys and practiced my target shooting. I always prided myself on how good I was at surviving but nobody else seemed to notice. I also practiced my knife throwing, running, and combat skills. I had to keep my skills sharp because I was under Pan's rulership.

When I finished, I sat down and drank some water to cool off. Eric decided to keep my company on my break, so I shot him a smile. "Hey, little buddy."

He smiled in return.

"I don't know much about you, Eric," I said.

He shrugged. "What do you want to know?"

Tapping my chin, I found the answer. "What is your favorite place on this island?"

"Zeeslang Waters."

I furrowed my brows. "But that's a dangerous place to go."

Eric giggled. "I like sea monsters. Back home I wanted to prove the loch ness monster was real, but I never did before I came here."

The boy amazed me with his interests. Kids were a force to be reckoned with. Sea monsters were intriguing, and I had to admit that much. I just wasn't about to prove the sea serpent was real by jumping off that cliff.

"What about you?" he asked me.

"Hm, probably the beach. We didn't have one where I lived." I laughed a little as my brothers came to mind. "I'm the middle child. I have a younger and older brother. My younger brother is reckless. He likes to get into trouble and disobey the rules. The older one, however, is more on our parent's side. He always gets us into trouble. He acts like he's the responsible one, but he does it to avoid a beating from our parents. Coward."

"What are they like?" Curiosity danced in his eyes.

They were the last people I wanted to think about in Neverland. "My parents are always angry. They never loved us. They're married yet they live in different worlds. Dad is a firm stickler for abuse. He believes there's one way to get a child to know their place, and that is by beating them when they can't fight back." I rubbed the scar on the top of my wrist.

He noticed. "What happened there?"

It ran from the middle of the top and down to the side. "I fell down the stairs."

"Were you pushed?" Eric could be so blunt, but most children never held back their honesty.

"I can't hide the truth from you, can I?" I gave a small smile. "Mom let us do whatever we wanted and get away with it. My parents' differences lead to many fights. They insist on raising us in opposite ways. How they ever got married is beyond me. I still wonder if my parents ever came to an agreement to this day." I looked up at the trees, zoning out.

Eric followed my line of sight. "Families should love each other and be together. I don't know why they get so messed up."

I nodded, my eyes meeting his. "I agree. They should. Our parents never loved us the way parents are supposed to. My brother was more of a parent than they were. It's crazy how that works. Even my siblings and I were never close. I wonder if they even know I'm gone. They have to know... Don't they? Twins have that weird bond. They just *know*."

His eyes landed on me in an instant. "What do you mean by twin? Is your older brother your twin?" He rested his jaw on his hand. "Twins are fascinating."

I realized now what I'd said. I'd gotten so lost in my thoughts that I hadn't realized my mistake. "Maybe we should get back to training."

"Aw, please tell me. I won't tell anyone, I swear." He pleaded with those puppy dog eyes.

I let out a sigh. "You can't let anyone know, and especially not Pan. I kept this hidden for a reason. I have a twin aside from my brothers. Three siblings in total. I never talk about her because even if we have our creative differences, I don't want her to meet Pan. She's not like me. She wouldn't survive here."

His eyes lit up at the mention of *she*. "She's a girl. Does she look like you?"

"She looks exactly like me." I pushed some hair behind my ear. "Her name is Lia. She isn't tough like me. She's weak. Lia cries more than most people I know, and she's got girlier tastes. She wears dresses to every event, even when it's freezing. We disagree on many things, so we aren't close, but she would never survive Neverland. She would never survive Pan." I ended the discussion there.

Eric didn't press on any further and for that I was thankful. I didn't want to talk about her. I couldn't risk Pan knowing. I always tried to forget about her and pretend she was happier now that I was gone.

We got up and finished our training. The perk of training was all the anger I got to release. It helped me hit the other boys.

We all went back to the camp and ate lunch. I avoided eye contact with

Pan, but he didn't bother doing the same in return. So when I finished my bowl of soup, I went back to my cabin.

I heard a knock on my door, and I answered it. I was surprised to see Kace, but I had to get over it at some point.

Don't say 'Pan needs to see you'.

I refused to go near, look at, or even speak to that demon. "I'm not going to see Pan. I'll take full blame, but I refuse. You have no idea what he did."

Kace didn't say much. His quiet nature intrigued me, and I questioned why he kept to himself so much. "I know what he did but this isn't about him. I want to take a walk and just talk."

I let out an uncontrolled laugh. "You're joking, right?"

"No." Not a single muscle in his face twitched. I couldn't tell he only ever joked once in a blue moon. I'd seen him laugh maybe twice, and that'd been pushing it apparently.

"Okay, but no Pan," I warned. This was more than a threat. It was a promise.

He agreed and turned towards the trees, following the trail behind our cabins. I ran until I caught up. Why did he always walk so fast?

"What do you want to talk about?" I asked.

He looked back at me, a smile holding my gaze. "Anything. I'm stuck on an island of boys. Pan hates conversations that aren't about him. He doesn't give me a chance to input my thoughts. Guys are perceived to not be talkative creatures, but when that option is taken away, we miss it. They say you don't know what you have until it's gone."

I nodded. "All right, simple enough. You want to talk. Go ahead. I'm here to listen and I won't tell anyone else." I zipped my lips.

He faced forward again. "I had a family once and I don't understand why they were the way they were. Whether you want to hear this or not, it's the truth. Pan took me from that. He gave me a better purpose. I belong here. We all do. He gave me a home I could be respected in."

"And what can I say about myself? I'm less respected here," I spat.

He shrugged me off. Asshat. "You will earn it. If I let you in on a secret, Pan doesn't respect anyone until they earn it. We all must prove ourselves, Lili. It wasn't just you. You're strong. You don't give up. Just keep at that, and you'll earn his trust. At least when you live here, you have a chance to earn the respect of your family."

I kept my mouth shut. I hadn't expected that answer and I certainly had no argument against it.

After clearing my throat, I changed the subject. "What do you want to talk about?"

Kace slid his dagger from his belt. "I was thinking maybe we could fight. You need more practice, and I would be a good challenge. I'm undefeated against the other lost boys."

"Sure, let's fight instead of talking," I joked.

He placed his dagger against the softest area of my throat. "Rule number one, never leave the vulnerable areas exposed." He backed away slowly.

I grabbed my own blade—one I was given earlier to join the teams during training. You always had to have a weapon. Survival here was key.

With every ounce of attention turned on him, I said, "All right." I got into a defensive stance and he took some jabs at me of which I did not block well. I was nicked and sliced a few times.

He took another swing. I successfully blocked his dagger with mine, the metals clinking together. I wiggled my eyebrows. "Not so bad, eh?"

He swung himself around, slicing into my side. "Never get distracted."

I took a few deep breaths to gather my strength, but he seemed to be just fine. Slow and steady won the race, they said.

He slipped his dagger back in its sheath, under his cloak. "You should keep practicing. You may be good against the other boys, but you're nowhere near good enough as a real fighter."

I put my dagger away as well. I got it with the weapon.

Kace gave me a look of curiosity. "I hear you have a twin sister."

I froze.

How did he know? Did Pan know, too? I swallowed the lump that formed in my throat.

He pulled forward his soothing voice. "Relax, I overheard you talking about her." With Eric?

I leaned against a tree and let a moment of silence linger between us. I scanned the area for any lurkers before confirming what he heard. "Yes, I have a twin sister."

"Do you miss her?"

A humorless laugh escaped as I nodded. "Of course I do. In a way, our little disagreements fueled me. But this is the price I have to pay so that she doesn't have to deal with this. I don't want her involved."

"I understand why, but I have to disagree. I'm pretty sure that twins need each other. They work best together. I'm also sure that Pan will find out. There aren't many secrets you can keep from him. He'll know. I won't tell him, but he will find out somehow. And she would be better off here with you. Pan may enjoy teasing you, but if she's your twin, I'm sure she is able to handle him." What a *fantastic* compliment.

I straightened my posture. "Look, Kace, I mean no disrespect, but you don't know me. You don't know Lia. You can't say what's best for her or me."

He choked on his own laughter. "What's best for you to have, is a family that you don't hate by your side. You and your twin are going to be best off with each other. I don't have to know you to figure that out." He stepped closer. "You have someone you grew up with—someone who is your other half. Don't give that up. That's letting Pan win. You have a chance at a family. Take it." He turned away, disappearing down the trail.

I wanted family by my side, but Nana was far past the age she needed to be that allowed her into Neverland. She was the one I wanted the most.

I could see why Kace was loyal to Pan. He didn't rebel or defy him. Instead, he taught people to trust Pan and that was his job. He was good at it. He was still loyal to the demon, but he was also trying to help people in the process. He was the devil's advocate. He played it so well, and why would he ever give that up when he had a purpose as clear as day?

I followed behind him, but the walk was built in silence this time.

He'd asked me to consider bringing my sister to Neverland, but I wouldn't give it another thought. I knew exactly what I wanted. I wanted her safe, away from this place. She was safer with our parents who cared more about her than the lost boys ever could. If that meant I never saw her again, so be it. Kace just didn't understand that and he never would.

We made it back to camp in time for dinner. The sun had set, and the fire was roaring. I didn't see Pan yet, and I was again thankful for that.

I sat down and grabbed a bowl of food.

The problem with this island was Pan. That was the sole reason that determined the deciding result in bringing my sister here. It was her or me. It *wouldn't* be both of us.

13: Pain

THE NIGHT BEFORE NEVERLAND

I WALKED INTO MY house, not bothering to announce it. It wasn't a place I enjoyed being, and I didn't get along with the people here.

I got to my room without any disruptions, but I hadn't even sat down before yelling filled the house. They were doing it again—fighting. My parents always fought like this. They never saw eye to eye. Polar opposites.

Why they hadn't divorced yet was beyond my comprehension. This family was hanging on by a thread.

While glancing at the old clock on my wall, I heard a voice say, "You need to do the dishes." I followed the direction of the voice to see my older brother in the doorway. I didn't want to do the dishes, but it wasn't a choice. The punishment for skipping out on chores was not worth it tonight. Last night's bruise still throbbed.

I took my sorry ass to the kitchen and cleaned dishes while my mom and dad continued to fight in the living room. The noise made anger rise within me like lava in a video game, but I never said a word about it. If I kept my temper under control long enough, I'd make it out of here alive. Only a few more months.

My little brother was running around and screaming until Dad directed his anger at him instead. He smacked him and ordered him to his room, to which my brother complied.

Mom got onto him for it, but he called her names to shut her up quick enough.

As soon as I finished my dishes, I migrated back to my room because I didn't want to get caught up in the mess. I had enough to deal with at school.

I spent my time trying to finish up homework. It wasn't an easy task, but trying to tell my teacher that my parents were raging monsters wasn't going to happen. I couldn't focus. The negativity, insults, and hate just made me want to shrivel up and die—*or* kill someone...

I decided to go out for a bit to clear my head.

I climbed out my window, but I was stopped before I could close it. "Where do you think you're going?" she asked. It was almost like talking to myself. She had my voice, my face, and my eyes but she wasn't *me*.

"Nowhere, Lia. Just leave me be," I said.

She stuck her head out of the window and stared me dead in the eyes—like looking in a mirror. "Where are you going?"

I hated her for interrogating me. She was the younger sister. She had no right to question me. "I'm going for a damn walk. Is it a crime to leave once in a while?"

Her eyes softened. "I have to make sure you aren't sneaking out to go drink or do drugs. I don't want to be an aunt."

"Gross, I wouldn't do that. I don't need to rely on boys to fix my brokenness." I rolled my eyes. I had already tried weed but it just wasn't my cup of tea. At the end of the day, it couldn't make my family disappear and I was searching for another solution. Right now, I needed a walk to think. I connected with nature best because it was peaceful. There was no such thing as a human who could destroy my life when I was down by the river.

The pitiful look upon her face said it all. I took that as my cue and shut my window. I took off down to the river as I planted myself in the sand by the constant current. I could stay like this for hours. The chirping birds and rippling river turned a switch that put me in a relaxed state.

I had to come here often, to make sure I didn't lose my temper through all the noise. I didn't want to be like my parents. I wouldn't choose the *dark side*.

The day passed.

Stars were twinkling, the moon its beam. Crickets paid no mind to the night. They *thrived*.

When I made it home, I snuck back in through my window, but someone was already awaiting my arrival. "Where have you been?" my brother, Jaren, asked. He got on my nerves far too easily.

"I was at the river. I had to go there to get some peace and quiet." It was always the same answer. I didn't know why he always asked the same thing.

He said one last thing, "Dad is looking for you. You're in trouble." He closed my door on his way out. *How nice.*

I let out a sigh. I needed a moment to figure out what I would tell my father. What would be my excuse to get out of this or would I get out of this at all? Most times, I didn't.

So, why do you still try?

I gathered what strength I had left to leave the security of my room and go to the living room where our dad was. The narrow eyes and blatant hostility said it all. He never loved anyone but himself, if he had any love left in his heart to do even that.

"Do you really think you can just sneak out and get away with it? You're grounded, and I don't even want to hear you complain. Do you know what it does to me having to worry about you like that?" he shouted.

He didn't care. It was an act. It was just his excuse to control us and treat us like dirt. It always worked, too, because nobody had a say against him. He was the head of the household.

Some days I made these stupid decisions to give my input where nobody asked.

Today was one of those days.

"I had to get out of the house. I can't stand the abuse. I can't listen to this all day. Do you know what it does to me having to listen to yelling and violence?" I had used his own words against him, but I realized my mistake too late.

He stood from the chair, towering over me. "Don't you dare talk to me like that." His hand came across my cheek in just one second. "You are the child, and you will respect me."

The tears in my eyes threatened to fall. "Am I not allowed to tell you how I feel? I *feel* unsafe. I feel like I won't make it out of here alive." I feared that maybe one of these days he would strike me hard enough to kill me. Just one wrong blow to my head and I'd never wake up again.

"How pathetic of you. Don't be *weak*," he spat.

My face turned red, but I didn't say another word. I wasn't weak. I liked to argue that I was strong for putting up with his shit for so long. He did nothing but bring this family down. He was the weak link—the *mouse*. He had to hit people weaker than him because he couldn't pick on someone his own size.

A lot of people would say they felt great for keeping their mouth shut, but I didn't feel a weight lift off my shoulders. My face was hot, my heart pounding. My mouth dried up. It was as if reality left, and every part of me went numb.

He dragged me to my room and locked me in.

Our locks were on the outside of the door, built-in just for my father's amusement.

I stood up, refusing to wallow in pity. I looked out my window and forced the tears to stay in my eyes. "I hate him so much. What did I do to deserve such a fate?"

I punched my pillow from my bed, repeatedly, to release the anger bubbling within. Maybe someday I could get out of this mess but what if that day could be today? No, it wasn't possible. Who would take in a broken girl? Where would I go?

Nana had tried to take me in, but the court had sent me right back here and Dad almost hurt Nana in return. I could never live that down if he succeeded.

Sitting down on my bed, I looked over at the small shelf in the corner of my room. There were old books on it, stories that I used to read to try and escape this hellhole. I didn't have anyone to read me a good book back then, and I could barely read to myself, so I would always form them based on the pictures.

When I became old enough to read, I did.

I learned about these stories, my favorite being Peter Pan. As a little girl who had an abusive family, Peter Pan was a dream come true. Which child wouldn't want to go to an island and fly with Peter Pan? I did. I always had, but reality set in shortly after. I had to face the facts—that Peter Pan was *only* a story.

Neverland did not exist. I would not be able to go somewhere where fairies existed to get away from this awful life. But lost girls had never been a thing in his story.

And I was no Wendy, either.

I grabbed the book and ran my fingers over the cover. If only fairytales were real. If they were real, they would have saved me before this family broke me.

Fairytales had happy endings. Life was composed of trauma and tragedy. The two could never intertwine.

I flipped through the pages and skimmed the words. Even if fairytales were real, how would one call Peter Pan? Would he even take me if I was a girl? I had no chance no matter what the outcome was.

As I put the book back, I leaned out of the window. The full moon lit up the night sky as if today had been another lovely day. Yet, I sighed to myself. I held onto the bottom lip of the windowpane. "Oh, Peter Pan, if you're out there, and if you're real, please, take me away. I want to go to Neverland. I need to get away from this life. *I'm begging.*"

I stared but nothing happened. No stars twinkled more than the others. I knew it was hopeless.

I lay back on my bed and gently put pressure on my cheek. The sting still tingled, the red mark was forming as clear as day. While looking up at my ceiling, I zoned out for the time being. How would I make these last months bearable? I could barely survive here as it was.

I seemed cold because I allowed my siblings to be treated this way, too, but my dad wouldn't care. Every time I said something, he would beat us both. We all got enough of it as it was. Sticking up for each other was no longer an option. We weren't a real family. We were strangers under the same roof trying to make it in a world of sin. It was every man for himself.

Someday you can change, but today won't be that day.

A pounding came through my door, causing me to jump. "Bedtime! I better not hear anything else from this room the rest of the night, ya hear?"

I swallowed my dignity and gave a short response, "Yes, sir."

His footsteps faded away and I was left alone.

I wanted to be strong. I wanted to stand up and defend myself, but my dad was so much stronger. He was almost triple my age. He worked out. He was tall, and tough, and he didn't take any type of bullshit from us. I wanted to change who I was for the better. I was just worried it would change me for the *worst.*

I heard some strange knocks on my window. I looked over to see something that I couldn't believe if I'd tried.

The black shadow came in through my window and looked right at me with those red glowing eyes. I wanted to scream, but who would save me? My family would never come to the rescue.

The shadow came closer and put his hand out for me to grab. I was baffled by what was happening before me as I backed up against my wall, on my bed. But this would be better than what I lived in now. It couldn't get worse than this.

I grabbed his hand, taking the leap. This was most definitely a dream, but even in those, I wanted to get away.

He pulled me towards the window and we both climbed out. As we flew up, my body became as light as a feather. I hoped to *never* wake up from this dream.

14: Blue Magic

Approaching the crops, I slowed down when golden locks came into my view. Something inside me lit up at the thought of making a *girl* friend. That's what I needed right now.

Wendy's bright, blue eyes gleamed as she turned to greet me. "Lili, hello. It's so good to see you again."

"Ditto," I said.

She furrowed her brows but dismissed the questions in her head. "Have you come to help with crops?"

I sat down on my legs in the dirt, beside her. "Oh, did you want help?" I asked, laughing a little. "I'm kidding. I'll help, although it's stupid that they make you do this."

"Do what?" She gathered some carrots from the ground.

I grabbed one, waving it around. "This. They make you do all the chore work because you're a woman. It's sexist and wrong. Crops should be a job for everyone. Chores should be everyone's duty because we all take part in living."

Wendy shrugged with a smile plastered on her face. "I enjoy this kind of work. It keeps me busy." She set the basket of carrots aside and moved over to the next row, gathering cabbage. "They don't have me working here because of my sex."

"How do you know?" I scooted closer, dirt scuffing up my black leggings.

Wendy lifted her fingers and snapped. Blue dust sprinkled the air around her hand. "Because magic is useful for helping with chores."

I paused, taken back by the scene before me. Magic? Wendy had *magic*. How did she get it?

She looked over at me, dismissing my worries with the swipe of her hand. "It's not harmful. Blue magic is harmless to most."

"How does magic help with chores?" I grabbed a head of cabbage.

"When we need water, I can provide it. I also move things with my mind." She nodded a little, placing a cabbage in my hands using telekinesis.

Seeing magic before me still rendered me speechless. "That's impressive!"

Wendy let out a cute laugh. "I can only move small things. My magic is limited here. Blue magic has limits, and green magic as well."

"Green magic—what is that?" I asked.

She finished gathering crops and took the baskets back to Pan's cabin. I assumed she was about to go inside but she walked around the back, onto his porch. I followed her the whole way, surprised at the little bucket pots. This must have been where the food was prepared.

As she washed the vegetables, she said, "Green magic involves spells. The spells relate to earthly matters, such as helping the plants or crops." Something of sorrow flashed in her eyes but she washed it away before I could ask about it.

Who had green magic? I'd never seen Pan use spells that related to the earth.

"What does Pan have?" A shiver ran up my spine as if I wasn't supposed to ask.

She looked at me and set the vegetables aside. "Gold magic. It's the kind of magic that runs Neverland. It's limited, yes, but also above blue and green magic. Gold magic isn't bound by elemental abilities. Without gold magic, Neverland couldn't thrive the way it does. We'd all age and die. *Pan* would die and everyone here would return to the shambles of their own homes."

Gold magic was what fueled Pan and Neverland. It made sense. Gold magic was like pixie dust in the fairytale I heard. Speaking of pixie dust, did Tinker Bell exist here? Where was she?

"Just one more question about this gold magic. What is it that Pan has limits to? He can teleport anywhere. He has the power to get anything he wants. It doesn't seem like he has limits." I shrugged.

Wendy finished washing and wiped her hands against her muddied dress. "He has limits. He can't make things appear out of thin air. That's a trick of the eye. What he's really doing is teleporting so quickly that it appears as if he's making stuff appear out of nothing. He can teleport, yes. He cannot create things out of thin air. He can fly, yes. He can also heal wounds but that comes with *risks*, so he rarely ever uses his magic for healing. The rest of his powers are based on potions he must create. Everything has limits, including Pan."

Pan had limits.

That was all I needed to hear today. The boy wasn't invincible. He was just a boy who used his magic to trick me.

"What could you two be talking about over here?" Pan asked as he leaned against the frame of his window. He stood inside his cabin, watching us, window open. Now I knew why she did her chores on his back porch. He needed to keep his eye on her at all times.

I approached him, arms folded. "Magic. I know that you're limited and much less powerful than I thought you were." The anger in his eyes was worth every word.

He leaned close, hands gripping the edge of the pane. "I can show you powerful, Little Flower."

"The most power I've seen from you is in your ego. You're the biggest ass on this island. Wendy doesn't get to experience adventure which isn't very fair to her. That is an asshole move." I gestured to her.

His eyes fell to his butt. "Well, never thought of it that way but I'll take the award for it." Pan then looked her over. "And I don't think she minds."

"Have you asked her?" I lifted an eyebrow.

His eyes landed on me again. "I know how to read people."

I choked on a laugh as I rolled my eyes. "She sleeps in a cage. How does anyone want that? It's an asshat move, Pan, and nothing else. At least let her sleep in my room."

He furrowed his brows. "For what? Are you *in love* with her?"

He was pulling the same crap on me. "It's called being a friend. You should try it sometime."

He leaned in closer until his lips were just inches away, whispering, "You sound a bit jealous."

Jealous? What could I possibly be jealous of?

As I turned to look at Wendy, her eyes were focused on the deck. She lifted them to see Pan, but her cheeks burned a bright red.

I widened my eyes as I realized she lied to me. She didn't sleep in the cage. She slept in his cabin with *him*.

My head whipped around until I faced Pan. "You're sick."

He chuckled and shrugged his shoulders. "It depends on how you perceive *sick*. Some people do think it's sick for a man and woman to share a room."

"Some people also think it's sick to take advantage of a woman," I said.

He put his hands up. "Back up and tell me who is taking advantage of a woman. I'm not forcing myself on Wendy if you're suggesting that."

"So, you admit you're sleeping with her." I glanced at her. Her blonde curls were still perfect despite living amongst a monster's clutches. Her skin was flawless, and her blue eyes could capture any man's attention. Could I blame Pan for wanting a woman who was willing to give?

He straightened his posture. "Now you *do* sound jealous and there's no denying it."

Wendy stepped between me and the window. "Pan and I are not that close. I promise."

"How close are you?" I asked.

She looked at him, but I couldn't see whatever she told him with just her gaze.

He glanced at me. "There was a time when Wendy and I used to...do things. It was never serious, and I assure you that."

I made a face. "You were friends with benefits?" They both looked at me as if they'd never heard the term. I'd often forgotten how old they were. "It means you guys were sexually involved without committing to a serious relationship."

Wendy grabbed a strand of hair, twirling it around her finger.

I backed away from both of them and shook my head. "I need time to process this." I turned on my heel and left camp as fast as I could.

I found myself at the beach and sat in the sand, watching the waves roll on by. The thought of an innocent Wendy giving Pan oral made my skin crawl. The childish fairytales I once knew were now anything but.

Of course I had to see the facts. They were both teenagers with hormones, but I could have always hoped that he wouldn't have had something with her. If the fairytales were twisted, I'd hoped that his infatuation with her was, too.

And it had been. Just not in the way I'd expected.

She had the accent to bring the whole thing together. What did I have? There was nothing I could offer any man that she didn't do already. Any man wanted her in their life if she could offer pleasure, rather than a lost girl who rebelled. I couldn't gain respect because she'd already offered him her promises.

Pan was not my type and not on my mind. I wasn't jealous of them, but it just made it feel more real when he told me the moments *we* had were just a game to him. He'd dance with me, sweeping me off my feet. He'd play in the waves with me, but at the end of the night, he went home to Wendy just so she could fulfill needs of his I wasn't willing to. That was exactly why he would never "respect" me.

There was Kace by my side, but he was a friend and nothing more. As attractive as he was, I wasn't interested in anything with him. I loved our friendship as it was.

Did Kace know about Pan and Wendy? Did he care? He probably didn't. He would just tell me that men had needs and Wendy was offering to please Pan's.

It wasn't so much that they were together that bothered me. It was that Wendy lied to me about it.

Pan pretended with me, but it wasn't that simple. He wasn't fond of lost girls, or maybe I reminded him of someone who'd hurt him. I'd assumed so much about him and now I'd realized I had no idea *what* to assume.

My question was why did Wendy do these things with him? What was the point? What did she gain? Was she brainwashed or was she just that desperate for love built upon deception?

Getting up, I pulled my shirt off and tossed it to the sand along with my glasses. Next, I removed my boots and socks, then my belt. My leggings came off last, and as soon as I was left half-naked, I ran into the water.

I tripped and got swept away by a little wave but caught myself soon after. I stood with the shake of my head. Why was this any better than home? No—this was home now. My previous life was nothing but a memory.

I couldn't trust anyone to have my back. They all had Pan's back first.

Facing the sun, I hugged myself, the reflection dancing off the water in just the right way. Picture worthy, even, if I'd had a camera. Pan had his thinking spot and now I had mine. The water was freezing but that didn't surprise me. I'd never been to a beach before this, but I knew that the water on the west coast had been below fifty degrees. On the east coast, it was bathtub water which was why they had hurricanes to worry about.

That didn't make the west coast safe, however. They were near fault lines and one bad earthquake could send a tsunami their way. However, in Neverland, there was nothing here that could do that. We were so far from disasters that we had *other* things to worry about. Like people. Men who played games and danced with magic.

I was thankful for that. I'd experienced an earthquake before, but it was terrifying. Everything shook and you couldn't do anything about it. You were powerless. I despised being powerless.

Just like Pan, I wanted to be in control of my life and who was around me. His shadow must have chosen lost children without his consent because here I was.

He didn't have control over who lived here, and I didn't have control over who was in charge. All I could manage was how I reacted. I wanted to fit in and be part of this family just like everyone else was, but I wanted Pan to show me some respect without expecting a *favor*. I worked hard to be a lost girl and he didn't value it.

I couldn't let this get to me. It was more reason to not trust Pan as a leader. He loved mind games more than his created family. He could do whatever he wanted but if he did that, I'd prove to him I could do the same.

Pan and Wendy could do what they wanted, and it wasn't my business. However, I would be working hard to be the best lost girl there ever was, and Pan would have to accept at some point that I was no Wendy Darling.

As hard as he tried to prove he deserved my respect, he, too, had to earn it like I did with him. He wasn't in charge of me. Pan was just another lost child. He just came with an inflated ego, and had some magic at his disposal.

15: New Arrival

Arriving at the training area, I felt the dagger in my hand to ensure my security. Everyone else might have been training for something big in the future, but I was training to defeat Pan at his own tricks.

I grabbed my bow and arrows and started to aim for the bullseye. The lost boys all gasped as if I hadn't shot an arrow before. I laughed while rolling my eyes. "You've seen me hit the target before. This is not a shocker. I thought we established this."

But they were looking at something else, something behind me. As I turned around, my breath caught in my throat. I'd been *cloned* in Neverland. "Lia," I whispered.

There she stood, studying her surroundings. Her brows were pointed inward while her face was scrunched just a bit. I swallowed, planted, and just hoping she wouldn't see me yet.

Pan walked out from behind her with that damned smirk on his face. "I see you have met our new lost girl. It's quite funny because she looks just like you," he mocked me.

I couldn't believe Pan knew about her. Kace betrayed my trust. He told

Pan about the only person I didn't want him to meet. He went against my wishes. I hadn't realized that I was supposed to keep my mouth shut when Kace wanted me to bring my twin. He was the one who suggested I bring her here for our benefit in the first place.

I didn't want to lose my cool in front of the lost boys, so I walked out of the training area, and Pan knew to follow me. Lia just came along because she was useless otherwise.

I stopped when they were far enough out of earshot. I faced him. "What the hell? You brought my twin? How did you even know about her? I didn't want her to come here!"

He let out a chuckle as he shrugged. "I know everything. You can't keep secrets from me. I wanted to bring her here because what kind of monster would I be if I allowed twins to stay separated? One was with me, and the other was in an abusive family."

I rolled my eyes once again. "Yes, because Lia was being abused."

He looked at my sister who wasn't sure how to answer, tilting his head out of curiosity. "Maybe I should give you my own personal tour of the island."

Anger rose in my veins, heating the surface of my skin. "You can't be serious. You're going to pretend to be nice now, for her? You are so far from such a thing."

He gave me a once over. "Little Flower, I think maybe you should get back to training. That's the healthiest way for you to let out your anger. I will be taking Lia here and we will be back tonight." He led her away, but she glanced back at me before disappearing into the forest.

I couldn't train, knowing she was alone with him. He would kill her.

I decided to follow them on their adventure instead.

The entire time I expected him to threaten and insult her existence and yet that never happened. It was just a tour of the island.

They came upon something I'd never seen during my tour. "The fairies light this river. They're along the entire bank, and they won't cause any harm as long as you don't do the same. Fee Abyss. Don't forget it." He pointed at the lights glowing through the fog. I watched his every move to make sure he wasn't going to hurt her—and he didn't. This baffled me. What made her so special that Pan treated her like she was a human? Why was he being so welcoming?

I followed them back to the camp as soon as the sun had set. Pan stood on the outside of the circle as the boys ate their dinner. "I will be calling it a night. Do make our new lost girl feel very at home." He turned to Lia. "You will be staying in my cabin. Come on."

Running forward, I grasped her arm and pulled her back. "No! You will not be taking her back there so you can use her, or worse—have a threesome. She's my sister and she'll be sleeping with me."

He chuckled as he grabbed her hand. "Don't be so foolish. I'm not going to sleep with your sister." He led her to his room, and they vanished for the night.

My fingers dug into my palms as they turned white, all color draining from them. To contradict my colorless fists, my face turned a deep shade of red as the fire in my veins heated my cheeks. She wouldn't believe me if I had told her he was cruel. Because like our family, she was treated like the victim, and not the criminal.

Why was he so bent on making her believe in the good? What made me different from her?

I gave my soup to Eric and headed towards my cabin when a familiar voice stopped me, "You're done for the night?" *Kace.*

I turned to look at him, throwing my arms up in frustration. "What do you want me to say?" When Kace lacked a response, I continued, "Pan is becoming best friends with my sister, but he hates my guts. Why on earth is he suddenly being so nice to her? What is he trying to prove? You told me everyone here had to earn his respect. That was clearly a lie." The anger flowed out in one breath, turning itself into exhaustion.

He strode over and ripped my dagger from my belt. He placed the handle in my palm. "We should practice fighting, to get your mind off the situation. Pan is right. Training is a healthy way to let it out."

I wrapped my fingers around the cold metal. "You should know I'm getting better. Soon, I'll be able to kick your ass." Of course, it was a very weak, empty threat.

He grabbed his dagger in one swift move, the blade nipping my side. "You'll never be able to do such a thing. You are far too inexperienced compared to me."

Kace never commented on Lia being accepted by Pan without earning it like the rest of us. Either he was ashamed he lied to me, or he, too, didn't know why she was the exception to the rule.

We continued to train to relieve some of the pent-up anger inside me. What those two were doing, or what Pan was doing to her, I never hoped to find out.

THE SECOND THE SUN began rising, I was knocking on Pan's door with all the piss I had. Confrontation. A great tactic.

He opened the door, frustration evident. "Is this necessary?"

"My sister is in there. This is very necessary. It's my job to protect her." I pushed past him and inspected the cabin. This place was huge, much more like a tiny home than just a room.

Over to my left, the bed stood against the wall. It was king size at the very least. His mattress had an extra layer of cushioning—something my mattress didn't get. The frame itself was made from bamboo, but it'd been built with extra care.

To the right was a tall dresser, much bigger than mine. He always wore one outfit, so why he needed that big of a dresser was news to me. What could he possibly need put in there aside from his pride?

In the corner was a man-made fireplace. Why would Pan need a fireplace in his room?

There was even a basic kitchen chair by the fireplace.

In that chair sat Lia. As soon as she saw me, her eyes lit up and a smile appeared. "Lili! I missed you so much." It was amazing how she could pretend we had a relationship before Neverland.

I turned back to Pan, looking him square in the eye. "Are you going to tell me what game you're playing? You know I didn't want her here so why is she? Why are you putting up this façade?"

He gave Lia a grin—much inconsistent with his usual smug look. "She didn't do anything wrong. Why shouldn't I be nice to her?"

I let out a laugh, unable to hold it in. "You've got to be shitting me." I didn't even bother to argue with him. He would believe whatever he wanted to believe.

Arms wrapped around my figure, squeezing me. "It's so good to see you again."

I peeled the arms from my waist and faced the one person I'd never wanted to see again. "You can't just pretend we're sisters. *Actual* sisters, with a bond and everything."

Her face twisted into an expression of despair. She touched her fingers to her face and let out a little sigh. "We didn't have a good relationship, but I hoped we could fix it."

"Fix? It was never broken. I want you to go back home. You belong there," I said.

"And you belong here?"

Pan cleared his throat, cutting in, "All right, take it outside."

I walked towards the door and Lia followed this time. I let her out first and peered back at Pan. "This isn't over."

"I'm only doing this to irritate you." A cunning smile appeared, one I desperately wished I could slap off his face.

I closed the door behind me, leading Lia to the firepit.

Her eyes took in all the wonders, unprepared for the reality that was going to set in soon. "This place is so cool! I can't believe Peter Pan is real." For now, everything would look so fun, and whimsical. But eventually the mask would bleed away and leave behind a rotten soul that Pan greatly took pleasure in burning.

"Don't get too excited," I mumbled.

She pushed hair behind her ear. "He's kind of cute. Who knew Peter Pan was that attractive?"

My nostrils flared. "Lia, we need to talk about this. I don't even know where to begin."

"He told me you summoned his shadow. Is that true?" She dropped the silly demeanor rather quickly.

"Yes."

"Was the house that bad?" She looked like a child who got into trouble, sticking to the lie that she didn't do it.

I shook my head. "I know we don't want to go down that road. Why don't we just..." I trailed off, not knowing how to end that sentence. I really didn't know what else we could do. I didn't want her here at all, and I knew that we couldn't pretend we were sisters. I dismissed my ideas, burying them in their nonexistent coffin. "Pan likes you, so stay on his good side." I started off towards the training center.

"This is your chance to make amends with your sister. I would take it if I were you," Kace said.

I spun around to face him. "Well, it's a good thing you're not me. I don't want to be her friend. I don't want to even fight about it anymore. There's no point."

"There is a point. You get a chance at the family you want. You complain about not having a family, but you push away the only ones you do have. We have to stick together here." He came closer. "You will regret not trying to build a relationship."

"So, you're telling me how to think now?" I slid my dagger from its cover, nudging the tip under his jaw.

He flashed his teeth. "At least I've planted some seeds."

"What is that supposed to mean?" I narrowed my eyes. Instead of answering, he left me to my own thoughts.

Now that Pan had brought my sister, my stress levels rose through the roof. I couldn't really seem to get a grasp on it, and it complicated everything. How was I supposed to save Pan, and stop myself from giving into my demons?

I didn't want to be best friends with Lia. I didn't like her, and just because she was my twin, didn't mean I was obligated to. However, I *was* obligated to keep her safe regardless of how I felt. I couldn't escape that no matter how hard I fought.

Protect Lia from Pan. Save Pan from himself. Don't give into the darkness.

Simple, right?

16: A Kiss

Lia sidled right up next to me, matching my pace. "Hello." Even her tone sounded so innocent—and I despised her innocence.

I kept walking, not uttering a word. I didn't want to have this conversation now. She would have to fend for herself here if Pan was going to make her life pleasant. Besides, it seemed Pan took a liking to her so he'd never hurt her, would he? Sure, he did it just to piss me off. However, it would always piss me off, which meant that he would *always* pretend to like her, and she would never be in harm's way.

Lia hummed with her head held high.

I jumped when a warm arm appeared around my shoulders. An arm appeared around Lia's, too. "Hello, lasses." Pan dragged the word *lasses* out just a bit.

Glancing at Lia, I was disappointed by her blushing. That girl could really wrinkle my skin.

Pan noticed and decided to use it to his advantage. When did he not use something to his advantage? His narcissism wouldn't allow for less.

He chuckled and took his arm away from me. "I think Lia is pretty cute."

He glanced at her first, then me, to get my reaction. She was a complete tomato by now.

I crossed my arms and shrugged my shoulders. "That means I am, too. We are identical twins, after all."

He pulled Lia's left side against his right. "She has more femininity in her."

"I'm not masculine just because I'm a strong woman. How the hell else do I survive this damn place?"

"Exactly." He shot me a look.

What? What did that mean? Of course he wanted her. It all made complete sense now. He hated strong women.

Inhale. Exhale. I did not want to give him control over my emotions like that.

"Fine, you can be that way. It's not like my job is to impress you anyway." I walked ahead of them, dead-set on ignoring their little interactions.

Sure, Lia wasn't trying to annoy me, but I could never be too sure. Pan, on the other hand, was in it to push buttons.

Pan had stopped walking with Lia as their footsteps faded into the sky. I pretended not to care or eavesdrop.

But I couldn't hear a peep. If veins were popping out of my neck, I wouldn't be surprised. I cleared my throat, asking, "Why did you follow us?"

Facing them, the sight before me ruptured the veins.

Pan had his lips plastered on hers. He was using her, and I knew that, but she didn't. She thought this was genuine. He was going to break my sister and murder her for sport.

He was playing her the way he'd played me. Still, I needed to keep my temper in check.

I stomped my feet through the dirt and twigs, grabbing Pan's shoulder and pulling him away. "Don't you dare touch her!" *So much for self-control.*

A devious smile danced on his lips as his eyes lit up. "What's wrong? Are you jealous?"

"Don't be stupid. You're only doing this to screw with her head. You're going to hurt her, and I won't stand for it."

Pan came closer, heat radiating. It had to be a result of anger. "Are you implying you care about Lia? You said you had no relationship, Little Flower."

"Do not call me Little Flower!" I screamed in his face.

He enjoyed seeing me get flustered. I could see all the little tricks dancing around in his iris'.

Lia stood behind him, a puzzled look wearing down her expression.

The hatred hanging in the air could be cut with a knife.

She approached Pan. "Why did you kiss me?"

He snickered in return, grazing his knuckles over her cheek. "It makes Lili mad and I love to see her eyes bulge."

Crossing my arms, I nodded a little. "This is the real Peter Pan. Not a nice guy. Murders people for sport. He just can't kill me because I beat his game."

Lia looked heartbroken but it didn't seem to be about Pan at all. The sorrow in her eyes spoke every word for her, and it got to me.

Pan's eyes darted between us. "Love is a useless feeling people want because they can't have anything else. Love *ruins* everyone." He vanished from that spot like a ghost.

Like that, I was left to fix what he had broken.

Lia's shoulders slouched. I slipped my hand in hers and took her back to my cabin. Once inside, I sat her down on my bed while I paced back and forth.

How was I supposed to mend this? I was not good at comforting anyone. I'd never been raised to be nurturing, and I certainly didn't want the role. We avoided people's problems at my house. "I don't know what to say."

She flopped back onto my bed and her hair flew out around her. How could I cheer up someone I hardly knew?

She lay there in silence, the awkwardness only thickening. I only let her lay on my bed because it kept her quiet. It was my job to make sure she was okay but being her sister was another field altogether. Protection—that I could do. But to nurse my sister back to health? What words did I use? Did I tell her to cry? Say it would be okay?

I grabbed her head and pulled her face into my view. "Do not cry over him. He's the villain here, and I do not want to see you give him that power. Why don't I teach you about this island and how to survive? Your only other option is to be killed, anyway."

"I couldn't cry if I wanted to. It was a small attraction and nothing more." She shook her head. "Is Peter really this mean to you?"

After pulling her up, I took her to the training area. I forced a knife into her hand. "First rule—don't call him Peter. He hates it. You'll eventually get your own weapon. I'm not sure about you getting your own cabin but I'm sure we can share." I pulled out my dagger. "This is mine. I've been training with Kace, mostly to defeat Pan."

"Who's Kace?" she asked.

I slid my dagger back into my belt. "He's Pan's second-in-command, but he's a lot nicer. Kace is easier to talk to. However, he's loyal to Pan no matter what. Don't go talking bad about Pan around him."

She studied the clothes on her body. A pink shirt and blue jeans. "Do I get clothes?"

"I can convince Pan of some decency. The keyword is *some*, so don't expect it to happen." I walked out of the training area and back to camp. "Don't be surprised if you get some boys who give you dirty looks. They're not welcoming to lost girls," I told her.

She followed like a lost puppy.

I paused. "Beware of the cage. I've been there a few times. Pan doesn't like to be disrespected in front of his lost boys. He will not hesitate to leave you in there overnight without dinner." I turned to face her. "And most importantly, do not wander off until I have taught you enough."

Nodding, she gave me a reassuring smile. "Are there other monsters here?"

"Monsters aside from Pan? The pirates, the sea serpent, and mermaids—all of them are enemies. I've personally never met any. There's also a deadly bush called mooie duisternis, made of thorns. Never ever go near it." I stressed that last sentence.

Lia admired the knife. "I'll make sure to be careful."

I gave her a tour of the island as Kace had done for me. I wanted to make sure she was as safe as could be. I would have to train her harder than I had, given she wasn't as skilled as I was. She'd never taken into account when she'd need to defend herself. She'd never had to worry about it before.

I'd teach my sister to be strong and independent, so Pan would have no effect on her.

When all was said and done, I took her back to my cabin and gave her some of my clothes. "Now that you're on Pan's bad side, you'll need to keep an eye out at all times. He's that pesky rat you can't get rid of."

She sighed. "He must be so broken if he thinks it's okay to screw with people. He directs his problems towards those who are the easiest target rather than dealing with them."

"Pan grew up in the 1900s and he doesn't know how to deal with his problems. We are the easiest targets, and that's what he does to avoid what is truly hurting him. He never had a real family. He couldn't have or Neverland wouldn't serve a purpose. His upbringing couldn't teach him compassion. How could he have known what compassion was? He's just a boy trying to lead an island and failing because they failed him. But he's always wanted a family because why else would he bring lost boys?"

Lia shrugged. "To recreate a family."

"He brings himself kids who have had bad families because he feels like he can help them somehow, but he can't entirely because he never figured how to do that—how to face his own problems. However, he's still a man so he only knows mostly about his own sex. He brings lost boys to make his family because it's easier for him to build. He wouldn't know the first thing about girls. In conclusion, Pan is just a homeless boy who created his own family based on what he experienced from his own." I tapped my chin.

Lia nodded. "Maybe."

"It's all I have to work with. I need to take him down, but now I need to find out what his parents did to him, too." I peered out the window of my cabin.

The boys were starting to circle the growing fire.

"We should go out and introduce you." I looked at her, smirking as a new idea formed. "I want the boys to get to know you. Pan must know that by bringing you here, he has added another lost girl." I'd have so much more fun messing with him. Lia and I would make him regret his decision—together.

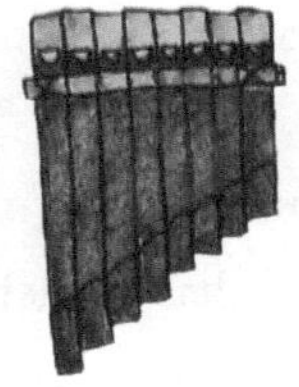

17: Acceptance

Lia sat atop the log, eating her soup while she watched the flames blaze. The boys in turn observed her. I focused on the soup, not taking a chance to miss out on any future meals.

How could I stay on Pan's *good side* while finding a way to defeat him? Easy—I could act. I could pretend to obey, but in my head, I would be planning his defeat. He wasn't a vampire. He was just Peter Pan. Everyone saw him as this god, but I knew he was anything but. My mind was a safe place to think about whatever I needed for this plan to work itself out.

Eric took a seat next to me. "Your sister is very pretty like you. What's her name again?"

"Lia." I swallowed my bite of carrot and celery. "Her full name isn't Lia though. It's a nickname, like mine."

"What do you mean? Her name isn't actually Lia?" He furrowed his brows, making the cutest face. He was becoming the sweetest little brother I'd always wanted, and I meant what I said. This brother wasn't reckless. Chaotic. Unloved.

"Sort of. Her name involves Lia, which is where the nickname stems from. Her full name is Celia." I patted his hair, earning a giggle from him. He leaped up and hurried off. He disappeared into the woods, leaving me to wonder where he was going. He was just a young boy. Didn't he need to eat?

I glanced over at Lia again. She seemed to be in a trance, and nothing could snap her out of this zone.

We finished our soup as the fire died down. Each boy retracted back into their cabin one by one, before all that was left was us.

"We shouldn't stay out here for long," I said.

Lia and I went to my cabin, none of us saying another word.

I used my blanket to make her a spot on the floor. We might have been sisters, but we hardly knew each other. Sharing a bed was out of the question.

I lay back on my bed and stared at the ceiling. How was it possible that a shadow could be separated from its owner? Anything was possible on Neverland, but it didn't make any sense because I swore the shadow was attached to him in the cartoons—or maybe I'd just been remembering things wrong. It was all one massive blur. This real version of Pan skewed whatever my previous thoughts once were.

HOLLERS AND SHOUTS WOKE me from my slumber, but I couldn't remember when I had fallen asleep. The shouts came from lost boys, no doubt. I leaned over my bed to find Lia already missing. Shit, she shouldn't have left without me. She needed me.

I didn't bother to change into different clothes before I left my cabin. I stopped dead in my tracks as soon as I had. What I saw sent my brain into a fit of questions. The boys were circling Lia, but not in an intimidating, power-hungry kind of way. They were celebrating *with* her.

She stood in the middle with a big smile glued to her face, high-fiving each of the boys. Was I just half asleep and imagining things, or was this real? How did this girl make friends faster than I could? Most of these boys were afraid of or hated me. They were not friendly towards new campers, but Lia proved me wrong. She always did. They loved Lia all because she was weak, and she *didn't* defy Pan.

Maybe that is why they accept her. She is more like them.

My face flushed an apple red, skin heating like a stove burner. I walked past the group, ignoring their cheers. I grabbed my bowl of berries and sat down, taking a huge bite to shut myself up before I lost my cool.

I finished my bowl a little too fast, stuffing more berries, which kept me from being able to say whatever I wanted.

On my way to the training area, a hand grasped my arm, pulling me. I turned around, expecting Pan to be there with a stupid remark but instead, Lia blinked at me and let go of my arm. "Good morning."

She had the audacity to say good morning after she took the attention I'd been working hard for? She was the twin here to steal my thunder.

She cleared her throat. "What is it? You're extra quiet."

I bit my tongue to keep my mouth closed as I looked sideways before returning my eyes to her. "How do you do it, Lia? Is that why Pan brought you here? Is this really how you're going to ruin me?"

"What are you talking about?" She looked confused, but she was a great actress.

"This!" I threw my arms up, gesturing to everything. "All of this. You suddenly show up and you somehow get everyone to love you. These boys hate me, yet they love you. I've been working hard to be accepted for who I am, and now you've proved that respect is not earned in Neverland, but rather I'm just destined to be unloved," I said.

Lia grabbed my hand, dragging me back to the cabin *we* now shared. I said that with no heavy meaning. If she was now their best friend, she would have her own cabin in no time.

Closing the door, she rested her palm flat against the door as she glanced back. "Maybe you're trying too hard. I can't control if they love who I am. I'm sorry, and I'll help you get what you want. If you want them to like you, I'll talk to them." She grabbed my arms, rubbing them to comfort me. It didn't work.

I pulled myself from her grasp, turning away before I punched her in the face. "No. If you talk to them, it will make things worse. I've been trying to earn respect. It's not fair that you get it before me and you've only been here nearly two days, three days... I don't know. I lost track. You're the twin who steals everything from me. I was trying to get away from this, and I won't have a chance here. I will always come second to you."

"I didn't do this on purpose. I'm not trying to make you miserable. You must understand that. If you got to know me, we wouldn't have this problem."

"If I got to know you," I scoffed while rolling my eyes. "What a load of bullshit." She sat down on my bed, dismissing my insults. She patted the spot next to her, which I chose not to follow. "I was supposed to help you survive but you seem to be doing just fine on your own. You don't need me. I should just pretend you don't exist and go back to becoming the best lost girl."

"No, stop. Don't you do that, Lili. I *do* need you. I'm a newbie here. I'll need your help with everything. I don't know much, but I do know Pan hates you. You beat him in a challenge which in turn earned you some sort of respect, even if the smallest amount. I need you to teach me how to do that." She reached out for my hand but pulled back when I ripped mine away.

With the shake of my head, I said, "You don't need me. You can just be yourself and everyone loves you, remember? That's what you said."

"Do you know what my favorite color is?" she asked.

"No. What does that have to do with anything?"

"Do you know that as your younger twin, I look up to you?"

"No... I don't see what any of this has to do with the subject at hand." Was she the cowardice type to change topics to avoid confrontation? Possibly. I wouldn't have put it past her.

"You don't know me. That's my point. Let us get to know each other. You can maybe figure out exactly what it is that makes the boys accept me."

I grumbled, knowing she was right. Why wouldn't she be? "Fine. Tell me about yourself."

A grin appeared as she straightened her back. "All right, my favorite color is yellow. I look up to you, and I always have. I consider myself a girly girl. And I'm a lover—not a fighter. That is why I need to learn how to fight and defend myself. If I'm going to live in the wild, I must toughen up. Anything else?"

"Yes, how the hell did you win over the boys?"

"I'm not trying to be one of them. I'm just being me. I don't care if they like me or not. My validation of value doesn't stem from the idea of someone else accepting my existence." She shrugged like it was no big deal.

Yeah, for her. I craved acceptance. It was all I ever wanted.

Once again, the girl was right. It drove me nuts, but I could accept her words or reject them. However, rejection would just make everything worse. It would make *me* look worse.

Lia sat there in silence, soaking in it. I loathed it. The silence admitted my defeat. She was right and I was *wrong*.

She got up after a few minutes and rummaged through my drawers. "The boys said Pan should give me my own cabin, too, like how you got yours. I'm not sure if it's true but I would love my own cabin. If he doesn't, it's still not the worst thing in the world because sharing a cabin with my sister would be a sleepover every night. You know, the one we never got to have." She looked over her shoulder at me.

I grimaced. Why did she have to say mushy crap like that? It ruined everything. "If this is going to work, you should know some stuff about me. I'm not exactly excited that you're here. I am working hard to fight and train to meet my goals, and I don't like girly things"—a pause—"and my favorite color is dark green." I snickered.

She did something icky. She gave me a bear hug. "Oh, that's great! We're going to finally be the sisters I swore I always wanted. Come—we can bond and we can teach each other stuff. I can hang out with you and the lost boys, and you can teach me more about Neverland. After all, you have been here longer."

I removed her arms from my neck and stood up. "Whatever. What first then, Celia?" I mocked her.

The grin widened. "Let the boys get to know the real you. Just be yourself." She grabbed my hand and dragged me from the cabin, near the fire where the boys were laughing and having contests. Burping contests, of course.

I didn't know if I should join in or be disgusted.

Just be yourself.

But that was so much easier said than done.

I took a deep breath while dropping my arms at my sides. A huge burp rippled through my throat, gaining cheering in response.

18: Lost Girl

Walking along the path back from the training spot, footsteps followed behind and I stopped in my tracks, narrowing my eyes. Pan, I swear... I spun around, gripping the handle of my dagger as I pulled it from my belt and held it up in front of me, in a threatening position.

Kace lifted his eyebrows. "You think that would work on me? Or were you expecting Pan? He would've won, too."

I mumbled some curse words and put my dagger away. "What is the reason for your appearance?"

"I see how much I'm wanted here." He put his hand over his heart.

I shook my head, eyes sweeping across the tree roots. "You know what I meant."

"Can I not just come to say hi? I thought we were friends." He frowned like a little boy. Granted, he was ageless on this island and never able to become a full adult, but he still acted like a boy much younger than he was.

Much younger in the eyes of Kace—and whatever his last name was.

I paused for a moment, brows knitting together. "You still think we're friends? I barely got the other lost boys to like me." I gestured behind me towards camp.

He came closer with a chuckle deep in his throat. "I thought we were friends the moment I helped you defeat Pan's challenge. At least, I know I never put it on pause."

My cheeks warmed. I had forgotten about how he helped me. "Oh, that. Yes, I suppose we are still friends. Thank you for helping me, again."

He shrugged and walked along the path. I started with one foot in front of the other as he said, "It's okay. I understand women work in different ways. You don't understand some of the things I say."

"We're not that complex. You make it sound like we're a different species." I choked on a laugh.

He *smiled*. It was refreshing to see a genuine smile in Neverland. "You are a different species to us. We've been here for so long now, just us boys. Wendy is never around because only Pan gets to see her. It has been a long time since most of us have been around a girl. It's like a new adventure for us."

I shrugged. "I guess I never thought of it that way."

He nudged me and lifted an eyebrow, a smirk forming. "Of course not. You're a woman." His laugh almost made the trees start singing.

We arrived back at camp and Hunter came running. "Pan said we could go down to the beach and make music! Do you want to come?" His eyes lit up in excitement, hoping my answer was yes.

I solidified that by saying, "Sure, let's go." The boys grabbed the drums for this occasion. But I didn't see Pan or Lia anywhere, and that worried me. One look over at Kace and I stopped. "You guys go ahead; I'll meet you there soon."

Kace's eyes flickered behind me. "You'll be walking with us."

I turned my head to find Pan and Lia catching up. Lia didn't look very happy, but she didn't look crushed either. That had to be a good sign.

She walked alongside me. "Nothing happened if that's what you're thinking," she said, eyes glued to the trail at our feet. I think a part of me was rubbing off on her.

Nodding, I glanced at Kace on my left side. "Kace, this is my sister, Lia. And Lia, this is my friend, Kace." I gestured between the both of them.

She looked over and gave a head nod in acknowledgment. "Hello."

He cleared his throat. "Likewise."

We all walked in silence the rest of the way to the beach as Pan trailed behind us. He kept an eye because at any moment, I could stray from the rules. I was known for doing that.

We arrived, mapping out a good spot to start our celebration. Some lost boys gathered rocks and sticks and built a firepit. I found a comfortable seat in the sand. "All right, boys, teach me how to play such music."

Lia sat beside me, her eyes questioning why we were here. I was just the only one bold enough to ask. "Why the beach?"

Kace got the fire going while the boys started dancing around it. Pan, flute in hand, looked at me as if I'd grown two heads. "Forget I asked," I mumbled loud enough for him to hear. I turned my attention to the waves that still rolled like clockwork, even at this hour.

The tide had been lowering.

He admired the crystal waters.

I was ready to pound my drum when he said, "Because the sound carries best here."

"And why do we need the sound to carry the best tonight?" I looked out at the ocean again, searching for what he saw. Would I ever be able to understand this place from his view? I had all of eternity to try.

"Because tonight is the night that we welcome Lia as a lost girl." His gaze met mine, dark green eyes piercing my contempt. Was he serious?

"What about me? I beat your challenge. She didn't do anything to deserve it." A little too late to reverse my words now.

Lia's face fell. A few tears slipped down her cheeks, but she wiped them away before more could follow. She knew that no matter how hard she tried, I didn't like her. And now she knew I was *just* jealous. I saw this as a competition between the twins, not as two sisters working side by side.

Pan chuckled. "Yes, and you got to live, with a fancy cabin might I add. You never asked for an initiation."

"She asked for this?" I whipped my head to face her. She didn't budge.

Pan shook his head and came closer, bending down to my level. It must have been uncomfortable for his legs due to his towering height. I hoped with every ounce of my being that it had been, and I'd revel in it. "The lost *boys* asked for this, Little Flower."

My heart would have cracked if it wasn't shattered already.

The lost boys asked for this. Why did everyone like her more than me? It didn't make any sense. I worked hard. She didn't do a damn thing.

I looked at the drum between my legs. I didn't know if I wanted to play for this. It wasn't fair. She managed to win once again.

Maybe this is why you truly don't want her here.

Kace planted himself next to me just as Pan sauntered away. "You're upset. I can see it in your face. Tell me how you feel, and I won't tell anyone else."

"And how did Pan know about Lia?" I redirected my judgment towards him. Everyone was getting a slice of it tonight.

"He probably overheard. I had nothing to do with it if that's what you want to think. I said I'm your friend. I may be old in Neverland, but I know how a friendship works," he stated.

I sighed in defeat and nodded. "I feel cheated. I feel cheated because I worked hard to stay alive here, to earn my cabin, and yet my *twin* gets everything handed to her. They all love her. How is that fair?"

"It's not."

I nodded, again. "Exactly. And she pretends to not know why I'm mad at her, but does she really have to be that oblivious? I belong here. She doesn't."

"What makes you say that?" His eyes moved to Lia.

A chilly breeze whispered my name, sending a shiver down the center of my back. "Forget it." Instead, I watched the flames lick for the sky, its kisses made of embers.

Pan put his flute to his lips and studied the faces as he started to blow.

Beauty was an understatement.

No, this tune he played, it was soft. Powerful. It broke through to the soul without you ever having a chance to run.

Captivating. It truly grasped the concept of Neverland. It haunted like a ghost in the halls of a mansion, searching for his long-lost love. It passed like a ship in the night—a wonder—never to be seen again.

It was a story told to friends.

But most importantly, it was the reason one picked up the paintbrush just one more time before inspiration hit.

Bewilderment settled on Lia's face. "Why doesn't it have sound? Is it supposed to be like that? Is there a trick to it?"

Pan stopped playing. I had never seen his eyes fill with so much discombobulation, not since I beat the challenge. He didn't say a word as the gears in his head began to turn. He glanced at me as if I had something to do with it.

I gripped the drum. "Can you at least answer this one, Pan?"

He cleared his throat and looked at his flute. "It's a special flute. Only boys can hear it, but you seem to be the one woman that can hear it. It is quite interesting."

I swallowed. This confirmed I was the only lost girl. How could this be? Of course, how could anything on this island be? It just was. Magic was real, so this flute could only be heard by certain people. Lia wasn't one of them, but *I* was.

Kace leaned in closer to me. "Now we know why she doesn't belong here. Who knew you could be so different?" You would think if I was special enough to hear it, my twin would be, too, but our bond was too severed to allow that.

"I did. I knew. I knew she didn't belong here. She didn't ask to come. She didn't believe. Pan kidnapped her himself." I scowled. She didn't belong here, and everyone knew. So why did she still get more love and acceptance than I did? I was the lost girl. I was unloved. I needed this place the most, and I needed them the most. But they chose *her*.

The lost boys continued to dance once, brushing it all off. Pan tried to move on from this new-found information, continuing to create wonderful music once more. I felt a little better knowing I wasn't crazy. At least I'd been right all along.

I started to bang the drum, using my one good hand to create a specific rhythm. The beat matched up with the flute, and the boys got even more excited. Much like monkeys.

Lia didn't fit in. This filled a piece of my heart I'd been missing. To know I belonged here. To know this was *my* home.

Kace sat in silence, not partaking in the dancing or hollers. He just enjoyed the festivity in his own way. Why didn't he ever celebrate with them?

The night went on as smoothly as a sailor who'd grown up on the seas. The sun had set, and the stars filled the sky. The moon had made like a flashlight and beamed down on us.

Lia sat in a very still position, squeezing her knees. She appeared to be upset, and who wouldn't be in her place? But I could care less. She now knew how I had felt all this time. A taste of her own medicine.

Our music filled the air to the brim. It couldn't get better than this. I didn't even hate Pan at this moment.

I hummed to the tune, utterly entranced. This really was a perfect location to celebrate. The beach calmed with its soft waves, as peaceful as the windpipe Pan used. At this exact moment, Neverland was *perfect*.

The music came to a stop, and the boys all froze. A voice echoed from behind me, asking, "What's this? A celebration with a few lost girls? Oh, but Peter Pan, don't you know the rules?" The boots trudged in the sand before halting before Pan himself.

His eyes darkened with a certain hostility even I could not bring about. His dagger appeared in his hand as he got onto his feet, stance ready.

I turned my head to see who he'd been so terrified of. A hook for a hand, and pirate attire to match. This was Captain Hook in the flesh. However, *her* body threw my disbelief for a loop. Captain Hook was a woman.

19: Heartbreak

She pulled her sword from her belt, pointing it at Pan. "Are you going to tell me why you're breaking your own rules or am I going to have to force it out of you?"

"It's none of your business," he growled.

A small smirk formed on her lips. "No? Does it perhaps have anything to do with chasing the same high you got when we were together?"

"It's bold of you to assume I'd ever be with another woman the way I was with you. I'd never wish that on anyone." He stepped closer, nudging his blade to her throat.

Her eyes darted over to Kace for just a moment before meeting Pan's again. "You didn't enjoy what we had?" She stepped even closer as a few droplets of blood began to form.

I wasn't crazy; the sexual tension was thick. Whatever happened between them caused a sour taste to form in the air between layers of salt, spice, and bitterness. The only taste missing was sweetness but that lingered only in my corner.

Pan's worst enemy was a woman, and now it was beginning to make sense. Whatever she'd done to him skewed him. She had taken something from him.

Kace pressed his dagger into her side. "It would be better if you left and never returned."

Hook narrowed her eyes at Kace before turning her attention back on Pan. "I guess we will just have to continue this another time. That's too bad. I could have given you so much." She moved away from their daggers and started back towards the ship a couple of miles down the coast.

Pan turned his body towards everyone. "We're going back to camp, *now.*" He gathered the lost boys, and they all took their journey back to the camp.

As Pan led the boys back to camp, I stayed behind. I glanced at Hook and ran to catch up with her. There were two sides to every story, right?

She cocked an eyebrow. "And just who the hell are you?"

I lifted my chin out of pride. "Liliana Stone. I'm the first lost girl."

She scoffed. "First lost girl? Oh, honey, he's going to discard you like he does the rest."

"That would be enlightening if Pan and I were sleeping together but we aren't. Wendy is his toy." I twirled my finger in the air.

"Wendy?" she asked. The tone of her voice implied that she had no idea who she was.

We approached her ship where I then came to a standstill. "Wendy is the English blonde-haired, blue-eyed beauty that lives in his cabin."

Slipping her sword back into the sheath, she shook her head. "I know Pan. He's not very interested in blondes. They bore him." So they did not have more fun. Her eyes racked my body. "But he'll take a deeper interest in you soon enough."

"Blondes bore him? Why would that be?" I was not interested in dating Pan, ever.

Captain Hook leaned against a palm tree, arms crossed and one knee bent, the sole of her boot flat against the trunk. "It's said blondes are easy.

Pushovers. The people who interest him the most are those who challenge him. She clearly does none of those things."

I made a face of disgust. "How the..." I didn't finish my question. I didn't need to think hard about how I challenged Pan. I was always pushing his buttons. That didn't mean much to me and he didn't seem intrigued either. He still went home to Wendy—not that it bothered me at all. What I felt for him was pure nausea.

She gazed up at the moon. "He'll come around, eventually. Just got to reattach his shadow is all."

"What?"

She shook her head and lifted her hook. "You told me who you are so it's only fair if I introduce myself." She rested the hook against her chest.

"Captain Hook, I'm aware." I nodded.

Again, she shook her head. "I have a real name. Captain Hook is what they call me because it demeans me to nobody important." She tipped her hat. "Name's Captain Kristin James."

Kristin didn't seem so scary. Everyone was afraid or despised her and yet she was just like anyone else.

I admired her transportation. "That's a nice ship."

"I bought it for a cheap price and fixed it up myself. It wasn't too hard." She shrugged.

"Let's cut the crap. Why does Pan hate me so much?"

"You tell me." By the certainty in her eyes, my purpose for coming here became clear.

"You did something to piss him off. You hurt him."

"Why do you care? Do you want to win his love?"

Rolling my eyes, I said, "In case you didn't notice, I'm stuck here with a man who hates me. I would like to at least understand what the hell you did." I closed the gap between us. "I deserve to know."

"Do you really think that though?" She lifted both eyebrows.

"Of course. I worked my ass off to stay here and get what I have now.

Why don't you want me to know? Is it because you think I'll direct my blame from him to you?" I balled my hands into fists, but she never took notice. I just wanted one person on this damned island to give me a straight answer for one. I was tired of riding ponies at the fair.

Her eyes fell upon the shore. "I used him."

"Used, abused, manipulated. He kind of mentioned he thinks women are like this. Come on, tell me the whole story." I gestured to her to give me the details.

She let out a sigh before giving in, "I made him fall in love with me. I played him like a fiddle. I broke his heart."

"Admitting you're the culprit—that's a first. It's more than that, isn't it?" I rested against a different tree.

I wasn't buying into this. She did more than she was letting on. Pan was willing to allow Neverland's venom to suffocate people. She did something to bring that out of him. She didn't break his heart; she *destroyed* him. He feared women wanted him because he had the power, and I think she was the one who tried to take that. I just needed her to admit it.

She put her hand on the hilt of her sword, ready to slash me to pieces if it came down to it. "I said what I said. Tell me what it is that makes you think it's more."

"He kills people. He enjoys every second of it. He treats me like I'm guilty of something. He is exactly what you made him be," I seethed. A filthy liar she was.

"Have you seen him kill?" she questioned.

"He would have had I not beat my challenge," I said.

She looked at me once more. "Your sister seems to be fine, and you, too. You were celebrating with the rest of the lost boys and having fun. I saw it. Don't lie to me."

"She doesn't belong here. Lia's just his ploy to blackmail me and have yet another reason to make me do his bidding. She's here to piss me off." Kristin was doing that very thing right now—pissing me off.

She pointed her hook at me. "Okay, so what exactly is it that you think I must have done? That isn't enough for you." She studied every muscle on my face.

I gritted my teeth, trying not to bite my own tongue. "He dangled me over mooie duisternis. I could've died. He made me sleep in a cage. Does any of this surprise you in even the slightest?" If she answered that with *no*, I'd have more than just punches to throw.

"Mooie duisternis is deadly, and I'll admit that much. I knew him when he was the good guy, and I can't truly say I know what you're going through. But it doesn't surprise me. Everyone is tested when they're backstabbed, and this was Pan's test. Spoiler—he failed." She clicked her tongue.

Pan became the villain when someone else screwed him over.

I swallowed my threats. "What did you do to him? What are you so afraid to admit? You confess to your sins, but you won't state what they are." Anger rose within. Darkness was threatening to take over, but I refused to be anything like Pan.

She stepped closer. "I told you. I broke his heart. I made him fall in love with me. I crushed his every fiber, and I played with his feelings." Her expression showed no remorse nor pleasure.

"You mean you took what was left of his feelings. I don't buy into this bullcrap excuse you're giving me. Don't think I'm too stupid to see right through it."

Kristin groaned, rubbing her temple. "I'm done here."

"I'm asking for details, Hook. You're denying what really happened but I know it's never just as simple as breaking someone's heart. Did you cheat on him?" Something flashed in her eyes when I asked her that. When she didn't reply, I yelled, "why can't you just tell me?" My temper bubbled at the surface as the gap between the violence and threats shortened.

With her hook, she twirled a strand of my hair. "And why can't you just drop it?" she whispered.

Before the top could blow, I inhaled. Exhaled. I couldn't let her be the death of me. "Forget it. You're not worth my time." Turning on my heel, I began to walk away.

While walking away, she said, "I'll have him wrapped around my finger again soon. Pan could *never* resist me."

She had a plan all along, and I had to warn Pan not to fall for her tricks.

I'd get her next time.

As I returned to camp, I found it empty. Everyone had already given up for the night, but I wasn't so tired.

I made my way to my cabin and jumped when someone said, "You're awfully late."

"Lia, don't. Not tonight." I cut her off, using my hand to slice the air.

She shrugged a little but kept her eyes focused on the floor. "Don't mind me. I'm just debating if I should go home. You belong more than I do."

With a scoff, I said, "Pity yourself for all I care. You can't belong everywhere you go. This is my turf now."

"Why can't we share?" she asked in a quiet voice.

I took off my boots and removed my glasses. "The same reason as to why we can't share the abuse at home." I sat down on the bed as I gripped the edge of the mattress, knuckles turning white. "I'm just sick and tired of coming in last to you. For once, I want to be better at something. I want to fit in somewhere you don't. I don't want to be the discarded twin any longer."

My night had been going exceedingly well, until a crow cawed at my window and a knock sounded on my door. Without waiting for an answer, Pan let himself in. "Let's go."

"Where the hell are we going?" I stayed put on my bed, leaning back as I folded my arms across my chest. Why would I go anywhere with this guy? Why did he expect me to ask *how high* after he told me to *jump*?

"Kace told me you need more training. So, Little Flower, we are going to train you."

"Me? You're going to train me?" My disbelief was suspended all right.

His smile flashed white. "Scared?"

Narrowing my eyes, I jumped from his bed. I supposed I did ask him how high. "Not one bit." I kept my eyes glued to him even as I walked past him and out of my cabin.

We approached the training area within minutes, long after the other boys had gone to sleep. "What first?" I asked.

The wind was knocked out of me as he swept me off my feet and my knees hit the dirt. "Come on. You want to fight me. Now is your chance." His brows shot up, eyes shimmering with suspense as I glanced up at him.

I dropped to the ground entirely before rolling, trying to grab his ankle. But he vanished between my fingers, and I cursed under my breath. "Not fair!"

A snicker here, a scuffle there. "Nobody said I was playing by any rules."

I scrambled to my feet and pulled my dagger from its sheath, lunging for him. Again, he puffed out like a ghost before I ever made contact.

"Try harder," he said from behind me.

I growled as I whipped around and sliced my blade through the air. A drop of Pan's blood was all I needed. That would be enough, like the final ingredient to complete my ritual. A ritual only I could hold, and the sacrifice would most certainly be his to bear.

"Love," his lips brushed my ear. "I'm right here."

I spun around to find him leaning against the tree and checking his nails.

"This is going to get boring really fast," he said in monotone.

His green eyes pierced through me as I ran for him, only to find my dagger stuck in the trunk of the tree I'd so carelessly stabbed after his departure. I braced my foot against the bark, yanking as hard as I could.

Fingers wrapped around my wrist and flipped me, Pan pressing me between him and the tree. His hand didn't dare loosen from my wrist which dug into the wood, as he glanced at the blade beside my head. "It's not that hard." With his other hand, he wiggled it free, but rather than handing it back, he pointed the tip below my chin, forcing my eyes up. "Better. I much enjoy you like this."

"What's that? Weak? Under your control?" I kept perfectly still so as not to puncture my own jaw.

"Precisely." He traced the side of my dagger down my neck before carefully placing the hilt in my palm. "But it's more than just that." He placed his hand around my throat. "It's the warmth. The soft of your neck." He rubbed his thumb over my pulse. The pulse that told him my heart was racing. Pounding in my ears. Chaotically and forever under his power. "The way you fear me, but not because I can kill you without a second thought. You fear the things I make you feel," his voice lowered. Leaning closer, he buried his nose in my neck. "Your scent, Little Flower. I've never come across anything more intoxicating."

I widened my eyes, swallowing whatever the hell I could. "My scent? The scent of sweat?"

"I can easily distinguish between your aroma and your odor. Much like a *crow*. I detect what nobody else is able to."

Pushing against his chest, he stumbled back and his hair fell in unruly waves. But delinquency roared in his eyes like flames as he disappeared before me, his laugh bouncing between trees.

Tightening my grip, I spotted him near a tree across the clearing and swiped when I neared him. I'd expected him to evaporate like he always did, and so I skid into the dirt and swung my arm around behind me, earning a hiss.

When I lifted my gaze to meet Pan's, he sucked the blood from his palm. Pride suffused in his eyes. His blood dripped from the tip of my dagger, and I stood to my feet until all that was left between us was a mutual promise. Neither of us would say a word. Not until Pan decided to, and that I could agree with. I didn't need the world to know, as myself was more than enough. We both were acutely aware of it.

Knowing I drew blood from the infamous Peter Pan was enough to fuel me for a lifetime.

20: Shattered

It was now or never, and I wasn't going to wait around for never. "Pan!" I shouted from across the training area. Everyone turned my way, but I ignored their piercing stares. His was the only one that mattered.

As I approached him, he asked, "What?"

Her words played over again in my head. *I'll have him wrapped around my finger again soon. Pan could never resist me.* I despised him but I couldn't let her make him worse than he was.

"We need to talk about Hook." That was enough for him to scan the area and take me somewhere more private. I guess he didn't want this getting out, too.

He ran his hands through his hair. "What did you do, Little Flower?"

He wanted to blame me, but I could be saving him right now. "Hook wants to get you back, and not in a good way. She's planning on hurting you again. She says that you could never resist her."

His posture fixed itself. "She wants me back to hurt me? What could she do that she hasn't already done?"

I opened my mouth to answer but nothing came to mind. There wasn't much she could do. Pan was already heartless and loved nobody but himself. She couldn't take anything from him when he had nothing left for her to take.

He circled me, and I twisted my body to follow. "I hate to ruin your perspective but there's nothing about her that can scare me anymore."

He headed back to camp, but he didn't stop there. He passed through and ended at Cannibal Cove. I followed him the whole way but he either didn't notice or didn't care.

A tall woman with brown hair appeared from behind the trees. "Look who decided to show up." Kristin pulled out her sword. "Here to kill me for breaking your law? You'd have to kill yourself, too, for breaking your own."

He lifted his hands in surrender. "I came to talk."

Her laughter echoed into the sky. "Talk? Pan wants to talk?" She closed the gap until the tip of her sword poked his chest. "We had a deal. No lost girls, and I would leave Kace alone."

If he was willing to talk, he knew there was something Kristin could take from him that he feared losing.

He used the palm of his hand to grab the top of the sword and push it down. "The deal is off. I can't control my shadow now, and you are the reason why. You've taken so much and you're still coming back for more. Why?"

She lowered her sword, expression softening. "You have no idea. Did your stupid lost girl try to tell you how horrible I am?"

He shrugged. "She may have mentioned you."

What was she doing? She told me herself she wanted to wrap him around her finger.

"She's wrong but you already know that. We shared something, didn't we?" She walked around in the sand, intently watching his every move. "Do you remember?"

He snickered as his eyes moved with her. "How could I forget? You used me for your personal gain."

She stopped, facing him, and shook her head. "No, Peter. I'm talking about when we fought together. There was a time when we both had it all. We were unstoppable."

"They always say not to let the flaws overshadow the beauty but you're not beautiful, Kristin. You *are* the flaw." He narrowed his eyes.

She grabbed her heart. "Ouch." She shifted her eyes to the ground. "What about your lost girl? Is she a flaw? Is it because of me?"

Pan disappeared and appeared right beside her. "Are you jealous?" I'd laugh out loud if she said yes. How could she be jealous of me?

Lifting her head, Kristin looked him in the eye. "No, but I hear she's jealous of this Wendy you have in your bed."

This caught his attention.

Why the hell did she have to say that? I was not jealous of Wendy.

He folded his arms, eyes focused on Kristin's. "The jealousy was painted on her face when I kissed her sister. It makes sense as to why she left when she thought Wendy and I fooled around. She always was a terrible liar."

I was not a *terrible* liar. I just couldn't act as easily. And I was never lying in the first place. Pan was always the one who kept secrets from me, and his biggest secret yet was his relationship with every woman on this island. I wouldn't be fazed if Tinker Bell was part of this group.

She let out a laugh. "Well, she doesn't know what she's missing out on."

Definitely not much.

"What would that be?" he asked with a smirk.

Kristin closed the space between them. "The way your lips move against even the most delicate of skin. Your fingers tracing every inch. Your hot breath fanning the top of my ear." She let out a small sigh. "You used to hold me as if I was about to slip away for good."

"And then you did," he said in a fragile tone. My heart cracked, the crack ever-growing as I held onto the tree to avoid falling.

Hook had slipped away from Pan and for once, I didn't blame him. He gave her everything and she sailed away with it all.

She grabbed his shirt, pulling him against her chest. "It doesn't have to be that way anymore."

He ripped her hand away from his shirt. "You don't get to crawl back here and beg for my forgiveness. You destroyed my trust. There is nothing you can do to fix it."

"You know I didn't mean it." She attempted to grab his arm, but he stepped back.

Venom laced his next words. "But you did. You don't accidentally end up with another man. You don't get to pretend you didn't use me. Emotions may fade but the memories don't. It disgusts me that you try to invalidate what you put me through. You feel no remorse. You're denying that you did anything wrong."

Turning away, he glanced back at her as if he wanted to apologize but he never said a word. He left her to wallow in her own shame.

I returned to camp shortly after him, and Pan was already being questioned by Kace.

Pan snickered. "She tried to seduce me. She thought we could just move past everything." He stepped around him, pausing, then he spun around to meet Kace. "She can't fool me anymore."

Kace's eyes met mine. "What about Wendy?"

"What about her?"

With a shrug, Kace said, "You still fool yourself by keeping Wendy trapped. Sooner or later you need to face the facts and realize you can't move past this. Think less about your pain and more about the example the boys need."

What the hell? He just totally forgot about Lia and I.

"And be more like you? Is that what you're suggesting?" Pan gestured to him.

Kace didn't seem bothered by his words. "No. Just be more like *you*."

That caught Pan off guard. He had nothing left to say to that and it didn't surprise me. Kace had a way with words. Pan needed to stop seeking validation in power so he could focus on healing from what Kristin put him through.

Both went their separate ways without another word but Kace came towards me. We walked to the well and waited until the coast was clear so we could talk.

"What did you hear?" he asked.

"Everything. I'm not here to judge. I just want to understand." I fixed my glasses before they fell off my nose.

He closed his eyes. "If I could tell you, I would. I am not a man who talks about other people's business. I just hope that when the time comes, you mean it when you say you just want to understand."

Understand.

Of course, I wanted to understand why Pan was the way he was. I wasn't about to excuse his actions, but I needed to show some humanity if I was going to be anyone else but my parents.

It wasn't a crime to show compassion and if I was going to fight my dark side, I'd need to do more of that.

What about Lia?

That was a question I couldn't answer. It was tough to pretend we had something special, but it was tougher to lie to myself about how I felt. I was jealous of her. I would admit that.

I was jealous of Lia because she was the one person who looked exactly like me and had everything I wanted. She never had to even try. Pan had accepted her, even if it was for a stupid reason. He threw her a celebration and brought her here of his own accord. However, when his shadow brought me, he refused to acknowledge that I deserved to be a lost girl.

"What do you think of Lia?" I asked Kace. He was the one who suggested she come here in the first place. He never even knew her, but he wanted her here. I just had to know if there was another reason behind it than just for my "benefit."

He shrugged. "She's not like you but that's not a bad thing."

Everyone loved Lia because she wasn't like me. She was funny and kind. She had something to her that I couldn't attain. I belonged here because I was unloved and unwanted, and that wasn't a good feeling. I ran away from home but even in Neverland, I wasn't desired. Its own king despised my existence. Yet, Pan had personally brought my sister here himself.

I ditched Kace and went to the training area to let off some steam before it drowned me.

Every time I shot an arrow, I missed the target. All my knives landed in the dirt. Today I just couldn't seem to master my skills whatsoever.

When Jacob entered the area, I tried to ignore his presence. However, when I was challenged to a fight by Jacob, I seized it.

His fist swung, but I moved my head to the right to avoid the blow. His knee came up towards my gut and sent me doubling over for just a moment before I fixed my posture.

Memories flashed in my mind of Jacob attempting to take off my shirt.

I swung my leg up and kicked him in the chin, but he came back like a warrior.

Jacob grabbed me by my tank top and pulled me close. "Don't think you can win this time." His knee went right into my crotch as payback.

I cupped myself and bent over to gather my sanity, but it wasn't anywhere nearby. The pain continued into my pelvic bone and I swore nothing would be the same again in that region. Both heat and a throbbing ache took over.

Kace entered the training area and grabbed Jacob by the arm. "You know the rules. Everything between the legs is off-limits." He shoved Jacob out of the way. "Lili, look at me. You okay?"

I barely lifted my head. "Do I fucking look okay?" I managed to get out.

He took me back to his cabin and pulled an ice pack from a small cooler. "This might help."

Sitting on his bed, I placed it between my legs while taking a deep breath.

"Does it really hurt that bad? I mean, you don't have a penis." He sat down in a chair.

I shot him a glare. "Does it feel swollen? Yes. Is my bone fractured? Possibly."

He threw his hands up. Unless a woman had really experienced it for herself, she wouldn't even assume it was painful but now I knew better.

I leaned against his wall and closed my eyes. "I swear the swelling will never go back down."

"Why did he knee you there in the first place?" What a stupid question.

"Because Jacob is an asshole. There's no more explanation needed. He's an asshole just waiting to tear me to shreds like a piece of meat. I'm not a human to him and I never will be." I meant nothing to Jacob, and the humanity in him didn't exist.

I was just another soul to steal. The question remained—would Pan get to me first?

21: Blood

The arrow whizzed through the air and hit the deer right between the eyes. All the lost boys believed it would be impossible for a girl to be any good with finding dinner, but I was going to bring back the feast of the night.

I approached the deer as it collapsed to the ground. I ripped the arrow from its flesh and wiped it with my shirt before placing it back in my quill. The birds had stopped singing as soon as I took out one of the animals that inhabited these woods. The crows, however, cocked their heads in wonder. I had to survive somehow.

I grabbed the deer by its antlers and dragged it back to camp. It came as no surprise when everyone halted in their tracks to gaze upon the meal I had killed.

"Impressive. You ready to cut it up?" Kace asked from behind.

Looking back, I rolled my eyes. I had no interest in cutting up a deer and seeing more blood than my period offered me. I had already killed the deer. What more did boys want from a girl? And if I said no, I would come off as *the* wimp. That was not a reputation I was willing to uphold, so instead

I chose the path that would help me get recognition from the lost boys. "Show me where."

Kace led me through the rest of the camp until we approached his cabin. "I'll help you out." A smile appeared as he opened the door for me.

Such a gentleman.

I got the deer into the main room and dropped its head onto the floor. "I imagine I have to skin it first."

Kace helped me with the deer. He provided tools and instructions so our meat wouldn't be contaminated in any way. The skin was removed, and the best parts had been cut off the bones for a better entree. I'd broken through a threshold I never thought I would have.

When all was said and done, blood covered me from head to toe. Pan entered the cabin and stopped upon the sight. His eyes went dark. If it were anyone else, they would have been ready to vomit. "All that blood looks good on you. It really brings out your eyes," he said in a low tone.

If he kept up with his games, it would be his blood on me next. Well, more of it. After drawing blood from our fight, I'd been very satisfied. But to say I wouldn't be pleased to see more of it would be a lie.

"You say that now and yet you still try to talk sense into Hook while playing with Wendy. Pick a girl, Pan. Not all women like to wait around for a man's pleasure." I wiped my dagger clean.

He shot me a glare before exiting the cabin. I said my goodbyes to Kace and ran out. I caught up to Pan, attempting to match his long strides. "What was that about?"

"You'll leave it alone unless you want your throat slashed," he said in a dark tone.

I slowed down so that I fell behind him. He always told me to leave it alone and yet it still festered within his soul to this day. How did he expect me to leave it alone when Hook was still on this island, reminding Pan of what he'd lost? I had to talk to her myself.

I couldn't leave it alone. I knew the story, but this was not it. I couldn't just let Hook walk away. I had a chance to solve a mystery and I was going to take it.

As Pan disappeared into the tree line, I decided to go the opposite direction, towards Cannibal Cove. Approaching, I studied the woman heading back to her ship. I broke out into a run to catch her before she left for good.

"What do you want now?" she asked as she spun around to meet my eyes.

I stopped in my tracks and bent over, grabbing my thighs as I took in gulps of air. I needed to work more on cardio if I'd survive here.

She cleared her throat.

I lifted my head a bit as I put up my hand. "Give me a damn minute to breathe, will ya?"

Her eyes almost rolled out of her head. "You're so persuasive."

As I straightened my posture, I rested my hands on my hips. "So, what is this I hear about you and Pan?"

"Why is this your business?" Her eyes narrowed.

I shrugged a bit. "Because I live here and you're screwing up my family. Coming back to screw Pan over again is a bitch move if I've ever seen one. I want to rebuild what I never experienced, and you're getting in the way of that. I'm just trying to be a good person by talking to you about it first."

Hook laughed. "And then what, you'll threaten me? You're no match against me."

She had no idea what I was capable of. I just couldn't let the wolf inside me escape.

"I'm trying so hard here, Kristin. What is it that you did to him? Maybe we can get everyone to move on. There is no good that comes from living in the past." I knew this myself when I saw my own sister.

She shrugged. "I tried. I tried to talk to Pan and he shot me down."

Now it was my turn to laugh. "That was a bullshit talk. You just wanted to mess with his head. You were trying to seduce him back into your schemes. I saw everything. You told him I don't know what I'm missing out on and proceeded to sex him up like a doll." That last line had my blood boiling to the brim of the stove pot. Something lurking within was clawing its way to the surface of my soul.

Her eyebrows shot up for a minute. "Yes, I did say that. Was I wrong? No. He was amazing in bed and I won't be able to deny that. I've been to your world, Lili. Men in your world are much less about satisfying the woman and more about themselves. It's a shame that men like that exist. They don't help a woman finish because they're just too selfish. It's cruel is what it is. Pan isn't like that. There was never a moment where I had to question whether I'd get my turn. I always knew. He destroyed that when he broke up with me. He took his *power* with him."

The darkness pounded on the walls, trying to break free. I gave in, allowing the walls to crash and burn as sweet, tempting immorality began flooding every inch of my blood.

Gripping the handle of my dagger, my skin paled, anger flushing out along with it. I swiftly pulled it from my belt, but her fingers wrapped around my wrist. "I wouldn't do that if I were you," she said.

"Then good thing you're not me," I spat.

I aimed for her side, but her hook blocked me. She pulled her sword from her belt and swung. I ducked just enough to miss it but when I stood back up, her sword sliced across my stomach.

She sneered. "Such a shame. You could have been smarter."

The blade flew from my hand as she sliced my arm. I dropped to the sand—pinching my weak hand in the process—and rolled away from her, dagger now in hand. While she was pulling her blade from the sand after missing me, I jumped on her from behind, knocking her to the ground.

She yelled and rolled onto her back as I moved out of the way. I scrambled back onto my feet and held my dagger out in defense as she stood.

Hook threw her hair out of her face. "You're pathetic for a lost girl. You have to do better than that."

"I can make it work." I spun around and our blades clashed together. She pushed against it, leaning close. I could smell the seafood in her breath. My lunch was ready to come back up the way it'd gone down.

I ducked my head as I pulled my dagger away from her sword. It swung around but missed me, and before she could recollect her focus, I plunged the dagger deep into her abdomen. "Don't underestimate what a woman is capable of. You should know that better than anyone." I twisted the blade.

She choked on her own blood as it spilled from her mouth like milk from a jug. Thirst-quenching. She held onto my wrists with no strength to defend herself this time. Neverland was timeless but it wasn't safe from the cruel clutches of death. Even here, he had reign.

Her hook fell from my hair and dangled at her side. A sorrowful look displayed in her eyes as she went down on her knees. I stepped back, admiring the way she collapsed into the sand, half of her body a victim of the waves with her legs folded underneath her.

As I stood over her, a slight smile grasped my lips. "Looks like I win." I bent down and pulled the dagger from her pale body. She grunted as much as she could manage but it was hardly anything at all.

I waded deeper into the water and waved my dagger around in the seafoam. It seemed to attract some human-looking creatures I assumed to be mermaids.

They dove, their fins slapping the water as they disappeared under the surface.

I walked back over to see Hook's chest still rising and falling. "The mermaids look hungry." The fear in her eyes was enough to tell me she knew they wouldn't hesitate to eat her. "It was a poor move on your part to assume you ever had leverage."

I had no idea what she'd meant by the deal with Pan, but it was my duty to protect him as well as everyone else here. If I wanted to save myself, too, that was...

Backing away from the shore as the mermaids swam closer to the captain, my eyes stayed fixed on her the entire time. She couldn't even scream as they ripped into her flesh.

I turned and walked back to camp where everyone else ate their soup in silence. It was the first I had ever seen of them seeing as most nights were filled with hollers and celebrations. She'd done something serious to Pan, more than she would let on. The boys all knew it, too.

The firepit had died long ago as I approached and took my spot next to Kace. Pan stood by the tree outside the circle. "You're late. No dinner tonight."

"Whatever." I smirked to myself, keeping my face from his view.

My smirk disappeared when I looked back at Pan. I think part of him knew what I had done, but he was trying to confirm if his suspicions were of any consolation.

I faced the firepit once again. Kace asked, "Why are you so late?"

"Why do you think?" Before he took my question as sarcasm, I added, "I'm just curious to know what your thoughts are." I shrugged a bit.

He pulled his hood down. "You want the answer as to why Pan is so rude. Hook could've given you those answers."

"Correct." I stared forward, keeping my secrets to myself. Anger no longer plagued my being. Instead, relaxation filled every crevice. Kace was safe, and maybe now Pan could heal since she was dead. The woman who caused his whole downfall became a meal for mermaids, and I felt like Neverland had a real chance here. Things could get better, couldn't they?

Pan clapped his hands together while facing everyone. "Finish your soup and go to bed. Nobody is staying up late. We have a long day of training ahead of us tomorrow." He disappeared into his cabin.

I wondered if he was training everyone extra hard because of the incident today. That would mean he wouldn't know what I did. Would he ever know? Not unless I told him. He couldn't know otherwise. I was sure of which abilities he had, and none of them involved him reading minds.

Kace stood up. "We should get to bed now. Pan warned us of a long day tomorrow and we will need all the rest we can get." He peered down at me.

I finally gave him my attention, but I didn't speak. They didn't even know my training had already led to the death of Captain Hook herself. I was not even close to defeating Pan by more than a slice of his palm, but I had taken out his enemy. Had he ever tried? Was he too afraid because of the love they shared?

Looking back at Pan's cabin, my mind wandered to what was going to happen next. Behind those doors, he could be using Wendy to get his mind off Kristin's death. I expected to see Pan change, and if he didn't, I was going to make sure he knew I was done with his games. Becoming who he hated the most was his biggest weakness and I'd use it to full advantage if it saved him in the end.

Revenge was a dish best served cold.

22: TRUTH

I AIMED AT THE target and let it fly. It stabbed just outside of the bullseye. "So close," I whispered in frustration. I was working hard to get this skill down, but I failed every now and then. Some days, my head wasn't with it. Anger fueled combat, but it didn't work the same with archery. If I had used an arrow to kill Hook, I would've missed by an inch.

"So close, Little Flower, but never quite there," the voice whispered into my ear from behind. I jumped and turned around, cheeks burning upon the realization of how close we were.

He pulled himself back. "I think we need to talk. Don't you?"

"Whatever could you mean, Pan? You never want to talk," I mocked him.

He stood up straight and clasped his hands together behind his back. "If you want real answers, you'll bloody shut up and follow me," he said as he turned on his heel, heading down the path.

I swallowed, dying to know what he was talking about. I hated him, but I needed answers to really achieve that. I also played into this idea that he was the *leader* so I could gain his trust and be able to achieve my plan effectively.

We came to his thinking tree and I stopped dead in my tracks. "No, absolutely not. Nope. I'm not doing this shit again." I turned to leave.

He chuckled. "No worries, I won't be doing anything like that. I'm giving you answers. Well, a few answers if you give me a few. We really *should* talk."

"Can you blame a girl for wanting to leave this place? We both know what happened here. This place gives me bad memories." As I crossed my arms, I faced him. "What answers do you want from me?"

He leaned against the big trunk of Hangman's Tree. He looked up at the branches before catching my eyes. "The memories weren't that bad. You enjoyed it." And he really took great pleasure in holding that over my head.

I threw my arms up. "That's just it, Pan! I am not supposed to be romanced by you of all people. I do not like you in the slightest." There goes my *pretend-to-obey* plan. "I'm mad at you for being a part of it."

"Well, then maybe now you know not to assume things about people." He shrugged a bit, lacking every bit of regret.

"Yeah, whatever you say," I mumbled to myself. "What is this talk about?" I raised my voice.

He pushed himself off that giant ass tree and stepped closer. "I took a walk along the beach this morning and noticed some sand stained with blood. Would you know anything about that?"

He knew. He knew what I did. But it wouldn't make him mad, would it? Unless he was humiliated that a girl could kill his enemy when he couldn't, then he'd be proud. I was dead to myself. "What do you mean?"

"You searched for Hook and kept insisting we talk about her. I'm sure you met up with her at some point. Now there's blood near Cannibal Cove. I need to know if you did something." His eyes darkened just a tad, narrowing.

"Why? Why would you need to know?" I was trying to undermine his authority again, and I knew it was a bad idea. I was in too far deep to be able to save myself now. I was all in for the ride.

He cocked an eyebrow. "Because this is my island. It's my job to know everything that happens in Neverland. That includes whatever you do at the beach. Confess now, or you'll fear the consequences."

I closed another foot of space between us. "Then kill me. I would love to get away from this hell you've created." I was cutting it close to punishment now.

He scanned my eyes. "You want me to kill you, leaving Lia behind to deal with me?"

"I don't care. Lia can take care of herself. She doesn't need me." Inhale. Exhale.

Pan closed the distance, lifting my chin with his fingers. "Then I can just torture you some other way. I'm beginning to figure out what makes you tick. You should tell me the truth about the blood before it's too late. You know what happened here last time."

I looked away, every thought running through my head. I'd let him get *too* close. "I killed her. I killed Captain Hook. Is that what you want to hear?" I couldn't let him do that to me again. Confessing my sins was my only option. He'd been right. I was terrified of letting him bring out the monster inside me.

He gave a slight nod. "How did you kill her?"

I didn't know why he was asking. Was there some way to creatively take a life? "I... I stabbed her. I stabbed her with my dagger, then I let the mermaids eat her." She'd still been alive when I fed her to those creatures... It began to hit me—the seriousness of what I had done. What was wrong with me? I'd gone too far. "I didn't mean it. I don't know what's happening."

He pressed his lips into a thin line. "But do you really? That's not something that someone with a heart does. You're finding your dark side, Love. You're finding yourself. Don't feel ashamed. Neverland doesn't judge you." His fingers stilled. I think I saw a hint of admiration in his eyes. No, that couldn't be.

"Don't. Don't you dare even say that. This is not who I am. This is not *me*. The demon will never claw its way out." *Oh, but Little Flower, it already has.* "I'm going to save you."

Lies.

I would probably lose myself instead.

He choked on a laugh. "Nobody can change me. Especially not a woman with crimson-stained hands."

"Hook did," I said.

This shut him up. I had finally caught him in his deception. It was refreshing to win every now and again.

"Hook was her own version of messed up. She never told me much about herself, but she did tell me that her father never believed she would be better as a pirate. She had been nothing but an incubator to him, a woman to marry off so he could have what he wanted. Being a pirate was her way of rebelling."

I swallowed as I dug the toe of my boot into the dirt. "And then she came to Neverland by accident I assume. How old was she when you met her?"

With a small shrug, he replied, "I didn't ask but she was probably twenty. She could never stay here long due to her age. Neverland isn't too kind to the adults."

"Yet, you're eighteen. An adult."

"But, you see, my power is what breathed life into the island. I am the cap. Nobody who enters can be any older than I am, or dreadful things will happen."

How dreadful? Just another question for the books. I was not just his resident and savior, but also a journalist. Lucky me.

He shifted his weight. "Soon you're going to see your shadow separate from you, and I'll be here, waiting."

"What do you mean?" Sure, his shadow was detached from him, but I figured it was because he was magical. How else would he find new lost boys? Right, fly to them himself. But that was asking too much of Pan, and he'd never be caught dead doing that much work.

He walked towards the tree. "Why do you think I have a separate shadow? Have you ever heard of shadows as good entities by themselves?"

"No..." I studied his every muscle movement. The way his calves tightened with each step. His veins in his hands became evident. His sleeve slid up past his elbow.

He stopped but didn't turn. "Exactly. Shadows are dark beings. They are part of us; they are our darkest parts. When we let our dark side win, our shadow becomes its own person, and then what do we have left? There's no more balance and the good in us can no longer survive."

"Are you saying that your shadow separated from you because you embraced your dark side, and your shadow then detached itself as its own person?"

He spun to meet my gaze. "That's exactly what I'm saying. Were you even listening? When we control our darkness, it resides inside our shadow. But when we let it continue to guide us, the shadow detaches as a form of defense. Without a shadow, your darkness has nowhere to go. It just stays within you, in full control."

"Who drove you so mad that you gave into the demon?" I asked.

He stepped down from the tree roots that reared their dirty limbs from the dirt. "Who do you think?"

Seconds passed before it hit me like a ton of bricks. "Captain Hook. I was right. She claimed she only broke your heart, but I knew she was lying."

Pan nodded a bit. "Now you're paying attention. Good for you."

"What did she do exactly?" I crossed my arms to deflect his insult. It wasn't considered attentive listening in body language, and that was my way of defying him. Any chance I could, I would.

"Is that your business?" He gave me a stern look.

"I killed her because she thought it wasn't my business. Does that answer your question?"

He paused for a moment, before caving. "She did more than just break my heart." I gestured for him to go on. Hesitance flashed in his eyes but as much as he wanted to keep his business to himself, he knew it would feel good to release the pain. After all, I'd killed her because of what she did to him.

"She *was* my enemy, but before that, she was never against me. Kristin was the captain who'd come and go from time to time. As the owner, I would always keep an eye on her to make sure she didn't do anything she shouldn't. She spotted me observing her every move. I was only watching her because I had to protect my island. I had to protect myself.

"I was wary, but I introduced myself. I might not have been evil before her, but I wasn't a pushover either. She took an interest. I didn't know at the time she was interested in ruining me." Our eyes locked, his gaze piercing the barrier I'd worked so hard to build. "Or as I like to see it, she was interested in making me into who I really should be. She kept coming back to the island. But it was I who made the mistake of trusting her."

I stayed silent, just hoping he wouldn't sense the crack in my heart.

After he finally returned from the depths of his mind, he continued, "She used my trust against me. She pretended to love me. She took advantage of the fact that I was a boy who'd never had experience with a woman. With Hook, I learned everything there ever was to know about a woman. She wasn't Hook at the time, though. She had two hands then, believe me." He snickered.

I scrunched my nose, getting an idea of what he was possibly referring to.

"She taught me all of it, including love." A frown caressed his face. "This is where the story turns sour. I let my guard down. I trusted her. Loved her. And she used me. She gave me everything I wanted, only to rip it away." He closed his eyes for a moment. "Then she did these things with my second-in-command."

My eyes widened. The three of them? I could barely picture Pan in love, but *Kace*?

Believe me when I said Pan was the kind of guy to accidentally entangle himself in messy devotion. Kace, however, had always kept his distance. He stood on the sidelines and watched everyone else enjoy themselves while he memorized their flaws, perfections, and otherwise.

To allow himself to be part of the action was unlike him.

"Kace never knew at the time that she was playing both of us. Kace loved her, too, but she didn't love either of us."

This was why the two were so loyal. They both had loved the same woman. They connected on levels no other lost boy could fathom.

Finishing his story, he said, "She had used me to get my power and the way I connected to Neverland—and she used my best friend. For that, I vowed to make her pay. I cut off the hand that ripped out our hearts. I wanted to do more, but she got away. She came back and threatened my lost boys and Kace. I made a deal that I wouldn't bring girls here and she wouldn't hurt my boys. She's the one who hated women, and that is why Wendy isn't a lost girl. If Hook had known, Wendy would be killed and so would the lost boys." He released the sigh that held all his woes. Closing the final gap between us, he lifted my chin. "You may as well let your dark side win. There is no good left in Neverland, Little Flower." His knuckles rested just above my throat, but it was his words that ripped me open.

There is no good left in Neverland.

Pan hated me because I was a threat to everything he built, but now that Hook was dead, that wasn't a problem anymore.

I shook my head as I pushed his hand down, making sure he was going to heed my next words. "You shouldn't let her win. She wins when you're miserable—heartless. You are giving her the power to control your thoughts. You need to take back that control and fight it. Show that shadow where it belongs and become the man you are truly supposed to be. That is how you defeat her. I didn't win last night, Pan, because in the end, I'd allowed her to control me. My monster got a taste of freedom. If the darkness has control, *nobody* wins."

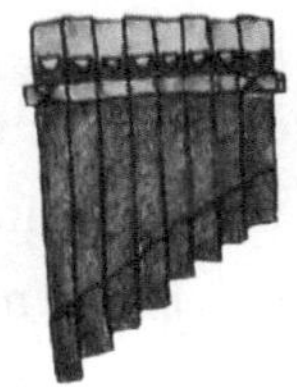

23: Unbreakable

The morning had already been treating me well. I ate my soup with Eric, laughing over silly little things with him, and when he finished his soup, we played a short game of tic-tac-toe. I won, as he'd had very little experience with the right moves.

Then he asked, "Where's Lia?" He was just a kid trying to be nice, but I didn't want to talk about her at the moment. She was the twin I wished I never had.

"I don't know. What do you want us to do today?" I changed the subject quickly.

His eyes lit up and he stood. "I have something to show you! Come, come!" He grabbed my wrist, pulling me.

I laughed. "Okay, okay. Let me finish this soup. I have one bite left." I shoved the final bite into my mouth and swallowed before I choked. "Done! Take me away, Eric," I joked with him.

He let out a laugh and pulled me to the place he wanted to go to. We ended up on the beach. "You wanted to show me the beach?" I furrowed my brows.

Eric shook his head and pointed to the mermaid tails flowing between the waves. "They're so beautiful!"

"Oh, of course, but they are also evil. They'll eat us. Why don't we do something that wouldn't risk our lives?" I bent down to his level.

He frowned. "But I love mermaids."

"Me too, but mermaids are not nice creatures in Neverland." They were sirens but more inclusive with their appetites. "I care about you. I don't want to see you get hurt." I held his face in my hands. "You're my *friend*."

"I'm your friend?" He grinned.

I smiled a bit and nodded. "Of course. Why wouldn't you be? You've given me the love I've always needed. You don't judge me, and you never have. I'm a girl on an island of lost boys. That alone makes me an outcast. Nobody accepted me but you always did. Even when Lia came, you still cared about me. *You* didn't forget about me."

"But you're a person, too. It would be mean to treat you any less." He put his hand on my shoulder. "We are in Neverland because we were unloved before. We are not supposed to feel like that here." Truer words had never been spoken.

A sad smile replaced the previous. "Yeah, well, I can't guarantee I don't feel unloved in some instances. Come on, let's go play somewhere safe." I stood up as we glanced back at the mermaids watching us. I grabbed his hand and off we went.

Sometimes I wondered if Eric was the only reason I was keeping the demon at bay. It was hard to make good choices when everyone around me hated my existence.

We came to the nice little lagoon, its waterfall as quiet as ever. "Do you know how to swim?" I looked down at him.

He gasped. "Yeah! I love swimming."

"Good. We'll swim her, and no mermaids will eat us." I took the first steps into the water. "It's so refreshing. Every day I wake up and I'm already in a sauna. It's like a hundred and ten degrees on Neverland!" I yelled.

Eric ran in while laughing. “It's cold!” He only went in deep enough until it came to his shoulders.

I dipped under and resurfaced. I pushed my hair back. “It is, but it feels great against the heat.”

“That's true.” He went under and drank the water but spit it back out like a fountain. “I wanted to ask how you brush your hair or wash it. It's so curly and long! We have short hair, so we don't have to wash our hair or brush it.”

I shrugged a little. “I have a brush. They’re really not hard to come by. I don’t use it as often as you might assume, either.”

“Jacob says you're sleeping with Pan to get what you want,” he said.

I choked, unaware I’d inhaled some water. “What?”

“Do you sleep in Pan's cabin? Why would that make Pan give you what you want? He likes to be alone.” He poured some water on his head from his cupped hands.

One swallow and I had gathered enough of my stability. “No, I am not sleeping in his cabin. I don't get what I want. If I got what I wanted, I wouldn't feel unloved, ever. You would be surprised to know that I only have some of what I need because I work hard to get it.”

“Oh. Okay.” He nodded.

“I normally use hair products and Pan provides me with some shampoo and conditioner. It gets the job done. The only way he gives it to me is when I don't undermine his authority, especially in front of you lost boys.” I released a sigh.

He made a funny face, tongue out. “That must be hard for you. You enjoy challenging Pan.” He opened his mouth wide and closed it, showing his teeth.

I laughed at both his comment and his facial expressions. “It is hard for me. Sometimes, I fail.”

We swam around for a little while longer. I had only wished I could've had this kind of relationship with my brothers back home. But I was in

Neverland now and I wasn't going back.

"Tell me, what was your family like back home?" I asked him.

He blinked like he forgot he ever had a family before Neverland. "Oh, I had a sister and a dad. That was it. I barely remember now."

"How long have you been here?" I questioned.

He tilted his head. "I don't know. I never counted. I would say for a very long time now. At least since 1923." *Wait, what?*

No, that couldn't be right. Kace told me that Pan had been born in 1905, and Pan told me he was eighteen. Neverland was created in 1923, and as far as I'd been aware of, Kace had been Pan's first ever lost boy. The numbers didn't add up.

I nodded a bit and screeched when he splashed me. I returned the favor, and eventually we broke out into a battle. There was nothing like a little fun to really lift the spirits around here.

Maybe things were looking up now that the cause of Pan's dark rulership was dead. Although, his shadow was detached, and we had to somehow fix that. If we repaired that separation, we could see the *real* Peter Pan again.

Peter Pan was supposed to be the boy who saved people from horrid home situations, providing them with what every human being craved. To be loved. He was never supposed to ignore our needs.

We finished swimming for the day and walked back to the camp soaked. I turned around to say goodbye to Eric, but he was already gone. How he moved so quickly, I'd never know.

As I walked to my cabin to put on dry clothes, Pan stopped me.

I cleared my throat. "What is it now, Pan? I want to change."

"We have some things we have to do together." He waved me over to follow him as we walked into the forest.

I wondered if this was a trick to piss me off again. What could he possibly want from me this time? He couldn't seem to leave me alone, despite claiming to not trust me at all. But maybe this was his way of keeping an eye on me the way he used to Hook.

"People think we're sleeping together and it's getting me what I want," I said. I didn't know who had started this rumor, but I sure didn't want it going around. I was enough of an outcast.

He glanced at me. "Okay. What do you want me to do about it? I'm not your parent. I am not here to make the bullies go away."

"Damnit, do you not realize why we came to you in the first place? We beg for your help because we believe you can. We believe in you, but you let us down. That makes you a failure." As my eyes brushed over a tree root I lifted my foot just in time to avoid, I shrugged.

He stopped, and I crashed into his back. I backed up as he turned around to face me. "Watch your mouth. Only you are being let down. You're ungrateful."

"Heaven forbid I want to be treated like a human!" I threw my arms up with the roll of my eyes. After a moment, I peeked up at him. "I could be evil; I could be heartless. I could be *just* like you."

"I could be stupid; I could be reckless. You know Neverland wouldn't thrive if I was anything like you." His eyes never wavered as the once-green iris' swirled in a thick cloud of *gold* smoke.

I scowled. "People think we are sleeping together. You may not care that your lost boys think you're screwing a woman, but I care what everyone thinks. I don't want them thinking I'm that easy." I began pacing, running my fingers through my hair. "Hell, I heard this from Eric. He's a little boy. He doesn't even know what it means. And yet, here you are thinking it doesn't matter that your lost boys think this about us."

Pan could push buttons that nobody else could do. Of course, it was in a man's ego to have everyone think he was getting in the pants of women. However, I didn't want everyone to think I was that readily available. Jacob was the one I had to convince the most. If the others were anything like him—and I feared they were all capable of it—they'd leap at the opportunity to put their needs before my safety.

"You don't care because it makes you look good and makes me look bad."

I let out a heavy sigh. "What the hell are we doing out here?"

He gestured to the mountains before us. "I want you to just take in the beauty of the nature around us. You worry too much about acceptance and what people think of you. Sometimes, you need to stop and smell the roses."

I pointed. "Mhm, yep, I see Skull Rock right over there. *So beautiful*," I said with sarcasm dripping from my voice. I stepped closer to the cliff. "What now?"

"You need more adventure in your life," he whispered against the top of my ear, his warm breath reddening my cheeks.

Before I could question what he meant, his hand met my back with a forceful push and I stumbled over the cliff, towards the rocks and ocean below. I tried to get a scream out of my throat, but my vocal cords shut down.

I closed my eyes to pretend it was just a dream.

Arms wrapped around my figure and I looked at them to make sure I was headed somewhere much more pleasant now. I was utterly disappointed.

Pan flew us across the ripples in the ocean's surface before landing on a giant rock at the base of the cliff. "Wasn't that fun? You can do that in Neverland. You should learn to be more adventurous. That's why you're here. Worrying about the things from your life before is never going to get you anywhere."

I sucked in deep breaths as I tried to understand what the hell had just happened. "I could've died!"

"But you didn't. Stop complaining, Love. I didn't let you die. Does that not mean anything to you? I flew you over a river. I don't do that for my lost boys. I don't even do that for Lia," he stated.

I started to catch my breath, looking around where we stood. I peered at the hard rock below my feet, thankful to be back on the ground. Nobody would've guessed I had a fear of heights. But I knew.

Looking up at Pan, I processed his words. "Why would you do this for me? Is this your way of warming up to me so that I let my monster loose and lose your game?"

"No game, no tricks. I simply just wanted to show you some adventure. I get tired of the complaining. I wanted to show you what it's really like to live here—in Neverland." He gestured to the island around us.

The wind here at the base picked up, my hair slapping me in the face. Pan's luscious waves only grazed his forehead before clinging to it. My heart almost skipped a beat when his eyes caught me staring a little too intensely.

Water crashed against the rock, soaking us. I lost the grip I had, sliding, but Pan reached for my arms so I didn't fall into the depths of the ocean.

When I regained my balance and pushed my hair away, I said, "I was already having a good day. I went swimming with Eric. Now I've been pushed off a cliff and flown over the bottomless sea. I think I have a good idea of what it's like to live in Neverland."

"Sure, but you have an idea as a lost girl rather than a lost boy." He stepped closer.

"Great, I'm still treated differently despite Hook being dead. She can't hurt Kace anymore, Pan. I'm a lost girl and it's okay to accept that."

He tilted his head a centimeter to the left. "Because you *are* different, Little Flower. I wouldn't do these things with my lost boys." His gaze never wavered from mine, and it kind of worried me. I didn't know what it was, but maybe it was a pimple?

Pan grabbed my face, thumbs just below above my cheekbones, pulling our lips together as they melded as one. *Unbreakable*—a kiss I would've never expected from Peter Pan himself. It was a mistake; it was all wrong and yet I couldn't will myself to stop. I tasted his sweet forgiveness, surrendering to him just for the moment.

24: Fee Abyss

The sun had set hours ago and Pan hadn't said another word to me since our adventure. Part of me was angry that I let him do it but the other part of me was curious to know why he did it.

Kace shot me strange looks from across the camp but he had no idea what had gone down, not unless Pan told him he kissed me. Had he? *Would he?*

Someone tapped my shoulder and I expected to see Hunter or even Eric, but not Pan. "What?" I asked in a quiet voice. When I saw people kiss on shows and then act awkward about it, I judged them. I always made fun of them for not talking about it, and now I understood why they avoided it. Talking about a kiss was a terrifying subject.

He turned on his heel and waved for me to follow him. Did I want to? He could kiss me again or reject me, making me feel so small—so worthless. Both options didn't seem tempting.

More lies.

I got up from my spot to follow him and as soon as I did, I asked, "Have you been shaving this entire time?" I gestured to the stubble on his chin.

He glanced back. "Did you think only adults grew beards? If that's true, you shouldn't have breasts."

"I just can't picture Peter Pan with facial hair. Maybe that's why you shave." I shrugged.

He laughed and shook his head. "I don't shave just because I'm Peter Pan and your book tells me to. I chose to shave because Hook liked the clean jawline."

"What about Wendy?" I asked.

This seemed to catch him off guard. "Wendy? Why would Wendy's opinion matter?"

I laughed a bit. "Because you're 'buddies', Pan."

He stopped in his tracks. "'Buddies?' We fooled around maybe once, but we never shagged." He turned to face me, but his eyes were filled with affliction. "You really think so low of me that you assume I keep her around for shagging when that's not true. Do I enjoy it? Yes. But that doesn't mean I'm going to shag any woman. Wendy and I get high together. That's what we do that you had to *process*. You just assumed, so we let you."

"Getting high? How... How do you get high?" I furrowed my brows.

Pan began walking the other way again. "I'd never tell you. Everyone would be abusing it." Not me. I tried to get high and it just never seemed as fun.

Chills covered every inch of my skin as we approached a cliff. Would we do it again? I peeked over the edge and tilted my head. Fog covered every inch below, but a few lights glowed through the thick blanket. *Fee Abyss.*

Pan halted me. "You might want to grab on."

I turned to look at him, but my foot missed the ledge and I fell back. The cliff rushed past and fog engulfed me.

Everything fell silent when the water ate me whole. I couldn't find my way back home. I tried to swim to the surface, but I couldn't locate where it went. How was that even possible?

Burning filled my lungs as I held my breath, denying the water entrance.

I flailed around until fingers wrapped around my wrist and pulled me out the opposite way I fell in. They pulled me into a small boat and wrapped a blanket around my shoulders.

I coughed up every bit of water that slipped in before taking big gulps of air.

Pan sat back. “Welcome to Fee Abyss. It's a river that never has a way out unless you're me. The fairies love seclusion. It allows their light to be contained.” He gestured to the glowing balls as we floated down the river.

“Why are you showing me this? I almost died and you didn't even catch me this time.” I shivered.

A look of betrayal laced his expression. “I saved you from the river.” When I didn’t apologize, he let out a sigh. “I tried to catch you, but the fog is impossible to navigate through. I wanted to show you this because it's part of our adventure.”

I looked around me to find some fairies lighting up the way. The fog was thick, but I could see Pan from where I sat. “That's great and all but I have to go pee now.”

“We're on a river. Where do you see a bathroom here?” He scanned the fog.

I looked over the edge of the boat and into the endless river. Fee Abyss finally became clear to me. “I really have to go, Pan. I can't just grab my crotch and hold it in.”

Another sigh. “Can't you cross your legs?”

If it were that easy. I was still a bit sore from Jacob's knee. “You scared me to death when I fell off the cliff and into a river with no way out. I thought I'd die. It triggered my bladder. I have to pee and I can’t hold it in. I'll just hold onto the boat while I'm in the river.”

He groaned. “Go.”

I put the blanket down and climbed over the edge of the boat. I kept my hands hooked over the side of the boat. It wasn't ideal but I wasn’t looking for a UTI on an island with no antibiotics.

However, I hadn't thought of how I was going to get back into the boat.

After a few minutes of trying to climb back in and failing, Pan asked, "Need any help?"

If I accepted his help, I'd have to also accept that he did so much for me that I wanted to do for myself. However, if I went under the water without a grip on the boat, I'd get lost forever.

"Fine," I said.

He reached over and gripped my arms as he pulled me back inside. I took my rightful seat back on the other end where my blanket was.

Pan admired the fairies flying by.

I leaned over the side of the boat, dipping my fingers in the river as the fog cleared a bit to allow the base of the cliffs some a peek at the beauty.

Glancing at Pan, I wondered what was on his mind or if he ever thought of anyone besides himself.

"I'm sorry." I swallowed my pride as I said those words.

He looked at me, a laugh coming out in a cough. "You're sorry?"

I nodded and closed my eyes. "I'm sorry for assuming that you and Wendy were having sex. I just thought that..."

"That what?"

No, Lili. You're trying to apologize. Don't ruin it by making excuses.

"Nothing. I'm sorry for assuming Wendy was your toy and Kace was your lover." I focused on the floorboards of the boat. Nope, no leaks here. "I forget that I need to work on myself, too. I always assume men just want sex from a woman. We don't build a better future by assuming horrible things about people. I also need to stop shipping two men together just because they're close friends. That's toxic for me to do. Men should be allowed to be super close and not be into each other. People should be allowed to be friends with the sex they're attracted to—or not attracted to—without it being romantic or sexual." Just as I was friends with Kace.

Pan wasn't sure what to say to that. It made me feel better because I didn't want him to tell me how shitty I was after I just told him I already thought that. My own criticism was more than enough.

The boat stopped against the side of something and I noticed a house hanging above us. What was this place?

Pan stood, grabbing my hand without giving me a chance to pull away. "Before you nearly drown again."

I squeezed his hand to give him the green light as he pushed us off the floor of the boat and into the sky. We flew until we were level with the door of what looked to be a treehouse. I stepped inside when he opened the door, grabbing onto the frame to make sure I was on the ground again. "What is this?" I asked him.

Pan followed me in. "This is where Hook and I used to go before she ruined it all. I haven't been here since I was with her. The memories are...overwhelming."

There was some furniture, and it looked almost like one of the cabins, but this treehouse had fancier lighting than our cabins. It was decorated to *set* the mood.

"Is this your shagging cabin?"

Pan sat down on the bed and looked at me. "I burned the sheets. I didn't want any of her scent left behind."

Now for the multi-million-dollar question. "Why did you bring me here?"

He ran his hands through his hair. "I wish I could answer this with something simple. I guess I was scared to come back here alone."

"Why me? Why didn't you take Lia? You don't particularly like me." That must have been why he kissed me. He wanted to piss me off because he never meant anything by it. I, however, wasn't upset. I always expected to be played.

Expect the worst—and hope for the best.

Pan stood from the bed and closed the gap between us. His fingers brushed across my cheek, but he was only moving hair back. "Why does everything I do have to be for a terrible reason?"

I swallowed the lump sitting in my throat. His lips were inches away and I wanted to just allow myself a moment to crave more.

Dismissing the feelings, I said, "Because it always is. How does bringing me here help you feel safe? I don't understand why it has to be me. Lia is the better sister."

His warm breath fanned against my lips. He was just one kiss away, but it was too far for me to try.

Pan's eyes shifted from my lips to the floor. "Yet she can't hear my flute."

I knew where that came from. Pan loved to prove me wrong but part of me also realized that he was telling me I did belong here, and *I* was the lost girl. I had no reason to be jealous of Lia.

"I'll help you," I whispered. "Whatever you need to move on from Hook and the pain, I can help."

He took a step back. "No, no. I... How do I need help? I'm here to face my fears because that's what leaders do. I don't want to change. I refuse to go back to the old me, Little Flower."

"Leaders also do what's best for their people. Nobody is asking you to be Peter Pan, the same man you were before your shadow detached. We just want to see the Pan who's good. It would be impossible for you to return to your old self after you've dealt with what you have. You've seen things and you've changed, but you need to let that change you for the better—and not for worse." I'd never seen Pan so vulnerable before, and yet I was just thankful he let me witness it. He was still human. He had a heart in there somewhere, just begging for someone to take care of it for him.

He approached the door. "What she did was tear away all the good left inside me. There is no getting that back. Stop trying to fix what isn't broken."

I choked on my own breath. "Broken? Pan, you are not broken. Broken would be a man who never let anyone back in, who didn't trust, and a man who didn't—"

He spun around to face me. "Didn't what?"

Pan was never broken. He was just handling his pain in the wrong way, but he had a chance to change his path. He kissed me because he wasn't sure of how to handle his distrust. He feared I'd become Hook, and I wanted to prove he was wrong.

"A man who didn't kiss me. A broken man would never kiss a woman the way you did. You'll never be able to pretend it was an accident or that you didn't want it to happen. You're the one who initiated it." I wanted to take a step closer, but I was too afraid of scaring him away. "And somewhere in there, you refuse to acknowledge that you want to do it again."

I knew because I did, *too.*

He snickered. "I didn't want to kiss you. It was just a stupid decision I made without thinking first."

I didn't press him further. I had to let him sort out his own actions so he could see for himself what the truth was. He had kissed me when we weren't being watched by those crows of his, and then he proceeded to take me to Fee Abyss. He needed me to help him heal from the memory of Hook now that her presence couldn't wreck his soul. He could never lie to himself that it wasn't true. I would be the one who helped him forget she ever existed.

I'd be the one to reattach his shadow.

25: Figment of the Imagination

Taking a deep breath, I walked into Pan's cabin. He looked up from the fireplace. "What are you doing, Love? This isn't your cabin." His brows furrowed. "And why are you always up earlier than everyone else?" He dropped his gaze into the flames.

I ignored his last question. "We need to talk about that kiss," I said. I couldn't continue to let it eat me alive.

His head shot up so fast, scanning the area. He jumped from the chair and covered my mouth. "Don't say it so loud! We need to go somewhere private for this."

Private? To kiss again? "Pan."

"If you want to talk, we need to go somewhere private." He pushed open his door and hurried into the woods. I followed, moving as fast as I could to keep up with him.

"You don't want them knowing we kissed. I thought you didn't care? They know we're sleeping together." I widened my eyes. "Oh. No. No, I meant that they think we are." My face heated.

He looked back at me with a small smirk. "Now I know what you really think of me." He stopped at Hangman's Tree.

I still never trusted this place. "Why the hell do you care about what your lost boys know?"

"They can't confirm their rumors about us shagging, but we *did* kiss. Besides, if they think we are shagging, they assume I'm getting what I want and I'm using you. If they know that we kissed, they know that I kissed you and they will think you're using me." Ah, yes, wouldn't want them to think that. He ran his hands through his hair. He was scared of losing his power, but I wasn't here to take it from him.

"But I'm not. You kissed me, and that's serious." I wiggled my finger at him.

"You want to tell me that kiss actually meant something to you?" Pan stood by the tree, mocking in his eyes. The smile was subtle.

It did, but telling Pan it meant something to him was fun. I needed him to admit the truth.

I shrugged. "It had to mean something to you. I'm no expert, Pan, but no boy can fake a kiss like that without it meaning something." I closed the gap between us. Why did I make such a daring move?

He pushed the hair behind my ear and grazed his thumb over my cheek. "You'd be surprised about what I can fake, Love. I have the power to make you believe in anything, including me."

"You're lying because you just don't want anyone to know that their leader is going tolerable. *Excuses.* That kiss we shared was very real," my words came out with every ounce of confidence I owned. He couldn't lie to me and get away with it.

His eyes softened, locked on mine. He straightened and lifted my chin. "You'll have to learn what is real and what isn't. This is my island. I control everything. It's a blessing yet a curse."

I pulled my bottom lip between my teeth, chewing. "What are you talking about?"

He closed his eyes to hide the shame. "That little boy, Eric, you've grown to be friends, he with isn't real. He's a figment of your imagination—a lost boy I made up. I am in complete control of reality. You can't tell the difference between my creation and your imagination. Hatred and fear are dangerous for me to possess. If I allow my emotions to show, things happen that even I cannot control. There are no happy endings in Neverland, Little Flower."

I brought my eyes to the floor. I didn't want to believe it. "Please tell me that it's not true."

He rested his forehead against mine, his voice now a whisper. "Have you ever wondered why you haven't seen Eric with other little boys? They can't see him because he doesn't *exist*. He's your imaginary friend created by my fear upon your arrival. Nobody else can interact with him but you. I created him like I created Neverland but not everything I create is good. I'm Peter Pan." He lifted his head, opening his eyes as he gestured to the island. "This is my home. This is *my* creation."

I ground my teeth together to keep from crying. I would never let anyone make me cry. Never again. "You can pretend that you're still the same boy that I first met, but that kiss showed me otherwise. Things have changed. I killed the woman who destroyed you. I know that makes you feel *something* for me."

Turning, I quickened my pace with every step until I was sprinting back to the cabin. I stopped at the sight of the camp, watching as the lost boys had a good time. Eric wasn't among them. He was nowhere to be found anymore because I knew the truth behind his existence. Eric had been just the fictional friend for my lost soul.

I entered my cabin and took off my belt, throwing the belt with the dagger to the side. I fell onto my bed and let out a sigh, but that turned into a sob.

I lay back on my bed. I thought I was finally getting through to Pan. I'd never expected anything like that kiss. It had to mean something, right? Of course it did. Pan kissed me, and that was not from his dark side. He couldn't make me think otherwise.

Lia came in and I sat up right away. She saw the look on my face and frowned. "What happened?"

"What do you mean? Nothing happened." I wiped a tear. He'd kissed her, too, but he did it to make me mad. Lia wasn't around when he kissed me, so it wasn't done in vengeance.

"Something did. I'm your sister. You can't keep secrets." She crossed her arms.

Rubbing my face, I said, "Pan kissed me." I didn't know why I told her, but she was persuasive. Either that or I was just too weak to argue.

She widened her eyes the size of a fifty-cent coin. "Wait, really? Why? Tell me exactly how it happened." She dropped her arms and sat next to me.

"It's not that big of a deal. He kissed you, too." I groaned once. My brain couldn't pick a side. I needed to protect myself, but if I could change Pan, I couldn't abandon him. I couldn't let the lost boys lose a chance at having a good leader again.

Lia grabbed my hand. "What is it?"

"That's just it. I don't know." I pulled my hand from hers.

"You have to tell me what you're talking about." She pulled her legs up onto the bed, sitting crisscross.

I shook my head, unsure of how to explain any of this to her. "He dropped me off a cliff, then said I was different, and kissed me. When I went to confront him about it earlier, he said it meant nothing. But he took me to Fee Abyss, and I hate to admit it, but it was romantic." I closed my eyes. "I had made a friend with a boy named Eric here."

"Who?"

Another sob escaped. "Exactly, Pan made him up. Eric isn't even real. I don't know what to believe anymore." I grabbed her hands for security and warmth. No matter how many times I hurt her, she always forgave me. Lia was a saint.

She squeezed my hands. "That's a part of being a girl, but also part of being around Pan. He never makes any sense. I think it sounds like Pan wants to kiss you, but he's scared of something else."

Yeah, scared of what Hook put him through. He probably thought I was also seeing Kace, but I wasn't. I never saw Kace as a boyfriend. He was more like the brother I'd always wanted.

"What am I supposed to do? I don't like him. I don't want to be like this. I need to build my walls higher." I let go of her and leaned against the wall.

"You may not need to though."

"I do. Pan has done awful things. People may change but memories don't, and my memories of what he's done will be there forever."

"What did he do? I want to understand, so I can give you advice. That is what you want, right?" she asked.

I looked at her. "I don't know what I want. I guess I could use advice." Where did I begin? "He's coy with me. He's always trying to get a rise out of me. He'd let Jacob threaten me."

"What do you mean?" She furrowed her brows.

"Jacob tried to assault me and I know Pan would never scold him. I know Jacob is the one who started the rumor that we're having sex." I lowered my eyes to the white sheets, picking at a thread.

Lia nodded a bit. "Jacob sounds like the asshole of the bunch, but have you considered that maybe Pan doesn't know? What makes you think he wouldn't reprimand him?"

"Impossible. He's Peter Pan. I once thought he didn't, but I was wrong. He knows *everything*. And he'd certainly never punish his own for my benefit. I'll never be worth that much." I sat forward. "What if he has a chance to change? I don't want to be the chance he has to be normal, and then also be the reason why he lost that chance because I make him fight my battles for me. It's too much for him to handle in his state. The lost boys deserve to have a leader who isn't wearing himself out."

She placed her hand on top of mine, threading our fingers together. "The reality is you must be able to help yourself first. If it would be a bad idea for you to go in circles over Pan and his shenanigans, maybe it's not a good idea to get involved with him. It was nice to be kissed, but you must care about your mental health first. I know you want to help Pan and his lost boys, but if it would hurt you, I would advise against it."

Lia was asking me to put myself first. She was right, as usual. *When would it ever be my turn?*

If it would cause me pain. It wouldn't be good for me to sacrifice who I was to help Pan if it wasn't *guaranteed* to help him and the lost boys.

I had to figure this out on my own from here, but what was the right course of action? Did I know if it could save him? What about saving Neverland—would it do that, too? Would it destroy who I was as a human being to save Pan from himself? Probably.

"Do you know what you should do now?" she asked.

I shook my head. "I will have to keep my trust in certain people and Pan is not one of them. I can't let us get caught up in something if it ruins me. I won't let the demon win." As to whether I was referring to Pan or my demon, I couldn't be sure. However, I guessed it was both.

She smiled a little. "I'm going to go eat breakfast. Are you coming?" She got up.

"No, you go ahead. I'm not hungry." I dismissed her.

She left after a little hesitation, but when she was gone, the waterworks rushed out.

The reality was that my true best friend on Neverland was never mine. He'd been just another pawn in Pan's little game, someone he created out of panic. It confirmed he was afraid I'd become just like Hook. Eric had meant so much to me, and my heart ached knowing he was just a delusion.

As for Pan, I'd figure this out someday, but I had the time to reflect on how to do that. Neverland was a place where time didn't exist, and I had all of eternity to spend in it.

Today, I just stayed in my cabin and grieved for the friend I'd never be able to confide in again. One less person to make me feel notable. A piece of my heart turned to ash in the wake of the fire Pan had so *lovingly* sparked.

26: Weakness

When I woke up, I caught sight of the body that lay across me. Lia. I hadn't even noticed she slept in my bed. Was I pissed off? I couldn't entirely tell. But maybe I wasn't as upset as I thought I'd be.

I began to roll her off me, but she opened her eyes and looked around, trying to make sense of what was happening. As soon as she saw me, she said, "Oh, sorry. I guess I fell asleep." She got off the bed while rubbing her eyes. Once she was alert, a knock on our cabin door sounded.

"Come in," I said quietly. Somehow, they heard me.

"Good morning." Kace nodded. "Get ready. Pan has a meeting for everyone today."

"Why? For what reason?" I asked.

He shrugged. "I know as much as you do."

Lia grabbed some clothes from my dresser, in which case my eyes snapped at her. "Excuse me, where are your own clothes? I don't have enough to share."

She glanced back at me. "I don't have my own."

"Then earn them fair and square like I did." I got up and took them from her.

A frown formed. “But I'm not as strong as you.”

“Then become as strong as me. It's only a matter of trying. I can't do everything for you.”

After contemplating, she nodded. “Okay...” She fiddled with her fingers, then lifted her eyes to see Kace. “Does Pan have anything I can wear? My clothes are dirty.”

He shook his head. “Nothing I know he would let you wear. I do have an extra cloak for you to wear in the meantime. I can grab it. Not sure it’ll help much, but the offer stands.”

She smiled a bit. “Would you? Thanks.”

He left to go grab her a cloak.

I changed into clean clothes. “We really should get going. I wouldn't want Pan to deem us late and withhold breakfast or something. He really grinds my gears.”

“So I've been told,” she said.

“Excuse me, what the hell is that supposed to mean?” I crossed my arms.

Lia turned her attention from the door to me. “Nothing.”

“No, it meant something. Tell me.”

“You say you hate him but that kiss you shared seemed to really change your opinion.” She shrugged.

I took a deep breath, trying to create an argument. I came up short.

“Listen, Lili, I can't tell you how to feel about someone. To me, you care about his wellbeing and the lost boys'. You want to make them all happy. We can't help how we feel. We only choose how we react. You are reacting differently from the way you feel. You want to hate him, but I think you might also feel something towards the man he has potential to be. The good in him is buried somewhere inside him, and you've seen it. That's the part you like about him.”

She looked over at Kace as he walked back in with a cloak. “Thank you.” She tied it around her shoulders. She bounced on her heels a bit. “It's heavy."

"You get used to it." He exited the room.

Lia and I left only seconds after, arriving at the meeting in the middle of the camp, and sat on the logs. I fixed my shirt to avoid Pan's gaze. I wouldn't let him affect me any more than he had.

Pan circled us. "I have called a meeting today because we have some good and bad news." Everyone watched him with curiosity, but I knew better. What was good news to him could very well be bad for us.

"The good news is Captain Hook is dead. I caught her sneaking around our island the other night. I made sure she would never come back, so I fed her to the mermaids."

I choked. He was taking credit for my killing. *Why* was I upset about it? I didn't want anyone to know what I had done. I wouldn't be proud of it. I did what I did, but it was out of defense, so Pan could find some peace.

His eyes locked on me, searching for a reaction. He got one. I was confused, mostly by my own emotions.

He continued, "The bad news is we have also lost one of our own."

This caught everyone's attention more than Hook's death. We *lost* a lost boy? I had no idea. A pin to my heart. I'd lost Eric and now we were another member down. That was nine boys in total.

"Who was it?" Hunter asked.

Pan's shoulders relaxed as a subtle smile entered his eyes. "Jacob. We lost Jacob. He got too close to the mermaids. I always warn you guys to never go near the mermaids, and was I ever wrong about that? Don't take my words as suggestions. They keep you safe. Take heed, children. They are not your friends," he said in an authoritative tone.

Jacob. He was the one spreading rumors about us sleeping together. Was it any coincidence that Jacob was the lost boy who was killed? Would Pan kill his own lost boys? He certainly was capable of anything.

Pan cleared his throat. "Go train." He retreated to his cabin.

As soon as I hopped off the log, I caught Lia.

Lia asked, "What is it?"

I shook my head before swallowing the thought. "Nothing."

Kace grabbed my shoulder. "I can guess what you're thinking, and I need to warn you to drop that thought."

Lia tilted her head. "Wait, what is she thinking?"

He walked off without another word.

I pushed my hair from my face, but it had a mind of its own. To no avail, in other words. "It's not important now." Anything to take my mind off of it. "I'm going to swim."

"It is important if Kace had to warn you against it."

I ignored her and grabbed her arm, pulling her toward the path to the lagoon.

When we arrived, my mind wandered right to Eric and the time we'd gone for a swim. It had all been a lie.

"Lili?" Lia asked.

I turned from her, coughing up the sorrow until it was no more. I couldn't cry. I couldn't allow a single tear to form. Instead, I removed my clothes before walking into the water, submerging myself, and letting all the pain and heartache wash away.

I screamed into the abyss of the pool.

Devastated. Furious. Vulnerable. Empty. Isolated.

This is every emotion that claimed my soul over the loss of Eric. I was back at the bottom with no friends by my side, except for Kace—who was loyal to Pan first.

When I came back up, I pushed my hair back.

Lia had been sitting on the rock beside the water. "You were under there a long time."

"I was." I swam further away.

I was having a hard time accepting that he was never real. It was as if everyone I loved was ripped from my grasp. Nana, and now Eric.

Nana had been the one light of my life before I came here. And as if the days had never passed, I reflected on if I should have said things a little differently.

"Come, Lili. Let's take care of that bruise," Nana said as she led me to the kitchen. She grabbed an ice pack from her freezer and placed it against my arm. "What did they do this time?"

She always thought it came from bullies. I was afraid to tell her the truth.

"It's nothing, Nana. I can handle it." I gave her a small smile. Being in her presence was enough to make me feel safe.

However, she pressed on. "Nonsense. I want to know exactly who did this. Nobody should ever lie their hand on you." She sat me down on her couch covered in dog hair.

With three dogs, it'd been inevitable. But their loveable nature made up for it.

Asa walked into the room, glancing at us both. He didn't seem all that interested in our conversation.

He was visiting, too. Nana had always tried to be involved in her grandkids' lives. She'd been very family oriented.

She looked over at Asa. "Boy, get your nosy ass out of here. Take the dogs outside for a little bit."

Asa grumbled but did as he was told. His mom, too, was not ideal for him to be around.

"If I tell you the truth, you're not going to like it." I frowned.

Nana let out a laugh. "I already don't like it. Knowing who did this is just the icing on the cake." Her mind took a detour. "Would you like some cake?"

I shook my head, then dropped it. "He's bigger than me. He hates me. He wished I were dead."

"Go on."

I feared what would happen when I told her. Would she be killed, or would she take their side? Whichever way the cookie crumbled, I'd lose her forever.

"Dad did this," I whispered.

When I peeked at her reaction, I saw pure horror in her eyes.

Maybe if I'd kept my mouth shut, she wouldn't have to worry so much about where I'd gone. All she knew now was I'd disappeared and Dad was most likely the culprit.

Lia asked, "What was Kace talking about back there? What were you thinking?"

"Nothing."

She scoffed. "Yeah, and I'm sure that's what you actually meant." She pulled the hood on, playing around with the strings.

I was ready to reveal what I'd been thinking about until *mother nature* came back. I took far too long to swim back to the shallow water where I could stand up and run out of the water. Every part of my uterus was twisting in every unholy position it could muster.

Lia widened her eyes. "What happened?"

I whispered, "It's back."

"What?"

My energy depleted. I was in far too much pain to form a coherent sentence. "Period."

"You're on your period?" She came closer.

I nodded a bit. I grabbed the rock beside the edge and pulled myself closer. I lay my head on it, hugging it. "You need to tell Pan to bring tampons."

"He has tampons?"

"Do it!" I yelled.

She jumped up as soon as I'd yelled at her. Her hood blew back as she hurried back to the camp.

Cramps—one weakness.

She came back far too late, bringing a whole box with Wendy running behind her. "I brought everything you asked for," Lia said.

She helped me grab my clothes. "We won't look." She nodded and glanced at Wendy who looked away. Lia turned her back, too.

Once my tampon was in and my clothes had been put on, I watched

Wendy. "It's been a while."

She faced me and took a seat in the dirt. "I didn't know you had a twin. I thought she was you for a second."

"You would think... She's different though." I held my abdomen.

Lia lowered her head out of pity. "Doesn't Pan have some cure to make you feel better? He has magic."

"Pan refuses to help using magic." I closed my eyes, wishing it would go away once and for all. Neverland wasn't a magical cure against mother nature. I wondered if maybe I was lost in this thought long enough with my eyes closed, maybe the pain wouldn't come back. However, it was only a delusion.

I opened my eyes again as Wendy said, "Pan doesn't care about any of us. He can't without his shadow."

Lia furrowed her brows in confusion, but she'd have to hold that thought for a little while longer. "Pan must feel something for Lili. He kissed her. He can pretend he's heartless, but if he's walking, he has a heartbeat. In the small of his brain, he's gotta be upset to see her in pain. Men can pretend they have no feelings, but they have just as many as we do." She let out a sigh.

I lay back on the grass. "It's no use. He is who he is. He may have feelings, but he has control over them and not the other way around."

The three of us sat in silence for a few minutes.

The rushing of the waterfall dropped the temperature a few degrees around the lagoon.

Wendy broke the silence first, asking Lia, "Who's cloak is that?"

"Kace's." She twirled the string around her finger.

"Pan's second-in-command? He lets you wear his stuff?" She lifted her eyebrows.

"Is he different with you?" Lia asked Wendy.

Wendy shrugged. "I never met the guy. It just surprises me that he would even lend out his clothes." She smiled a little. "Are you doing okay now?"

She directed her question towards me.

My eyes lifted to the sky. “I'll never be okay as long as I have a period. It brings me to my knees. It forces me into a fetal position. Cramps feel like a punishment, and I believe they are. I just don’t understand what I did that was so horrid to deserve them.”

“Being a woman sucks,” Wendy said with a sigh.

Lia nodded. “Ditto to that.”

“Neither of you can tell Pan. If he knew what made me weak, I’d be over. As far as he knows, I'm not a weak woman.” My eyes moved back and forth between them.

“Fair, we won't tell him a thing.” Lia zipped her lips.

An English accent echoed from the trees, “To keep it a secret, that would require me not listening.” Pan came out, his eyes studying every inch of my language. “Now I know exactly what makes you rot.”

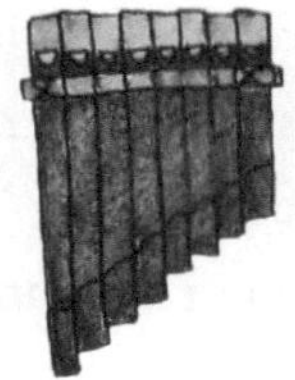

27: Sisters

My feet created a small draft as I paced back and forth on the floor. He could use it against me at any time.

Any time.

"You've been doing that for a while," Lia said.

"Pan knows my biggest weakness. What do you expect me to do with that?"

She shrugged. "I expect you to rise up and show him you're not afraid. He's still Pan and if you're right about the things he's done, he would never use it against you. Any man who uses your biggest weakness against you deserves to *rot* in hell, and he knows if he went that far, you two would never have a chance."

I leaned against the wall. "But that's it. What if he is so adamant about proving that the kiss meant nothing that he goes as far as using the weakness against me?"

Lia leaned forward from sitting on the bed. "What is it that he's so afraid of? Why is he so scared to admit it meant something?"

"He thinks I'm going to become Kristin." I closed my eyes. "He told me what she did to him. She cheated on him with Kace, stringing them both along for the ride. Now I'm best friends with Kace, and Pan probably thinks that we have a relationship."

"Do you?"

"No. No, not at all. Kace and I are just friends. I don't see him like that. He's a great guy and all but he's just... He's..."

She finished for me, "He's not Pan."

I scowled at the thought. I didn't like Pan that way. I refused to go that far. Attractive, yes. A good kisser, oh hell yes. But to see him as a potential partner? Never. "Ew. I need to talk to Pan and Kace *together* so we can tell Pan that we're not lovers. We're just friends. We're really good friends."

As I turned to leave the cabin, I stopped in the doorway. What was I doing?

I turned around and faced her as I closed the door. "I'm sorry."

She lifted her brows in surprise. "For what?"

I closed the space between us, taking a seat next to her. "For being such a bitch to you. You're my sister and I treat you like shit and every time I do, you never retaliate. You're better than me."

Lia smiled a little. "I'm not better than you. I'm just your sister."

I wrapped my arms around her, squeezing. "I'm so sorry." There weren't enough apologies in the world for treating her so poorly.

She wrapped her arms around my torso and whispered, "I don't hate you."

That's what she said to make me feel better, but I knew better. She hated me somewhere in there and I had to make it up to her.

We both pulled away.

I said, "We should do something together. We need to do something that proves to everyone you're here to stay."

"What? But you don't want me to stay." She furrowed her brows. Nobody would ever be so lucky enough to experience this girl's compassion but me. What an utter tragedy.

Standing, I explained, "Yes, I do. I need my sister here to keep me grounded. I need you because nobody else here is going to understand me the way you do. I have an idea." Grabbing her wrist, I led her from our cabin.

We walked through camp, past all the areas where Kace showed me places I could go. I was finally going to climb the mountain and Lia was going to do it with me.

"What is this?" she asked.

I pointed. "We are going to climb. Kace told me that climbing a mountain is a good way to earn respect in the camp."

Her laugh cut short. "I have respect."

"It's going to prove you belong here." I leaned against the side. "Get climbing."

After giving me a look, she pointed to the mountain. I nodded for her to go on. First, she took a deep breath. Then she removed her cloak and began to climb. She placed her left foot on a small ledge as she reached for the higher one.

Jacob was dead this time around so I didn't have to fear him coming back. My hand had barely healed.

"I'm doing it!" she yelled. She continued to climb higher, showing me up. Crap.

I placed my foot and pulled my body up, putting every muscle into it. "I'm coming for the win!" I climbed faster.

She laughed, looking down at me. "You wish!" She pulled herself up another foot.

I followed, quickening my pace.

After many laughs and harmless threats, we made it to the top of the mountain without dying. I was surprised, but she had worked hard. She definitely did deserve the credit.

She planted herself on a flat edge and admired the island. "It's so beautiful up here."

I sat beside her with a nod. "It is. Is there anyone here who...stands out?" I poked her.

Lia met my eyes with uncertainty. "What do you mean?"

She had no idea what I meant. Was I that bad at this or was she just not very bright sometimes?

"Is there someone on this island that you want to make out with?"

She laughed a bit. "Uh, no. Pan was cute until he wasn't. Nobody else here..."

Her eyes flashed with something of desolation, and a hint of fear. It had never occurred to me until now that Lia was hiding something, but she was *scared* to reveal it to me. She, too, had her own things going on.

"Tell me what you're going to say. I'm here to listen." She wanted to share; she just needed me to nudge her.

After some hesitation, she nodded a little. "Back home, everyone was always so quick to tell me how great sex was. The kids at school. I didn't fit in because they'd talk about it and I had no idea what it was like. They told me that I needed to try it."

I frowned. "I mean, sex is probably good but...it's not the end-all, be-all." If that was how the saying went.

She shrugged. "I always felt like something was wrong with me because when I saw an attractive man, I never got aroused just by his abs, or his face. When I discovered that asexual people existed, I felt like I was close but sex didn't turn me off entirely. I just didn't want to sleep with people I saw as attractive but knew nothing about. I...wanted it to be with someone who meant something to me. I thought that was weird.

"I just didn't understand why I was so out of place. I could never explain to people why I wasn't having sex. It made me feel like I was in the wrong." Her eyes fell shut. "But then one day, I found it. I came across the term when I was in a conversation about sexualities, and I found one that explained exactly how I felt." She opened her eyes. "I'm demisexual. And maybe it sounds stupid, to admit that like it's some big secret. But as a teenage girl in a sex-sells world, it feels like I'm always the butt of everyone's joke. I'm the one out of the loop, the one who can't seem to get a man."

I had no idea what a demisexual was.

She continued, "I'm not sexually attracted to anyone I don't have an emotional connection with. Just being able to understand this bit of information has been a huge relief. I could finally explain who I was. It was weird, but putting a label to it *lessened* the judgment. I simply tell people I'm demisexual and they,"—she paused to take a deep breath—"understand me. They're so much nicer. More forgiving than they were before. It's like the label tells people I have a sexuality different from theirs and they have no choice but to accept it. If they don't, they'll be labeled the assholes."

Smiling, I lay her head on my shoulder. "That's how this world works. People don't understand sexualities until there's a name."

Lia laughed. "Try explaining to people why online dating makes you uncomfortable. My anxiety would rise when I tried to explain why I didn't want to try it and yet when I mentioned I was demisexual, it just fell into place. It's not as simple as talking to someone I like and asking them out. The anxiety leaves when I think of just becoming friends with them first. I can't jump into the ring. I need to take things slow if I want to make things right for our relationship.

"So, to answer your question, no. Nobody stands out to me because I don't have any friends here aside from you, and given that you're my sister... Without an established friendship, I don't have romantic feelings for anyone, and therefore, I don't want to makeout with anyone." She lifted her head from mine.

There were some things I'd never understood about Lia but this I could. She was her own person, in her own world, and I loved that about us. We looked the same, but that was as far as our similarities went.

Lia screamed as her foot slipped and she slid. I grabbed her arm and used my other to hold onto the mountain. The rocks dug into my skin but the adrenaline rushing through my veins made them bearable. The thought of losing Lia *wasn't.*

I struggled to pull her back up. She attempted to get a footing but her arm was slipping through my fingers. "Lia!" I yelled.

The terror in her eyes sent an arrow through my heart. She'd been petrified to die.

Time went by too fast the minute I lost a grip on her. She slipped down the mountain and rolled to the ground. I climbed down as quickly as I could manage, skidding from time to time.

I made it to the bottom and kneeled next to her. "Lia!" I yelled. I checked her pulse. She was still breathing but she had cuts, bruises, blood, and—I was certain—broken bones.

And she wasn't conscious.

Standing, I pulled her up and wrapped her arm around my shoulder as my other arm went under hers. I attempted to carry her, but I just couldn't carry that much weight. I had to drag her back to the camp while trying to keep her off the ground as much as I could.

When I entered the camp, people ran over to see what had happened, but I moved them away from her.

"What happened?" Pan asked me.

I slumped my shoulders, keeping her upright. "We climbed the mountain."

Her nose gushed blood, her head lolling side to side. Cuts ran along nearly every inch of skin that'd been exposed, but the cloak had managed to keep most of her vital organs inside her body. I couldn't say the same about internal bleeding.

Pan waved someone over and Kace came. "Take her to your cabin to tend to her wounds."

Kace nodded and took Lia from me, actually carrying her back to his cabin.

Pan moved in front of me, searching for injuries. "You climbed the mountain?"

"It was my idea. I told her that if she wanted to prove she belonged here, we needed to climb the mountain. We made it to the top but...she slipped." I swallowed. "It's all my fault, Pan. I think I might have killed her." A sob escaped me, and once one came out, more followed. "I can't lose her. I can't lose her," I whispered through the cries.

He closed the small space between us and reached out, wrapping his arms around me. He pulled me against his chest. "She's going to be okay. I'll make sure she's okay. Kace is a great medic. You're not going to lose Lia," he said in a quiet voice against my hair. My thoughts were too scrambled to focus on Pan, though. Instead, I just let the waterworks flow freely while Lia fought for her life.

28: Delirious

I WAS THANKFUL PAN hadn't made fun of me for crying the other night. It was a vulnerable moment of mine that I'd given to my sister.

"Where's Pan?" I asked Hunter as I passed by him. I held a basket of vegetables between my arm and stomach.

He pointed northwest. "He went that way a while ago."

I nodded and thanked him before dropping my basket off with Wendy. I had to check up on Pan and ask him if I could bring extra soup to Lia.

Following the direction, I approached the mooie duisternis patch. Why would Pan be here?

As I closed in, a boot on the ground came into my view. I walked around to find the leg attached—and Pan unmoving. "Shit!" I kneeled.

I checked for a pulse. Weak, and his skin had lost the little color he had. I knew this wasn't a joke. He didn't make jokes like these.

I also inspected his body and found a small cut on his arm.

Dragging Pan wasn't easy, but I dragged him far enough away from the venomous plant. I slid my dagger from my belt and tore through his sleeve, rolling it up to clear all skin from any irritation.

"What do I do now?" I asked myself. "Think, Lili, think."

It came to me the moment I hit my head against my palm. I ran back to the camp and fetched a bucket from the well, filling it up with water. I took it back to Pan and used a piece of cloth from my tank top to soak the water and wash away the venom.

"Please let this work," I whispered.

However, his appearance wasn't improving. I wanted to ask Kace for help, but he was already watching over Lia. I had to do this on my own, but if Pan died, what happened to Neverland? Everything here would vanish, and we'd be left with *nothing*. Not even our own bones.

I had one other idea, but I wasn't sure if it would even work. Still, it was worth a try.

I grabbed his left hand and placed it over the cut on his right arm. "Come on." I leaned down until my lips were near his ear. "Heal yourself. *Heal.*"

When I pulled back, I noticed a faint glow beneath his palm. A cough erupted from him and he opened his eyes just slightly.

"Pan? You're okay. I did my best to get rid of the venom," I said. I grabbed his shoulders and helped him sit up.

He studied my face before realizing who I was but instead of feeling ashamed or getting angry with me, he poked my nose. "You look so real."

I helped him up from the ground with a sigh. "I am real."

His laugh became infectious. "What? I let a girl stick around? It's about time I changed my mind." He lay his head against my shoulder.

The venom had done a number on his grip of reality. It didn't shock me that he was acting the way he was. He was a man drunk on the defense of a thorn.

This was perfect. "Pan, Lia's still in bad shape from falling off the mountain. Is it okay to bring her extra soup?"

Bingo.

He gasped. "Another girl? Who is she?"

"You've met her many times now." I got him back to the camp and of course, every lost boy stopped to stare. "Nothing to see here!" I shouted. They all went right back to work as I led Pan into his cabin and dropped him onto his bed.

He sat up with a sigh. "I don't want to sleep."

I took a seat in his chair. "I know, but you need to rest regardless. The venom is still leaving your body."

"Venom? Why would I allow myself to be so careless with it?" he asked.

The tone of his voice as he asked me caught me off guard. Had he intentionally tried to cut himself or was it an accident? I hoped it was the latter. But Pan didn't make mistakes.

As I leaned back in the chair, I crossed my arms and said, "We need to pass the time. You're not very stable and you can't leave the cabin. You also don't want to sleep so I'm really not all that sure what to do with you."

When I locked eyes with him, I got the idea. He was delirious. Now was a better time than ever to ask for the truth.

He fell back on the pillows. "I don't know what to do with me either."

"A few weeks ago—or what I'm assuming was a few weeks ago—you kissed me. You told me it meant nothing, but I want to know why you would do such a thing if it meant nothing to you." I tapped my foot.

His eyes landed on me. "I don't know. I probably thought you were pretty."

I swallowed as my cheeks reddened. "My sister is identical to me and you kissed her, too. I want to know exactly why you kissed *me* and not some excuse that applies to Lia, too."

Pan rolled onto his side. "I don't know, but I'm famished right now."

"Wow, this is absolutely useless." I stood. "I'll be back." I left the cabin and gathered some fruit. When I returned, I found his bed empty. "Pan?"

At the sound of his name, he exited the bathroom without any clothes on. As a reflex, my eyes moved down his body and took in every detail.

He approached me and grabbed the food. "Wonderful, I was questioning eating myself." He sat back down and leaned against the headboard.

The entire time, my eyes memorized every muscle I normally didn't get to see. I wanted to look away, but it was hard to.

No, no, Lili. He's basically drunk and if you were drunk and naked, you'd want the other person to respect you.

I grabbed the blanket from the bed and covered his lower half. "Trust me, you'll feel better without everything hanging out."

He bit into the nectarine as a warm smile crept up. "Do you ever just eat fruit and thank the universe for making it?"

I rested back in the chair, shrugging. "Never. I am more of a vegetable kind of woman."

"You like to be in a coma?" He took another bite, some juice slipping from the sides of his lips. It was certainly tempting to lick it...

I glanced back at the fireplace. "Do you still have trouble getting over what Hook did?"

He paused, his eyes focused on one single berry. "All the time. It's hard not to think about what someone did to you when you loved them. Sometimes we think we're strong enough to deal with it all, but we realize we're just as weak as we feared." He attempted to throw in a laugh.

Despite his laughter, his eyes conveyed just how much he'd been hurting. Pan thought he was strong enough, but he realized he wasn't. Even with her gone, those scars would never disappear.

"What makes her so special?" I asked.

His eyebrows knitted together. "I think it's because she reminds me of the love I could have had. You think people care about you, but they really don't. I was young and stupid. So young and stupid then. I thought I would be the best guy ever if I shagged an older woman."

But he wasn't. It just destroyed him in the end. She took advantage of him, and he wasn't to blame for that.

Pan rubbed his stomach after finishing his food. "She was fantastic though."

"I'm sorry," I said.

"For?"

"For what she did—using you like that. It was wrong. At least she's rotting in hell now. But I should go check on Lia. I'll be back soon." I got up and walked over to Kace's, knocking.

He opened the door and put his index finger to his lips. When I stepped inside, I found Lia sleeping in his bed. She looked so peaceful and yet I'd also never seen so many bruises on a person before. She'd been bandaged in some areas, and a handmade brace peeked out from under her shirt. Her ribs were fractured—and all because of *me*.

I turned to face Kace. "Pan was cut by mooie duisternis. I managed to get the venom out and help him heal himself. He's in his cabin and I've been keeping my eye on him, but I wanted to make sure Lia was all right."

He nodded. "She's been doing fine. Nothing seems out of the ordinary. How is Pan?"

"Incoherent. He thinks everything's a joke, but he also forgot who I am. Is that normal?" I glanced at Lia.

Kace shrugged, rubbing his neck. "Depends on what you consider normal. But for Pan, yes. When he...loses touch with reality, he forgets some of the bad parts. You know, to revel in the little happiness he does have."

He forgot about Lia and I because we didn't make him *happy*.

I stopped on my way out the door, twisting my head to look at Kace. "And Pan said she could have extra soup if needed." He'd never answered my question, but it couldn't hurt to lie while he wasn't going to remember this anyway.

I returned to Pan. I was about to ask him some more questions, but he'd passed out. He needed sleep, so I wasn't about to wake him up.

Taking a seat, I lowered my head. He'd forgotten about me because I was *bad* for him. What was I supposed to do with that information? Now I knew the kiss really did mean nothing to him. He'd only acted on impulses, and in that moment he was told to do something irrational. But irrational didn't always mean good. In fact, rarely did it ever mean anything positive.

I wanted to apologize but what could I apologize for? There wasn't anything I'd done wrong. He was the one who'd judged me when I arrived. He made me feel like I didn't belong here because of Hook.

He would take me to these wonderful places but in the end, he lied to my face and told me they meant nothing.

What else could have been bad?

Fear. Fear was wrong in some ways. Sometimes it drove us to do stupid things we'd regret later. He was afraid of so many things, but it drove him to create Eric. Then, when the terror dissipated through our kiss, my heart was ripped from my chest and squeezed as the blood poured between *his* fingers.

Pan had always been too confused with his own feelings to admit what was deep inside. Men weren't taught to be in touch with their feelings and yet they still had them. When their feelings surfaced, they had no idea how to deal with them. I wanted to be the one to teach Pan how to deal with his.

I never understood why humans told men they had to hide their feelings. What made feelings feminine? Nothing. It was just a concept created by men back when our days began. They feared that if they showed emotions, they would be vulnerable and weak. They associated that with women—feminine traits.

I leaned forward and brushed my thumb across Pan's cheek. "It's okay," I whispered, "You don't have to be afraid anymore. This is your island, and no adults can tell you what to do. *You* make the rules."

He shifted his body but never woke up from his deep slumber. He needed time to rest on the idea that he could do what he wanted. He didn't have to let the fears of adults control his life anymore. Things were meant to be different here. Our families taught us that feelings were a sin, but if I could teach Pan otherwise, maybe Neverland could be the fairytale we'd always dreamed of.

29: Sick

As I brought soup back to the cabin, I jumped when Pan asked, "What the bloody hell are you doing here?"

I set the soup down on the chair. "You were cut by mooie duisternis. I had to help you recuperate."

He grabbed the soup and eyed me. "You saved me? Why?"

A shiver ran up my spine. "Because I don't want to see you die, believe it or not." I sighed. "Did you cut yourself on purpose or was it an accident? Neverland may be a magical place that grants everyone immortality, but it does not protect you from depression or any other mental illness."

Pan shrugged. "I didn't cut myself on purpose. I promise you that."

"Can we at least talk about what's going on inside your head? I just want to make sure you're stable. I can't..." I sat down on the floor and pulled my knees to my chest. "Lia hasn't been waking up."

Don't cry.

"How long has it been?" he asked, his voice softening.

I released the breath I'd been holding in. "I don't know. A few days. It's like every day that passes that she doesn't wake up, I lose hope. I saved you because I was scared to lose yet another person when my sister, too, might be dying."

He took a small bite, his skin still paler than normal, bags around his eyes. "I'm sorry," he whispered.

There was nothing inside me that gave me the energy to tease him for apologizing. My chest hurt too much to bother.

Closing my eyes, I said, "How does this seem fair? She was all I had left. I finally made the move to bond with my sister. I wanted to have something special, and as soon as I tried... She's lying in a damn bed, unconscious. She's fighting for her life and it's my fault. She's about to die because of me. Lia opened up about things that meant something to her and now this is what she gets in return. I've made her feel like shit from the first day she arrived, yet she has always forgiven me. Now she's the one paying the price."

Pan didn't respond to that. The silence was kind of nice.

I leaned back against the wall and dropped my head. It should've been me. It should have been me who fell down the mountain.

Pan finished his soup in silence, lying back on his bed. "What's the world like now?"

I lifted my head and looked at him. "Different from 1905. We have electronics and the internet. Interracial marriage is legal. Gay marriage is legal."

He turned to his side to face me. "Interracial marriage? When did that happen?"

I swallowed. "1967. That's when it was legal in every US state, anyway. As for England, I'm not too sure." I wasn't too great at history as Kace pointed out ever-so-lovingly, but I knew that answer because it had pertained to me.

He nodded, clearing his throat. "That's good. It would have always been legal in Neverland, if we had residents who were old enough to marry."

I chewed on my bottom lip. "Yeah, we're no longer segregated from white people but there are still those who believe in staying within your own race. They're the vermin of the earth."

Pan snickered, throwing his head back against the wall. "I'm not surprised. If people have the choice to choose wrong, they will." He coughed and leaned over the edge of his bed. "I thought for a second my food was coming back up."

I rushed over, sitting in the chair. "That's what I'm here for."

His laughter echoed throughout his cabin. "Lovely, you're here to take care of me."

Frowning, I said, "Yeah, I also saved your life. Don't act so surprised."

"That kiss must have gotten to you." He patted my hand.

"And it never got to you," I mumbled.

If he could forget about me without a second thought, the kiss hadn't affected him in the slightest.

Pan threw an arm under his head and coughed a bit more. "I'd kick you out if I could."

I leaned back in the chair. "Sure you would. You must enjoy having someone here to take care of you when you're sick. Speaking of which, I'll be right back."

I left the cabin in a hurry and grabbed a bucket with a rag. I brought it back to his cabin and heated it in his fireplace, setting it beside his bed. I soaked the rag and wrung it out before folding it up and laying it across his forehead.

"Why?" he asked.

Shrugging, I fell back into the chair. "Why do I do anything?" I moved my arms in circular motions as I wiggled just a bit. "Why do I do anything at all?" I sang.

He winced. "You're such a horrible singer."

"Screw you, too."

A smirk rose upon his lips. "Well, if you insist."

I made a face of disgust. "Never. And just for the record, you tried to show me your penis and I declined."

You declined out of respect, moron. It wasn't because he's ugly or small.

Amusement displayed in his eyes. "When was this?"

"The other night, of course. You were so out of your mind that you just took off all your clothes. I had to put a blanket on you." I crossed my arms, just wishing I'd grabbed a cold drink of water before I came in.

Some days I hoped that Pan would disappear, but I never asked for him to be be...venomed, in other words. When I saw him lying there, *dying*, something inside me snapped and all terror flooded my body. I was afraid to lose people, *including Pan*.

I couldn't even imagine what could have been running through his mind the moment it happened. Was he afraid to die or had he been alive so long that he welcomed the idea?

Death scared me. I wasn't ready to give up my life. If I were surrounded by people I loved, I'd be ready, but nobody here loved me. I didn't want to die without becoming a story to tell. Who would be willing to tell it?

Lia lay in a bed with her life hanging on by a thread. Kace said she would be okay, but I feared he was wrong. She could be trapped inside her mind for a long time, so was she really alive and well?

There was nothing I could do to get her out of it unless I talked to her. There was no way talking to her would even work.

If she survived, maybe she could finally belong here. Who fell off a mountain and said they survived? I couldn't say that. Lia had done things that even I hadn't.

"What's on your mind?" Pan asked.

"Lia."

He didn't need to ask questions as to what about Lia I was thinking of. She meant everything to me, and now I'd realized that she was my other half. I *needed* her to survive. How convenient that I needed her around now that she wasn't and possibly wouldn't ever be again.

She was just a sweet soul who deserved to live more than I did.

"The world is a really dark place..." I said in a quiet voice.

Pan sat up and used his thumb to wipe the tears from my cheeks. "I would heal her... I just can't. I'm too weak. My magic is useless at this rate."

I shook my head. "It's not your fault. It's mine."

The tightness in my chest didn't dare leave. An ache settled in the pit of my heart. I had no idea what I'd do if she never woke up again.

"Have you ever lost someone?" I asked.

He furrowed his brows. "Do you mean as in death, or in general?"

I closed my eyes to avoid the thought but I'd already started down this road. It was too late to turn back now. "Death."

"I haven't. I've never had to worry about it." He wrapped his arm around himself.

It must have been nice to never worry about losing someone. I wish I had the same experience. Instead, I sat here and questioned everything I ever said or did to Lia. She didn't know I loved her. She had no idea that she was my soulmate.

Despite not giving permission, my body released the pain through cries. I curled my hand into a fist and placed it over my mouth to quiet myself, but it didn't make much of a difference.

Pan was too sick to save Lia.

And I couldn't live without her. It was comforting to know that someone out there *loved* me. She had always loved me, and I needed to show her that I felt the same way.

The fear of not knowing flowed out for a while until my body had no more tears left to produce. What remained now was the pain growing inside me. I had nothing without her.

I left Pan's cabin to give him some rest and allow myself some privacy.

The walk from his cabin to the beach was longer but when I arrived at the one place that gave me any kind of peace, I dropped to the sand.

"Come back to me, Lia." I looked up at the stars, begging and praying that she would return. She was all I had left to live for. I was afraid of what

I'd do if she disappeared forever.

If she woke up, I would spend the rest of my days making it up to her. I would make sure she knew I loved her, and I'd never stop. *Nothing* could stop me from loving her.

The darkness hugged the edges of my figure but the moon battled what it could, promising me protection. The waves licked the sand before rolling back out to sea, providing me the relaxation that ate away the worry. Mist carried through the air and cooled me as a favor for feeding the mermaids.

I glanced at the ship in the distance, forever anchored at Cannibal Cove. I'd taken out one of the main characters from Peter Pan's story. How could I do something so cruel, so twisted, and so repulsive? Why he hadn't taken my life yet amazed me.

There was nothing in this world that could justify what I did to Kristin in her last moments. Maybe now I was paying the price with Lia's life. She'd gotten caught up in my karma. Karma had its own mind on how to screw with people. You got through to people the most by hurting those they loved. Lia was the only person I truly loved in this world.

"I'm sorry!" I yelled into the sky. "I'm sorry for being such a screwup! Please, don't take it out on Lia." I lowered my head. "Please, not her..."

Whoever was up there didn't listen. After hours at the beach, Lia hadn't stumbled from the trees. I'd really messed up this time. How could I make things right? How could I change it so karma made me suffer instead of us both? She didn't deserve to die because of my recklessness.

I could climb the mountain and fall but that wouldn't be good for either of us. Asking Pan to heal her was out of the question. The only option left was to go to Skull Rock myself and try something. I'd be able to use Hook's ship to get there and maybe I could talk to Pan's shadow about how to save Lia another way. Maybe I could save Pan, too.

30: Skull Rock

I stood at the edge of the cliff, overlooking the endless blue below. I'd been warned not to go, but I couldn't follow the rules. Lia's life was on the line. I was too much into this mess to be able to turn back now. My life here continued to spiral out of control the more Pan got involved.

I knew the mermaids would be waiting for me.

The waves attacked the base of the cliff, roaring.

My hair flew in my face. I pushed it away, wondering where the wind had come from. My best guess was that I was on the edge of Neverland, and the wind picked up the closer I got to leaving the island. Convincing. Persuading. Warning.

"What are you doing?" Kace's voice cut through the air.

I stumbled, taken back by his arrival. "What are you doing here?" I asked him in return.

He shrugged. "I'm here wondering what you're doing. Your turn."

"I'm trying to find a way to get to that rock." I pointed in the distance.

He laughed *at* me. "Skull Rock?"

"Because it's forbidden, and I need to know why." I crossed my arms. "I just need a ship." I narrowed my eyes, turning around and walking back down the grassy cliff.

Kace followed me this time. "Where will you get a ship?"

"You should stay behind. It would look suspicious if we both leave." I scanned the trees, only spotting the crows, ensuring Pan wasn't spying. How many times had this boy eavesdropped on me?

Kace shot me a crazed look. "You expect me to keep this quiet, don't you?"

"I'm doing this for Lia and Pan." I glanced at him. "Just go back to camp and do whatever it is you do." I gestured.

He let out a sigh. "Good luck on this journey." He pulled the hood of his cloak over his head as he walked back with confidence. He'd need it to tell a convincing lie. I shivered as I started my way back to that beach—the scene of the murder.

I swallowed when I stepped foot in the sand, remembering exactly what I did. If it wasn't rigging me with despair over Lia's accident, I would have been plagued with guilt over Hook's murder. It was not something I should be proud of. It wasn't me. Sure, she hurt people, but I went too far with the killing and I even enjoyed it. That's what scared me the most; I *relished* taking a life.

My nerves gnawed at me as I walked towards the large vessel that waited just a few miles down the coast. I quickened my pace, impatient. I needed to get to this ship and check out the never-ending mystery of Skull Rock.

After breaking out into a run, I reached the ship. It was intimidating in all its wooden exterior, and when I walked up the steps, looking around, it wasn't any less overwhelming. The cloth rippled in the wind, begging to go on an adventure. I pulled the plank up and straightened my posture. I noticed the gold metal wheel up at the front of the ship, staring me down. I peeked around the side to find the anchor and a way to bring it back up.

Once I'd found the lever, I reeled it back up with enough force. It challenged my strength no doubt, but I'd won in the end. "Damn you,

Lili. You can't drive a ship. Who do you think you are? You're not Captain Hook. You are not going to replace her."

But you are.

I peered up at the sails, studying how they worked. They were already out, which I assumed was where I needed them. Now it was a matter of steering. None of it made much sense, though. It was nothing like driving a car, and I'd barely known how to do that. The only time I ever got to drive was with Nana, to run her errands. She knew she wasn't supposed to be driving anymore.

The ship started sailing away from the shore. I went to the wheel and spun it the way I wanted to go. Glancing back at the sails, I forced all my insecurities down. I was already in it.

I tried to keep the sails against the wind, while I steered the ship. The ship started to turn too sharply, and I pulled the wheel in the other direction. "We have to get to Skull Rock. We have to defeat Pan and save Lia."

While taking deep breaths, I was terrified I was in over my head now. I didn't know what I was doing, and the internet couldn't help me. I just hoped I survived.

Steering the ship around the island wasn't easy. I did run into a lot of mishaps like going the wrong way and leaning over. I almost ran into the island and some rocks as well. I was struggling to stay afloat and yet somehow, I was managing it okay.

As the rock came into view, I widened my eyes. My eyes darted around the area.

I straightened the wheel and ran to the lever, cranking it to drop the anchor. I watched as I neared the giant skull made of rocks before dropping the anchor completely. The ship slowed before coming to a stop, now bobbing in the waves.

The rock appeared much more frightening in its proximity. My insides became mush. My balance faltered. I was entering a forbidden place.

I wasn't close enough to walk onto the rocks, but I was close enough to jump and swim to them without being eaten. I used one hand to protect my glasses while the other pinched my nose. I jumped from the edge of the ship and into the water, not going far before my feet hit the rocks. I then pushed myself back up to the surface, gasping for air. I swam to the rocks, grabbing on and climbing onto them. "That water is freezing!"

I blinked up at the rock, but my vision was off. I put my glasses back on and began to climb. It wasn't too hard. The rocks were all connected, so it wasn't like I had to jump from one to another.

Climbing into the mouth, I stood up and began to take in every detail I could. After all, I'd probably never be able to make it back here.

The entire cave was lit up by a ball of light, surrounded by jagged rocks as they protected it like a trophy.

Something shiny caught my eye, and I looked over to find a hook hanging on the wall. I approached, brushing my fingers over it, wondering if this was the *original* hook. He appeared to have stolen her hook, so I had to give him credit for that.

He tried.

Red eyes began to glow from the corner, growing ever so slowly. My scream echoed through the cave as I backed away, nearly tripping over my own feet. The shadow came out into the orange lighting, but he didn't make any sudden moves.

I scanned the area, hoping to find a way out before he told Pan about me. I wanted to do this discreetly, and *this* was not discreetly.

"I remember you," it said in a much deeper accent than Pan's.

I choked on my own saliva. It could talk? How the hell...?

This was Neverland. Anything was possible. I had to remind myself of this.

Gulping, I took a few more steps back. "Of course. I was just leaving." I turned to go but it echoed again.

"Why are you here?" it asked.

I stopped, not sure how to answer. It was Pan's shadow after all.

"I-I'm..."

"Speak up," he demanded.

I spit out, "I came here to find out all I could about Pan because I plan to save him. I'm also here for my sister who's in a coma as we speak."

He came closer, towering. Like Pan, the shadow was much taller. Unlike him, his shadow happened to be *much* taller. "I'm not going back to him. I live right here, where I belong."

I nodded quickly.

His shadow was just a dark entity, with no beating heart. It couldn't feel remorse. Angering it was no way to go. "Okay, I'll just leave."

"What is it that you want to know?" he asked, suspicions rising.

I dropped my gaze to the ground, unable to meet his red eyes. They glowed with such judgment. Such hatred. "I want to know what Skull Rock is. I want to know why it's forbidden."

"I live here—that's why." It flew a few feet away, its feet finally meeting the ground. "This is where it happened."

"Where what happened?"

"Where I left Pan." He turned to look at me with full, well-intended threats. "This is where Pan's darkest secrets lay."

I laughed a little. "But I know his darkest secrets. He told me what Hook did to him and Kace." Did that all happen here, on Skull Rock?

"This is where Pan confessed his love for her; this is where she used him. This is where Pan found out his lover was sleeping with his best friend. Skull Rock lets Pan have eyes on the entire island. He saw what went on between them. This is where Pan embraced the darkness and finally let me go," he said with a smug look.

As I gripped the handle of my dagger, I realized I couldn't even hurt the shadow. It was just that—not solid. I loosened my grip. "What is this light for?"

"This is the life source of Pan and Neverland." He touched the glass that encased it.

I furrowed my eyebrows. "Why do they need a life source? This is Neverland. There is no time here." I rubbed my eyes.

"Because if Pan dies, the countdown to Neverland's end begins. If Pan is killed, the light dims and that then gives Neverland only an hour left to survive before it becomes smaller and smaller, vanishing into nothing." He looked at me, making sure I wasn't planning to do anything stupid. I couldn't make promises.

Nodding, I said, "I see now. So, this is it? Skull Rock is kind of a disappointment," I mumbled.

"Sorry to let you down." He snickered. "It isn't paradise." He moved back towards the darkness. "We don't trust you."

"The feeling is mutual," I added. I couldn't trust Pan, so I felt the same towards whatever stemmed from Pan himself. I turned towards the opening of the cave. "I'll leave you and get out of your hair now." I glanced at his form. "Or your transparent head, whatever it is." I left the cave and climbed down the rocks. I found the ship, muttering curse words.

I swam around the hull to where the anchor hung down, grabbing onto the chain and climbing my way back up. The links pinched my skin here and there but when the edge of the ship was within my reach, I grasped it and pulled myself back on deck.

I rubbed my shoulder and got to my feet. "Thanks for nothing, Shadow," I mumbled. I pulled the anchor up and struggled to turn the ship around, but eventually I got it.

Issues rose once more while I headed back to the shore of the island. I neared the shore, but the ship started to tilt too much. "No... No, no, no!" I screamed as it continued to tip on its side, going under. I grabbed the wheel before dropping into the water.

I thrashed my arms and leg, finding the surface. I had no time to waste my breath before the mermaids were already rushing to eat me.

The shore was just within my reach as I pushed harder as if I'd won a medal in the swimming Olympics.. The mermaids were much faster than

I was, and I kept choking on the water, swallowing.

A hand grabbed hold of my wrist and pulled me from the waves, flying me over the ocean before dropping me back on the beach. The fins dipped below the depths.

I glanced up at my savior. His bright green eyes didn't leave mine for even a second. "Tell me, Love, why were you swimming with the sharks?"

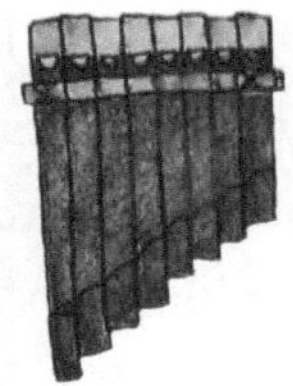

31: Zeeslang Waters

Pan tapped his foot impatiently. Could a girl get a chance to breathe? "I'm waiting for an answer."

I looked up at him, standing up to appear more confident. Well, after almost getting devoured by man-eating mermaids, that was a stretch. "No reason." I cleared my throat and crossed my arms. Why tell him the truth?

He rolled his eyes. "I'm not stupid. I know you went to Skull Rock."

"Then why the hell did you ask me?" I threw my arms up.

He looked at my arms and then back at my face. "I was trying to give you a chance, Little Flower. I was giving you a chance to lessen the punishment by being honest, but it appears honesty isn't your strong suit. Not that lies are, either."

I swallowed. "Oh."

He sighed. "I'm disappointed in you. Am I surprised? No. You always seem to go against me, and why would you obey me now?" He stepped forward. "I know your weakness. Are you asking for punishment?" A frown cursed his expression. "Why must you always be so rebellious?"

I held back a laugh. "Rebellious. Stubborn. My own person. Call it whatever you want."

"Are you going to answer me?" he asked in a stern voice.

"What is even the point? You hate my guts. We kissed, but that doesn't mean I can trust you. It just means you're a typical man who can't seem to control his feelings. And for the record, I am not Captain Hook. Sure, I sailed her ship, but I am *not* her. You're gonna continue to hate me regardless, so why would I bother obeying you?" I shrugged off his threats.

He started to speak but I cut him off. "I'm never going to gain your respect. I don't really care anymore either. If the reason you despise me is because I'm trying to fit in with the boys, so be it. I don't care about what you'll do to me because you'll do it anyway." I gestured to him.

He pressed his lips into a thin line. "Fair enough. You're smart; I'll give you that. It's just too bad because I cannot stand people who disobey me." He curled his fingers into a fist, squeezing.

I locked eyes with him, waiting for pain to bring me to my knees. However, no pain came. Had he lost his magic or was he just pretending to try and use it without *actually* trying?

As his fist tightened and twisted, nothing happened to me. My legs stayed straight and my organs intact. What Pan was attempting to achieve was beyond my understanding. He knew my biggest weakness and yet he wasn't using it against me. Nothing could come close to that kind of pain, igniting it within, but *someone* could. Pan could. However, he hadn't even exhausted himself.

I couldn't keep my curiosity silent any longer. "What the hell are you doing?"

He dropped his fist and narrowed his eyes. "My magic is just weak from the venom." I could see the lie coming from a mile away. His magic wasn't weak anymore and we both knew that. Who was he trying to put on a show for? Himself?

"Punish me if you will, but don't pretend that you're trying when you're not even lifting a finger." I pointed to the sunken ship. "I did this because

Lia is still in a coma. This was never done with ill intentions."

His eyes returned, the hatred flushing away. He gulped whatever pain he held inside and nodded, before vanishing into thin air.

I waited, attempting to regain my strength. I didn't have much left. I didn't want to keep doing this. I just wanted to live peacefully in Neverland with Lia so we could be sisters. Why did Pan have to be so selfish?

Deep inside, I wanted to feel guilty for what I did but I couldn't. Pan never fazed me with his rules and he hardly ever followed through with his punishments. Maybe he wanted to be a villain, but his heart wouldn't allow it.

When I gained back some energy, I walked back to camp. I made it to my room before I fell onto the bed. I didn't want the lost boys to see me as weak, but nobody here could understand what it felt like to be burdened with the fear of a loved one. Had anyone on this island loved anyone at all?

Lia. The lost boys loved her. She had some sort of power over them, enough to show them how I felt inside. She could never make them understand, but she could still at least let them know that it was no easy battle.

I lost every single one, too. Now, I had nobody to help me fight the war. No army. No allies. I was screwed for all eternity on this island.

To protest the laws, I ran towards forbidden locations. I had expected to end up at Cannibal Cove but when I stood over the cliff where a sea serpent lived below, I was afraid of my own stupidity.

"Lili, what the hell are you thinking?" I asked myself.

I didn't know what I was thinking. What was the point of coming here? It wouldn't save Lia. It just proved to Pan that I was reckless, and I didn't want that to be true.

Something hit the back of my leg, sending a sharp pain up my thigh. My knee buckled and I fell forward as my hands caught the edge. I'd almost gone over but I caught myself just in time.

As I glanced back at what happened, my hand slipped down the cliff and

I hung over with just half my body holding me up from danger.

My hair fell in my face, I only seconds from falling into a monster's territory.

Well, *monster* wasn't the right term. Monsters were scary, ugly, and myths. Sea serpents were just massive water snakes that had babies with dragons.

I attempted to scoot my body back, but a pair of hands grabbed me by the shoulders and pulled. I flipped onto my back to see who they were, *relieved* to see Pan.

"What are you doing?"

How did I answer that? I wasn't about to tell him I was trying to show him I didn't have to listen, but I had no other valid reason.

"Would you believe me if I told you I was saving Lia?" Yeah, because that didn't make me look bad...

He peeked over the edge. "How does this help her?"

I had hoped he wouldn't ask because I didn't have an answer. Instead, I shrugged.

He grabbed my hand and lifted me onto my feet. "The sea serpent will kill you. You are aware of that, correct?" He gave me a judgmental look—one that told me I was the biggest moron to exist.

"I'm aware." And yet I didn't make any moves to get away from the edge of death.

Pan began walking back to camp and I left with him shortly after. I was thankful he didn't say anything to make me feel more of an idiot than I already did.

"Zeeslang Waters. Zeeslang is Dutch for sea serpent, the same way fee is Dutch for fairy. Mooie duisternis is also Dutch for beautiful darkness. As you've noticed, we use Dutch here in Neverland. It's a beautiful language," Pan said.

When I didn't respond, he continued, "The sea serpent is dangerous. It will eat anything it can. Can you blame it? It's hungry."

"Is there nothing in this ocean for him?" I furrowed my brows.

Pan glanced back at me. "The mermaids get to it first."

Branches moved out of the way for us. Clouds were rolling in as a sign of a storm of some sort. Had I ever seen a storm in Neverland?

He stopped next to the lagoon and spun around to face me. "Is the sea serpent in your fairytale?"

I shook my head. "Not that I know of. It's just you, the lost boys, Hook, Wendy, and Tinker Bell."

He nodded. "Our sea serpent is similar to a shark. He can smell you the moment you're within a radius. Sharks can normally smell your blood and that's what attracts them, but this serpent can smell even the slightest scent. He can smell your sweat, pee, and whatever it is that makes you human."

"Why is he here?"

Pan shrugged. "He came with the island. I've never stopped to ask him why."

I narrowed my eyes. Smartass. "What do you know about him?"

"His name is Jack," he joked. "I don't know much else. I control Neverland but he isn't part of that. I can't just tell him to stop eating people. If you had fallen in, I wouldn't have been able to tell him to leave you alone. I don't have that kind of power. I couldn't control Hook or the mermaids, either. I control this island but not the living creatures. Well, the vast majority of them, anyway." What did he mean by that?

Taking a deep breath, I said, "You controlled Eric."

He looked away, afraid to look me in the eyes. "Eric wasn't living. He was from my imagination. Everything you told Eric, I heard because his ears were my ears. He was just a manifestation of my fear."

That was how he found out about Lia. Every time I told Eric not to tell Pan, I hadn't realized I was telling Pan myself. Eric *was* Pan.

"When you took in the venom, you were delirious. You forgot who I was, and Kace said you forget the bad things in that state of mind." I swallowed. "Are you afraid of me because I represent the bad things Hook did to you?"

He didn't have to respond. I knew my answer. Pan was afraid of me because I reminded him of Hook. I didn't want to be like her and that was why I continued to fight the darkness inside me begging to escape. I wanted to prove that I would *never* follow in her footsteps. I may have killed her, but it was to protect us. If she'd still been alive, she could have killed us all and used Pan. I had to protect him from her.

I stepped closer to him. "I'm going to show you that I'm not her. I don't want to be her. I don't even like you. She had no problem admitting her crush, but I do."

Oh, real subtle.

"I don't have a crush, is what I'm trying to say. I don't want to date you. I just want to prove to you that I'm capable of being here just like the boys. I'm capable of being the good guy and I don't want to end up the villain in your story. That is *all* I'm trying to prove to you."

32: Jacob

As I approached Cannibal Cove, waves rolled onto the sand, taking but never giving back. That was what Hook did. She stole from Pan but never gave him anything in return.

Something stuck behind a rock caught my eye. I hurried over to check it out, but once I recognized the object, I slowed. Picking it up, I eyed the shoe in my hand. It was Jacob's.

What had happened to him?

I placed my hand over my heart and jumped when someone behind me said, "What did you find?"

I turned to face Kace. "Nothing, just Jacob's shoe. I assumed he was killed but I never knew why."

Kace came over and looked at the shoe. "Pan killed him."

Snickering, I said, "I knew it. Why did he do it?" Why was that important to me?

"Do you know Jacob despised you?"

"I think that became clear at one point or another.."

"Do you know why?" His eyebrows lifted high on his forehead. With a shake of my head, Kace added, "Your cabin was Jacob's first. You showed him up during the test."

Pan gave Jacob's cabin to me? Ew, why did that make me want to vomit? On one hand, I didn't want his hand-me-downs. On the other, I took pride in knowing Pan had demoted Jacob so quickly when I asked about my prize. Jacob really didn't mean anything to the Demon King himself, and that soothed every inch of my soul.

He cleared his throat. "As for his death, it's not a pretty story but I suppose I have time." He pulled his hood down. "It starts where Pan finds out the truth..."

Kace told the story so vividly I felt like I'd lived it myself. I'd never truly noticed before today that Kace had been a master storyteller at heart. And now all those nights of him watching the action made complete sense.

Pan never seemed to mind Jacob, and when the rumors began about us sleeping together, just a tad did Pan's view of Jacob sway. However, one thing that did get Pan's attention.

Jacob was telling the lost boys Jacob himself slept with *me.*

Like any curious leader, he wanted to ask Jacob about it. The two took a walk after dinner one night along the beach, here in Cannibal Cove.

As to whether Pan knew the water would be his demise, nobody could answer.

Jacob got tired of the stalling and asked Pan why he wanted to talk. Pan told him about the rumors he heard, and Jacob had assumed he meant the rumors about Pan and I.

When they were about us, it didn't matter because we both knew the truth. They meant nothing. However, when Jacob told everyone they were about him and I, Pan had no idea what the truth was.

The truth was Jacob had tried to assault me and then when he didn't get what he wanted, he lied about it and said we had sex. Pan must have suspected something was off if Jacob's first rumor was a lie—and surely the second one was, too. Pan wanted to get to the bottom of it.

Can you blame him for trying?

He asked why Jacob was so interested in spreading rumors that weren't even true.

Jacob told Pan that it wasn't his intention to anger him for the rumors. His intention had been to humiliate me the entire time, and yet it never worked. If he wanted to humiliate me, he would have told everyone the truth. Jacob wanted to get laid but I was too prude to do so.

Jacob said it was all just a *game* to him.

"Pan tells Jacob that he's the king of games and Jacob's just playing with fire." Kace glanced at the horizon. "Jacob has the audacity to tell Pan he likes fire."

That earned some threats, of course. Pan told Jacob that if he played with too much fire, he'd eventually get burned. Ironic—since Pan would end up drowning him instead.

Being as stupid as he was, Jacob told Pan he was humiliating me for Pan. His response to that was, "If it was for me, we wouldn't be here right now."

Kace furrowed his brows. "I'm not supposed to tell you this next part, but I consider us friends."

I nodded as he kept going.

Jacob asked him why he was being treated so poorly when lost boys were above lost girls.

That was the moment Pan admitted to someone out loud he felt something for me that he couldn't explain. No, it couldn't be true. He would never. He hated me, right?

Pan was made fun of for what he said. As soon as Jacob made jokes with enough insults to get under Pan's skin, Pan asked him about what happened between Jacob and I. This had shut him up quickly.

What could he say that was believable? He attempted to say we had sex but Pan just brushed off the idea saying it didn't sound like the whole story. Kace had told Pan earlier that Jacob kneed my crotch during that fight and knowing it was against the rules, Pan accused Jacob of being angry at me for no good reason.

He was right about that. He *was* angry for no good reason. He tried to claim rights over my body and threw a tantrum when he didn't get his way.

The beneath-a-scumbag tried to defend himself and say he had a good reason, but Pan dismissed his lies and told him what he really thought happened—that he assumed Jacob had gone too far and tried to do things I didn't want to do. I hadn't expected Pan to ever come to my defense, but it was a relief to know he never faulted me for it.

It had never been confirmed nor denied that Jacob forced himself on me, but it had been implied that was what happened.

"As soon as Jacob tries to leave, he asks Pan, *'What do you want from me?'* Pan notices the hungry teeth waiting in the waters, just beneath the surface." Kace leaned closer, pulling me in by my collar as if the best part was coming up.

"Pan twists his head to look back at Jacob, and without a single misstep, he says, *'I want your silence.'* That comes as the biggest threat. Jacob is a little too close to the waters and so, the mermaids snatch him up as Pan approaches with slow strides."

He tried to fight back, to apologize, whichever would work in his favor. Neither did.

Pan told him he was ashamed to have Jacob as a lost boy. He couldn't tolerate a predator among his boys. He refused to get behind anyone who ended up like their parents. A rapist, an abuser, or anything near those heinous acts. He reminded him that he had to take care of his own and if that meant killing the threats to his family, he would take that path in a heartbeat.

Underneath the cold exterior, Pan was filled with warmth. He cared about us whether he liked to admit it or not.

Just as the mermaids reached for Jacob, Pan grabbed him from their grasp. Jacob thanked him but Pan laughed it off. He wouldn't save Jacob. Instead, he fed him to the mermaids himself because he knew that they wouldn't bite the hand that fed them, unlike Jacob had already done.

"Pan revels in the taste of revenge. Sweet. Cold. Bloody, and merciless for years to come," Kace said.

I could picture the scene before me now. Jacob screaming and begging for mercy like the coward he was. Fighting for his life while beautiful monsters emerged from the endless blue to devour every bit of flesh on his bones as if they'd been starved.

Eventually, his screams ceased to exist as they tore out his throat and swallowed in one final gulp. When they tore apart the very asshole who tried to ruin me, I was envious of them. I also admired the cynicism. Jacob got what he deserved, and I never felt the least bit sorry for him. He died knowing what he was.

Kace glanced out upon the water. "Pan doesn't hate you. He gets too scared to show it, so he makes jokes about not caring. The last time he opened up to someone, she used him for her own gain."

I released a small sigh. "I heard. She cheated on both of you. But I'm not here to fall in love and have a happily ever after. Well, I am here for a happily ever after, but my ultimate goal isn't falling in love. I just want a family. Besides, I feel nothing romantic towards you. Pan is silly to think I would want to date you. You're a great guy but you're definitely...not my type." I tilted my head.

In what way is Kace not your type? He's perfect.

I continued, "My point is, I'm not attracted to you at all. It's important to have a relationship with some kind of attraction, and I don't see you as a romantic partner. I see you as a best friend."

Kace chuckled. "Relax, Lili. I'm not interested in pursuing a romantic relationship with you, either. You're great and all, but it would never work."

How could it never work? Was he saying we clashed or that I was just not datable material? I resented both opinions.

I had to ask the question that had been nagging all day. "How's Lia?"

He shifted his posture. "She's still in a coma. I've been keeping a close eye and trying to wake her, but there's not much I can do. Her entire body is in a vegetative state right now. The good news is she's healing as she sleeps, faster than if she was awake."

Chills covered every inch of my body. Still, the question persisted. Why her?

"Thank you for taking care of her. She means the world to me. I know I've treated her like shit, and I didn't want her to come here but... I don't mean it. I mean, I did but I regret everything I've said. She's all I really have, and I need to appreciate that. She's a kinder soul than anyone I've ever met, and I forget that it wasn't just me who was abused. We both were. Yeah, I got the worst end of the stick but that's not her fault. That doesn't give me the right to make her feel bad just because I had it worse. We both had awful parents. What she went through is just as valid. She's the strong one for not letting it control her," I said as I looked at the sky. I was the little shit who'd always antagonized my father.

Kace smiled a little. "She's strong and there's no denying that. However, you're also strong. You've recognized your mistakes and owned up to them. Not even many adults can say they've done that, and they're supposed to be the wise ones. That's why Pan started this. Adults are the biggest hypocrites of them all."

I couldn't deny that. They would say they loved you but as soon as you did something wrong, they would call you every name in the book. They were making you feel ashamed for *existing*.

That's what my dad did. He would make me feel like I never mattered. When people would tell me that I had an impact on the world, he would say it wasn't true at all. Everything I did made no difference because I wasn't of any significance.

I eventually began to believe it. Nothing I did made a difference.

What if that was the same here? Was helping Pan making any impact in Neverland? I feared I wasn't of enough importance to sit on that kind of throne. There were billions of people on this earth. Why did *I* matter? There were many lost boys here, and Lia, too. They loved her, so why did I think I could ever save Neverland? I couldn't. That was the simple answer.

Kace's eyes focused on something important behind me. Footsteps came running down the shore and I turned back to meet the eyes of Pan. Why run when he could just transport himself everywhere he went?

"What is it?" Kace asked him with a curious expression. I, too, had that same look.

Pan pointed back towards the direction of the camp, shaking his arm. "Lili, you need to come back now." I'd never seen a more serious yet genuine expression on Pan's face.

I stood from the sand and wiped it off my leggings. "Why?"

"Lia's awake."

33: Fear

Lia gave everyone strange looks as we all stared at her. She thought maybe she grew a third eye, but we were just shocked she woke up.

I was the first to approach, and without warning, I wrapped my arms around her. "I'm so thankful you woke up. I was scared, Lia. I am so sorry I was the worst sister ever."

She returned the hug. Now I could spend eternity proving to her that she was everything to me.

"I remember falling off the mountain," she said.

I pulled away with a sigh. "Yes, you did. I'm sorry I told you to climb it. You're okay now and that is what matters." I grabbed both of her hands and squeezed them.

"So, I guess this means I can eat more? I've been deprived of food, haven't I? I'm starving." She smiled a little.

Kace glanced at Pan who nodded in return and gestured for him to go. Kace left the room and returned minutes later with a bowl of salad for her.

She frowned as she stared at the food. "What is this? Am I an herbivore now?"

"It's a salad." Kace twisted his nose in confusion.

"It is bug food is what it is. Bugs eat this. Am I a bug to everyone? I just woke up from—" She cleared her throat, asking, "how long was I out?"

I lifted a finger. "A few weeks I believe. Hard to tell, really." However, she didn't wince as she breathed which meant her bruised ribs were healing. It confirmed that she had been out for two weeks at least.

She crossed her arms. "I was in a coma for a few weeks and I want to eat real food, not plants."

Kace and Pan both looked at me, to which I shrugged. "I'm the only one in our family who likes salad."

Kace hurried out and grabbed something else. This time, he grabbed her soup and the roasted leg of a small animal.

"Now this is food. Thank you." She smiled and began to eat.

I nodded my head towards Kace and Pan. "We should give her some space, to settle back in. I'll be around." I spun my finger in the air and exited the room.

I headed back to my cabin and cleaned up the blanket on the floor. Maybe Lia and I could plan a sleepover. Sure, we slept in the same cabin, but what was the point of having a sister if every day wasn't a sleepover with your best friend?

What could we even do? There was no TV or cute boys to talk about. We had no makeup or dresses. We had nothing to do to *make* this a sleepover.

We were in Neverland, known as the first lost girls. We could use that to our advantage and create a lost girl sleepover. It sounded cheesy but I'd have to work on it.

Well, we could train. We could do something safer that didn't involve climbing mountains. Swimming was an option. I'd offer skinny dipping if it wasn't weird already.

Lia and I could figure it out tonight. Spontaneous decisions were much more exciting anyway.

I grabbed my dagger and pulled it from my sheath. I spun it around, practicing new tricks to appear more coordinated than I was. However, that didn't work in my favor.

The blade cut into my hand and I dropped it, shaking my hand and sucking the blood. I was glad nobody was around to witness.

Except those damn *crows*. Flapping their wings. Beady eyes pinned on me.

Pan would have taken the chance to humiliate me. Of course, I needed to practice but I wasn't a newbie, and I didn't want it thrown in my face that I sucked.

Taking a seat on the bed, I folded my hands together.

I couldn't express how grateful I was to have Lia at my side again. I had denied it for so long, but I knew now we had been twin sisters for a reason.

How hard could it have been for her? She was in a coma the entire time and had no recollection of anything. She also hadn't lost any time because it didn't exist. She got a good rest and woke up just fine, all injuries healed. I was the one left reeling.

I had suffered through the agony of watching her almost die. The fear festered inside me, and she never felt a thing. Every day I had to question whether she would make it and what would happen if she left me.

While she went off to heaven or wherever people went after death, I would be forever stuck here, living with the shame—the grief of losing someone I love. So really, she got the easy end of it.

No, it was wrong of me to think of it like that. I needed to just be appreciative that she was alive.

As soon as I thought that, Lia came running in. "Lili, we have great news!"

I groaned. "Better than what I just went through?"

"Yes!" She clapped her hands but paused, a frown wrinkling her face. "Wait, what?"

I shook my head. "What's the news?"

She spun around and laughed a bit as the hood of the cloak fell from her head. She looked directly at me. "I'm officially a lost girl! I know that my original initiation was interrupted but Pan just told me I am a part of the group. The lost boys are excited about it. We're going to go eat and dance. Come celebrate with us!"

I was not in the mood, but I had no choice. Lia pulled me up and took me out to the fire and sat me down. The flames before my eyes mesmerized me, and I focused on that to keep myself level-headed.

Everyone got their bowls of food and scarfed it down so they could continue dancing. I, however, took my time to savor the meal.

Lia pushed me a bit to my left as she came over. "I can't believe they've accepted me. Who gets to say they were a part of Pan's lost group? I do!" She squealed. She took this far differently than I did.

Maybe she was afraid of Pan seeing anything but excitement about it. She knew that he was capable of anything, and he knew what periods could do to a woman.

I struggled to keep my eyes open as I looked around the camp at all the others present. Exhaustion hit me, coming on at once, out of nowhere. "Hey, Lia, I need to go sleep." I got up before she could reply and headed back to the cabin. As soon as I hit the mattress, the world went dark.

Someone was watching me. Lia. She refused to sleep if something bothered me.

I turned my head and opened my eyes, rubbing them and groaning at the sight before me. *This* was just irritating to wake up to.

"Hello, Love. You seem to be very tired. Any idea why?" Arms crossed, Pan played dumb. I knew better.

"I'm sure you played part in it." I sat up, pushing away the idea of being so much more vulnerable to him than needed.

Be alert.

Wake up, Lili.

He furrowed his brows. "Why would I put you to sleep?"

"Why not? I'm only that much easier for you to use. I don't know exactly what your plan is, but I expect it." I got off the bed, but Pan didn't move. It was not my idea to be this close to him. "You've already done your worst. What more could you possibly want from me?"

"I haven't even come close to doing my worst on you." He cleared his throat. "I wish I were sorry, but I'm not. I am just a man without his shadow."

At that moment, I realized I could kill him, but that would take Neverland and all of us with him, and then where would we be? I had to reattach him with his shadow. That was my *only* solution.

"If you must know, I had slipped something into your food to get you to sleep. You needed the rest after all the worry about Lia. You wouldn't have allowed yourself to rest on your own," he said.

Pan cared about me more than he liked to admit.

Clearing my throat, I gazed at the crows on the windowsill. "You seem to know so much about things in my world—things I never would have guessed you would know. Why is that?"

A small smirk appeared. "Maybe I'm just that intelligent."

"Or maybe you still visit my world, but I don't know why."

His smirk fell. "Why does it matter to you?"

I knew the direction of his question wasn't anywhere I wanted to go, so instead, I changed the subject. "What do you want from me?"

"I don't understand this show you're putting on for everyone. As far as I know, you lost Eric. You pretend to be fine, but you're not. You go and visit my shadow for Lia. Is there something I should know?" He lifted his left eyebrow, a cunning smile creeping up where it perfectly fit.

I shifted weight from one foot to the other. He took notice, and now he knew I was nervous. There was no use in lying. "You want the truth. I have vowed to become someone else on this island. Everyone treated me like I was an inconvenience to them and all I wanted to do was prove that I was meant to be here. It hadn't worked in the way that I wanted, unfortunately."

"Where is this going?" He sounded bored already.

I replied, "I refuse to change for you Pan. I can't be weak anymore."

He came a bit closer. "I refuse to change for you as well, Little Flower. You don't get that, but now at least you can understand how I feel. Kace may trust you, but I can't. You are exactly like her. You are the Captain before the Hook." He exited my cabin, a heavy layer of hostility the only sign his presence was here.

Was I the Captain before the Hook? He was saying I was showing signs of becoming just like her, but I wasn't. I couldn't be. I refused to *believe* Pan.

Looking down at my hands, I studied the lines that ran across my palms in multiple directions. I widened my eyes as soon as I understood what he was getting at.

Pan was afraid of me. Pan was afraid of me because I was stealing his best friend and becoming what he feared. I had the trust of Kace, and maybe I had the trust of Pan, which explained why he pushed me away. What else could he be so terrified of? Nothing else scared him as much as Kristin did.

I had control. The way Pan kept pushing onto me the idea that he controlled me—it told me that I was the one who had control over *him*.

I dropped my hands and peeked out the window, watching Pan admire the celebration. I couldn't help but grin, feeling better for the first time in a while. Peter Pan dreaded me because he was my little puppet.

And he secretly adored it.

34: Firewood

Staring off into the trees, I asked, "Have you ever noticed that the mermaids are everywhere now?" I looked over at Wendy.

She gave me a look. "I guess I wouldn't know. I don't get to go down to the beaches."

Remorse washed over me as I reminded myself that I'd been a terrible friend, and a liar. "I'm sorry. I promised I would get you a cabin with me. Now I share with Lia, and she never asked to come here. She can't hear his flute at all."

"Neither can I." Her eyes lowered to the dirt.

I tilted my head. "What? Wait, so I'm the only girl who hears his flute?" I'd thought maybe Pan made it up to boost my ego to play me. Oh, how wrong I'd been. "How does that even work? I wonder if Hook could hear his flute," I mumbled the last sentence.

The silence enveloped us, but I wanted to squash it.

"Tell me more about yourself. How did you get here?" I asked Wendy.

"I asked to come here the same way you did."

"Was your family awful?"

She smiled—but sadness drenched it. “They wouldn’t accept me.”

“What wouldn’t they accept?” Wendy got high but that didn’t make her a bad person. Did her parents find her getting high? If she had been here a while, maybe getting high in her land wasn’t an option then. So, what did they hate about her?

“I’d rather not say.” She peered around the area as if trying to scope out something specific. “We should do something. This is the only time I get to be out and about.”

“Right, my bad.” I cleared my throat. “Let's go enjoy the beach. It should be fun. Sure, the mermaids are invading every area of the water now, but the beach should be okay. You can at least enjoy it.” I grabbed her wrist and led her down to the beach.

“There you are!” Lia came running. She skidded in the sand, a big smile plastered on her face. “Girl’s day? Yes, please!”

Wendy let out a small laugh and buried her toes.

“Does Pan not give you any shoes?” I asked her.

She wiggled her feet, shaking the sand off. “I choose not to have shoes because they become very bothersome in a short time.”

I also asked, “Pan mentioned you two getting high together. How does that work?”

Her eyes shot to mine. “High? Oh, right. It's supposed to be a secret, so nobody abuses it. We do it near Hangman's Tree.”

“Wait...” I paused to think. “That's where...” I couldn't finish the sentence. Hangman's Tree was where Pan won the game. “I've never seen you guys get high there.”

“As I said, it's a secret, so nobody can steal it,” she repeated.

I thought back to the size of the tree. It was huge. Did they eat from the tree to get high? If it was Pan's thinking place, why did he insist on getting high there? It was probably because he knew nobody would bother him there.

Changing the subject, I said, “Let’s teach you a little about freedom.”

I ran to the water and fell to my knees. "Come in! The mermaids are staying away." Our gazes met, but they simply watched us as if we were a movie and they couldn't interact at all. I didn't know why, but it wasn't like I was complaining.

Lia came in after me and splashed. The heat of the sun was no match against the refreshing ocean waves.

Wendy soon followed and the smile on her face spread. "Do you really get to do this all the time?"

"Eh, usually as we want to, when we aren't training." I splashed them, grinning. While I did prefer boys as friends, it was still nice to get some girl time as well. They could understand my period pains, and my hatred for Pan better than any lost boy. "You're kind of like Pan's high buddy and I'm his water buddy." My laugh got caught in the waves as I toppled over.

When we finished splashing around, we got out and dried off.

Unapologetically, I said, "I despise Pan." I hated Pan for kissing me and playing with my feelings. I was still trying to figure out who I was in this damned place.

Wendy smiled a bit. "You've said many times."

"I know, but it feels so good to talk about it with people who understand. Do you know what I mean?" I ran my fingers through my curls.

She nodded, hand spreading in the sand. "Lia was only brought here to use you. You're *the* lost girl." Lia's eyes began to water as it caught her off guard, and I questioned why. She climbed a mountain and survived it. Was she really about to cry over this?

A cry emerged. "I'm sorry. I just want to be able to call myself a lost girl. What am I supposed to do with that information?" She struggled to hold back the rest of the tears in her eyes, but she failed. Her eyes glossed over like fresh rain on a layer of snow in freezing temperatures.

I grabbed her shoulders, forcing her to focus on me. I planted my feet as I narrowed my eyes. "You do exactly what they wouldn't expect. Don't cry.

You fight, and you prove that you deserve that title. Prove you belong here just as much as the rest of us."

She swallowed the lump in her throat and nodded. "You're right. I'll fight. *I promise.*" She wiped her tears with a sniffle.

"Good." I let go of her and swung my arm in front of me, scooping. "Continue to train. As you said, you just have to be yourself. The lost boys already love you." I winked. Pan trusted her quicker than he ever trusted me.

She released a nervous laugh—broken up into segments and much quieter than her others. "Yes, and the leader who kills people." She nodded a little. "He did kill Hook."

Wendy's eyebrows shot up. "Wait, Pan killed Hook? That took forever. The boy brags about his kill list but couldn't even kill her for almost three decades."

Lia asked her, "How did you know?"

"He only talked about her in awful ways. Whenever she came, he would become a sour puss, and worse than I've ever seen from him. I've been on Neverland longer than anyone can remember. Who knows how long it has been at this point." She began to wander into the depths of her mind.

I stood there as it ate me up inside. Jealousy was an *awful* thing. As if bugs were burrowing into my organs until I ripped them out.

"I killed Captain Hook!" I yelled.

Wendy and Lia looked at me with wide eyes. "What?"

Taking a deep breath, relief washed over me. There'd be more to come. "I killed Hook. Pan just took the blame because he knows I hate myself for it. I was the one who stabbed her and fed her to the mermaids. I'm the monster."

Lia grasped my hands, gently squeezing. "No. No, you're not. You regret it. Monsters don't regret their decisions."

Wendy stepped forward. "Why did you kill her?" I assumed she was judging me and it made no difference. I judged myself.

"I killed her because of what she did to Pan. He couldn't do it, so I did." I pulled my cold hands from Lia's warmth.

Lia folded her arms across her chest and gripped along the edges of the cloak. "What did she do to Pan?"

"They had an affair, but she used him. She used Kace, too. She wanted Pan for his power. She told him he couldn't have any lost girls and she'd leave the boys and his best friend alone. Pan embraced his demon. I *regret* what I did." I regretted the satisfaction it gave me. I rubbed my arms, goosebumps rising. One couldn't feel the warmth from a cold heart mixed with shame.

Lia nodded to reaffirm her argument. "You're not a monster. You didn't enjoy it, nor did you believe it was right. You were only defending Pan. It's sweet. You hate Pan but you also understand that he didn't deserve what she did."

I sent her a small smile. I couldn't tell her that I did actually enjoy it. That's what confirmed my thoughts into believing I was a monster. What else was I if not a demon myself? Human, sure, but humans were the worst monsters of all. That was why Pan brought us here in the first place—away from all the other demons that bred us.

Wendy touched her dry dress. "We should get back. The day is ending soon..."

I let out a sigh. "All right, let's go."

We all walked back to camp, but I stopped when I saw Pan. I grabbed Wendy's arm to stop her.

She looked back at me. "What are you doing?"

"Just hold on," I whispered. I marched up to Pan. "I want to help Wendy cook dinner."

"Ah, I see you're finally willing to help out?" He phrased it more as a question.

"No, I just think it's good for two girls to bond." I tried to keep my smile to a minimum, but I purposely said it the way I did to get my point across.

He furrowed his brows. "Two girls bonding?" He started to really question my intentions. Pan wanted me to help, but to what extent? We had power over him, more than he was willing to let on. He would soon know that I knew.

I nodded with a smile. "That is correct. I need girl time, too, on an island full of boys. Is there a problem?"

He cleared his throat. "Not at all; no problem here. However, I already have a job for you."

"You have a job for me? In the span of three seconds? Where was the mention of this job before? There is a problem, isn't there?" I cocked my eyebrow.

He glared at me before grabbing hold of my bicep. "Let's go." He pulled me to the woods. I feared he would tell me that Wendy was fake, too, but everyone could talk to her. "I want you to collect firewood for next week's supply."

"But you're Pan. You're magical. Just make the fire out of thin air." I gestured to his hands.

"I don't like using magic for everything. I would like to teach you guys how to survive on your own." He disappeared into those wicked trees of his.

Why would Pan want us to survive without him if he wasn't planning on leaving us to fend for ourselves?

I rolled my eyes and gathered up firewood, scratching up my arms. Red marks now covered what was once smooth, medium-brown skin. I gave up on having nice skin a while back. Cuts and bruises were a frequent thing here.

"Ow." One of the branches had been just a little too sharp, enough to break the skin. I shook my finger and sucked the blood that began to emerge.

I heard footsteps behind me and quickly turned, dropping all the branches, and sliding out my dagger. Kace was dancing his way through the trees, causing me to stumble over the wood. I'd never seen him dance before, but the way he moved told me he enjoyed every second of it more than anyone else here. "Kace, what are you doing?" I asked.

He turned to look at me before realizing I could see him. His eyes went wide, his cheeks a deep red. He didn't want to answer.

I put my dagger away and gathered my branches once again.

He shook his head and cleared his throat to dismiss my question. "I actually wanted to ask you something, now that you're here."

"I'm kind of busy right now," I grumbled. The bark was so damn rough.

He stepped forward. "I wanted to ask you about Lia."

I'd feared he wanted to talk about what damage there might have been from the coma. That'd been a terrifying thought.

"What about?" I straightened my posture. What else could he want to talk about involving her? Was he here because he wanted to get rid of her now? He was the one who told me she needed to come here because we shouldn't be separated.

He shifted a bit. I had never seen him do this, so now I was really interested. "I have a question about...her training. How she's doing."

Maybe he knew something I didn't, and she was a different person behind closed doors. "Fine, why? You think she's like Pan? Are you worried?" I laid the sticks on the ground.

"Just the opposite, actually." He nodded.

The opposite? What was that supposed to mean? "You think...she's good? You came to tell me this, why?"

"I know you have some feelings of jealousy and I am aware she doesn't technically belong here. But screw technicalities. I want to ask if I can be the one who trains her from here on out."

"You want to train Lia?" He was asking to take that time away from me.

"I am better than you." He shot me a grin.

Why did he want to train her?

"All right. Fine. But I expect good results or I'm coming after you, and

I also expect you to continue to train me as well. Capiche?"

"Capiche."

"No, the proper response is capache. I don't know what it means, but I know that's how you respond." I gathered my branches again.

Kace chuckled. "Yes, let's use terms that we have no idea the meaning of."

"That's the spirit."

Kace was more forgiving than Pan. Kace saw potential in women. We needed more of that here in Neverland. I just still couldn't put my finger on why he was so adamant to train my sister.

35: Crows

I CIRCLED AROUND PAN'S cabin to his back porch. Now that I had less time with Lia, I figured I could take up some time with Wendy instead.

I'd expected to find Wendy sorting through pots and pans, preparing lunch.

Instead, I found Pan.

Relaxed was an understatement. With a taste of curiosity.

On Pan's back porch was a wooden chair, or more like a throne. The way he sat certainly made it look like his throne as he watched Mermaid Lagoon while the crows cawed.

Half a dozen crows perched themselves on the railing and headrest of his chair.

The monster himself was tilted more towards his left, a leg up over the opposite arm of the chair. His dark waves fell across his forehead while a crown made of twigs sat atop.

His forefinger was pressed against his lips as his gold eyes flickered to me. "What is it that you want, Little Flower?"

"I was looking for Wendy but she's not here. What the hell is this?" I squinted at the birds.

He glanced at his crows, shrugging. "We're enjoying a nice day. Is that so terribly wrong?"

"Are you...friends with them?" My eyes sparked.

The gold dimmed, his iris' returning to their bright green. "Are you asking if I talk to them?"

"If that's how you took the question..."

Without hesitation, he said, "Yes. We talk. They're how I keep an eye on the island and everyone around here. They tell me all I need to know."

"Wait, your shadow said that Skull Rock is how you have eyes to Neverland. It's the crows?"

"Well, Little Flower, yes. Skull Rock is where I talk to the crows. My eyes to the island."

“So it’s the crows, and not Skull Rock?”

"Both. When I'm at Skull Rock, the crows will relay to me their findings. That's where I speak to them, or in other words, where they speak to me. I have no idea what they're saying right now." He gestured to the one squawking above his head. "I think they just like to hear themselves talk sometimes."

"You talk to the crows." I almost didn't believe it. Why was that unbelievable of all the things that happened here?

The corner of his lips curved up a bit. "Are you jealous?"

"Wendy's not here so I'm going to go somewhere else. Enjoy whatever this is." I waved my hand over his crows as I left camp.

With the sun scorching the earth, I headed right for the lagoon past Hangman's Tree.

Nobody was around today, so I discarded every piece of clothing and dove in. When I came up for air, I squeaked at the sight of Pan standing over my clothes. Instinctually, I covered my chest. "What the hell? Do you have no manners?"

"This is a public lagoon, Love. The question is do *you* have any?" He glanced at my bra. "By all means, do what you want. But don't act surprised when one of us stumbles upon all your naked glory."

I swam further back, ensuring I was deep enough that he couldn't see beneath the surface. Paranoia was a force to be reckoned with. "Can you at least turn around? I'll put my clothes on."

"No need. I'm not here to stay. You're looking for Wendy?"

Shivers slid down my backside. I nodded.

"Well, if you do find her, you might not want to be naked when you do."

"I wasn't planning to go looking for her without my clothes."

"No, no. But if she came here... She loves someone else. Just keep that in mind." Someone else? Wendy? In love? It didn't sound right, but I would ask her later.

"Wait, Pan. Can't you just tell me where she is? Your crows know."

He cocked an eyebrow. "They do, but they're mine. I'd never use them for your benefit. You should learn to find people without my help. I might not always be around."

I lowered myself further into the water, barely hitting my lower lip. "If you're not around, we won't survive, either."

He'd turned to leave but twisted his head to look at me. "Maybe I wasn't referring to my death."

"You always do that. Say things with no full understanding, leaving me questioning more. Whatever, Pan. Just go." I spun away from him and watched the waterfall. Any closer and that thing would take me under.

After a minute of silence, I heard some movement behind me. I looked back to find Pan undressing. "What the actual hell are you doing? Peter!" The name had slipped, without a second thought lingering behind it. Regardless, my eyes went wide as I faced the waterfall again.

"Since we're skinny dipping, I'd be rude not to join. You said I leave you with more questions. Now here I am." He waded into the water until I could feel the ripples from behind me. "Are you going to ask any questions?"

I shook my head. "I'd rather not give you the satisfaction."

"And what about the waterfall? Are you going to stare at it all day, or are we swimming underneath?" He leaned so close to my ear that I sunk a little into the water just to avoid the temptation.

Furrowing my brows, I said, "Are you crazy? I'm not willingly drowning myself."

He swam around me and flipped onto his back, floating towards it. "Don't let me show you up, Love. Let's go. You won't drown. I swear it."

My eyes darted to the sky, away from his full...display. "No thank you."

"Suddenly the lost girl is afraid? You've never had such hesitation before."

"Water scares me."

"Then why swim in it?"

"Because swimming doesn't scare me. But the deep ocean. The big waves. Waterfalls. It's terrifying. Staring at it now, my heart is racing just by the thought of rushing water pushing me under. Getting caught in the undertow. Never being able to find my way up."

"Oh. I see." His tone was soft, laced with compassion. "You're afraid of the fast water. Unpredictable water."

Shutting my eyes, I nodded a little. When I opened them, I almost gasped from the proximity between Pan and I. *Inches.* How had he moved so quickly? Magic—right.

"I believe sometimes facing our fears puts more adventure in our life. I'll be here, every step of the way." His fingers closed around my wrist, pulling me.

"Pan..."

"I won't let go." He slid his fingers up my palm before intertwining them with mine. "You're safe, Little Flower."

"I don't feel safe," I said in a quieter voice.

The waterfall's roar filled my ears until I couldn't hear Pan's soothing words anymore. He slipped under the waterfall, and then I went under, the weight forcing me down. A tug. Harder. Then I surfaced from the other side, intaking all the air I could. I swam to the rock, placing my back against it, Pan's hand still locked in mine.

He swam closer, blocking my view of the fall as he lifted our interlocked hands against the wall. "See? I told you I wouldn't let you drown. You don't trust me."

"You give me no reason to trust you," I breathed.

A look of pride. His eyes darkened just a little as he eliminated almost every remaining inch between us, all but two. "I like when you call me Peter." He brought his hand up, running his thumb across my lip. "It sounds enticing coming from you. A spell, even."

"A spell?" my voice came out so small.

"Call me Peter."

Questions hit me. What if I called him that in front of his boys? What would happen? Why Peter? Why now?

He leaned in, his throat vibrating as he spoke lowly, "Call me by my name."

I'd give into him in a heartbeat. I desperately wanted to. If he'd just kiss me, we could end this now. Nobody would ever know. Nobody could ever find us.

"And if I call you by your name?" I asked.

"Little Flower, you're treading dangerously close," he growled.

“Danger is my middle name, *Peter*.”

The remaining gap was snuffed out like a flame on a candle wick. His kiss became my every emotion, his taste all I asked for at the end of the night.

Surprise. Wanting.

He’d done this dance so many times that I didn’t have to question how he felt. I knew. With me, his vision cleared.

And the way his lips took a firm stance, captivating me, begging me for more.

I’d give in...

Kace shouted, "Pan!"

"Mm." I reached out, palm flat against his chest as I pushed him back. "Your best friend needs you."

He brushed his fingers up my throat. "This isn't over." Before I could respond, he dipped out under the waterfall.

I threw my arm out, eyes big as I realized I'd need his help. "Don't leave me here!" But he couldn't hear me anymore.

After contemplating every life decision, I finally slid along the wall until I made it around to the edge of the lagoon. Much to my humiliation, Kace and Pan hadn't left, and they stopped to watch me crawl out, ass in the air. I dropped with my knees to my chest. "Carry on. Nothing to see."

Kace side-eyed Pan before they headed back through the forest.

"Oh... I'll certainly call you Peter all right. Just when you least expect it. In front of everyone." And that was a *threat*.

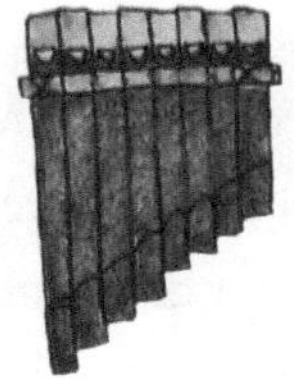

36: History of Neverland

Mermaid Lagoon was still unsafe to venture to. Like Pan's private beach, as if he told us to steer clear so he could have it to himself.

But the mermaids were dangerous in every part of the island now. Including Cannibal Cove which had once been only a threat to us because of Hook. Once she'd died, you'd assume it would be safe following that.

But the mermaids I fed her to hadn't been in their own territory. They'd been hanging out in *hers*.

There used to be a difference. Now, I couldn't be so sure.

No, mermaids eat humans—not other mermaids. Cannibals eat their own kind.

I looked over at Pan as he exited his cabin and ventured out into the woods. I was careful when I decided to follow. I wasn't sure of how sneaky one could be around him, but I was going to find out.

He approached Hangman's Tree, the tree opening up for the first time. It wasn't some huge light that emerged from the tree in the shape of a door. It was more so just an opening that blended so well with the bark that one wouldn't notice it existed. As soon as it closed after he disappeared inside,

I rushed over.

What was he possibly doing in there? What was there inside this tree? I touched the bark and traced the edges, questioning how I'd get inside.

Jumping back, an evident line appeared, shaping into the form of a door. A bit of light illuminated from inside, and I slowly slid in. The opening closed behind me and I walked down the tiny stairs into an area that came straight out of a study hall. All of this was really inside his thinking tree?

Sure, the tree was huge but that didn't mean I wasn't surprised at how much was inside it. This was much more than I could have ever imagined.

Papers littered a table in the center of the room. Along the walls were shelves of books, and some potions. Lights hung from the ceiling in a chaotic order, and pots of plants graced a few shelves. One of them draped over the edge.

I caught sight of Pan as he crossed his arms. "Have you mentioned anything to Lili that she shouldn't know?" he asked Wendy. "Does she know why I go to solid ground?" What the hell was solid ground? Was he a *ghost* now?

Did he haunt his own island?

Kace, too, wanted to keep things from me involving Pan, but he didn't have the same trust issues as Pan. That much was clear.

Wendy nodded and cleaned up the tables. "I haven't told her much aside from the blue and gold magic. I didn't even tell her how we get high together."

I saw the sickening smirk on his face. "Good."

I rolled my eyes. He might have had power over her, but he knew he had none over me.

Pan circled the room. He investigated a book that laid on the table. "You know, I think Lili is getting somewhere." What would this boy say about me when I wasn't around to hear it?

Wendy cleared her throat and kept her gaze on the table. "What do you mean?"

"Lili is going to lose—lose this battle with her dark side. She is trying to change me, and I'm aware. But a woman is only willing to handle so much before she breaks. She almost lost her sister, and her one friend here turned out to be a figment of *our* imaginations." He wandered into his thoughts, intrigued by whatever he saw.

Wendy broke him from that daydream. "What do you have planned?"

"It would be quite a pity if I exposed my plans to anyone. I wouldn't risk it with you, but I will see to it that Lili breaks. What else am I best at?" He stared in my general direction, but never spotted me.

I noticed he had used my real name multiple times. I was always *Love* or *Little Flower*.

Wendy's eyes followed Pan as he moved around the room. "What about the mermaids? Lili said the mermaids have been swimming more out of their territory around the island. They no longer stay within their designated beach. They even stayed away from us when we swam."

Pan lifted his brow. "Yes, I am aware. The mermaids know their future. There isn't much in store that includes their death but that's not any of your concern. You are just here to get high." He turned back to his book.

Wendy kept her arms at her sides, compliant. "What are you looking at?" she asked so softly.

He looked at her and leaned his hands on the table. "It's the history of me and the history of Neverland."

"Oh. You keep a book?"

He nodded. "I won't always be around. It keeps record of my legacy."

"Well, you are connected to this island. But if you disappear, so would the entirety of Neverland." That'd been exactly what I told him.

"Indeed. You'd take the book with you to your world." He chuckled, then his face dropped. "My parents didn't exactly want me. I was born in England, just like you. Brighton, England. In 1905. My parents were selfish, deciding I wasn't worth it. They were too afraid to give me away publicly, so they secretly left me alone by the beach, and then claimed I died during birth." He flipped a page. "England was a waste of space and you know that, Wendy. That's why I took you away from there. You know which area always intrigued me? The Netherlands. It caught my attention, and maybe because of the strange name but...their language was much more than people perceived."

I felt bad for Pan, but I wouldn't let his sob story make excuses for his actions.

"I'm not really sure what happened there. The Netherlands had a strange name, and I wanted a place to exist like that. I hadn't yet decided on the name Neverland, but it was inspired by the Netherlands. That's why I use their language to name things. The Netherlands was always a better story than England, and England didn't have its own language that made Fee Abyss, mooie duisternis, and Zeeslang Waters sound like mystical locations." He faced Wendy. "But I despised adults for being so judgmental towards minors. I despised families and parents who neglected and abused their kids. I wanted a place for people like me to get away from that life and that is where I created Neverland." He pushed off the table and paced.

I gripped the spindles in the dark shadows on the stairway.

He halted. "But things don't last forever, Wendy Darling. Neither do I."

I covered my mouth. If Pan caught me, I'd be a dead woman, and he preferred me dead rather than alive.

He grabbed his dagger and eyed it. "Because I created the wish with magic, I am the source for keeping this wish alive. If I die, everything I wished for goes along with it. This dagger will just end up on that beach waiting for a new owner once more." He placed it on the table. "Magic is real for those who believe. Magic is real for those who are desperate. I was desperate just enough for the magic to choose me.

"You know better than anyone that if Lili knew why I go to solid ground, she would use that against me. Hook was my weakness but now she's dead. Without her, my focus is on what's left in England—*who's* left in England. I need to know what happened to my parents when they left me. I need to know if I have any family left there."

Pan called my world solid ground, which meant Neverland wasn't actually *solid* to begin with. Maybe just the faint what-if of our dreams.

Without his permission to leave, I couldn't use it against him. Was he afraid I'd find a way back? I wished to see Nana, but there was no way I'd risk losing all this and he knew that more than anyone else here.

"Little Flower, how did you get in here?"

My breath caught in my throat.

How did I get in? The door just opened for me. Did it not do that for anyone else?

Pan stood before me, leaning down into my space.

Swallowing, I said, "I was..." I didn't have an answer. "How did you get in here?"

"It's my tree. It opens from my command."

Seemed so simple, yet that was unlikely. Well, likely for him and unlikely for me. He didn't command it to open for me, but I'd somehow opened it on my own accord. Did it have anything to do with why I could hear his flute?

I still didn't possess any magic.

He grabbed my wrist and yanked me onto my feet, leading me out of the tree. "You never obey, and for it you are dearly going to pay. You will fear me before dusk falls on the next night." Was he trying to conjure some spell to make that happen? Why the secrecy?

"I doubt that," I said as matter-of-factly.

He stopped, spinning me around to face him as he straightened his posture. "Don't test me. You may have your little hate-love relationship with me, but I can manage to squeeze in some fear in just the blink of an eye. Remember, Love, I am capable of *anything*."

37: Exposed

I DIDN'T KNOW WHAT Pan had in store for me now, but I was certain it wouldn't be all that wonderful on my end. I'd still rebel regardless of what he did. He would have to accept that I wouldn't change for him one day.

Gazing out of the window of my cabin, I kept an eye on the camp. The boys were at training and I wasn't allowed to go.

I noticed Pan walking up to my door, and I leaned back from the window with a look of disgust. "What is he doing here?"

Pan entered. "Let's go."

"Where are we going?" I asked.

He spoke more clearly, dismissing my question. "Let's *go*."

I followed him out and stopped when I saw a familiar structure of bamboo. "Really? This is my punishment? I've survived this before."

He opened the door to the cage. "All right, then you don't mind me using it." He waved me inside and I listened. He closed the door behind me. "Twenty-four hours. If any issues shall arise, I will have to worsen your punishment." He said that but he never meant it.

He left my sight, and I leaned back against the wall.

What was a girl to do in a cage?

I sang to myself for some time. When I got restless, I began to reposition myself, but it wasn't any less uncomfortable.

My stomach began to claw at my insides for food. I groaned, rubbing it. It was supposed to help the pain die down, but it never worked. My hands did not withhold magic as Pan's did. Lucky me.

For hours on end, my stomach tortured me for not feeding it, but eventually it gave up. I moved to the corner and curled up since I hardly had space anyway.

Goosebumps covered my skin. I noticed that it wasn't because of me this time, but because the air was a bit chilly. It struck me as odd that Neverland could get cold.

I EVENTUALLY GOT SOME amount of sleep, but it was interrupted when someone grabbed my leg. My reflexes kicked in and my leg shot out at whoever.

"Love, please don't make it worse on yourself."

My dry mouth somehow managed to muster up a terrible taste. "Then don't grab my leg when I'm asleep," I warned.

He grabbed my ankle anyway and dragged me out of the cage. I looked up at him as he let go. He stood, making me feel puny. I was quick to scramble to my feet to squander that.

Pan turned and walked towards the center of camp only a few feet away. I followed, stopping just as he did.

He faced all the lost boys, taking turns with each one until he had their attention. "Everyone, gather around. We need to teach our lost girl a lesson."

I peered up into his leaf-green eyes, confusion racking my body. What could the boy do now? I survived the cage. Did that not mean anything?

He looked at me, but his eyes showed utter animosity. "How dare you spy on me?"

He kept his eyes on me, tearing into my every being. I hated this stare. It was nearly the same look when he saw Captain Hook—a look soaked with sorrow and shame. "I own this island. I created it. I can take you out with a simple thought."

I kept my mouth shut this time because this was not a good time to stand up to him. It would make everything much worse.

"You continue to undermine my authority and disobey. You try to make me out as the bad guy in front of my lost boys. You couldn't fix your family, so your only hope is to fix ours." He swallowed the guilt.

My face heated. It wasn't my idea to expose Pan's vulnerability to everyone, but I couldn't stop him now or he'd go off like a rocket.

"You are just a human girl!" he shouted. "You cannot get away with anything here!" His eyes never left mine as they glossed over. I was terrified to look away.

"They're *my* family. I brought them here and you cannot take that away from me." He laughed without a hint of humor in his voice, pointing his finger at me.

If cartoons were real, I would be shrinking, and he'd be growing.

Reality began to fade away into nothing. Everything went numb. This was the only family he had, and I was taking it away from him, and not for any good reason.

"Look around you, Little Flower. Nobody here is your friend. Real friends don't exist." He gestured to everyone who stood and watched.

"Kace is my friend," I said in a quiet voice.

"What? I can't hear you," he said, cupping his ear.

I shook my head to forget what I was saying. I didn't want to start any problems that I couldn't promise to fix.

"That's what I thought. Your only friend was Eric, and he's not real," he spat.

I just nodded. What else could I do? I was starving and tired, so I wasn't in the right state of mind to tell Pan that nobody loved him any less.

"Pan," someone said in a threatening voice. Only *I* ever defied Pan. Nobody else had the guts to.

"What, Kace?" He snapped his head towards his second-in-command.

Kace's gaze darted between us both. "I think she's had enough."

Pan narrowed his eyes. "Who are you to decide when she's had enough?"

"I am your second-in-command, your first lost boy, and your best friend. I understand you're trying to get your point across, and I think it has been well received from the looks of it," Kace spoke with confidence to his leader. It was the first I'd seen from him, but it was also nice to know that he had a backbone, and he wasn't just a lost puppy. "I don't want you to humiliate yourself any longer."

Pan glanced back at me as I pressed my lips together. "I don't think she has had enough."

Kace was looking out for his own but Pan was too prideful to even listen. He was the one humiliating himself. It wasn't about me. It was about *him*.

He turned to face his lost boys. "All of you know the rules. You know what I will do if you disobey. But our lost girl thinks she is an exception to these rules. Why? Because she's a girl!" He threw his arms up. "They think they're so special and they don't deserve the same standards as boys. This is my island, and everyone has the same set of rules to follow." He spun towards me and came closer.

I swallowed, afraid of what else he could say. I took the cage. I starved. Why was he attempting—and failing—to humiliate me? That wasn't the deal.

"That includes you. You spied on me, and you broke into my tree. I've had quite enough of you by now. I am not your friend; I am your enemy. I will crush you." He lifted his hand and began to curl his fingers into a fist.

He was attempting to inflict cramps but as to why he was holding back, I couldn't say. Maybe he was afraid to hurt me, or maybe he just didn't want to.

Or maybe he can't.

He thought he was humiliating me by exposing himself, and now I was beginning to wonder if he was doing it on purpose to assert his leadership without making me feel like crap. And I did feel like crap because he was humiliating himself for my sake.

The boys watched intently, but nobody had an answer except Kace and I. I wanted to hug Pan and tell him it was going to be okay.

"She must be immune to my magic. Maybe this plays a part in why she can hear the flute." He faced his lost boys, lies lacing his tongue. "She feels nothing when I try to inflict pain."

I did feel something, but it wasn't pain. I felt pity.

He began to circle me, making sure I wasn't about to do anything stupid. Honestly, I wasn't going to do anything stupid anyway. "You haven't quite understood yet what the consequences are. I will continue to break you until nothing is left." He stopped behind me, hand on my shoulder. "You will never have any desire to go against me again."

He let go as I whirled around to face him, locking eyes. He *was* broken inside. He had been ripped to pieces and nobody ever offered to put him back together.

Kace stepped closer. "Pan, I do think she gets the point now."

Pan shook his head. "No, she doesn't. Not yet. I can tell." He lifted my chin, forcing me to look at him. "I can see it in your eyes. There's still just a hint of you that wants to defend yourself." I wanted to defend *him*.

I didn't know what else he could possibly do. I was already letting him do all of this. I wasn't trying to fight back. "I surrender," I whispered, only loud enough for him to hear it.

He chuckled. "It's pathetic that you think that works here. Neverland plays by different rules."

I swallowed, shaking my head. "Please... I'm sorry."

"But do you actually mean it?" His eyes never faltered.

I was trying to get him to shut up, but he wouldn't listen.

"You make me look like the villain in front of my lost boys, and maybe I am. I couldn't protect Kace from Hook. I couldn't protect you from Jacob. What good am I, Lili?" He lifted his eyebrows, suggesting I do something to him.

Taking the bait would have been a stupid move. He was trying to get me all riled up so I would act out. I didn't want to give him what he wanted.

Lowering my head, I tried to keep my emotions under control. I couldn't let him break himself for me.

He continued, "I have so much control over you that I even led you to believe Eric was real. He was fictional. He was only my creation because I'm afraid. I'm a puddle because of you and now everyone knows because every time you step out of line, I let you get away with it."

He could tell he was getting into my head somehow. "Maybe I never taught you a lesson because I didn't want to hurt you. Maybe every lost boy knows what I feel for you, but you don't care. I'm not supposed to have feelings," he kept repeating it, to get me to react. I'd held myself together for as long as I could.

But today, I couldn't hold myself together anymore. The dam broke, unstoppable. A massive rush of tears down my cheeks.

Pan froze in his spot.

I sobbed for Eric, my lost friend. I cried for myself. I wept for Kace, what I did to Hook, Lia, and Pan most of all. "I would never...." I peeked up at all the faces that watched *me* break. The grief continued to wreak havoc. "I just wanted a family..."

38: Pan's Origins

After hearing a bit about his past, I wanted to know more. No, I *needed* to know more. Whatever happened to him while he was still in England had to come to light.

I had to revisit Hangman's Tree.

I approached the tree with caution while scanning my surroundings for any danger. Pan was in his cabin as far as I knew, questioning what he'd done to himself.

Entering, I admired the inside for the first time. Without a limit, I could check it out for myself. Everything looked so cozy. It was something you'd see straight out of a treehouse magazine.

A few tables lined the walls, littered with books. If I hadn't known better, I would have painted Pan as an innocent boy who loved magic and adventure. He wasn't so sweet, however.

I gasped at the sight of his dagger. He left it here? Was he so out of his mind that he left his weapon alone?

I hurried over and grabbed it from the table.

A heavy dread washed over my soul. The tree had transformed into Pan's cabin and I was sitting on his bed, head hung low and eyes glued to the floor. However, not an ounce of comfort caressed me.

I screamed as I dropped his dagger, stumbling back.

What the hell was that?

Something had taken over my mind when I touched it. I saw things that weren't actually in front of me, as if I was seeing things through someone else's eyes. It couldn't be possible. But here, anything was. In Neverland, nothing was controlled by *never-going-to-happen*.

Picking up the dagger again, I wrapped both hands around the handle and closed my eyes.

The nightmares return, overwhelming my being. Everything inside me is placed in this dream I can never awake from. They come for me every time I close my eyes, and I fear they may never allow me to be at peace.

Opening my eyes, I inhaled. Then exhaled. These weren't my own thoughts. I couldn't control what was inside my head. I feared I was inside Pan's, now and I couldn't go back since I took the leap.

I pretend I'm not afraid, challenging these nightmares to haunt me. I welcome them with open arms but only after that do I regret my decision.

A ten-year-old boy stood in the middle of the road with his backpack. His entire body tensed up at the sound of his mother's voice calling him over. "Thomas, get inside!" she yelled.

Her eyes blackened the closer he got but as soon as he stood in front of her, she was ready to rip him limb from limb. "What have I said about standing in the middle of the road? You are a disgrace to our family name." Her hand met his cheek, but the child never winced. Instead, he took the slap as a badge of honor.

Pan witnessed other children getting abused and yet he could never stop it.

The scenery changed. The ocean shore took its place and now I saw what appeared to be a beautiful family making their trip to the beach with their new baby boy.

His father glanced at him and gave a fake smile the baby had never seen but would soon come to despise. "You get to experience the sea for the first time."

His mother placed a hand on the father's arm while shaking her head. "We're not bad people. We're doing this for him. Someone will find him."

Little did they know, nobody ever found me. They ran from their responsibility while I agonized in solitude.

The baby was ecstatic, not aware that this beach would be the scene of all his night terrors. He had no idea that they were not giving him a positive experience, but rather leaving destruction in their wake.

His parents placed him down in the sand, showing him a view of everything a beach had to offer. The boy admired the wonders and chewed on his own fingers as he studied the seafoam forming from the waves.

Behind him, his parents began to back away, heading back towards the road.

Look back! Don't you see that they're abandoning you? he screamed into my head.

Just as I could hear his thoughts, I could feel the emotions that ran throughout his body. His heart ached. A feeling of dread plagued his entire soul, promising him a life of misery.

That didn't make a difference. The baby watched the ocean with curiosity and reached out towards the water. As soon as his parents were out of sight, he looked around for them. Without them by his side, he was left without security or a kiss goodnight.

This little baby made a few noises, hoping to capture their attention. When that didn't work, he began to cry. Nothing he did made them realize he was still in the sand with nowhere to go and nobody to keep him safe. He simply craved warmth. He needed to be *loved*.

The aching in my heart grew without warning. A lump formed in my throat as I faced the truth that a baby boy was promised a nice day at the beach and discarded as if he were trash.

Why did you leave me? Why wasn't I enough?

The baby's cries grew louder until eventually exhaustion overtook his little body and put him to sleep. He could only hope to wake up from this bad dream and see his parents once again.

The scene faded and another one took its place.

Before me stood a teenage boy no more than fourteen, scavenging through the trash for food to eat. He'd spent his entire life on the streets and he knew nothing better than this.

When I caught a glimpse of his face, I was shocked to find Pan hidden beneath the dirt and torn clothes.

Citizens nearby pointed at him in mockery as they walked past. Pan ignored their stares and insults, his focus solely on surviving.

He found bread in the trash and scarfed it down to fill the emptiness in his stomach. It was enough to keep him alive just a bit longer.

Across the street, a father was yelling at his son. The boy was shoved by his father—a man too drunk to keep his own balance in check.

Save him, Peter. He needs you.

Pan approached them, shouting at the father, "What the bloody hell are you doing?"

"Who are you to talk to me like that?" the man asked as he faced Pan. His words came out more slurred than he intended.

Pan got in his face and stood his ground. "Who are you to treat him with such disrespect?" He moved between the two.

The man rolled up his sleeves as his whiskey breath wafted in Pan's face. "You don't have a right to tell me how to raise my son."

The fear etched on Pan's face stemmed from his strength compared to the man's. While living on the streets—eating trash—it wasn't easy to build muscles with no nutrition.

"Father, please, don't hurt him," the son pleaded.

He shot the boy a glare. "Watch your mouth or you'll get it, too."

Forming a fist, he sent a blow to Pan's face. Pan tried to defend himself, failing every chance he got to block the punches. Bruises began to show, and blood seeped from his nose. His silence provoked the father to punch harder.

Please, stop. Make it stop.

Pan dropped to the ground as he wished all of this to be over, but the man didn't stop. His punches became kicks to Pan's ribs. "You're as worthless as the trash you consume."

Every eye on them ignored the situation. They were all either afraid to step in or they didn't care much about children who came from abusive households.

The boy tugged at his father's arm, begging him to leave Pan alone. He just wanted to go home and daydream to his heart's content. The last thing he wanted to witness was a boy being beaten for protecting him.

Giving in, the father growled before leaving.

When his father was out of earshot, the boy bent down to look at Pan. "I'm so sorry. Meet me out here tomorrow and I promise to bring you food," he said in a hushed tone.

Pan nodded, in far too much pain to move any more than he could due to the injuries.

"Harry, get over here!" his father yelled.

The boy said, "Thank you." He ran off as soon as the rain began to pour from the sky, pelting Pan's cold skin as he curled in a fetal position.

You tried, Peter.

This flashback skipped ahead to an older version, a version of Pan who looked far more homeless than any version I'd seen before.

He couldn't sleep so he took a walk towards the beach where he'd first been abandoned by his parents.

The moon on this particular night had been full as it reflected off the surface of the ocean and left a small glow over the entire beach. As soon as he stepped into the sand, a chill ran down his spine. Something eerie lingered in the air here.

An object caught his eye as it shimmered under the moonlight. Pan approached with curiosity and reached down, pulling it from the shore. The dagger was a strange object to hide on a beach, but he picked it up anyway. He made sure to hold it as if it were a piece of delicate glass that needed to be protected at all costs.

As he wrapped his fingers around the handle, he wasn't blind to how perfectly it fit in his palm. Pan swung the dagger to test its strength against evil but something else sparked inside his soul. Power radiated from within and at that moment, he knew right away he wanted more.

The dagger began to glow, a light that the moon couldn't possibly project, causing Pan to drop the dagger in a panic and take a step back.

After eyeing the blade that no longer lit up, he grabbed a stick and poked it a few times to make sure it wasn't a weapon that had a mind of its own. "I assume you're the closest thing to a human." He moved closer.

The dagger began to glimmer again based on Pan's voice. It was responding to his assumption. However, he didn't notice.

"Humans aren't the most wonderful creatures alive. These parents will abuse their own children to feel better about themselves. They find joy in hurting their own flesh and blood and I try to step in and tell them to open their eyes, but it never works in my favor. I want to give them a taste of their own medicine. I've been on my own for eighteen years and it's as if it all plays no part. How would this help anyone? I need a purpose," he said.

He had so much to let out.

"I see the pain in their eyes. I understand the feeling of never being enough. I want to help them escape and have a better future but how could I give them that? Unfortunately, there's nothing I can do for them at this point. Where would I begin?" he asked.

The glow from the dagger grew but still, he didn't notice.

This gleam grew until it became blinding, overtaking the moonlight. Pan shielded his eyes and when everything returned to normal, he lowered his hand. He couldn't recognize his surroundings. He was still on a beach but this one was surrounded by trees instead of homes and buildings.

Pan approached the trees further up the shore, studying every inch.

I took a wild guess that I was on an island. I'd certainly heard of them before.

His wish for a place to escape to had been granted. Children would be able to live out their wildest dreams and adults could never step foot here.

He tightened his grasp on the dagger that had now appeared in his palm, keeping it close to his body. Peter had found his forever home. "A place where children can thrive—and I shall call it Neverland."

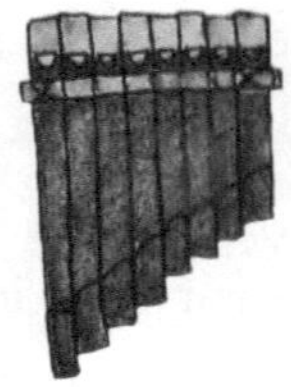

39: Storm

THE DOOR OPENED TO reveal Pan and he stepped down the stairs, eyes on me the entire time. "What the bloody hell are you doing here?"

"I wanted to understand more. Don't I get to know that?" I kept his dagger behind my back, swallowing my fear.

He approached me. "This is my place and *my* mind. You do not get to barge in whenever you please. What is it that has you thinking you don't have to follow any rules?"

I shrugged. "I'm not breaking rules just to piss you off. Skull Rock was for Lia. Zeeslang Waters was out of boredom. I spied on you and Wendy because I wanted to know what was inside Hangman's Tree. After I heard a bit about you and how Neverland came to be, I wanted to see more about it and then...that happened. Nothing was done with ill intentions. Everything I did was because I wanted to help someone and believe it or not, I want to help you."

"I don't want your help." He reached behind my back and grabbed my wrist, showing me his dagger that still warmed my hand. "I want to be left alone."

I laughed, not an ounce of humor in sight. I nodded towards him. "Yeah? If that were true, you wouldn't be so interested in making me follow the rules. You wouldn't have kissed me. I never intended on kissing you at all, Pan. I just came here to get away from my own family and be part of a new one. It was you who decided it wasn't enough."

He studied my eyes that told every lie on my tongue. "You kissed back, Little Flower."

Lifting a finger, I said, "To be fair, I was in the moment. It never meant anything. If it meant nothing to you, it was the same for me. Two can play this game, Pan."

He grabbed his dagger from my hand and put it back in his belt. "But then I know it's not true. You're only saying that because I am. For me, it's true. For you, it's just meant to get my trousers in a twist."

I took a step back. "You wouldn't know what it means to me. You can't read my mind." I left the tree, but Pan followed me out.

He asked, "What did you see?"

I slowly turned on my heel to face him. "What didn't I see? I saw what you saw. I watched as your parents left you on the beach. I watched you get beaten by a boy's father for defending him. I heard your thoughts." I let out a sigh. "I know that these are recurring memories you can't make go away."

He shrugged. "It's part of being human. We all have memories that never let us be. I'm no exception." He leaned back against the tree.

When I began walking the other way, I heard something strange echo between the trees. I glanced back at Pan whose intense gaze never left mine. I studied him just for a few seconds longer to see if what I heard was true.

The glistening tear that escaped the corner of his eye confirmed I wasn't crazy. I'd heard Pan *choke* on his own pain.

He wiped the tear, but it didn't make any difference now. I'd already seen it.

I walked over to him and stopped just inches away. "You're no exception from feeling what we feel."

He said nothing. Maybe he was afraid if he tried to speak, he'd lose control of his emotions. But sometimes, he needed to.

"It's okay to cry. It's okay to let it out. That's how we heal ourselves. We all have emotions, Pan, and we have every right to let them show." I reached out and grabbed his hand, interlocking our fingers.

He lowered his head. "It's never that easy. People expect you to be emotional. You're a woman. Nobody expects their leader to cry."

I squeezed his hand. "Screw them. Fuck anyone who judges you for crying. If you weren't allowed to cry, you would have been created without the ability to feel. I will personally punish anyone who thinks it's funny that you're in pain. You were not made to be everyone's rock. You saved everyone here by taking us away from our homes. Let us save you, too. You can't be everyone's hero all the time and not feel the repercussions of it. We have limits and we need to acknowledge those."

Pan released a deep sigh. "I'm not going to show weakness."

"Weakness? Who the hell said crying was weak? It shows strength to cry when everyone else may judge you. That takes courage most people don't have. This comes from someone who hates to cry in front of other people. You know I won't hesitate to threaten anyone who insults you for crying." I gestured around us. "Besides, they know not to bother you at Hangman's Tree. You have privacy. You can go inside and cry there. I won't even watch if it makes you uncomfortable."

His eyes searched mine. "You're trying to tell me to go cry. Does this not sound like your evil plan?"

"Evil would be telling you to hold it in. If you keep bottling it inside, eventually it's going to explode at a horrible time, and you won't be able to control it. It's better to do it in a controlled environment, right now." I let go of his fingers. "Trust me. The last thing you want is to break down in front of someone you're afraid to show your emotions to." It hadn't come as much of a surprise that I was afraid to show him my emotions.

When he didn't respond, I turned to leave him some privacy. If I left now, I could say I'd never actually seen him cry. If anyone made fun of him for it, I could defend him with that argument and a few threats.

"Don't go. Please," he pleaded in a quiet voice.

Glancing back at him, I watched his form shrink a bit. He wanted me to stay but I wasn't sure why. We weren't exactly friends. We couldn't even be considered acquaintances.

He lifted his eyes to meet mine.

I nodded and walked back over to him. "I won't go."

Pan wrapped his arms around me and rested his chin on my shoulder. I hadn't expected it, but I wrapped my arms around his torso to give him comfort.

"I had to name myself Peter because they'd never named me. Now, Peter reminds me of the miserable life I lived before this, and I want it to all go away," he whispered.

A few sobs left him, then more followed. I told him to cry, but I never thought he'd listen. He was the last person to listen to me.

However, I could never hold this against him. To save him, I had to let him express how he felt. Even villains had vulnerable moments.

There were a few moments where his cries were uneven, sudden, and sharp. As he wept, he forgot to breathe.

It would have been too easy to kill him if that were still my original goal here. I'd be no better than him if I resorted to violence. I didn't want to give into my dark side and let him win.

After a while, Pan went silent and neither of us pulled away. I wasn't about to tell him to let go of me and he was too embarrassed to even say anything after exposing his feelings.

Every now and then, he was reminded of what he never experienced before us. Love *or* a family.

It was no different from a child growing up without parents and then becoming one. They were finally part of a family but that hole of never having parents to love and protect you would always exist. Between having a parent and being one, they only had the chance to experience one. That filled a person with far more pain than they should ever have to carry. Having parents was a necessity but it wasn't up to the child whether their parents cared about them or not.

Pan had been a homeless kid because his own parents didn't think he was good enough. That was a hurt that would never be erased and even long after he would heal, he'd always feel that ping in his heart. He would always wish he had a chance.

He withdrew and turned to face the tree. "You should go."

I caught a glimpse of his face. His eyes were red—bloodshot—swollen, and his cheeks stained from the tears. I'm sure he had a headache arising from dehydration as well.

"I'll be at my cabin if you need me." I left him alone and returned to the place I slept when I wasn't out causing trouble.

If you could call making Pan cry trouble...

My cabin hadn't changed at all since I arrived. Lia and I shared the bed and dresser. We were treated as if we were twins with no separate lives of our own.

I loved Lia, and there was nothing that said it wasn't true. I just wanted us to have our space, so we didn't smother each other too much. Otherwise, sometime down the road, we could be so sick of each other's presence that we'd end up in a nasty fight.

I furrowed my brows as the sound of thunder boomed. Storms? There were no storms in Neverland. Where had it come from?

The thunder grew louder, and light flashed outside my window. I opened the cabin door and stood in the frame, admiring the clouds roll in as rain began to pour.

Lost boys from every direction came running, headed to their own cabins. Everyone wore confused expressions due to the sudden onset storm, but I guessed where it possibly came from.

This island was connected to Pan and his emotions tonight were something we'd never experienced before. This storm was just the island's way of expressing how Pan felt without letting everyone know what had happened to him. Maybe Kace knew but nobody else did. They weren't close enough to Pan to know how his magic worked in every shape and form.

The pain picked up and everything was soaked within seconds. I'd never seen rain pour this hard before, like a bucket pouring water on a child's head at a waterpark in the kiddy pool.

Lia came running from the woods. I moved to the side as she rushed by, but her cloak was drenched in rainwater. She pulled it off and dropped it onto the floor, taking a deep breath. "It came out of nowhere." She approached me, eyes fixed on the lightning illuminate the night sky. "I've never seen this happen."

Keeping my promise to Pan, I shrugged and said, "Yeah, I don't know what's happening. This island has many secrets."

I'd wondered where she'd been but I'm sure she and Kace had been training. She was being trained a lot more than I'd been doing when she was my student.

Lia closed the door and shook her head. "Whatever it is, it's telling us we should get some sleep. We have a long day ahead of us tomorrow. I'm barely getting anywhere with my archery skills, and tomorrow is all about practice. It's important to me that I have those skills if I'm going to help gather the meat."

What? She wanted to gather meat, too? Lia was the last person I'd assume wanted to see blood. However, this would be a conversation for another day.

My eyes grew heavy, and my body was begging me to lie down. I needed it, and I knew Pan would just as much as I did. He had finally released the pain that'd been locked in his heart after all these years.

40: Venom

I SAT IN SILENCE. I hadn't said a word since yesterday's breakdown. I refused to. He deserved privacy and so did I. He spent so much time trying to prove to everyone that he was tough, but he couldn't pretend forever. They saw every part of Pan and yet had no idea what was really going on.

Lia came in and knew right away I wasn't in a chatty mood. She kept her mouth glued shut, and instead grabbed her dagger from the dresser and left. There was nothing she could do or say to fix this. It just had to handle itself.

All day, the cabin stayed quiet. Kace and Lia had gone to train. Pan left me to dwell in my own pity. I pitied him for having to hold up a front. I pitied myself for having to grieve over an imaginary friend.

That friend would be able to fix you right now if he were real.

Lia came back during the night and she went straight to sleep. I stared at the ceiling, wondering what else I could do. Nothing. Pan's point came across clear as day. He had the power. He controlled everyone and everything here. I tried to be brave and rebel. I resisted him for a long time. How much longer could I hold out?

I barely got any sleep. I only got up to pee, and that was it. I never got up to even eat. Lia brought me food earlier, but I didn't touch it. I had lost my appetite when I realized Pan's weakness. He'd lost everything.

THE SUN BEGAN TO rise and display its beautiful, warm array of colors.

Lia woke up and looked at me but didn't say a word. She got up and left the cabin, letting me think in peace. Was I thinking or was I burying my shame from the monstrosity of Pan's entertainment?

It wasn't until midday that I finally got my sorry ass out of the bed. I walked out of my cabin and stared at the fire everyone ate lunch in front of. All eyes turned to me, growing bigger, filling with curiosity. I walked over to the circle and sat on a log, grabbing a bowl of salad.

I began to eat while I let the fire warm up my cold insides. It was getting harder by the day to keep up. When I finished, I peered at all the eyes still on me. They all stared, making me uncomfortable. I never even said a word.

I got up and headed down to the beach. Those alluring mermaids were watching me. I thought for a moment that just maybe I could conspire with them. I thought against it, not ready to die yet. I didn't know why I had any will to live after what happened. I should've given up on that and yet I was more determined than ever to save Pan.

Sitting down in the sand, I wondered what our parents or brothers thought about our disappearance. Did they care? They probably assumed we ran away. Mom would be crying to the police, pretending she loved us. The police would believe she gave a shit.

I looked out at the open sea, wondering what it would be like to be swept away in the waves. It would be so easy to do it. It would end with the mermaids devouring my flesh. Yet, I still sat here in this sand. I didn't move even an inch closer towards an effortless suicide.

I'd been so engrossed in my own head, just wondering about all the possibilities of what could've been that I didn't notice the person until they sat down next to me.

The blonde wisps of hair gave it away. I had to start the conversation, or nobody would. "You're the only person who didn't see what went down."

"No, but I got the idea. Pan wouldn't stop talking about how he made a mistake..." Wendy looked my way, but I never looked hers. "I had no idea. I thought you had it easy because you had your own clothes and a cabin. I thought..." She didn't finish her sentence.

I finished for her. "You thought you had it worse. Now you think I do. Nobody has it worse. This isn't a competition. I'm not here to pity myself anymore. We both got treated like shit by our families and we both deserved better. Let's leave it at that."

"Fair enough." She gazed at the waves that would rush to the shore and flow back into the ocean only to repeat the process.

I enjoyed the silence. This serene moment in a timeless place where I could see good in the world, even if for just a second, was all that I needed to keep my sanity on the surface.

Wendy left before I did because she had to go check on Pan. I couldn't blame her for following orders. My fate was not something anyone deserved—a fate where seeing Pan cry was a raw moment and not just a fantasy.

I walked back to camp just before sunset. It amazed me that night and day existed in Neverland where time refused to. Night and day indicated the days passing until the world ended. Would Neverland end when my world did?

I ate dinner alongside everyone else. Thankfully, only half of the eyes were on me. It would lessen over time if that was possible here. I disappeared back to my cabin after I finished my soup.

I lay down on the bed, but sat up as Kace came in. "Why are you here?" I tried not to come off sounding like a bitch.

"I didn't realize how tough it was for you," he said.

"Please don't pity me. I don't need that right now."

"He wanted a friend, and I couldn't even provide that. I tried to be there for him. I didn't want that to happen but as you can see, there are things I can't provide for Pan that you can." He nodded, his head just a bit too heavy as he dropped it.

"No need to put yourself down over it. That's not going to help anyone. It's over now and we can't go back and fix it. Move on. Capiche?"

He smiled a bit as he met my eyes. "Capache."

I laughed a little, but my smile faded and I sighed, glancing at my dresser. "Why am I still here? Why hasn't Pan just killed me? I've disobeyed so many times. Why has he kept me alive?" It didn't make sense because he bragged about killing people. He enjoyed it but he avoided killing me no matter what I did. "He says he has feelings for me, but I just can't forget that he said his bloodlust is far greater..."

"I'm not actually quite sure why. If you were someone else, he would've killed you immediately. On the bright side, I'm glad he hasn't. As I said, I consider you a good friend."

"Don't get all mushy on me. I hope this isn't your subtle way of saying you like me romantically," I joked.

Now it was his turn to laugh. "No, no. I don't see you that way."

We'd established this before, but I just needed to confirm it one more time—for Pan. I didn't want him to assume the worst of me.

"Good, because I don't either. It would be awkward if any of us did." I placed my hands on my stomach, lying back down. "Where's Lia?"

"She went for a walk. She said something about clearing her head, whatever that means." He furrowed his brows.

"Clearing your head means you need a quiet place to think. It means getting yourself back on track." I rolled my eyes playfully, a small smile dancing on my lips.

He lifted both eyebrows. "Really? I didn't know what it meant." He choked on his laugh. "Of course, I know what it means. I just don't know why she needs to clear her head. It's you who witnessed...his vulnerability," he said it gently as if I were a fragile, able to break at any word.

"Lia isn't around me all the time. She has her life here, too, and who knows what that is? Maybe something we don't know about is going on and she needs to process that. Lia is still her own person even if we did come from the same egg and sperm." I shrugged. "I'm assuming that's how identical twins are made." My eyes met his.

He cleared his throat. "All right, understandable. I think I've got the message now. I just thought you would know because twins usually have some mind-reading ability."

"No, we don't. What we have is just a connection. We share everything. We share DNA as well. We can sense and feel what might be going on, but we can't read each other's minds. It's just a gut instinct."

"The one that only recently came to be?" He lifted just one eyebrow this time.

I smirked a little. "Yep, that's the one. And because it's recent, we aren't very good at reading each other. I have no idea what could be going on. I have my own shit to process, so we just handle our own problems for now." As I peered up at the ceiling, I wished for stars instead of a roof over my head.

The commotion outside increased with every passing minute. What could be happening now? I got up, worried, because Lia was not with us and Pan wasn't stable at the moment.

We both went out to see what the fuss was about. It wasn't Lia. Lia wasn't anywhere in sight.

Pan closed the gap between him and Wendy, eyes falling on me, and when they did, they lit up with wonder. "Nice of you to come to watch the show, Little Flower."

"What's happening?" I didn't need anyone else to take the blame for what I did. Had someone said something bad about Pan's emotions?

He looked at one of his lost boys, Trevor. He was an older lost boy, probably the replacement for Jacob. "Bring it here." He put out his hand, waiting for something.

Trevor brought him a little bottle and stepped back. Pan nodded towards me. "I will need some of you to hold Lili back."

I widened my eyes as Trevor and Levi came over to grab me. I struggled but lost the battle as they held my hands behind my back and gripped my shoulders to keep my feet rooted. "What is this Pan? You already got what you wanted from me!" I yelled at him. Wendy didn't deserve this. She was just a girl.

He shook his head. "It's nothing you did wrong. It's what Wendy has done wrong." He put on a thick, black glove before opening the bottle.

I pleaded with Wendy but she returned the same energy. She nodded, telling me it was okay.

It wasn't okay. None of this would ever be *okay*.

Pan took something out of the bottle. I began to struggle again when I realized what it was. They were some of the mooie duisternis vines—venomous. I was terrified of what he was going to do.

"No, Pan, please!" I begged. I adjured for Wendy more than I asked for his own mercy just a few days ago.

He snickered. "What I'm doing is justified. She is not who we thought she was."

"Kill me!" I shouted at him. "Please, kill me instead."

"That doesn't do *me* any good. If she's going to pay for her crimes, I need to make sure you stay alive." He grabbed her arm and gripped the thorns. "And you get to experience the mess you created," he said to her.

He dragged the point down the inside of her wrist, breaking skin, slicing into her muscle just enough to let it seep inside. Everyone fell still. The silence made my head throb.

After a minute, Wendy began coughing, her breathing shallow and raspy. Her skin paled in a grayish tone. I tried to turn away, but I couldn't stop myself.

Her eyes glossed over as she collapsed. She clawed her own chest, trying to tear out the venom eating her alive. Her movements slowed and eventually came to a full stop. She'd gone into a coma, trapped inside her own body as the venom devoured her.

This lasted for what seemed like days but were merely just hours or so. As Pan warned, mooie duisternis was slow and agonizing, and nobody could save her now. As hard as I tried, the boys kept me in their grasp, their fingers digging into my skin.

Pan bent down and checked her pulse before standing and facing everyone. "Clear out. The show is over." He left the camp as the boys cleared out, allowing me to fall to my knees.

I gawked at her body while struggling to catch my own breath. Pan had no mercy, and now I saw how apparent that was. Wendy Darling lay in the dirt—void of all life.

41: Rumors

Nothing made sense right now, and I didn't want it to. "She didn't scream. She didn't fight. She didn't struggle. Why? Why did she let this happen?" I looked at Kace.

"She didn't feel there was a better choice. She had done something horrible and she'd rather take the only route out of this place, as long as it meant she was free," he said.

"Everyone keeps saying that." And that was all I could say. I was trying hard to understand this, but nobody was telling me what she did.

Kace left to go help Pan discard her body. I wasn't really sad. I mean, it was sad, but I wasn't sad for her. I was more shocked than upset for Wendy. Something had to be seriously wrong with me, too.

I went down to the beach to free my mind. I hadn't been to any beaches before Neverland, but now I observed it to be the most peaceful setting. Even if the mermaids did watch me, they didn't try to kill me.

I found myself walking closer to the water. My feet buried themselves in the sand as the tide washed over them. "Why do you guys watch me?"

"Why would we? Do we bite the hand that feeds us?" the redhead asked me. It didn't surprise me when they spoke. Pan's shadow could speak, too.

I swallowed.

No. "I fed you once, and I regret it. Please, don't treat me like your mother."

The brunette came closer. "But you are... You fed us and we like food. Pan is going to feed us, too. He said he has more for us."

Wendy. He was going to feed Wendy to the mermaids. I couldn't let him do that. It was insulting. "Did Pan say anything else?"

"He said that as long as we don't eat you, you will bring us more food. He promised us. He fed us a boy at one point," the brunette said.

I narrowed my eyes. "Jacob..." I turned to walk away but paused. "Consider dinner canceled." I left before they decided to make *me* their meal.

I had to find Pan. I would find out later as to why I wasn't affected as much by Wendy's death, but I had to make sure she wasn't fed to the mermaids at the very least. I had respect even if I didn't have any remorse. Was that possible?

Marching up to Pan's cabin, I knocked. I had tried to bang on his door, but my fear of his emotional state stopped me. I couldn't let him do that again.

He opened the door. "Oh, Love, what are you doing here?" He didn't seem angry or surprised. He'd expected me.

"We should talk."

"About what I did?"

"Yes and no. It's something you did, but not just that." I couldn't even come to the idea that she was dead. It didn't feel right saying she was murdered.

He lifted his eyebrows in question. "What did I do?"

"The real question is what didn't you do?" I moved him aside as I entered. I turned towards him. "First off, do not feed Wendy to the mermaids. She doesn't deserve that. Why don't we burn her body? That's more fitting."

"More fitting than being eaten by mermaids? This is Neverland. She was killed by mooie duisternis, so I think it's safe to say being mermaid food isn't out of the ordinary. If I died, I'd still want to help the island. I would rather be mermaid food than rot. At least I'm helping with something. It's also a unique way to get rid of the body. Plenty of people burn." He closed the door and turned to look at me.

I tapped my foot impatiently. "*Fine*, but I do want to talk about something else, too."

"All right." He seemed pleased by my agreement.

"You killed Wendy and I don't know why." I couldn't get my foot to stop tapping the floor.

"Why does it matter? She was making up rumors that hurt your feelings." He shrugged.

"It hurt my reputation. There's a difference," I paused. "Wait, *she* was making up rumors? No, you said Jacob was doing that."

He shoved his hands behind his back. "We thought it was Jacob. Turns out it never was. Jacob tried to force his way into your tights, but Wendy started the rumors. She was trying to turn you into a whore so she could humiliate you and keep me to herself. When you get high with someone, they develop Stockholm Syndrome, and she got jealous."

I swallowed. "She started the rumors. You killed her over that?"

Pan let out a sigh. "These rumors were more than rumors. They were lies. They forced people to judge us for no reason. It's not my intention to hurt you but Wendy is not your friend. She was using you. She's the one who started the rumors to turn you into a whore. She wanted to make people hate you."

I shrugged. "It never worked. They hate me for other reasons."

"She told Jacob you were easy and willing to give it away. She's the reason why he went after you," he said.

Freezing in my spot, I kept my mouth shut. Wendy? No, it couldn't be true. Would Pan lie about this?

Never.

"The people you think you can trust, you can't. Those you think are against you are on your side in the end," Pan said.

She was jealous and for what? Getting high? She wanted Jacob to rape me so she could see the shame and hatred spread. I would have never talked to Pan again had that happened. And she'd known that, which was why she did it...

"I had to kill her because she was destroying this family. She let her emotions ruin the good in her the same way I did." He stepped forward.

"You do care, Pan. You care that she made me out to be a whore. You also care that she made up lies about us both. You killed them both because they wanted to steal my body from me." I closed my eyes. "Most men don't mind rumors about sex. They like for the boys to think they are getting some. They don't see the pain that comes with sexual assault but you—you see much more. You killed them. There's still *some* good in you."

"That's not why." He crossed his arms. "I don't want to create a world where anyone who comes here is receiving the same treatment they were on solid ground. Wendy didn't seem to care about that. I also didn't enjoy that rumor."

I shook my head, cutting him off with a swipe of my arms. "Don't lie. You surprise me sometimes with your goodness. You didn't like a rumor that benefitted you and hurt me."

He scoffed, rolling his eyes. "No, that rumor was gross. They made up lies about me. That is not okay in Neverland. They are not supposed to make up lies about me."

"Why? You make up lies that you feel nothing for me when we both know the truth. You lie about why you kissed me." I gestured to him, throwing my arm.

He glared at me. "Lili."

"Is it not true? It is. Your excuses are lame, Pan." I smiled a bit, but my smile faded shortly after. "You rarely call me by my name. You always call me by nicknames."

"I like those nicknames. I think they suit you." He moved closer.

"You think *Love* and *Little Flower* suit me? Me?" I laughed, the crows perching on his windowsills.

"Your name is that of a flower. You're little compared to me. Little Flower suits you perfectly. Would you rather me call you twat?"

I furrowed my brows. "I go by a nickname already. My full name is Liliana. Lili is just my nickname."

"Liliana sounds like the name of a pretty flower," he pointed out.

My cheeks reddened. Did Pan just call me a pretty flower? No, that couldn't be right. Just a few days ago, he was trying to humiliate me.

Why was I blushing over this? Something had to be wrong with me. First, Wendy's death didn't affect me. Second, I agreed to let the mermaids eat her. Third, I was blushing at Pan's compliments. Most importantly, I had killed Hook and *enjoyed* it.

"Pan, can we talk about me?"

"A little narcissistic don't you think?" A sly smile slid onto his lips.

I placed my hands against my chest. "Something is wrong with me. I need your help to figure it out." I now played a worried—desperate expression. Desperate times called for desperate measures, including going to Pan for help.

"You need my help?" He tilted his head, amused.

"That's what I just said."

He nodded a little. "What do you need to figure out?" For once, he didn't ask in an irritated manner. He was asking a genuine question. A little dizzying to say the least.

"I don't know. I'm not affected by death so much. Let's put it this way. I'm here having a normal conversation with you now despite what Wendy did."

"That's because you're afraid of me. You can't get back at me," he joked.

"Pan, please. This is serious. I'm actually scared of why this is happening to me." I was more upset about not being upset than I was actually upset about Wendy's death.

He shrugged. "You may have known deep down that she did something awful. I've said it before—your dark side is fighting to win. I can see it. You can't feel remorse if you don't. It doesn't just happen."

"Listen to me. I do not want my darkness to win. Why is it even becoming this hard to fight it? I was abused *at home*! Shouldn't *that* bring out the demon?" I asked in a louder tone.

He came closer, mere inches away. "I am right here, Love. No need to yell." He pinched the bridge of his nose, eyes closed like a disappointed lover. "Yes, it could've come out then. It didn't. But now I'm here. I am encouraging your dark side and that's why it's becoming stronger. You had people you loved holding you back."

"This doesn't make any sense. Your encouragement shouldn't matter."

"It does if you like me." His eyes searched mine.

"I don't. *I don't.* That doesn't make sense." I shook my head, rejecting it.

"What doesn't make any sense? I am explaining all of this as clear as day. I recall it was you who got all upset when I rejected the kiss. You were the one who kept pushing the idea that it meant something." He pointed his finger.

"Because it did mean something! You kissed me, *twice* might I add!"

"And you kissed back, Love. Because you like me." His eyebrow shot up.

I put some space between us. "Let's get back to the subject. Something's wrong with me. This further proves it."

"Yes, and that was on topic. You like me so it makes it easier for my darkness to bring out yours. You're being influenced by me. And here, you've been trying to influence me. It didn't work out too well." He chuckled lowly.

I cleared my throat. "You kissed me, so it seemed to work out in some way. You like me even." A smirk formed in light of my revenge.

"No, I don't. We've been over this. I only do these things to trick you." He nodded as if he was trying to force himself to believe it.

"You called me a pretty flower. Even if your goal is to turn me dark, you still like me. You may like this idea that I can be your partner in crime. However, you still like me, which gives me power over you." I wiggled my finger towards him.

His eyes darted down to my body for a split second. "You do not have power over me."

"Do I?" I grabbed him by the collar and pulled him close. This caught him off guard, his Adam's apple bobbing. "I think it is very safe to say I have power over you. You can try hard to deny it, but I'm beginning to learn that you can't kill my spirit."

"I'm not planning to. I'm only twisting it," he said. "And I also have power over you. You are more affected by the kiss. You're this close because you want to kiss me again."

"And you *want* me to kiss you again." I let go of his shirt as his eyes filled with surprise. I backed away. "I won't turn out like you. I refuse to."

"Not feeling remorse is you being on your way to this side of the island. You cannot create remorse."

"Or maybe, I knew that she'd done something wicked so I couldn't feel sad watching her succumb to the venom. She deserved it." I rolled the kinks from my neck, rubbing. "I know I can't create remorse, but I can at least create excuses that make me feel better for not feeling it."

He stayed silent. Planning my ultimate demise? I wished.

He won't kill you. He likes you.

I choked from that thought.

But he still made my life hell. It meant I had some power over him, and I would build on that control. I would influence him enough to turn him good. This was the key to saving Neverland.

"All right, well, I guess I will see you around, Pan." I let a cunning smile slide onto my lips as I turned and left his cabin.

What he didn't know was I wouldn't be seeing him much longer. I was going to leave Neverland if it meant I kept my sanity. I feared I couldn't win this war.

42: Tinker Bell

I PACED BACK AND forth, running my fingers through my hair. "I like Pan. He's supposed to be my enemy!"

"What exactly happened?" Lia asked.

Sitting on my bed, I released a loud sigh. "I *like* him. That's what happened." I threw my arms up.

She laughed. "But what made you come to this realization?"

"I went to ask Pan some questions, and...well, we got to talking. He called me a pretty flower, and we got close. He told me that I liked him and now I'm realizing that he's right. I don't just want to kiss him, Lia. I want to call him my boyfriend. Peter Pan—my boyfriend."

"Wait, as in..." she trailed off.

I nodded. "Yes, I want to date him. This is the man who wanted to murder me when I arrived. Why do I want a man that wants to watch me bleed? My monster wants him—uh-huh. That's it."

"That may be true... Lili, remember what our family is like. Our family hurt us, too. We're used to it. Some people from abusive homes will fall into the same patterns. It's what you're used to." Her face softened.

"That's why I'm telling you this. I need you to help me stay away from him. It's for my own good. I shouldn't want someone who hates me." Yet he wanted me, too.

"Okay. Okay. I can do that." She stood and pushed her chest out.

I lifted my eyebrow. "The cloak makes you more confident."

She smiled like a little girl who found a kitten. "I know I'm supposed to give it back, but I like the way it looks and makes me feel. I feel like I belong here now."

I swallowed, afraid of what I'd say next. "I need to find a way home."

Lia's smile faded. "What?"

"I need to get home because I'm afraid I won't win this war otherwise. When we go home, we can just run away to a new life. We know how to survive on our own now. Come with me," I pleaded.

She put her hands up. "Whoa, Lili. I'm sorry. I like it here. I like training with Kace and being independent. I want to stay. I don't want to go home and be the runaway. I want to be a lost girl." Her eyes fell as her shoulders slumped.

"You're not going to come with me?" I scratched at the fabric of my tights. My toes curled from the anxiety. I couldn't believe that my own twin was going to leave me.

"I like it here. I really do. I'm sorry."

"If you're sorry, then look at me damnit," I demanded.

She looked at me. She didn't say another word before she left our cabin to go do Pan knew what.

I gulped. I was going to have to get out of Neverland alone. Lia desperately wanted to bond but now she wouldn't even come with me. This is why I never wanted to make friends with her in the first place.

Getting up, I went outside. I started off in some direction, not sure where I was going. Heavy boots caught up to me. "Where are you off to?" Kace asked.

I turned to face him. "I'm going home. I'm finding a way off this island because I don't want to lose. I have to leave before I become Pan's ruination."

"You can't leave."

"Don't start. I may miss you guys, but it's for the best."

"No, I mean, you can't leave. Pan will find out your plan. There is no escape." He cocked his head to the side.

I groaned. "Kace, please stop. My future here is going to be far worse if I don't attempt an escape now. You need to let this go. Let me go. Stop worrying. I can handle myself because I am a big girl. I know what Pan is capable of and I am still making my choice to leave. I cannot become Pan."

"What do you mean? Did he propose? Are you going to be Mrs. Pan?" He stifled a chuckle.

"Pan doesn't propose. I wouldn't even say yes." I rolled my eyes.

He thought for a second. "Then what did he do to make you want to leave?"

I threw my arms in the air. "What hasn't he done? He's done everything in his power to make me miserable. Kace, if you really want to know, I like Pan. Romantically. I can't allow anything to happen between us. You saw the waterfall incident. I refuse to join the dark side. I am going to find a way home, and you can't stop me." I walked forward until Kace disappeared from my sight. *Good.*

I ended up at Hangman's Tree again. This was the only place where I knew to find secret information about the island. It would be my best bet.

I touched the bark and the door opened. I went inside and scanned the area first to make sure I was alone. I hurried down and looked through some books on a shelf to the left. Most of them were just rules for this island. Then I found the book about Pan's and Neverland's history.

Grabbing it and opening it up, I skimmed the pages. Surely there had to be some mention of a way to leave this island without his permission.

One page had the mention of a *certain* fairy. "Tinker Bell, eh? I was beginning to wonder if fairies existed in Neverland. It makes sense that you'd be my way out. Of course, in the original story, she's Pan's ally. But this is surely not that story. You're talking to yourself, Lili. You're losing it." I rolled my eyes.

I kept reading.

I was going to find Tinker Bell and go home. Pan really thought he could keep this hidden? He was clearly not the only way off this island. The boy was stupid enough to think that I would believe him. He always was a liar. But where did Tinker Bell live?

I put the book back in his place and left. Walking south of the tree and then west, I came upon a cliff. "Clearly this is not the way to find her." I gazed at the water below. If I ever got into trouble, I assumed Pan would be there to save me. Of course, this was in situations in which I could not save myself.

As I turned, I admired the rest of the island. It glowed with such beauty under every ray of the sun.

My eyes moved multiple directions. If I were a fairy, where would I live? If I headed to my right, I would end up by Cannibal Cove.

Where else would she be? I looked straight ahead, towards the range of mountains in the middle of the island. "All right, Tinker Bell. Let's figure out where you are so I can go home."

Impatience controlled me. The more time that I spent here was more time that Pan had to turn me to the darkness.

I booked it towards the mountains. I reached them within twenty minutes or so and studied the rocks. I'd have to climb these mountains, wouldn't I?

After a few failed attempts at climbing, I made it to the top.

I spun in every direction, my eyes peeled. "Tinker Bell. I am not sure how this works or where you are, but I could use your help. I know you exist," I spoke to whoever was listening, hoping it was just Tinker Bell herself.

After a moment of waiting for any sound of a fairy, I let out a defeated sigh. "I just want to go home! Is that really too hard for a girl to ask for?" I yelled into the sky.

"Depends on the girl," said a female from behind me.

I whirled around and took in her appearance. "You're supposed to be a fairy." Green attire. She was taller than I was, nearly six feet.

She rolled on her heels as a bit of green magic glistened in the light. "I am. Who's asking?"

"Lili. I want to go home. Pan is going to destroy me if I stay." This was a twisted version of the story.

She tapped her chin. "How so?"

"I've been fighting my darkness. If it wins, Neverland will be forever lost as we know it. I can't win this war against Pan anymore."

She let out a small laugh. "What do you want me to do? Take you home? I don't have that kind of magic. I wouldn't be sure if I could use it on you." She was stubborn for a fairy.

"Why not? This is your home, too, isn't it?"

Tinker Bell stomped her right foot. "I can leave and go as I please, but I cannot help you."

"Why are you doing this? I thought you were supposed to be a nice fairy?" I crossed my arms. Ah, yes, insult your own way off the island.

She glared, approaching me, and beginning to circle. "I refuse to help someone I don't know. You got yourself here, you must get yourself back. I am not your taxi." She mumbled a few words and headed down the mountain, as if I couldn't see her. A bit of green magic trailed behind her, fading into the air as it pleased.

"Damnit."

"That kind of language is not attractive," a certain English accent sounded from behind me.

I jumped, catching my footing just before I tumbled like Lia. "Shit, Pan! Stop doing that!" I faced him. "You trained her well."

"She doesn't work for me," he said calmly.

"She should. She would be a perfect fit," I suggested with sarcasm. "If you're hiring."

"I am hiring, but for a certain position. The requirements must be met first." He stepped closer until barely any space was left between us. "She is required to know how to fight. She must be a lost girl. She must have proved herself. Most important of all, she *must* let her demon win."

43: Love

As I left my cabin, a human-sized fairy blocked me. "Ah, look who decided to come back." I crossed my arms.

Tinker Bell straightened her posture while her arms stayed at her side. "Well, I wanted to hear your offer." She shrugged, eyes focused on something else.

Why was she so interested in me now? She made it clear that she had no intention of helping.

"If we're going to talk about offers, we might want to go somewhere else." I gestured to the camp. It was crowded with boys and I was worried about Pan.

She nodded and turned to face the other way. "Follow me."

I did as she said, and we arrived at the beach. I had no idea that Tinker Bell had any interest in the beach, but I guess I should have known by now that nothing here could be predicted. I thought if Pan was evil, Hook wouldn't be. I was wrong. I thought maybe if that were the case, Tinker Bell would be nice. I was wrong, again. I was always wrong about Neverland because this place was nothing like the fairytale. There were no good guys in Neverland.

Pan never told a lie about that. I feared I'd be the next to follow in their footsteps.

She shoved her bare feet under the sand and folded her hands in front of her. "I've been told that you assume a lot about this place because our stories are told somewhere else. Well, whatever you think about me, it's got nothing to do with Peter Pan."

"What does Peter Pan have to do with us? I was told you were going to hear my offer."

Tinker Bell gestured for me to go on. "Yes, of course. The offer."

"I want to go home. I'm not sure what I can offer that a fairy might want, so we should probably talk about that." I nodded a bit.

She snapped her fingers as green dust dispersed into the air. "Yes! Of course. Well, I've been banned from interacting with Pan's lost boys. As the only fairy here, it gets lonely."

"Banned? But you just walked into camp and he didn't even care." I scoffed.

She bent down and grabbed some sand. "Yes, because I'm magical. I have a form of magic called green magic. With the right ingredients, I can make myself blend in with nature and nobody knows I'm here. It's not quite like invisibility but more like camouflage."

I squinted. "But I can see you."

"I've really only mastered it with boys. Have yet to figure it out with girls. Not that I'm too concerned with girls seeing me anyway. I prefer girls." She dropped the sand. "Have you ever wondered why you're special?"

"You just told me why."

Letting out a sigh, she turned to face the ocean waves. "I'm not blind to what happens. I live here and I keep up with current events the best that I can. I know that you can hear Pan's flute and no other woman can. You don't seem to understand why this is, but I know why."

Everyone knew I could hear his flute, as if Neverland had a newspaper and I the headline.

I swallowed my fear. "Why? What makes me so special?"

"It would be stupid of me to say you're here to restore Neverland and save Pan because it's not as if this was destined to be. However, it does seem odd that you are the exception to the rules. You're skilled. You survived getting lost in Fee Abyss. You're connected to Neverland in ways others never will be. You're connected on a higher level than your sister, higher than Hook was, and almost higher than the lost boys." She glanced at me.

I gestured for her to spit it out.

"You're the female version of Pan," she said.

I choked. "What? I am not. I am nothing like that bastard."

Her eyebrows shot up. "Nothing like Pan? You're exactly like him. You're both stubborn and refuse to follow rules. You both get yourselves into trouble. It was Pan who was at risk of losing to the darkness and now it's you. The only difference is that you don't have magic because Pan's still the one who keeps Neverland alive. But that doesn't mean you aren't connected to it."

Walking towards the shallow water, I stopped just before it hit my boots. Was she right? Was I just like him? *I* may have been what I feared most. "Why am I connected to this island?"

She approached and draped her arm around me. "There are some things I can't explain. But I'm beginning to believe if Pan died, Neverland would thrive with you in its place."

A gasp left my lips. "Kill Pan? You're asking me to murder him and take his place?"

She spun me around. "Lili, this is our only chance. Pan is a horrible leader. Look at him. He's chosen darkness over light. Neverland can't survive forever on just evil. Just think of how much could happen here. Women would be allowed to be lost girls. We could prove to him that a woman is just as capable."

"Capable? What did Pan do to you?" I asked.

She stepped back. "Nothing. He just hates me."

That didn't sound like *nothing*. She was hiding something. I needed to know what it was.

"I won't even consider this plan until you tell me why you despise him so much. You can't just say you want him dead because he hates you. He did something." I furrowed my brows.

Tinker Bell kicked the sand. "Why? Can you not just believe it's a solid reason?"

"No, because in my world, we have thousands of people who kill for no *good* reason. I'm not about to kill him or do whatever it is you're afraid of. I simply don't want to discuss murdering Pan over something I know nothing about. It wouldn't even be a worthy kill if I didn't hate him just as much."

Her eyes almost rolled back into her head. As far as I knew, Tinker Bell was just an unreasonable fairy. She'd always been jealous of Wendy, right?

I lowered my voice and asked, "Is this about Wendy?"

That caught her off guard. "How did you know?"

Chills ran up my spine. "Are you jealous of Wendy? I'm not surprised if you have a crush on Pan. That's how the story goes."

Tinker Bell turned around and shook her head. "No, no." Yet the way she twirled a strand of her black hair told me otherwise. "I was jealous, yes, but not of Wendy."

"Who?" I asked. Seconds later, it hit me. I lifted my eyebrows but blinked the surprise away. This fairytale continued to amaze me. "You were jealous of Pan."

Her shoulders slumped. "It's not exactly something I enjoy admitting to."

Maybe there'd been a time when Wendy had a pure heart. That was when Tinker Bell must have had a crush on her.

"Is Pan mad at you for...being gay or is it another reason?" I scratched the back of my neck.

Her green eyes landed on mine. "I think he just despises me because he wanted Wendy to himself. He keeps her locked in his cabin so she can't sneak off and see me."

Nausea swirled around inside me. "That's gross. I mean, it should be her choice." It wasn't going to be my place to tell her that Wendy was killed. I didn't want her to see Wendy in a darker light. "I might not particularly care for her, but I don't think anyone deserves to be held captive from seeing those they love."

She glanced back at me.

I knew that look. She wanted to know why I didn't like Wendy. Well, aside from the fact that she had supported Jacob raping me, I just had a bit of jealousy inside myself from her relationship with Pan. Maybe I wanted to be the one getting high with him. In a figurative manner of course.

"I'm the one jealous of Wendy," I lied.

Tinker Bell fixed her shirt. "So, I assume killing him is a no go. You're in love with Pan."

A laugh burst from me without me even trying. "In love? Hell no. I could never. Maybe I'm attracted to him but it's not like I can help who I'm attracted to. I'm certainly not trying to be with him. He just... Forget it."

The ping in my heart couldn't be ignored. It hurt me to know that Tinker Bell had cared about Wendy in ways Pan never could and yet he took her from her. I couldn't support Wendy and her horrible choices but that didn't mean I couldn't understand how *Tinker Bell* felt.

Pan said Wendy had been jealous of me but now I knew that wasn't true. She wanted Jacob to ruin my reputation and steal my dignity because if he did, I'd never talk to Pan. She tried to take away his happiness the same way he took hers.

"Before Pan found out, we were happy. We weren't open with our relationship, usually sneaking around, but we were still trying. Wendy was the only one who had magic like me. Nobody ever understood why she did, but I wondered if it was always meant to be with us." She let out a sigh. "Can I ask if Pan's accent attracts you?"

Lie. Just lie to her.

"It does."

Why the hell didn't you lie?

"That's how I was. I'd never met a British person before I came to Neverland but, nevertheless, I was still desperate to hear it every day. I hated hearing my own, and hers was just so...pure." She shook her head. "So, you want to leave, or you could just replace Pan but that's out of the question since you love him."

"I don't—" I waved my hand, dismissing it. "Whatever. I want to leave. I want to go home and I'm willing to offer you anything."

She stepped forward. "I have something in mind." A small smile formed. "Could you get Wendy her freedom? I just want to see her one more time."

My heart shattered. What did I tell her? Looking away, I wiped the tear that threatened to fall. I couldn't tell her the truth, but I couldn't offer her Wendy, either.

"That's not possible. I'm sorry. I can't," I whispered, my voice cracking.

"Why not? Is Pan that ruthless?"

I closed my eyes, blocking out the sorrow in hers. I couldn't see her face when I told her. "Wendy is dead."

Silence came in thick like fog. What was running through her head? Did she want to kill me?

Opening my eyes, I faced the heartache before me. Tinker Bell didn't move as tears formed in her eyes and spilled over. Her entire body went numb as she collapsed into the sand. The feeling in my legs left me as well but I kept my strength for her. Tinker Bell needed a shoulder.

I kneeled beside her, pulling her into my arms. Her entire body shook as she screamed into my shoulder. When her throat was raw, she let the sobs kick in. I ran my hand over her hair, resting my chin on her head.

I couldn't imagine the pain she was going through. She'd lost her love and I'd never experienced anything that excruciating. She just needed someone to comfort her and be her shoulder and I couldn't leave now after creating this mess. I needed to be there while she fought her own mind.

"I'll be right here. I promise," I whispered.

She never said another word. Instead, she sought the comfort I promised. I knew what I'd have to do later. Pan was going to hear the worse end of this. He had to know that what he did to Tinker Bell was a wicked move.

In fact, he'd need to explain to me why the hell he would pull such a horrible fate. He ripped them apart for his own gain. He was a *monster*.

After the way Tinker Bell and I ended the other day, I was surprised that we were here now, and she was in my arms. I'd intended to make friends here, and now I understood that meant seeing everyone else's perspective on things. Nothing was black and white. Things were always so much more than they appeared, and Tinker Bell appeared as a selfish fairy who didn't want to help anyone, but the truth was, she was anything but. She was a broken fairy who wanted to experience love again until that love was torn from her forever.

I'd lost my Nana when I came to Neverland. If someone had kept her away from me, then killed her, I'd be screaming and crying, too. I didn't love my Nana the way Tinker Bell loved Wendy, but I could empathize as much as allowed.

Tinker Bell was lost—and I needed to be the one to guide her through her grief.

44: Regret

As the moon replaced the sun for its shift of the night, I recalled the pain Tinker Bell shared here on this beach. It was the kind of pain I'd never wish on anyone, and not even Wendy herself.

"You never told me what you did," I said to Pan as he approached from behind.

He sat beside me. "What did I do?"

He was playing dumb. How smart. "When you couldn't have true love, you denied everyone else the same privilege." I swallowed.

"I denied someone true love?" he asked.

I faced him. "Don't act stupid. You're an asshole is what you are. You stole Wendy away from Tinker Bell. You're disgusting."

He nodded his head a little. "That's what this is about."

Standing up, I towered over him. "Don't you dare do that. Don't play the victim. Don't pretend you didn't do a shitty thing. Tinker Bell and Wendy were in love. You destroyed that for your own sick game. I had to be the one who told Tinker Bell that Wendy is dead."

"I never made you tell her that." He shook his head.

I pulled out my dagger. "If you had let them be together, Wendy would never have been here. She wouldn't have told Jacob to target me. She would be happy with someone she loved instead of spending her eternity with you. Nobody wants to be around you and only you, Pan. You're not that remarkable." Well, I told myself that to sleep at night.

He let out a little sigh.

"I'm not here to justify what Wendy did but I will still try to understand what led her down this path. We don't treat people like shit. It will just hurt more people later down the road. You'd be surprised by what humans are capable of," I stepped closer, my dagger pointed in the soft of his neck.

Pan pushed it away. "I'll be surprised if Lia is the one who loses her shadow instead of you. I'm not all that surprised otherwise."

I groaned from the frustration bubbling within. "You tore two people apart. I know you have no idea what that feels like because your lover screwed you over, but Wendy and Tinker Bell had a good thing going. You ripped that apart. It was not love destroyed from the inside this time. You did this. You took that away from them."

"I know."

"They were happy before you came along and—" I stopped, narrowing my eyes at him. "Wait, you know?"

He shrugged. "I know, Lili. I'm not proud of everything I've done. Am I proud I killed Wendy for what she did? Yes. Am I proud that I ruined love for everyone else because it was ruined for me? No." He stood from the sand and brushed it from his butt. "There are some things even I regret doing." He pulled his shirt from his body and dropped it. "I regret forcing Wendy to live with me." He removed his shoes and belt. "I regret kissing Lia to make you mad." He took off his socks and his leggings, straightening his posture. "I regret making you think I was playing a game this entire time."

I watched him as he walked towards the water. I was shocked to hear him say he regretted these things. Pan didn't seem like a bad guy when he tried. The keyword was *tried*.

He closed his eyes as he walked into the ocean. "I'm not playing a game anymore. I can't just pretend I'm okay with this."

"Okay with what?" I asked. "What are you doing?"

"I'm going for a swim. I'm recreating the first time we had fun together. I don't want this relationship to be based on games, or *hostility.*" He glanced back at me. "I can't pretend I'm okay with just being a player. This isn't about winning anymore."

These words rattled me to my core. These were words that had left his lips, laced with his thick sincerity. What did I say to that? He wanted a relationship, but I couldn't be too sure yet. I was stuck between killing him or just being together. Which one was the better option?

I let out a nervous laugh. "Okay, to be fair... I assumed I was your pawn."

He shook his head. "I can't keep denying the truth. It just messes with my mind."

Sighing, I said, "Fine, whatever. I don't know what you want me to say. I want to kill you but then I want to kiss you. It's a difficult battle. You make it so hard and you don't even realize that."

He scoffed. "And you do? You're the most stubborn woman I've ever met. When I first kissed you, I expected you to slap me."

He wasn't wrong. I would have slapped him hadn't I already been so confused by my own feelings. "Pan, I can't express how much this throws my thoughts for a loop. One day I want to comfort you and hold you close and the next day I'm ready to cut your head off. "We can't make this work."

He came back to me, droplets of water settling on his skin. "There's one option." He grabbed my hands and pulled me closer. "Just let the dark side win," he whispered as he leaned his forehead against mine.

"I would be no better than the donors who conceived me." I closed my eyes, shoving away the helplessness. "I don't want to be like them. I want to show them that they didn't win."

His fingers grabbed my chin, lifting it, nearly brushing his lips against mine. "They didn't win. You live here now."

I let him take my lips captive with his for a moment. The taste of salt lined his lips. I didn't want to let go of this between us. When he kissed me, he reminded me why I didn't want to kill him. I didn't think I could.

I pulled away, inhaling and exhaling deeply. "I can't do this. I'm sick of the mind games. They're not fun anymore." I stepped back.

He furrowed his brows. "Who says these are mind games? It was meant to be in the beginning but at some point, it stopped being a *game* to me. I just never told you when."

"We share things that others don't share with you. I cherish those things, but I don't want this to be a one-sided relationship. I don't plan to change for you, and you've decided the same. It can't happen." I turned and walked up the shore. "Come talk to me when you're ready to reattach your shadow."

"Why do you have to make everything about our differences? Why can't you just let a good thing be?" he asked.

I spun. "A good thing? This is good?" I gestured between us. "No, Pan, this is toxic. We're two different people. You want me to kill people and I don't want that. You tear lovers apart and I would never do that. I don't support caging people as a punishment. We are opposites in the way of our morals. You say I'm fighting my demon, and I *am* because I refuse to be anything like you. I don't want to take pleasure in taking a life," my voice cracked. "Even if it was Jacob and Wendy who tried to destroy me."

He opened his mouth to say something, but nothing came out. Instead, I left the beach and gave myself time to think.

I took a walk up towards the other side of the island, where the cliffs were. After a while of thinking, I came upon Fee Abyss and asked myself how I would get down there without dying or getting lost in the river. The answer was simple. I needed to make the longest ladder I'd ever seen, or I needed to make stairs that went down the cliffside. Either way, I needed access that didn't require Pan's help.

If he chose the dark side over me, I'd have to let go of the idea of *us*. That meant not wanting his help as much, if at all. It would be too awkward to bother him if I'd rejected him after we went a whole five yards.

I headed back to camp and gathered supplies I would need to build a ladder. The boys gave me strange looks but they'd thank me later. Maybe. Pan would be pissed if I gave them access to Fee Abyss but in my defense, he showed me the beauty before I had a chance to say no. That was his mistake—not mine.

Laying out the sticks, I tested their sturdiness by stepping on them. They were thick, as thick as medium-sized tree stumps. However, I was planning to cut them in half so I could have a flat surface to step onto when climbing. It lessened the risk of slipping into the bottomless river below.

I set a log onto a flat tree stump and grabbed the ax, bringing it down on the log, splitting it down the middle.

"What are you doing?" Kace asked.

I set another log on the stump. "I'm making a ladder." I swung down, splitting. "I want to get to Fee Abyss without Pan's help. He's an asshole, and I made sure he knew that."

"You're fighting again?" He chuckled.

I stopped chopping wood and looked at him. "It's more than that. He had the audacity to tell me he wants more between us but he's refusing to consider being a good leader. He likes the monster, and I don't. Neither of us wants to change. It can't work. The kiss was a three-time thing and it'll be nothing more." I shook my head, picking up the ax again.

Kace nodded, eyes fixed on the logs. "Makes sense. Although, it may have helped you both if you realized this all before you got caught up in the moments."

I shot him a glare. "No shit, Sherlock. And where the hell is Lia? I swear I haven't seen her for a few days." I scanned the area.

He shrugged. "She makes it to training so I don't question her business."

"You had no problem questioning mine," I mumbled.

I set another up on the stump and pulled the ax above my head. I pictured Pan cowering in fear. Screaming, I brought the ax down and chopped the log into two.

With wide eyes, Kace asked, “You okay?”

I snickered. “I haven't lost my shadow yet. I think I'm doing just fine.” I grabbed the halves and dropped them into a pile. “This will take a while for me to build. That cliff is tall.”

He backed up. “I'll give you your space.” He turned on his heel and disappeared into the trees. I didn't care where he went right now. I needed to focus on building a sturdy ladder so I could visit Fee Abyss as soon as possible. I was sure it was so much more mesmerizing while alone.

Without an annoying English accent criticizing my every move, I could admire the beauty for what it really was. I wanted to see the fairies and feel the mist of the cool water against my skin. I needed to experience the serenity of Fee Abyss in pure silence.

The rest of my night was spent chopping wood. Even as Pan returned for supper, I barely gave him any attention. I skipped dinner just to finish my project.

When all the wood was split, I used a thick metal tool to stamp the holes on either side of the logs. I had strung a rope through each, tying knots below each to keep them from sliding down. I didn't want to need Pan to survive here. He meant nothing to me—or that’s what I used to tell myself when I could still tell a lie and believe it. Now, I knew deep down that Pan meant more to me than I wanted to admit and *both* of us recognized it.

45: Desperate Pleas

The morning I woke up, I found the camp empty. No sign of the boys or Pan. I checked Kace's cabin, then the training area. Nobody was in the area, and I didn't know where they went.

I checked the beach. I glanced down towards Cannibal Cove but saw no movement there. I even ventured back to Hangman's Tree and the lagoon. Still, nothing. Where had they gone? Was this some cruel dream, or was this a sick joke?

I went to the cliff overlooking Fee Abyss. My ladder had been mounted, two stakes securing it to the edge. I certainly hadn't done that, which meant someone else had. Who? And why?

Nobody was around, so I made the decision to climb down. I placed my foot on the first step, testing it. If it was unsafe, I wouldn't find out up here.

Continuing down the ladder, I hung on tightly as it wiggled beneath my grip. To say my heart was pounding was an understatement. No, my entire body was shaking and I had to keep telling myself not to look down.

Yeah, the ladder idea was a nice thought. Executing it had been a whole other plan.

The climb down took far too long, and by the time I reached the bottom, I opened my eyes and looked back behind me. Behind me was a newly built bridge. Who the hell had the time to do all of this?

Pan was the only one with access. But would he really do it?

I carefully put my foot on the first plank, ensuring it was steady.

I dropped onto it and fell to my hands and knees, taking in all the gulps of air I could. I lifted my head just as a glitter of gold announced the sign that said:

STRAIGHT ON

I stood and followed the bridge across the wide river, a few twinkling fairies here and there. "Yes, hello. Hello." I nodded at them as I approached a corner. Another sign popped into view:

SECOND RIGHT

It made little sense, as this had actually been the first right. But I rounded the corner anyway and followed on. When I approached what once looked like Pan's treehouse, the final sign said:

'TIL MORNING STAR

Pan's flute whistled from inside, lights on through the windows.

This treehouse appeared bigger than the first time he showed it to me. It had once been just a small room with a bed. But when I entered the door, it had become the size of a small apartment.

"Little Flower, you made it." Pan grabbed hold of my arm, leading me over to a separate room. "You were right about making this into something different, something I was proud of."

"Did I say that?"

He swept his arm to the lost boys who danced. Kace was watching from a corner, and Lia had been twirling in the center of the event. "The opening of Fee Abyss. What do you think?"

He was screwing with me was what I thought. I'd wanted to piss him off and gain access to this wonder myself, without his help, and he turned around and threw it in my face. After I told him we couldn't be together.

After things had gotten just a little too real.

"Why now?"

"Why not now?" He snapped his fingers, a tux replacing his usual attire. That asshat. "You can't come to a party dressed like that. What color do you prefer?"

Lia spotted me and rushed over, squealing. "You made it! Isn't this place so stunning? I could barely believe my eyes." It was then I noticed the blush pink gown. Simple, and subtle. But perfect on her nonetheless. It definitely fit her personality far better than the jeans and shirt.

"Color," he repeated.

My sister glanced at Pan. "She loves dark green. Forest dark green."

Pan's lips brushed my ear. "Forest green it is."

His fingers trailed across my shoulder as a heavy gown weighed on me in seconds. "I hate dresses," I said with a scowl.

Another touch of his fingers and the weight disappeared.

I now wore straight leg dress pants in black, a dark green silk blouse with some lacing detail and buttons, and flat-heeled brown boots.

"Real subtle," I said to Pan.

He circled around to the front of me and held his hand out. "Dance with me."

"Dance with you? In front of everyone?"

"That's what I said."

Regardless, I still took his offer and we moved to the center of the boys. They pretended not to notice whatever game Pan was playing. I needed to stay one step ahead of him the same way he did me.

"So, Peter," I started, "what are we really doing here?"

Boys shot their eyes at us in surprise when I called him by his first name.

He leaned in close, deepening his voice, "Careful, Love. The challenge you want to engage in is a solo kind, only one pawn. You might not even be the victor."

"You saying I'm the pawn?"

He chuckled darkly. "If the shoe fits."

I tightened my grip on his shoulder, pulling out chests together. "Where does that leave you?"

Gold gleamed his eyes. "Right where you left me. Waiting for you to say *yes.*"

It was never going to happen. Not even with the flick of his wrist, the flitter of his fingers across my waist, or the gentle kiss of his nose on my cheek. His dancing couldn't even affect me.

"Is this entire thing supposed to be some set up? To win me over? My answer stays the same, Pan. No. We're far too different with different goals in mind."

His dark hair fell into my eyes as he leaned close to my ear. "Hardly. We're the same. You just have no idea what you want yet."

I ripped myself from his arms and narrowed my eyes. "Excuse me? What do I want?"

The music fell silent, desperation clawing its way up everyone's throats as awkwardness hung in the air.

He gestured around us, to the lights and the plants draped in every corner. "It's one thing to admit you enjoy the taste of blood and you want to revel in such fantasies, but another to deny it entirely just to prove a point. If you had just come to me and told me that you would rather Lia not watch you fall down the rabbit hole, I'd have believed you. But seeing as you continue to live in this pretty little land of perfection, you will fall deeper into the darkness. You cannot continue to fight what you so desperately crave."

Feeling around my hips, Pan worked his magic until my dagger returned. I wrapped my fingers around the hilt for comfort. "I did tell you exactly why. I told you I want to be nothing like our parents. You care nothing about my well-being if you're so hellbent on turning me into them."

He stepped back. "And you, Little Flower, are nothing like your parents. I do not intentionally bring kids here to slap them around. I feed them.

I clothe them. I train them to defend themselves. I let them have fun the way they were never allowed. Have I ever hit you? Have I *ever* called you by a filthy name? The worst I've done is kill those who do not believe here. That is hardly a crime, seeing as it was you who took Hook's life, and not I." Gasps ensued. "I killed Jacob for you." More gasps. "I killed Wendy for you. I have never done anything with the intent of punishing the innocent. It has always been about taking revenge on those who deserved every last ounce."

Ripping my dagger from my belt, I sliced the air. "I never asked you to defend my name, Pan! I asked you to treat me the same you do these boys! You've always seen me as a body to hunt, and you said so yourself the day I arrived. Your intent was never to keep me around."

Nostrils flaring, he strode over and stood merely centimeters from my face. "I was protecting my boys, and you bloody know that!" His chest heaved as he stumbled back. "You know they always came before outsiders. If a killer came into your home and told you to choose between your sister or a stranger, who would you choose?"

"So, why, then can you not just join me and leave your demon behind? Why must you fight to keep him around?"

His heavy breaths were all that could be heard now. "Because, Love, if I give up the monster, I'll return to the meek leader I once was. I can't risk that for my family. The confidence—the backbone—it's all I have left when you told me we could not share the same bed."

Inhale. Exhale.

"And I can't say yes to someone who chooses not to care about me the way I've always asked."

I pushed past Pan and the boys before exiting the structure and leaving Fee Abyss altogether. The cries that bubbled in my throat, and the boiling in my blood were enough to fuel me up the ladder without a second glance. Okay, there might have been a glance or two.

I swiped at branches as I trod through the forest. Just a few feet away, a crow scattered and the scent of fresh kill drifted in my direction. I carefully closed in on the small rabbit and moved it with my blade. "You poor thing. Never had a chance, did you?"

Behind a bush, another small animal squeaked.

I found a young rabbit with blood coating its soft, white fur. It tried to hop, but alas, it could not go even a foot. I did what any self-respecting person would do. I grabbed it by the head and sliced its neck clean until it was violently put out of its misery.

The sight of vibrant crimson dilated my pupils just a tad.

So when I got to my feet, I stalked out smaller animals, preying on them and taking them home for dinner. Camp stayed empty, but I made a pile of the animals before setting on another hunt.

I squatted behind a bush, scoping out the next victim from here. A deer, if I got that lucky again. I mostly came across squirrels and rabbits tonight.

"It was you, wasn't it?" Pan said out of the darkness of the trees.

"Just go away. This doesn't concern you."

A bitter laugh escaped him. "Yeah, you keep telling yourself that." He grasped me by the arm and spun me, pinning me to a tree by my throat.

I reached for his wrist, trying to shove him away, failing. "What are you doing? Let go of me."

"You wanna play dark, I'll show you a real demon." He squeezed a little, a lump settling in his throat. In a thick disarray of betrayal, he said, "What the bloody hell is this disappearing and hunting the entire wild? Fuck, I care about you!" Animosity swirled in his iris' as he dropped his hand before sliding his fingers up my wrist and into my palm.

"You care about the idea of me. But this—hunting—it's who I am. It's what I want, Peter. To help you. I saw the way you looked at me when I killed Hook. If you couldn't even be proud of me for defending you, you would definitely not want me to kill for fun. I live a much simpler life this way. Besides, when you're immortal, it's best not to get too attached to people. You've made it abundantly clear you won't be around forever.

But you know what will be around forever? This darkness." I met his gaze. "That monster is dangerously close to being unleashed."

"Yeah, I figured that out. You think you are the only one consumed with darkness? Once everything happened, it all clicked. I just find it so hilarious how you made all these promises of never leaving Neverland for my sake, yet you high-tailed out the second you saw the darkness. I guess that's what you truly love, right? My stupid mistake of being vulnerable when I promised myself I wouldn't go down that road again. I bet you laughed in my face when you made fun of me afterwards—the villain in your story finally admitting his feelings. Do you get off on killing animals? Because hey, I've killed many, but you don't know half the things that come with it." He chuckled lowly. "Not one clue."

"Fuck you." I spat on his face. "Always making everything about you, huh?"

"Aren't I?" He let a smirk slide onto his lips while he wiped his cheek. "You want to see real killing? Come on. I'll show you. I'm a real expert on that. Do you like seeing the life leave their eyes? The sweet sound of their last, choking breath? The feel of their skin turning cold?" his voice dropped to a whisper. He pressed against me, slipping his fingers between mine.

Shivers ran down my spine, but I pushed against him despite how the rest of me felt. "Get off me!"

"I thought you wanted to know the secrets to killing! I'm here for it, Little Flower, because it's one thing to snuff out a life and relish it, but it's another thing with what comes after." He licked his lips, eyes searching mine.

"I'd rather learn on my own, with hunting, and not from the vain demon. You don't need me around, Pan. You never wanted me here in the first place." I elbowed him, just enough to loosen his grip while I hurried from his embrace.

I'd never fall victim to Pan. Never again.

The second I did, I'd have lost the entire war.

46: Falling Victim

His warm breath fanned across my lips but all that ran through my head was the way he tore us apart. We could have had it all. "Pan, you're a little close there." I swallowed the fear, giving space for my confidence to return.

"I've been this close plenty of times." Those damned messy waves across his forehead.

"I refuse to be like you. I..." I didn't know how to finish the sentence.

He leaned in, his lips so sure of their statement.. "You like me. It's been obvious for quite some time."

"Obvious or not, I've told you this cannot happen. Why are you so insistent?" Narrowing my eyes, I straightened my shoulders. I'd be a moron to let him intimidate me.

He twirled a strand of my hair. "Because for once I've finally found the perfect star and I'll be a fool to let you slip away. Hook had been rotten, infecting my very being. You, however, are fruitful. Addicting. Intoxicating. Whatever you want to name it, I must have more. Come. You're not going home." He started on his way back to the camp from Fee

Abyss, and I followed not long behind.

When we arrived, he walked towards his cabin. I headed to mine, but he called out, “Where are you going? My cabin is this way.”

I looked at him and hesitated for a moment.

He considered me fruitful. He acknowledged the control I had over him, and he even dared me to come and take it entirely.

I would probably regret this. Although, I seemed to have a hard time learning from my mistakes. I went with him instead.

“I assume this is in regard to how I treated you the other night. What's my punishment?”

He stopped by his fireplace, angling his body my way. “No punishment. I expected this from you. In all honesty, it's no use punishing you. You don't listen anyway.”

I faked a gasp. “What made you come to this conclusion?”

He shook his head and ignited a spark until a small fire began. “You just love to make fun of me.”

“Of course. That's part of the fun. You have such an ego and it's very entertaining when I get to crush that.” I wore a smug look.

He came over to me and held my chin between his thumb and forefinger. “What about your ego?”

“What about it?” Chills slid down my spine.

Pan leaned closer. “It's fun to build and crush your ego as well.”

“I didn't say I build your ego to crush it. I just crush it as it is,” I said in a quiet tone. “Although, good idea. I might just do that.”

He whispered, “Oh how I hate to love you.” He closed the remaining gap, bringing our lips together in a deep kiss.

I told him I couldn’t get involved with him if neither of us wanted to change, and yet I didn’t find myself pulling away.

I’d tried to go home but that wasn’t an option. I couldn’t kill him. All that I had left was to save him by reattaching his shadow and I could do that. I’d have to. So, with that hopeful thought, I allowed myself this moment.

The taste of plums. The scent of pine. The sound of waves in the night as a ship sails by. The touch of a shattered man who so desperately fought to piece himself back together.

It was wrong in every aspect. But I'd been raised on flaws. What was just one more?

I kissed back, my fingers tangling in his shirt. Breathing became a secondary thought.

He pulled away, both of us realizing his hands were on my waist. He didn't even remove them. "We both know this can't end well for one of us, but at the same time, it is bloody obsessive."

Before I could respond, his lips met mine again. I let go of his shirt but only to grab the hem and remove it from his body. Pan was right—this *was* intoxicating.

As our kisses became so infused with one another, we backed up as he pulled off my tank top. We toppled onto the bed, but he pulled away as soon as my back hit the mattress. "Why are we doing this?" he asked.

I propped myself up on my elbows. "We both *never* follow the rules."

He grabbed my boots and pulled them off. "Rebel we shall." He removed his boots before climbing back on top. I'd be lying if I said I wasn't craving more of him.

As he kissed me again, I ran my fingers through his dark locks. A groan buried deep in his throat escaped.

Eventually, all the clothes came off and we did things I couldn't tell anyone else about. If people found out, things would get worse for me and I wasn't about to go back down that road.

"I SHOULD PROBABLY GO back to my cabin," I said as I sat up.

"Do you just give yourself to every man and then leave?" He watched every move intently.

Was I about to boost his ego by telling him he was my first and the best I'd had? No. I lifted an eyebrow. "I'm going so nobody suspects anything." I grabbed my bra and put it back on, glancing at him.

"Why does it matter to you what they think of us? I may not show them much, but I do have feelings, Love." He placed his arms behind his head.

I shrugged. "I have to go think this through."

"Usually, people think before they shag." A coy smile lingered on his lips.

"Yeah, well, congratulations. I happen to be a stupid human who thinks about the choices after I make them." I slid my underwear on. "You make it impossible not to act on impulses." I yanked my leggings up, fixing them until they were even at the ankles.

"You can't put this on me. I may have control over Neverland, but I can't force you to sleep with me. I wouldn't want to. It was you who led us down that hill. I like my women to be willing." He turned his body to me.

I huffed. "Oh, so there's more than me and Hook?" I pulled my shirt over my head. I bent down and put my socks and boots on, tying them.

"It's just an expression. I've only been with two women. I don't have to have left a string of broken hearts to say I prefer sex over assault," he argued.

Standing up, I put my dagger belt back on. "I still need time. This can't happen again, Pan, and you know it." I fixed my hair and grabbed my glasses from his dresser, putting them on.

"I wish you'd just call me Peter." He picked at a thread on his sheet.

"Goodbye." I exited the door of his cabin.

He yelled from inside, "Make sure to go pee right away! You'll thank me later!"

Not sure what he was getting at, so I walked back to my room.

Lia wasn't there. Just for the sake of it, I listened to Pan and peed before I went to find my sister, but I ran into Kace instead. "Where's Lia?" I asked.

He shrugged. "I don't know."

I sighed. “Great.”

“Why?” He looked at me funny.

I rolled my eyes. “It’s not really your business, Kace.”

“All right.” No objection? Why couldn’t Pan be that simple?

“I did something I was trying to avoid. Lia was supposed to help me stay away from Pan. That didn't quite work.”

He nodded, a small laugh slipping up. “Pan is confusing at times.”

I scrunched my face. “That’s an understatement.”

“Understatement or not, I’d be careful around him. You’ve got him wrapped around your finger but if you hurt him, he could do something drastic and take us all with him.”

“Are you implying that I date him just for everyone else’s safety instead of my own will?”

“Not at all. All I’m saying is be prepared for the worst. When you do break his heart—and you will—be ready to have to help me save our asses. Pan takes drastic measures when things don’t go his way. You may have dodged a bullet.”

Dodged a bullet? I’d just slept with the guy and here Kace was congratulating me for saying no. He’d be sorely disappointed.

I sighed, shaking my head with my hand against my forehead. “I think I'm losing my mind. Don't you?” I lifted my eyebrows, waiting for an answer.

He shrugged. “I can't be too sure. I think both of you just have a complicated relationship.”

“But... Kace, I'm not supposed to be letting him get inside me. He is not the hero in this scenario. If we continue with this, I'm afraid I will go dark. It's getting harder to fight it. If I take him to Skull Rock, I have to win.” I shivered and hugged myself. How on earth was I so cold?

Pan spotted us, stopping just a foot away. “You leave a man alone in his bed to go talk to his best friend? You're becoming just like her,” he said with venom in his voice.

That stung. "Stop with that bullshit. Kace and I don't see each other in that way. Stop accusing me of stuff I'm not doing."

He rolled his eyes. "Here I thought we shared something special."

"I am here because I need to talk to Lia about this and I can't find her. Kace was warning me about you." The hair rose on my arms as goosebumps formed. "Damnit, why am I so cold?" I yelled, "this is Neverland!"

Kace looked over at Pan. "I have noticed it's been dropping in temperature quite a bit."

Pan shrugged, arms folded. "I haven't noticed. Although, I am sure it's because I'm the King of Neverland."

"The Demon King," I corrected.

His eyes locked on me, a feral glint evident. "That I am."

I tapped my foot repeatedly. "That's why I'm trying to find Lia. She'd know what to do."

"You're afraid of me because you know I'm winning you over."

Just lie.

"Uh-huh, sure."

He shrugged. "You're a terrible liar and have been since day one."

"Pan, you can't just call me a liar and hope it sticks. It's a piss-poor comeback," I said.

He furrowed those brows of his just to bother me. "You can't trust me to listen to you." Then he wiggled them.

"That is not when you wiggle your brows."

"Then when am I supposed to wiggle my brows, your highness?" He threw his arms up in the air. "Suddenly it's your world."

"It's your world, too." I shook my head.

"Not anymore," he said in a small voice.

After swallowing the sympathy, I dropped my gaze. "Let me go home to visit my Nana at the very least. That's all I ask."

"I can't let you do that. If I let you leave, others will assume they can, too, or else I'm giving you special treatment," he said.

I knew that was just an excuse. He had a choice and chose to keep me captive. "You already are."

"You're right, I am, but you asked me to come here. My shadow granted your wish and now you can't leave. Those are the rules." His green eyes showed the sorrow he would never admit to.

I yelled out in frustration and stomped my way back to my cabin. I slammed the door and fell face-first onto my bed, screaming into the pillow. This couldn't be happening now. I had done something as stupid as letting Pan have sex with me, and now, I was in defeat.

How was I going to get out of this one?

You won't.

I would get out of this, and I would attach Pan's shadow. I would figure something out. I couldn't just give up now. I had no other choice.

And where the hell is Lia in all of this?

47: Shadows

Lia walked in at the buttcrack of dawn, laying her dagger on the dresser. I was sitting on my bed in the dark corner, waiting for her arrival. "Where were you?"

"What do you mean?" Her brows kitted together.

"I needed you most, but you weren't there for me."

She frowned. "Don't say that," she said with such confidence. Oh boy, was I about to crush that.

Scoffing, I said, "Can't I? You weren't around when I needed you. I had no excuse to not go to Pan when he told me he needed me. In the end, it only led to my weakness. What do they call it again? Sex?" As if it didn't matter anymore... Did it matter? I couldn't be sure these days.

Gasp. She ran over and plopped on my bed. "Lili, tell me this isn't true. You are not supposed to be this stupid! Can you not say no?"

"That is exactly why I asked for your help." I rolled my head, rubbing the muscles in my neck. "But you failed me."

"You, of all people, are telling me this? Really? What happened to the girl who used to tell me that I needed to stay strong and show people I wasn't weak? You used to tell me that I need to go against stereotypes and be myself. Now you're blaming me because you said yes to Pan? I don't control you," she argued.

Sly girl—trying to get out of this. I knew better. "Damn you, Lia, if you don't want to be there for me when I can't always be strong, then don't promise to be there at all."

I got up from my bed and left her behind in the cabin.

I went off to find Pan, in which case I found him at his tree, of course. Where else would this boy be? "Hello, Pan."

His eyes met mine. "Look who came running back for seconds." Chuckling, he shrugged.

I stalked closer. "Hardly. What happened can never happen again." I needed to make that clear, at least before he tried it again.

"Why are you here? I told you I'm not taking you home." He closed the door to the tree.

"I don't need you to take me home." What I had in mind was different. I needed to simply reattach his shadow on my own accord before things spiraled further out of our control. He wanted to date me, and I'd only ever consider it if he had his shadow back.

I'd use it to my advantage.

He narrowed his eyes. "What is this? What game are you playing, Little Flower?"

I put my hands behind my back. "No game. I just had a good night's sleep. I thought about yesterday's events, and I have come to a conclusion. I don't want it to happen again. But I do want to stay here forever, until it ends—as they say."

"Yeah, right. I can't believe that." With a shake of his head, he started to walk back towards camp.

I hurried to catch up with him. "There are no tricks. It's no use in fighting anymore. When the method no longer works, try something new. Otherwise, it's insanity."

"Why would I believe this is no trick? Games are all you know how to play." He shot a look back at me.

"At least do something with me. Have a little fun. Surely that was never a trick on my part. Let's go to the beach." I grabbed his hand and dragged him before he could reject my offer.

We stepped into the sand as it reformed itself beneath our boots. "Just have fun." I took off my belt, glasses, boots, and socks.

He ran into the water with me, and much like the first time, we splashed one another. He tackled me into the waves, but we jumped back out as quickly as could before I drowned.

Real laughs. Genuine smiles. Even if I never wanted to sleep with him again, I wanted *this*. I wanted to remind him of the good times and what was waiting for him when he reattached his shadow. I'd be here the entire time. I wanted more of this Peter, and less of Pan.

It was a recreation of the first real moment we had together. I wanted to use this moment to create something old but new. I had to change him as he was, and *if* he was going to change...he would change because he had his shadow back at his feet.

We walked back to camp, and once Pan had begun to head towards his cabin, I called out his name.

When he paused to face me, I pushed some hair behind my ear. "Can we visit Skull Rock?"

He carefully eyes me, tilting his head slightly to his right. "You want to attach my shadow. That's your real goal, right?"

Busted.

I was never a good liar anyway.

"You do know me, and I can't lie." With a small smirk, I implied a test. One last game. Everything else had been a failure and seeing as this was our forte, it seemed like the right move to make.

"And you know me. I can't resist a good challenge."

Now would be my chance to shine. "Then it's on."

"Remember, I never fail. You can attempt to get my shadow attached, but you'll lose."

He grasped my hand tight and pushed us off the ground, flying us over the island. My darkness was stronger than ever, and I had to make Pan whole again. If I didn't, I would lose myself, too, and Neverland would be lost forever.

We landed inside the right eye of the skull. His shadow came into view upon our arrival. "You brought her here of your own will?"

"She thinks she can get us back together. I think I can turn her dark." He approached me, but I'd been ready the second our feet touched rock.

I lunged for him, shoving him towards his shadow, but his shadow moved out of the way.

"Nice try, but there are two against one," Pan warned.

A look of madness glinted in my eye. "Just because I'm a girl, doesn't mean I can't handle the challenge. We know what my streak looks like."

Pan closed his fist, causing me pain throughout my body. "Yes, but I know how to hurt you." He'd actually used it against me. After all this time of faking it...

I bent over, hugging myself. "You bastard, that's cheating!" I yelled out.

"Nobody said there were any rules."

His fist loosened as his fingers uncurled while he watched me regain my cool. He shot out some magic, but I ducked and ran towards him again. Just as he moved out of my way, the shadow caught me. "He's right. You won't win." It let go of me, and I stumbled forward before I caught my balance, fixing my glasses.

I put my arm out. "Hold up, I need to breathe. Does anyone have water?"

Pan shot me the most judgmental look I'd received yet.

"Damnit, I need water. If you're so confident in your success, you won't feel threatened by my need for some strength." I bent over, putting my hands on my thighs to breathe slower. "Food would be appreciated, too."

Pan grabbed me, spinning me as my back hit his chest. He wrapped his arm around my neck.

I struggled against him, elbowing and kicking. I would be the most embarrassing woman in all of Neverland's history if I lost now.

He kept a firm grip despite my attempts. He gave a heads up to his shadow who read the signal. His shadow came over to me, and I kicked outward but that didn't do any harm or even slow him down.

He bent down and gripped the arms of my shadow, yanking.

I twisted in Pan's arms, trying to throw him off me. I bit his arm and he cursed, losing his grip.

While trying to run, I tripped over something—or someone. I got up, putting on the glasses that'd fallen off, and wiped off my leggings, looking back at Pan and his shadow.

There, next to his male outline stood a female figure. She didn't stand as tall as his, but she beat me by six inches. Her eyes lit up red, gaze fixed on me. "You lose," she said.

The monster had once been an unhatched egg. Waiting patiently for its turn to come into the world. With the death of Hook and a few encounters with Pan, that shell cracked. Claws came out. But they'd always retreat back to the safety of its home.

The pieces continued to drop. Cracks unstoppable. And when there was no longer a strong enough barrier to keep the monster under control, it broke free. Left behind was a broken cage once meant to protect those around it, and not the one locked away.

A scratch here and there, along the veins. Venom bleeding into the wounds. Spreading. Searching. Tainting everything in its path. Like a tree planted and ensuring its roots were permanent. A tree here. A tree there. Sprouting one after the other, overlapping. Until the view beyond the forest didn't exist. The only view left were the dead woods as the wind whistled and crows cawed.

Now free, the monster spread its wings.

Dark. Cold. Heavy. And *certain*.

With certainty, it took flight, and oh how I'd bathe in all the terror.

With sinful intentions written in my smile, I approached Pan. "I think it's only fair we go back to the island and announce me as your new queen."

"Who says you're going to be my queen?" He narrowed his eyes a bit.

"I do. If you meant it when you claimed you wanted us to be together so bad."

He hesitated—but ultimately gave in.

"Shall we?" I put my arm out for him to link his with mine.

He groaned, running a hand down his face. "Great, now you think you own me." He linked his arm.

My deep chuckle paired well with the devastation in my eyes. "Silly boy, I have always owned you. Now I just have nothing to get in my way—not even you."

He flew us back to the island and we landed in the center of camp. He waved his arms, calling everyone over. "Everyone, gather around!" he shouted.

The lost boys hurried closer as they formed a circle. Kace stood off to the side, eyes glued to the chaos waiting to ensue.

"We're missing someone." I scanned the faces.

Pan noticed it, too. "She might want to hear this." He snapped his fingers and Lia appeared in front of the boys. She stumbled forward, circling her arms like airplanes before catching herself.

I glanced at Pan. "I'll let you do the honors."

He straightened his posture and faced every curious body among the small crowd. "We have a new ruler."

There were whispers among the boys.

"...she did it..."

"...she changed Pan..."

"...is Pan a good guy now..."

Pan cleared his throat. "Quiet!"

Everyone stilled.

A sharp smile formed, claiming his lips as my own. "I am introducing everyone to the new Demon Queen of Neverland. I expect everyone to listen to her just as you do me." He glanced at me and I nodded in approval. He leaned in close to my ear. "Anything you would like to say, Love?" he whispered.

One thing plagued my mind. Neverland was *mine*, now. Soon I'd rid it of his stench.

I stepped forward, wearing a wicked smile so wide even those on solid ground could never miss it. "Welcome home, lost children."

Here's a sneak peek at

To Believe in the Demon King

from *Monica Shantel*

01: First Snowfall

The air grew colder as night fell, darkness surrounding my warmth. I pulled the cloak tighter, mentally thanking Kace for having lent it to me in the first place.

Neverland was not as it first was when I arrived. Lili was now Pan's equal partner in crime. She lost, and I only had *myself* to blame.

I walked back to my cabin but stopped as I saw a white snowflake pass before my eyes. There was no such thing as snow in Neverland. Until now, that was. Was it an annual season, or an anomaly?

I placed my palm flat out, catching another. "Where did you come from?"

As I peered up into the gray sky, millions of snowflakes began to fall freely. They almost looked like little delicate creatures trying to make a soft and happy arrival as if trying not to anger the island itself. They could have been.

"Snow on Neverland. That's new. I guess your sister was right," Kace said from behind me.

I turned to find him watching the fragile designs of winter itself. How utterly lovely to experience such beauty in a land where beauty existed in many different ways. A unique pattern had never been one. Neverland thrived on routine. At least it had before my sister let Pan claim her soul.

"Why is this happening?" I asked him.

"I would like to say it's because of the balance of Neverland being shifted. With two rulers and two shadows inhabiting Skull Rock—which is basically the heart of Neverland—the island must adjust somehow. Neverland was Pan's wish alone so it could only inhabit one in charge. I expect more changes to come." He stepped closer. "Let's get you back to your cabin. We will need to keep warm or die trying."

I followed him to my room just a few feet away. I opened the door but stopped and turned on my hell to face him. "I won't let this happen. I am going to have to find a way to get my sister back and change Pan along with her. But I can't do it alone. I'll need your help." I gave him my best hospitable look, hopeful that he would maybe work with me *again*.

He gave me a small nod in response. "Consider me your ally for this mission. We will restore Neverland if it's the last thing we do."

I closed my door and scanned the bed. After taking off the hood of my cloak, I set my dagger on the dresser. I still had memories every night of Lili and I sleeping in this room. Now she slept in Pan's. I hadn't been a good enough sister and that was on my part.

Climbing into bed, I tugged the cloak as close to my body as I could get it.

I still hated Pan with passion, and even more so as he had taken my own sister from me. Together, they were destroying our home.

A scowl escaped me at the thought of his existence, I wanting nothing more than to take him out completely. He was a scoundrel. He was the scum from the bottom of my shoe.

While gripping the handle of my dagger, I imagined slicing his head clean off. I wanted to watch the blood squirt from his neck, tainting the ground as a reminder to never allow anyone that much *power* again. I wanted to watch him suffer.

He deserved misery and pain, and I was destined to give it to him. I wanted him to feel the wrath of my fury for what he had done to Lili. Pan was going to fear me—for my hatred of him fueled my determination.

As I lay down on the mattress, it sank with my body.

I couldn't be too sure about how we were going to save the island from itself, but we would. I had to ensure Lili would come back to me.

Drifting into a peaceful sleep, I forgot all my troubles of today for just a little while.

WHEN I AWOKE, I was shivering, nearly freezing from the air that now surrounded me with its icy touch. I couldn't get myself warm enough, so I jumped out of my bed and ran to Pan's cabin. I pounded on the door, my own breath forming before me. The snow was colder than I'd ever experienced back home. And now it came up to my ankles. How long had I been out?

Pan opened the door with an unpleasant look just waiting to be slapped off. "Why the bloody hell are you bothering me at this hour?"

"It's freezing. You must do something. Please," I begged.

He studied my shaking limbs and chattering teeth, lifting his eyebrows. He glanced back into his room and faced me again. "We're finding ways to warm up. I suggest you do the same." He closed the door in my face.

I contorted my expression into disgust, unable to comprehend that he was sleeping with Lili. I was not going to go do that. He had to know I wasn't anything like her.

Turning away, I released a small sigh. I ended up back at my cabin and tightened the cloak around my body. As I sat on the bed and closed my eyes, I thought of ways I could stay warm.

Train.

Jumping up from the bed, I briskly walked to the area and pulled my dagger from my belt. I began to swing and jab at the air, pretending it was

Pan I was fighting.

"What are you doing?" I heard the familiar voice behind me.

I turned to give Kace my attention, still swinging my dagger at nothing to keep my body warm. "I'm trying to practice *and* keep warm. I'm killing two birds with one stone."

"What does that mean?" Kace questioned.

I held back a laugh. "It means I'm killing two birds, warming up and becoming a better fighter, with one stone by doing them at once. It's a figure of speech."

He rolled his eyes as he stepped closer. "I know what that means and what a figure of speech is. I was asking what does it mean to practice when you're by yourself? You don't have the skills." He smirked a little.

I allowed my laugh to slip this time. "Shut up. I have skills, okay?"

Kace laughed inwardly in return and came over to me. "I have to warm up, too, so let me help you practice." He pulled his silver dagger from his belt, wrapping his fingers around the embossed, bronze metal. "Ready? You are just as bad as Lili when I first trained her."

I faked a gasp. "I am not that bad." I pouted and jabbed his side.

He waved his blade around. "That was too easy."

We both began to train, sharpening our skills. *Pun was intended.*

Kace swung around, slicing my cheek. He straightened himself and stepped back. "Lia, I am so sorry. I did not mean to do that."

I gently touched the blood. I brushed it off as nothing by swinging my blade at him, across his hand. I gave him an artful smile. "Never let your guard down." I looped my fingers under the string that formed a bow where the cloak came together around his neck. "Keep your friends close." I yanked him towards me. "And keep your enemies closer," I whispered.

I took notice of how close we had gotten, letting go and clearing my throat while he fixed his cloak, saying, "Let's continue, yeah?"

"Yes. The snow isn't stopping anytime soon, so neither are we," I replied.

We continued to train all day, keeping our body temperature up against the cold. We finished and went back once it got too dark for either of us to see.

I turned back and told Kace goodbye before I retreated into my cabin. However, some commotion was going on in the middle of the camp. It could be heard throughout the whole island if I knew any better.

I stood and tightened my belt around my hips as I went outside to solve the problem. I moved the boys out of my way as I walked into their circle, stopping just inside.

Looking down upon the new boy that sat in the middle of all this, his eyes met mine, a piercing stare the only welcome I'd receive. There was a reason why, but I couldn't let anyone else *know* that.

I shook my head and cleared my throat, not giving him any leverage to threaten me. "What's your name?"

"It doesn't matter to *any* of you." That was the wrong move. I was the easy one to deal with. I couldn't say the same for the two who ruled this dreadful island.

Lili emerged from the circle with Pan, eyeing the guy. She snickered and shot a look at Pan. "You brought another lost boy? What about girls? Haven't I proven we can be just as strong?" She knew who this new member was. *We both did.*

Pan ignored her with the cross of his arms. "State your name."

"I said no." He had guts but then again, he didn't know the things Pan was capable of.

Pan slowly squeezed his fingers, cutting off his air supply.

The guy began to struggle for air, scratching his throat as if he could tear it open and inhale. Pan closed in on him and let go, the guy coughing endlessly. Before he could speak, Pan conjured up the clouds of black smoke in his eyes. "When I ask your name, you listen to me. What is your name?" he asked louder this time.

The teenage boy finally stopped choking, his lungs most likely irritated and in need of hot tea. "Asa. My damn name is Asa."

Lili looked over at Pan with a smirk. "Asa? What an interesting name. Never heard of it before."

Lies.

Asa rolled his eyes, but she still caught sight of it. She looked at him and tilted her head a bit, admiring his ability to rebel against the authority. "I used to be just like you, Asa. Now I'm ruling with Pan himself. The dark side is much more intoxicating." She looked toward Kace. "Show our new lost boy around the island. Don't forget to inform him of our rules." She spun around and walked back in the direction of their cabin. Pan followed behind like her new puppy.

Kace waved Asa over and led him off into the woods. Asa knew he had to comply or else. I just hoped he wasn't stupid enough to go exploring the *or else* option.

With careful consideration, I trailed behind my sister and her lover.

Lili pulled Pan down to her level and kissed him, whispering something I didn't quite catch. She gave a long sigh and frowned a bit. "Could you imagine if I never came here? I would still be stuck at home with my parents. All I want is the chance to love and be loved. I deserve that."

Her words cut my throat like a knife. I couldn't help but assume that she had only done all of this for love. The broken girl had craved what she never felt. Did I not love her enough?

I thought I had.

Pan cupped her face, rubbing his thumb over her cheek. "I can't imagine it because I don't want to. You're here now. Forget about your parents." He paused, "although, you could tone it down on the power trip."

Her fingers reached up and grabbed his that still held her cheek. "You like it." Before he could respond, she closed the gap and locked their lips together once again.

I wish I could say it disgusted me, but it didn't. It sunk its teeth into my heart more than anything. The kiss between them wasn't filled with hostility or poison. What passed between them was desperation and a craving that only two halves of a whole could produce.

I left the two of them in their privacy as I disappeared back to the cabin. I turned to watch all the lost boys as they danced while they waited for their breakfast. I couldn't focus on much, but I could try to form a plan to save my sister and her new boyfriend. It surely wasn't any easy task. Nothing was going to be the same as it once was.

Snow now blanketed the island. Two beings ruled over everything that took residency here. Worst of all, the new lost boy—*Asa*—would never know what once had been.

Also by

Monica Shantel

THE FEATHERS AND FLAMES TRILOGY
Beauty of a Crimson Soul
Beauty of a Burning Flame
Beauty of a Permanent Love

ACKNOWLEDGEMENTS

Thanks to my mom for always supporting my writing, even as a valid career. Thanks to my brother who's asked questions and made me think about my plots, and to the other family members who have picked up my books just to say they were proud of me.

To Ashly for always supporting me.

And thank you to my beta readers for pointing out the rights and wrongs of this book to help me make it the best it would be. This book needed all your help.

About the Author

Monica Shantel has always had an interest in artistic and creative hobbies of sorts, including but not limited to: drawing, crafting, graphic design, and painting. Although all she has is a high school diploma under her belt, she is not new to the writing community. At the age of twelve, she began building stories to escape reality and find hope in life once again. Her debut novel is Beauty of a Crimson Soul. Along the same genre, she writes dark tales of mythical romance which only add more to the growing fantasy worlds inside her head.

www.ingramcontent.com/pod-product-compliance
Lightning Source LLC
Chambersburg PA
CBHW020340310726
48979CB00015B/2445/J

* 9 7 8 1 9 6 0 6 9 6 0 6 9 *